Star Commandos

Book 10

Watchdogs of Space

Books by P.M. Griffin

Star Commandos *series*
Star Commandos
Colony in Peril
Mission Underground
Death Planet
Mind Slaver
Return to War
Fire Planet
Jungle Assault
Call to Arms
Watchdogs of Space

Coming Soon!
Star Commandos *series*
Pariah
War Prince

Star Commandos

Book 10

Watchdogs of Space

P. M. Griffin

SPEAKING VOLUMES, LLC
NAPLES, FLORIDA
2025

Watchdogs of Space

Copyright © 2003, 2014 by P.M. Griffin

All rights reserved. No part of this book may be reproduced or transmitted in any form or by any means without written permission.

ISBN 979-8-89022-285-5

To my friend, Marianna Shacker,
whose unflagging interest in the series fired
—and pushed—me to write this book.

Chapter One

Commando-Captain Varn Tarl Sogan lay in his flight chair. He stared somberly through the surplanetary viewer at the array of starships berthed around him in this portion of Horus' huge Navy spaceport. All of them were small like his *Fairest Maid*, two-man and five-man fighters mainly with a smattering of ten-class ships sprinkled here and there among them. The bigger vessels, the fifty-, one hundred-, and five hundred-class battlecraft, planeted in other areas designed to provide for their specific needs. He could not see any of them from his present position even with magnification, a fact which pleased rather than troubled him at the moment. He was conscious enough of the *Maid*'s inadequacy . . .

The major starships, those of one thousand-class and larger, never came on-world at all but docked in near-space. One of those was reputed to be out there now, one of the Federation's best.

Varn, may I come up?

He straightened at the touch of Islaen Connor's mind. He and the woman who was both his commander and his consort, or wife as they more commonly said in this ultrasystem, shared the ability to communicate through thought, to link mind with mind, a fact both took care to conceal from all but the other members of their tightly knit unit, that and the other, differing abilities their strange talent gave them.

Aye, Islaen, of course, he responded after carefully raising his shields to screen the feelings, the thoughts, he did not particularly want her to read. Surface communication could take place without betraying what lay in the inner mind if he were careful and not too deeply or powerfully troubled.

The woman sighed when she felt the barriers rise, but she had expected that and gave no sign that they bothered her. *I knew I'd find you here.*

Sogan smiled physically and in mind at the sight of her, as he nearly always did.

Islaen Connor was an extraordinarily lovely woman, comfortably tall, her slender body lithe and carried with the grace of one well familiar with space.

Her features were delicately chiseled, her brown eyes large and thickly lashed. Her hair, tightly confined in the braid that was the almost universal style adopted by women who ranged the starlanes, was a rich auburn color, and her complexion was exquisitely fair, the mark of all those born of Noreen of Tara.

She was clad in typical spacer's garb, as was he—tunic, close-fitting pants, and high boots capable of giving good support and purchase either on the deck of a starship or in a surplanetary wilderness. Around her narrow waist was clasped a heavy, multipouched utility belt, and its holster was not empty.

The small, winged creature perched on her shoulder whistled happily to see him, and he cupped his hands to receive her. When she flew to him, his fingers closed gently around her to both cradle and caress her. "Welcome, Small

One," he said aloud, as both he and Islaen addressed her when alone with her, although she could share their thoughts as readily as they did hers. "Did Islaen give you a good breakfast?"

Yes! Varn's good, too! Long ago. —Varn not sleep long!

"Space!" The gurry had a talent for broadcasting information he would sooner hold quiet, but he had just about given up protesting. It was a war he was not going to win.

Bandit was decidedly the oddest member of his unit. The little feathered mammal looked to be nothing more than an exceptionally delightful mascot, barely seven ounces in weight and brown in color apart from the black stripe circling her head and crossing the equally dark, merry eyes like the mask of a pre-space Terran thief. Those eyes were set forward in her face, affording excellent binocular vision.

Her bright yellow bill was supple, giving her round face a wide range of expression. Her legs and feet were also a vivid yellow, and the prehensile toes functioned as did a human's fingers.

She was appealing, aye, but she was also a great deal more. The gurry was intelligent as humans defined the term, and she could communicate in thought with those with those she was bonded to as well as understand verbal speech in any language comprehended by them. Beyond that, she could broadcast an enormous volume of goodwill, influencing anyone not totally depraved or gripped by some overpowering, usually violent emotion to respond favorably to her and to her companions—all facts Islaen's unit guarded as closely as they did their commanders' equally strange abilities.

As for her love and her courage, those had been proven time and again since she had bonded with Islaen Connor and, through her, with Varn on her homeworld, Jade of Kuan Yin.

The Commando-Colonel smiled softly as she watched the two of them. Varn never denied the little gurry his affection or tried to disassociate himself from her even in the times when he became aware of what an odd and rather ridiculous companion she was for a War Prince of the Arcturian Empire.

Connor studied this former enemy she had come to love even as she had battled his forces as head of Thorne's Resistance and whom she had once believed dead—executed by his own people for giving life to the world he had invaded at the War's end.

He was moderately tall by the Federation's broad standards, and slight of build. At the moment, he was too thin. He had been hard hit on several of their assignments, and one had followed the other too quickly to allow him to regain those lost pounds, although he was otherwise fully recovered.

Physically recovered. That nearly sleepless night Bandit had mentioned hinted at one wound that was not yet closed. Varn had the pride of his kind, and he conducted himself in accordance with their stern code. When the needs of their mission had compelled him to violate that on Amazoon of Indra, he had wanted—and had been promised—vengeance. Now, all chance of exacting that was gone.

She sighed in her mind. He was angry, with himself and with the fate that had brought him to his present state, and he was hurt, and there was nothing in space or beyond it that she could do to help him, nothing he would allow her to do. He would not permit her even to share his misery. He would not open himself sufficiently to so much as let her see it.

Sogan carried himself like the soldier he was, with the balance and lightness of movement of one who had spent a large portion of his life in space. The air of command rested on him like a cloak, as well it should. He had been bred to lead a fleet in time of war and to rule star systems in peace.

His hair and eyes were the same dark brown color, a trait found only in the ranking officers of the Arcturian warrior caste, and among them only in those whose families were closely linked with that of the Emperor himself. He had the olive skin of his people and their well-formed, rather harsh features—features that could mean his death should they be recognized for what they were, given the hatreds engendered in the recent War. On several occasions already since they had been together and on unnumbered times before that, his life had been threatened when suspicion of his race had been aroused in the wrong place.

She sat on the arm of his chair and made herself face the planeting field outside. A direct approach would probably be the best. They both knew what was driving him beneath those tight shields.

Thatcher's execution took place this morning.
Aye.

Her eyes flickered toward him. *I'm sorry, Varn.* She had promised Sogan personal vengeance against the man. The Federation's formal justice system had prevented him from claiming it.

It could not be helped. The fact of the atrocity would have remained in any event.

Not atrocity! the woman snapped. They had been through this so often, always to no avail. *You believed you could manage Amazoon's leeches, and you thought the river would serve as a refuge for those thugs. What happened was beyond your ability to control. It was totally against your will, and you damn well nearly died trying to stop it.*

What I believed or willed is of no consequence. Only what occurred. The man shrugged. *That is over, Islaen. I must accept the loss of that part of my honor along with the destruction of so much else I had valued.*

Connor cringed in her mind. He meant that, and she found his resignation harder to endure than his previous anger. There was so much of defeat, of despair, in it.

Islaen thought it best to turn the topic and seized upon the increasing activity outside.

It promises to be a busy day, she observed. *There are some new arrivals in port, large ships, and I understand that Gray Jack Dundee's* Terra's Charm *is in the near-space dock.*

So our mechanics have informed me, he told her carefully. He grimaced. *I suppose that means the end of work on the* Maid *and the* Jovian Moon *for a while.*

She gave him a strange look. *You should know our lads better than that, Captain Sogan. These ships are their pets. They'll see a visiting Chief Admiral sit in his dock for quite a while before they neglect us.*

He chuckled and raised the gurry so that he could look at her from eye level. "That is your doing, my feathered comrade. You have worked your magic well on all of them."

Crews nice! Like Bandit!

"Everyone likes you."

Islaen laughed. Bandit had indeed done her part, but the maintenance staff would work well for Sogan without the gurry's influence now. They were not many starship captains who labored alongside their support crews as readily and frequently as did the former Arcturian admiral. He knew and appreciated their skill. He respected them, and he listened to their ideas, to the extent that the unit's two ships were essentially experimental craft, the fastest and most advanced of their class, maybe of any class, in the Federation Navy.

I suppose I did wrong them, he admitted.

That, you did, my friend.

She studied the seemingly frenzied yet actually highly ordered activity outside with a shake of her head. *The* Terra's Charm*'s a five thousand-class,* she mused absently. *I wonder what she's like?*

"She is a big starship."

Islaen's head snapped up as if she had been struck. The abrupt switch to verbal speech and the accompanying slamming shut of his shields even over his surface thoughts graphically informed her that Sogan wanted her to have no further part of his mind or that nerve she had just savaged.

Damn him! Someday, she was going to tear him a new set of tubes for this.

The woman gripped her temper with more than a little difficulty. "That was unnecessary, Admiral," she said coldly.

"I am no admiral," he told her bitterly.

"You are by talent and training. By blood." She forced the annoyance out of her voice. "It's hardly a disgrace to admit that you want the ships to go with the ability. I wish I could get them for you, Varn, or at least a proper single command. I've failed you there, too."

"You have tried?" he asked, ashamed of his curtness but still afraid to open the discontent inside him to her reading.

"Aye. So has Ram Sithe."

His eyes lowered. "The Navy cannot risk so much with a former enemy," he said dully. "It does not matter. I have my starship. She suffices for my needs."

"It does matter, or it should," Connor told him angrily. "Accepting that you cannot have a fleet or battleship command is one thing. Refusing to accept that you are entitled to want one is another. That drives me right into the next galaxy." She glared at him. "Or doesn't it work that way in the Arcturian Empire?"

"No," he responded evenly, "it does not, not when the desire cannot be achieved. A member of the warrior caste must only accept those throws of fate that he cannot change."

Islaen forced her mood to lighten. This conversation was becoming too painful for him. "Varn Tarl Sogan, if you Arcturians were so flaming accepting of the dictates of fate, you'd never have left your original homeworld, much less built yourselves an interstellar empire and damn nearly whipped the starlight out of us."

The man smiled slowly. *Your lot were even less accepting of fate, apparently. You did the whipping in the end.*

She acknowledged his tacit apology and held out her hand to him. Suddenly, all her love for this man, all her awareness of how often and how closely she had come to losing him, surged through her. *I love you so much, Varn. These two years have been a miracle.* She smiled at him. *Two years ago today, you took on a Federation commission and a Federation consort. Any regrets, Admiral?*

None whatsoever, Colonel Connor, save that I wish I had done so several years sooner.

I wish you had, too, she said softly.

He came to his feet and drew her into his arms. *I did not have so much even when I had everything, my Islaen.* The kiss he gave her was neither casual nor short lived.

Regretfully, he released her at last. *Later, we shall celebrate properly. For now, I have a starship that needs parts, and I promised Sergeant Lampry that I would see if the depot had them in stock.*

Her brows raised. *Captains now run errands for sergeants?*

They do when they want the work on their ships to continue without interruption and the sergeants head up the maintenance staff. —Check on the crew's progress while I'm gone. Turn Bandit loose on them if the lads seem to be slowing down.

Chapter Two

The War Prince shivered and fastened his jacket to the throat. Space, but Horus was cold this time of year. He had decided to walk into the port facility both because he enjoyed the exercise and because he wanted to clear some of the shadows from his mind. Now, he regretted not having brought the flier or rover. He would be well chilled by the time he got back.

Maybe it would serve to cool off his temper, he thought sourly. His performance this morning had hardly been creditable. Islaen's remarks had not been intended to provoke him and should never have done so. As sure as space was black, it was his problem, his alone to settle or bear, that he seemed to be incapable of resigning himself to the command and duty laid on him by fate and the cruel gods of his Empire. He had little enough cause for complaint. Two years ago, he had nothing at all, existence only without purpose or glimmer of hope . . .

Sogan's thoughts returned to his surroundings as he left the planeting field and entered the port facility, the great city-within-a-city that serviced the spacers' needs and interests, military and civilian alike. The news of a number of new ships in port was accurate, he saw. The streets were crowded, and a lot of the faces were completely unfamiliar even here in an area frequented more by Navy personnel than by civilians.

Watchdogs of Space

The Arcturian carefully scanned the other passers-by without seeming to do so. It might have been a mistake to come here today. He had become a fairly familiar figure to those frequenting the Horus military facility with any regularity and so had grown to feel somewhat secure about being here himself. All these strangers raised the old sense of threat in him. Every one of them was a potential danger, a potential assailant.

He came in the end to the large supply depot that was his goal and went inside.

The big room was comfortless and drab. Its walls were almost completely covered with boards listing the materials available, along with their prices and stock codes. One notice announcing that other, less common items were also on hand broke the tedious columns. It drew the eye and invited inquiries.

A long counter ran the length of the chamber opposite the door. One clerk manned it at the moment to cater to the fairly steady flow of customers all such establishments on this part of Horus enjoyed. A closed door behind the counter led to offices and warehouse facilities.

For once, fortune was with Varn, and no crowd was gathered there. A woman finished paying for her bulky package, which she slung over her shoulder with the ease of one well accustomed to handling cargo, and then it was his turn to speak to the attendant.

The Horusi behind the counter looked at him without much interest. "How may I help you? Captain, is it not?"

"Varnt Sogan of the *Fairest Maid*."

He used the half alias smoothly. It was a pitiful defense against anyone suspecting who he really was, but when the desperately injured War Prince had been pulled out of space at Dorita, he had responded to his rescuers' questions with his own name, fortunately in the Basic in which he had been addressed. The Spirit ruling Space had so far smiled on him that his voice had been low and his speech unclear, and this was what his listeners believed he had said. When sufficient awareness returned to him and he realized what had happened, Sogan had been forced to adopt the name. He would have aroused too much suspicion had he attempted to alter it at that stage.

"Your requirements, Captain Sogan?"

At that point, luck deserted him. Nothing on his fairly extensive mental list was in stock. The Commando had to content himself with placing an order and accepting the clerk's assurance of a speedy delivery. It was not a short process, and by the time it had been completed, several others, individuals and groups, had come inside. All of them were waiting with the usual mixture of resignation and impatience for him to finish.

He turned to go only to find himself faced with a line of five men in the uniform of Navy yeomen. None of them had drawn his blaster, but all had their hands upon them.

"Freeze, you son of a Schythian ape," ordered the centermost man. "Grab the moon."

Sogan made no move. "What appears to be the problem, Yeoman?" he demanded. His voice remained low, but it was cold as the breath of an ice planet, and his words stung with the whip of one accustomed to giving rather than receiving commands.

"I've seen a lot of nanos in my day, and I saw a lot of live Arcturians at the surrender ceremonies. I see a live Arcturian now, and I'm wondering what he's doing in civilian clothes snooping around a Federation spaceport."

"I happen to hold a Federation commission," the Commando replied even more coldly.

"Right," said a second yeoman, "and I happen to be a Malkite. You probably don't know what Malkites are, Redjacket, but they're mutants, big, ugly bruisers—"

Someone cleared his throat behind the shipmen. "Now, if that isn't a blaster bolt straight through my sensitive heart! Imagine calling someone like me a big, ugly bruiser?"

Varn Tarl Sogan found it difficult to keep his expression impassive. Despite the seriousness of the situation, he was hard pressed not to laugh aloud.

The speaker and the other three individuals accompanying him were huge men, not extraordinarily tall although distinctly so, but showing the almost grotesque development of chest, shoulders, and the muscles of arms and legs characteristic of Malki's race.

Their complexions were a fiery carrot red, their hair coarse and black, their eyes well spaced and dark. Features were heavy with a particularly strong beetling of the brows, which met in an arch above the nose.

The lips were thin and were drawn back at the moment to reveal the most visible sign of true mutation on them, the very large teeth, which were well separated and distinctly pointed.

The four newcomers strode around the yeomen and calmly took their places beside the War Prince.

"You'd best let us handle this, Captain Sogan," the leader advised in a voice intended to reach and impress their opponents. "Officers really shouldn't get into brawls with yeomen. It spoils the fun for the poor bastards to know they'll all wind up in the brig after it's over. Now, my mates and I were just wandering around, wondering how in space we were going to work up appetites for lunch. A bit of exercise here would be just the thing."

"That won't be required, I think."

Sogan had already come to attention, and now the Navy men did as well at the sound of the deep voice behind them. He felt sorry for them. They looked as if their eyes were about to eject from their sockets.

A stocky man in the working uniform of a Navy admiral strode around the line of yeomen following the route the Malkites had taken a moment before. His features were pure North Terran, his eyes blue, his hair the odd steel gray that had been his trademark since it had turned so in his very early teens.

Gray Jack Dundee glanced at the Commando. "Relax, Captain. What is going on here?"

"An unfortunate error, sir. These yeomen thought me to be an Arcturian and took the steps they believed necessary to block a perceived security threat to the spaceport. Captain

Zubin of the *Rounder* and his crew know me and came to my assistance."

"So I observed." The famed admiral's eyes sparkled. "You have my apologies, Captain."

He showed no similar consideration to his frozen crewmen, as the insignias on their uniforms proclaimed them to be. "You scramble-circuited microwits have just insulted the most highly decorated soldier in the Federation military. This is Commando-Captain Varnt Sogan. You have heard the name, I presume," he added sarcastically. "Vishnu, Astarte, Jade, Mirelle, Omrai, Anath, Tambora, and, now, Noreen. — Did I miss any, Captain?"

"No, sir, but I am not insulted. This is a situation that I have encountered before. It is inevitable given my appearance."

"You're a generous man, Captain. I am not, but if you don't wish to press charges, I suppose I must let it go at that."

"No charges, sir."

Dundee glared at his crewmen. "Get out of here, and thank your pet stars that you won't be spending your time here scrubbing tubes rather than on ill-earned leave."

The yeomen cleared, moving as rapidly as they dared to distance themselves from their commander.

The admiral waited until they had gone and then left the depot himself. Sogan and the Malkites followed. "I'm glad I spotted what I thought was trouble and investigated," Dundee said, "though Captain Zubin and his lads would probably have taught them a salutary lesson about using a modicum of discretion when on-world."

The Malkites grinned broadly. Varn smiled as well despite his discomfort. He always felt the humiliation of his disgrace when he was forced into the presence of Ram Sithe, and this man was even more, the Chief Admiral of the Federation Navy. They had once been near equals. Now . . .

The Terran turned to him. "Have you finished in there, Captain Sogan?"

"Aye, sir. I was just about to start back to my ship."

"Where's your rover?"

"I walked."

"You'll ride back with me. My transport's up the next block.

Four men moved down the busy street. All were tightly wrapped in heavy hooded cloaks whose like covered most Horusi civilians at this time of the planet's year, although none of them visibly cringed when one of the frequent, sharp gusts of wind bit at them.

All four were Arcturians.

Colonel Barnak Fran Urtine led the group. Beside him was Captain Harnid Form Lassur, and behind walked the two lieutenants serving as their aides, Trion Sorn Gidon and Sivor Dord Mitree.

The commander was sunk in his own thoughts. It was strange and anything but pleasurable to find themselves in this facility of their enemies, no more welcome than the diplomatic mission to which they had been assigned.

Welcome or not, it was important. The Arcturian Empire had been badly hurt in the War they had lost, the first major defeat in their race's long history of combat. The Pirate Stars were becoming a serious challenge, as were smaller but no less vicious raiders from all over the galaxy, every one of them seeking to nibble away at the shipping and planets of the poorly patrolled rim. The former, a loose confederation of independent star systems, was a serious threat and had grown so daring as to establish a base in Federation space near the long-disputed border and to station a major battlecraft there. Four Arcturian colonies had already died as a result. He and his comrades were on Horus to request permission to bring in battlecraft of their own to eliminate the raiders before they could cause any further havoc.

At least, it was no lessening of himself or his Empire to work with the officers representing the Federation. He was, rather, honored. Dundee and Sithe were among the finest admirals in either ultrasystem.

They were the finest, he amended with a mental grimace. Only the renegade Varn Tarl Sogan had been their equal in the final decade of the War. It had been said of him that he thought more like a Terran than an Arcturian, and in the end, that had proven both the truth and the man's undoing.

In a sense, it had been a pitiable case. Had the madness of his superior been recognized at the time, Sogan would probably have been commended rather than condemned for his refusal to burn off that accursed planet. Unfortunately, he had believed himself to be dealing with a competent officer, and his refusal to comply with his orders had merited court-martial and the heavy discipline required by Arcturian law.

Urtine shrugged and returned his thoughts to the present. He and his associates had been brought secretly to Horus of Isis to meet with the Federation military leaders. They had been well received by those few who knew of their presence, and they were assured that they were not considered prisoners, but clear warning had been given of the powerful hatred of their kind that existed throughout the victorious ultrasystem.

That, he did not doubt. Many had died in the fighting in space. Many others had perished on the planets the Arcturian hosts had overrun in their advance, particularly where commanders had used stern measures to control restive populations. This was a mongrel system comprised of menials, however well those same menials had fought, and he did not question the probable result if his party were identified and overtaken by a mob harboring such animosity. They would have to be circumspect indeed in their conduct.

Their hosts had been thoughtful enough to supply the four with civilian clothing including these cloaks to afford them some degree of freedom of movement, and they had at last chosen to avail themselves of the protection the garments provided. It was good to walk, and all were pricked by a desire to see the spaceport, to have a look at some of the starships they had battled for so long.

They stopped suddenly as Admiral Dundee emerged from a building whose door sign proclaimed it to be a supply depot. Others followed. Four were subbiotics, mutants of particularly hideous form. The fifth man . . .

He heard a gasp from one of the lieutenants, Mitree, he thought. "Silence!" he hissed.

The man was beardless now, his expression guarded, his body far leaner than in the past, but there was no mistaking who he was. Varn Tarl Sogan, alive and apparently on familiar terms with the Federation Chief Admiral.

The two men spoke briefly together and with the other things before walking away, fortunately proceeding up the street, away from the watchers.

Urtine steeled himself. He needed answers, and the mutants were apparently acquainted with the former admiral. They should be able to supply some information.

He would go himself. There was a degree of danger in approaching them, and the contact would be unpleasant enough in itself that he did not like to inflict it on any of his companions.

He walked over to the four as if in casual interest. "Your friend is singularly honored by the admiral," he observed with apparent good humor.

"The admiral is honored by our friend. That's Commando-Captain Sogan. He's got enough stars sparkling on his dress uniform to start his own baby galaxy, eight of them at this point."

Urtine fought to stay steady. "A difficult achievement."

"So were the things he did to win them."

"I expect they were."

The Arcturian returned to his comrades and told them what he had learned. His voice was low, as if the former admiral's shame were his own.

Captain Lassur swore. "A mercenary in the enemy's pay. He did not even have the sense of honor to alter his degraded name."

"He did not have the honor to die. Why should this other failure surprise us?"

"Let us keep walking, my Colonel," Sivor Dord Gidon warned. "We shall begin to attract notice."

They started moving again.

"How could he have survived?" the second lieutenant wondered.

"No matter. He did and has chosen to continue his wretched existence." The colonel's mouth twisted. Sogan might at least have remained aloof from things like that mutant. He felt soiled, physically ill, after his own brief involvement with it.

"What are we to do, my Colonel?"

"Continue with the mission assigned to us. That, and make report of this encounter as soon as we return to our quarters."

Sogan and Dundee stopped beside the admiral's vehicle, a comfortable-looking four-wheeled ground transport.

"Shall I drive, sir?"

"No, thanks. I'll do it. I like to hold the controls." He glanced at the other. "I imagine you do as well."

He nodded. "Aye."

The transport's engine started with a smooth purr. "You'd probably have felt compelled to make that offer to drive during the War as well. I'm Chief Admiral. You didn't hold the equivalent post in the Empire's Navy." He shrugged as the younger man stiffened. "What's the point of pretense? I had to approve both your original Navy commission and your transfer to the Commandos. I've had no cause to regret either, I'm glad to say."

His manner became less abrupt. "Power down a little. I've been wanting to meet you. —Did you know you were considered the single most dangerous man in the Arcturian military? If your Tactical Command hadn't made the incredible blunder of tying you down on Thorne of Brandine, you could have kept the War going for another five years and maybe another ten, though the result would've been the same in the end. It was the Empire that was beaten, not you."

"Then I am glad to have been denied the opportunity," Varn said quietly, then smiled slightly. "You headed our version of that list."

Dundee's shaggy brows raised. "I thought that was Ram Sithe."

"Different categories. He as a combat admiral, you as an overall commander." His dark eyes lowered but raised again. "I had not thought ever to meet you. It is an honor."

"I have business in the Sector." The transport slowed a little. "That is your portion of the planeting field up ahead, I believe."

"It is."

"I would have asked you and Colonel Connor to join me for dinner, but I understand from Ram that your unit has some better plans for the evening. It's your anniversary, is it not?"

"Aye, sir. Our second."

"Twenty-four most fortunate months for the Federation. Congratulations, Captain."

"Thank you, sir." For the first time, his smile reached his eyes. "I consider myself the fortunate one in this."

Chapter Three

"You did remember to make a reservation, I hope. It would hardly do to show up at *The Lioness* only to find no free table." Commando-Captain Jake Karmikel, a Noreen like Islaen, was a relatively big man. He was more than a head taller than Sogan and considerably broader of shoulder, although he was by no means muscle-bound. He was handsome by his own race's and by Terran standards. His eyes were a clear, bright blue and his hair a fiery true red.

"I did, but I left it too late. The private room was already taken. We have been promised a good place, however."

Jake eyed the War Prince for a moment and shook his head in mock disgust. "No one has a right to look that comfortable in a dress uniform, Admiral Sogan."

"This is comfortable. Those in which we fought were scarcely better. Our court uniforms, on the other hand, are pure torture. They do look magnificent, though."

"I'd put credit's down that they do." He smiled suddenly, warmly. "The pair of you are married two years. It's hard to believe—two years and ten missions."

"Nine," Varn corrected. "Vishnu happened before our marriage."

"It was close enough to count, friend."

The Arcturian's face became grave for a moment. "They have come too fast. It has been hard on Islaen."

Karmikel gave him a sharp look. "You've been chopped up worse than any of us."

"She is commander. That responsibility doubles the burden." He had not always done well in helping her bear it, either . . .

The redhead glared at the core ladder, the usual form of access between the decks of smaller starships. "The eternal motto of the military," he grumbled. "Hurry up and wait."

Their two female colleagues had elected to go in Thornen dress and were taking their time with the details.

As if in response to his complaint, the women joined them. Varn's eyes glowed at the sight of his consort. Islaen Connor was beautiful, but it was her competence that most people usually saw. It delighted him when she chose to reveal this aspect of herself as well.

Her gown was of pale golden Thornen silk and followed the lines of her body like a second skin. It was modestly cut, but its neck was low enough to perfectly frame the fabulous gem suspended with deceptive simplicity from its slender chain. The river tear was over thirty carets in weight and of finest clarity, and its rarity put its value well beyond any mere diamond of equal weight and quality. It had been an honor gift presented to him by the citizens of Jade of Kuan Yin, Bandit's homeworld, the first, the only, object of worth that he had been able to give to this woman who was all the universe to him.

Her normally severely styled hair was woven into an intricate pattern accented by thin wires of gold.

Her eyes glowed in delight at his pleasure and pride in her, and she was quick to open her mind to him so that Sogan could read her own equal response to him.

Her companion, Commando-Sergeant Bethe Danlo, Jake's wife and copilot on his *Jovian Moon* and the unit's demolitions expert, was a small woman. Her features were attractive and of a Terran cast that proclaimed the origins of the spacer clan into which she had been born. There was the steadiness of one willing and well able to bear responsibility in her slate blue eyes. Her softly styled hair was blond.

She, too, wore Thornen silk, a rich blue accented with silver. Her dress fitted her as closely as did her commander's, and she supported it no less well. A circlet of blue stones collared her throat.

Although not as striking a woman as Islaen Connor, her beauty shone as well in this setting, and Jake Karmikel's face was alive with his glory in her.

Bandit rode the Commando-Colonel's shoulder, taking great care that her claws did not snag the delicate material of the gown. She whistled eagerly. *Go to* Lioness *now?*

"Aye, Love," Islaen assured her. "We know they won't let you starve there. —Are you two men ready, or are we going to have to wait for you?"

"We've been ready—" Jake started to explode. He gave up and held out his wife's cloak. It was a cold evening, and the women, especially, would need the additional covering.

"Hold up, Jake," Connor told him. "I believe we'll have an audience. I noticed that our maintenance lads were hanging around after hours. They want a look at us wearing something besides spacer togs, I think."

Her assessment proved accurate. The Commandos returned the uncommonly precise salutes of the small group lounging in seeming idleness by the ramp, then Islaen and Bethe drew the cloaks about themselves and boarded the flier.

The main room of *The Lioness* was brightly lighted and elegantly appointed. Its proprietor had taken the really good restaurant she had received from her grandfather at the conclusion of her enlistment and had made it into the finest on this part of Horus, drawing both top ranking Navy personnel and high-level locals for its clients.

Their table was a good one and reasonably secluded, set as it was in a rear corner so that it stood basically alone. Seating in *The Lioness* was well spaced in any event, permitting its occupants full freedom of conversation. Still, Sogan regretted his failure to secure the private chamber. He would have felt better knowing there would be no other eyes on them.

Karmikel saw him glance toward it. His comrade's seemingly perpetual wariness could be annoying at times, but tonight, he was minded to be tolerant. Besides, it was amusing in this setting. *The Lioness* was not exactly some pleasure district dive. "Never mind, Admiral. No one is going to challenge us to a blaster duel in here. Our hostess has an equally warm heart for good fighters and cute gurries and will see to it that we're not disturbed."

Once they were settled in their places, their waiter for the evening approached carrying a bottle with considerable reverence.

"I hope you do not object," Varn said. "I took the liberty of ordering the wine when I made the reservation."

He went through the ritual of tasting and approving the beverage, then the waiter poured a glass for each of them and left the four to themselves again.

Jake sipped the pale liquid. His eyes widened, and he turned the bottle to read the label. "I think this part of it should be a four-way split, Admiral."

"Not tonight, my friend. I carry this evening myself."

"You're a foolish man. Bethe and I have huge appetites. So does Bandit."

The gurry had been sitting patiently by Islaen's plate. She knew she was forbidden this type of liquid treat and was awaiting the arrival of something interesting.

Varn rubbed the top of her head with his fingers. The sight of her eager little face sent a twinge of guilt through him, and he looked about. The table was supplied with dishes holding both sugar and solid honey triangles. He took one of the latter and placed it before her, to her immediate delight. "That is better, Small One. I cannot see you here with nothing and hope to enjoy myself."

Islaen shook her head but said nothing. All the unit, herself included, spoiled their Jadite companion shamelessly.

"You could have held off stuffing her a bit longer, Varn," Bethe Danlo remarked. "I have a feeling she's going to be very well fed in the near future. Here comes *The Lioness'* owner herself."

May Smythe stopped at their table, as she did with all her patrons. Instead of the usual greeting and polite inquiries, however, she promptly picked up the purring gurry. "How is my little lady tonight? I'll put credits down that your humans have been simply starving you."

Bandit answered with a whistle and a battery of lower-pitched chirps. She looked up expectantly into the civilian's beaming face.

Smythe turned her attention to the humans. "I hope everything is to your satisfaction thus far?"

"Everything is perfect," the Noreenan woman responded.

"Would you permit me to borrow Bandit? My kitchen staff has threatened to mutiny if I don't bring her back for a visit."

"By all means. Don't let them overstuff her with treats. She needs real food as well."

"I believe a miniature banquet has been prepared for her."

"No doubt an excellent one. —Go with May, Bandit," she ordered, as if speaking to an animal.

The gurry whistled. *Yes, Islaen!*

Keep linked with us. That was a discipline her humans insisted upon whenever Bandit left them in any port area. There was almost no danger that anyone would injure her, but there was always the chance that someone might covet her themselves or see her as an exotic pet for the inner-system market. She was never permitted to enter any starship or confined space with a stranger without their knowing it and being near to hand to effect a rescue if necessary.

Islaen brought her attention back to her goblet. Sogan had excellent taste . . .

She felt her husband's eyes on her and raised hers to meet them. *Varn?*

I love you, he said softly.

And I you, more than all the universe besides, Varn Tarl Sogan.

Their meal was nearly finished by the time the highly satisfied gurry returned to the unit.

She flew to her usual place between Islaen Connor and Sogan. *Dinner good! Dessert soon?*

"I do not believe it," the Arcturian muttered. "I do not know where she stows it."

He translated what she had said for the benefit of their two companions who could not share her thoughts.

Bandit's careful! she protested. *Bandit visit Admiral Sithe?* she added hopefully.

"Sithe?" the colonel asked in confusion. "How does he figure into this?"

Admiral Sithe likes Bandit! Admiral's here!

"Where?" Sogan demanded.

In our room.

"The private one?"

Yes! Another man, too!

He repeated the gurry's intelligence. "What are they doing?"

Eating dinner! Talking! Very serious! She read the tension in him. *Bandit scout?*

Islaen hesitated. The gurry had proven an adroit spy on several occasions. She was small enough to go unnoticed and would pass for an animal if observed, and between her mind contact with her bonded humans and her ability to link her senses directly with Varn's, she could make the pair a virtual party to whatever scene she witnessed.

"No," the colonel decided in the end. "We're not working tonight, and it's not so odd that he should be here. Admiral Dundee is in port. Where else would Sithe be expected to bring him?" She smiled. "We're just about ready to consider the dessert selections, remember? I suggest we concentrate on that and forget about Navy brass for the time being."

Varn yielded. Although he still felt uneasy, he recognized that to be irrational and used his will to leash, if not entirely to quell, the unwelcome sensation. He turned in his seat to look for and summon their waiter.

The man had been watching for that signal and started for the table. To Sogan's surprise, he was bearing another bottle.

He presented it to the War Prince. "Compliments of Admiral Sithe, sir, with his congratulations."

"Please convey our appreciation to Admiral Sithe," Islaen said quickly, then smiled and indicated that the Horusi should open the bottle for them.

Sithe's gift proved to be a Hedonite dessert wine, golden in color, sweet as a dream, rich and complex.

"A fine gesture," the colonel said aloud. *Now, my friend,* she commanded, *sit back and enjoy it.*

"It is indeed," Karmikel agreed. "Let others ruin their digestion by working through what should be a grand dinner. We're here to celebrate." He eyed the War Prince. "If the admiral, here, will split a bottle of opaline with me after dinner, we can make a proper night of it."

Bethe Danlo glared at him, knowing he was running their comrade over the jets. Arcturian officers drank only fine wine and that in utter moderation. To Sogan, the rest of the Federation's prized potions might be compared with strong poison for all their appeal.

Varn only smiled. He ran his fingers over Islaen's hand. "Sorry, Captain Karmikel. I do have plans for making this a proper night, and they do not include obliterating my wits."

Jake flushed hotter than did the colonel, and Bethe laughed heartily. "Beautifully done, Admiral! If it weren't for the table, this big ape's jaw would've hit his boots!"

"You're getting a galaxy too good at this game," Karmikel grumbled without any loss of his previous good humor.

Islaen recovered her composure. "A masterful stroke, Admiral," she agreed, but her smile was for Jake. The shadow which had touched and threatened to blight their evening had vanished once more.

The wall of the private room was constructed of single-way optical laminate. Although invisible themselves, the

Federation admirals seated within enjoyed a full view of the glittering room beyond.

Gray Jack Dundee watched while the Commandos were seated. "Colonel Connor is exquisite," he remarked. "It's a little difficult to envision the best Commando leader in the Navy looking like a princess out of some story nano."

"Colonel Connor is a princess," his host reminded him.

"Aye, the wife of a War Prince."

"Also the adopted daughter of Thorne's Doge."

"I'd forgotten about that. I'll put quite a few credits down that those four won't waste their opportunities on that merchant world, either."

"They won't be depending upon Navy pensions to fund their retirement if any of them should live so long," Sithe agreed.

The Chief Admiral studied the unit curiously. Their table was reasonably close, and he could see a tiny feathered creature flitting from one to the other of the party. "What in space is that?"

"A Jadite gurry. The team's mascot. She's a very nice little thing and has managed to make herself the pet of just about everyone in the port." He glowered. "That's certainly true of the maintenance staff. The *Fairest Maid* and *Jovian Moon* get top service whenever they're on-world, whatever about any competing demands."

"A large portion of those crews are mutants, aren't they?" Dundee asked carefully.

Ram Sithe's eyes narrowed. Arcturians were notorious for their intolerance of peoples widely divergent from prototype ideal, to the extent that they had eradicated every such race discovered in their own ultrasystem. "Captain Sogan doesn't seem to have a problem. Sure as space is black, he hasn't caused one."

"How is he managing, Ram? You know I had some serious doubts about the wisdom of commissioning him in the beginning."

"He's adapting, even if it's a struggle for him. It's death pure and simple if he does not. As for the rest, Sogan knows he has no other option. He chose to continue living against everything his kind would call reason. If his existence is to have any purpose or offer any shadow of satisfaction to him, he has to throw his lot with the Navy. There isn't anything else for him. His life in the starlanes was nightmare only."

"It isn't likely that he'd make it as a trader, I suppose. The bargaining and other necessary nonsense must have been killing for him even if he could manage it at all."

"He was making it—barely—but by taking on what amounted to suicide runs. Vishnu was the rare exception until he got mixed up with Islaen Connor and everything novaed on him. Afterwards, he jumped at the chance at real service, and we owed it to him." He grimaced. "I also did not want to lose Colonel Connor. She'd never have let him face the universe alone again and would have found a way to go with him, as a space hand if not as a wife."

"And now? He still has to live here, on Horus or elsewhere, when not actually in space."

"Sogan keeps to his own ship and his own unit for the most part. I deal chiefly with Colonel Connor, which is probably for the best. I find it uncomfortable treating a man who should be my equal, even on the opposite side of the starlanes, as a subordinate. I dislike even to imagine how he must feel. Admiral Varn Tarl Sogan was, if nothing else, a proud man. I doubt that has altered since his fall."

"I can understand why he sticks close to his own. That incident with my lads today could have been unpleasant."

"At least, they kept their heads cool and their blasters holstered. It's not always that easy."

"It happens often?"

"Not frequently on Horus now. The unit's pretty well known among the regulars, and there are plenty who'll come to their defense. On other planets, aye, to the Federation's discredit."

"I saw the defense part. How do those Malkites fit in?"

"They're the crew who assisted the unit on Tambora."

"Ah, aye, I remember now! The captain, Zubin, was one of those who planeted immediately after the volcano blew to get Connor and Sogan out?"

"The same man. The ground was still smoking at the time."

The other made no reply. *The Lioness'* owner was passing near the transparent wall while carrying the gurry toward the kitchen. He peered closely, trying to get a good look at her. "Odd little creature. It's hard to believe so small an animal could be of use for more than emotional comfort and good public relations, yet the unit's reports indicate that she's been instrumental in saving the lives of all of them on one occasion or another."

"So she has. Colonel Connor assures me her reports on the subject are not exaggerated."

"Has the gurry been tested to determine her actual intelligence and potential? I've seen nothing about that."

"You won't, either. Jade of Kuan Yin is adamant with respect to that. Her colonists will not permit any off-worlders to study their fauna and will allow none of them to be exported. Bandit is decidedly an exception and is formally covered under that ruling."

"I suppose it was hard to refuse her to the people who had saved the whole colony twice over."

"Damned hard." Sithe shrugged. "I once suggested doing some testing anyway in jest. All four of them promptly offered their resignations. They have the right, too. It's in their enlistment contracts."

The other man chuckled. "More power to them! —A tight team?"

"All my good ones are."

"All mine as well."

Dundee fell silent for several seconds. "You know what I want, Ram. Do you think they can handle it?"

Sithe, too, was quiet before replying. "As an admiral of the Federation Navy, aye. Those four can handle just about anything. They've proven that."

"As their commander, you would say something else?"

"As their commander and as a man, if you weren't Chief Admiral."

"Ram, damn it, spit it out! I'm not talking a training exercise here!"

"You wouldn't give Sogan a proper ship. Now, you want to haul him and the others off into space on yours."

"I couldn't give Varn Tarl Sogan a battleship, Man! What we've done for him already is more than unorthodox. Not all the commanders who survived his attentions during the War, particularly some of those whom he repeatedly outfoxed, would be prepared to be as generous as you are. A few of them occupy high places. They'd see to it that he'd lose everything he's gained, and if by some miracle, he held onto it, they'd make sure his life was one everlasting siege in hell."

The other sighed. "Aye, I realized that, Jack. It's the injustice of it that chokes me."

"I don't feel so very happy about that myself."

Gray Jack's eyes flickered to the four for a moment, then returned to fix on Sithe. "You have no other reservations?"

The black eyes met Dundee's. "Just one. Giving a man doomed to die of thirst a single drop of water isn't a kindness. It's a torture. I don't want to see the finest Commando unit I have, the finest anywhere in the Federation, ripped to shreds, in whole or in part."

Islaen Connor carefully folded her cloak and lay it on the table in the *Maid's* crew's cabin, that in which those aboard the starship spent their nonworking waking hours.

It was a small cabin, as were all those aboard the little fighter, but it was comfortable. A high-backed, padded bench stood against three of the four walls. Cabinets set into its base contained the nanos and other materials used by the crew to pass the time on the sometimes long voyages between the stars. At the blind end of the room, a table was set between the benches. Two doors led from the other, one going to the core ladder, the other to the tiny, well-appointed galley.

The Noreenan's eyes were bright when she raised them to meet her husband's. *Thank you, Varn. This was a wonderful evening.*

It was, he agreed. *It was a small gift for a War Prince to offer his consort, though.*

Patience, my friend. We should begin seeing some proper return from our investments fairly soon, even before we can begin introducing nectar to the ultrasystem at large on any major scale.

He let her feel his amusement. *You are beginning to sound like a merchant princess already.*

Islaen laughed softly. *You haven't been exactly slow in assuming the role of merchant prince, my friend.*

Varn looked surprised. *I?*

I've sat in on some of your strategy sessions with the Doge, Admiral. You don't play a minor part in them. You've also taken over the task of selecting the freighters to carry Thorne's goods, and you've been spending a lot of time and effort doing it.

I owe Thorne of Brandine, Islaen, and Harlran Lanree personally.

Aye, although some would say that giving a planet her life on two separate counts is cause enough to win her people's support.

The woman smiled as she studied him. *I also think you like having a few credits at your command again, over and above those required for bare survival, and that you're anything but averse to increasing your stock of them.*

The War Prince started to scowl but then surrendered. He removed his own jacket. Even with the temperature dropped for the night, the starship felt warm in comparison with the biting chill outside. *You are right,* he confessed. *It does feel good. I was able to give you nothing at all for our marriage.* That poverty had been a bitter dose when the wealth and rule of star systems had once been his.

There's the little matter of the river tear, she reminded him.

That came after the fact. It was only a present.

Only a present worth half a small planet.

That is an exaggeration, Colonel Connor.

A precious little one. Islaen came into his arms. *You gave me yourself, Varn Tarl Sogan.*

Then the touch of her mind altered. *You mentioned having plans for the remainder of the night, Admiral. Perhaps we should begin discussing those.*

Chapter Four

Karmikel and Danlo were already in their usual places when the Arcturian entered the crew's cabin.

"You two are early."

"You're just late," Jake told him. "Mission accomplished last night, Admiral?"

Sogan only smiled, refusing to rise to the good-natured bait.

Bethe administered a rabbit punch to her husband's ribs that drew a gasp from him.

"Ease up, Sergeant!" he protested. "Sure, if I didn't jink him now and then, he'd be calling in the medical staff to attend to me!"

Varn laughed. "Let him be, Bethe. I think I am good enough to hold my own with him."

"Too good at times," the other man grumbled, rubbing his side.

The War Prince watched him with amusement and also with some envy. Jake and Bethe Danlo were fortunate in their open ease together. He could not play like that with his consort even mind-to-mind. It was only recently that he had become able to do so openly with Bandit.

His eyes softened momentarily. Islaen and he had shared another freedom last night . . .

"Is the colonel still abed?" Karmikel asked.

"On the bridge. The surplanetary transceiver finished routing us out."

"Well, breakfast should be ready. Bethe programmed the range when we came aboard. Since you're standing, you might as well do the serving."

Varn complied, leaving Islaen's portion until she should join them.

His eyes brightened a moment later at her mental greeting, and he turned to face her as she came into the cabin. "Sit. I shall have your share ready in a minute."

"Thanks, Varn." She accepted the plate and inevitable cup of jakek from him. "We have an invitation for lunch the day after tomorrow," she informed him.

"With whom?"

"Chief Admiral Dundee. We're to meet him in *The Lioness*. The private room, naturally. After that, we're to return to headquarters with him."

Bethe Danlo frowned. "What does that son of a Schythian ape want?"

"Sergeant Danlo, is that any way in which to speak of our Navy's highest ranking officer?" asked Karmikel in mock shock. "Of course, I echo the question. Ram Sithe's our commander. It's his business to meet with us, or with the colonel, now and then, but the head of the Federation Navy just doesn't up and leave the inner-systems and journey all the way out to the rim merely to eat lunch with a couple of Commandos, however famous they happen to be and however illustrious their past lives."

"He has obviously arranged to borrow us for a job," Sogan stated, "and it is sensitive enough that he does not want to discuss the details in a public place. The lunch is a courtesy."

"That's my reading as well, Admiral," Islaen concurred. "As for the details, I suppose we shall just have to wait until we hear them."

"In the meantime, I have the *Maid's* tubes to scrub. I dislike leaving it entirely to Sergeant Lampry's lads. I also hope to pay a visit to the coast later, so I had best get down to business."

"I'll give you a hand," the redhead offered. "The work will finish faster that way."

"You're an arrogant bastard, Sogan."

The Arcturian pulled off his work gloves and laid them on the table beside Karmikel's. "It is part of my inheritance. A War Prince is given high rank at what your sort would consider a very early age, star systems to rule, and a large measure of arrogance."

Bethe Danlo put down the nano she had just selected for reading. "Let him alone, Jake," she warned, cutting off the reply he had been about to make.

"Why defend him?" the Noreenan grumbled. "I'm your loving husband."

"You provoke him. He just gives back as good as he gets."

"I give back better," Varn interrupted in an injured tone.

"See, he doesn't need protecting," Karmikel said.

"You both need protecting. Islaen and I can't trust either of you out of our sight."

The colonel appeared in the doorway at that moment. "Are they at each other again, Bethe?"

"We'll be quiet," Jake promised. "It doesn't do the troops any good to give their commanding officer a headache."

"I'm grateful for the consideration," she told him dryly.

Islaen turned to Sogan. "Are you still planning to go to the coast?"

"As soon as I steam off this grime." Any work involving a starship's tubes was always as dirty as it was physically difficult.

"Jake needs the flier, and I have to use the rover," she informed him.

"I can walk. That is my reason for going."

"It's six miles to reach the coast at all, much less any part of it deserted enough to be of interest to you. Jake can drop you off where you want to go before heading into the port."

The War Prince frowned. "That is an imposition on him. It would be completely out of his way."

Karmikel smiled. "I hate martyrs, Admiral. You'll just have to owe me."

"I'll pick you up," Connor promised.

"Islaen—"

"I hate martyrs, too," she informed him briskly. "Will two hours be sufficient, or would you like more time?"

"Two hours will be fine. This will probably be my last chance for a while," he added in explanation to soften his answer and also by way of thanks to his comrades. "Even if we do not lift as soon as I anticipate, winter is coming on rapidly. In another couple of weeks, it will be too cold to venture near the ocean for any such casual purpose."

Two men in the coverall working uniform of Navy mechanics stood together. They were tall and thin with the flat, lipless features of Lemura's offspring. The bright sunlight made an iridescent glory of the small scales covering their heads and hands, the only portions of their bodies open to its rays.

They watched the officers enter their flier and drive off.

"The dark-haired one is Sogan. The redhead's Karmikel," Maintenance Sergeant Max Lampry informed his companion.

"They look like any of the space hounds hanging about the civilian part of the port."

"Commandos do not normally wear uniforms on their missions for obvious reasons, and they usually stick to spacer togs in general, at least, these four do. They put on dress finery only for special reasons or when they have to deal with the brass."

"And those are their starships?"

"The *Fairest Maid* and the *Jovian Moon*," Max replied proudly.

"When are you going to stop playing with little splinters like these? You're a fine mechanic. I could get you on any system aboard the *Charm*."

"Thanks for the offer, Pete Ospry, but I like my present assignment. So do my lads. We work with ships. We don't spend our lives turning one specific screw on one valve in one system. We also get to actually know the captains and crews whose vessels we service."

"Knowing Commando-Captain Varnt Sogan isn't much of a bargain from what I've heard. Rumor has it that he's half an Arcturian when it comes to mutants like ourselves. The story goes that he doesn't even like to have one of us touch his exclusive person—"

Lampry's oddly round eyes flashed. "Listen to scuttlebutt if you want, Pete, but don't go spreading it, not about Varnt Sogan. He looks like a damned Arcturian. Any rumor mentioning the word could get him killed. Captain Sogan's a fine officer and, as far as I know, a good enough man. I'd hate to see him burned down because someone shot off his flaming mouth at the wrong time. Look what happened with those flyboys from your *Charm* yesterday."

Report of the incident had received fairly wide circulation, and the other mechanic shrugged. "They got carried away."

"The *Rounder*'s Malkite crew didn't seem to mind stepping in on Sogan's side, did they?—As for the rest, Sogan doesn't have to care for us. He has to let us do our jobs, which he does. He also works beside us, as does Captain Karmikel. I somehow can't see your Admiral Dundee or Captain Broderick soiling their fine uniforms crawling inside the tubes."

"They don't have to. The *Terra's Charm* has a large enough crew to handle all that," the other man protested.

"Precisely. —These two go further than just working with us. It was Sogan and Karmikel who recommended me for sergeant last year, and my crews and I have done so much experimental work on these ships that I rewrote the manual. Sogan read what I'd done and had Colonel Connor present it to Admiral Sithe. It'll be the new Navy standard come next month. My name's on it and on the rights that go with it."

That silenced Ospry. "All right, power down. I'll give you that you've got a fairly good berth here even if I still don't envy you it."

"No more than I don't envy you your spot, Mate."

Karmikel kept the flier at a good pace but did not try to push the drive to its top surplanetary speed. This was no race, and there was no pressure on them.

He glanced at his companion. The Arcturian had been silent for most of the journey, responding to Jake's occasional remarks but offering few of his own. "I may have been off the charts today," the redhead said, "only a wee bit, mind you, but off them."

Sogan smiled faintly. "I am the one who should apologize. You had no need to make this trip."

"I don't have any more luck than you do in saying no to Islaen Connor, my friend."

"Still, this is my own concern, not the unit's."

"I wish you'd let me help with it," Karmikel said.

To his surprise, the War Prince neither bridled nor retreated behind the wall he could raise so expertly to separate himself from the rest of his species. "I wish that you could, too, Jake." He shrugged. "It is nothing very dramatic or important, just something I want to try to put to rest before we lift again. This method works for me."

The other smiled. "I thought you always vanish onto the *Maid*'s bridge to do your heavy thinking."

"That is for serious matters." He was too ashamed to admit his true reason for setting a different course this time.

They had come well out from the city. The road below was empty of traffic. The coastline looked bleak and forbidding and was completely deserted, as was to be expected at this time of the year. The tumble of barren rocks on the opposite side was even less inviting.

"Will this do, Admiral?"

"Perfectly, Captain Karmikel." His paused. "I do like walking, you know, and I like oceans, including this one."

"I know. Arcturians are all mad."

He eased the flier to a stop. "Last chance to change your mind. It looks cold out there. You can't tell me you like that."

"I do not, but I shall stay warm if I keep walking."

"Have the joy of it, comrade, but I'm thinking you'll be very happy to see the colonel when she finally shows up to collect you."

"You are probably right, Captain."

Varn Tarl Sogan left the vehicle. He gasped despite himself at the slap of the wind. It had a bitter bite.

He braced himself against it and walked over to the chest-high wall that separated the road from the cliff dropping down into the sea sixty feet below.

It was a wild, cold scene that met his eyes. The cliff itself was rugged and straight, although no special skill or strength would be needed to climb it. The stone comprising it was dark. It spread out in this place at water level into a broad ledge that tapered gently down about six feet until it disappeared under the waves. During Horus' wild storms, fierce surges would roar right up the rock wall, but normally, this much, at least, of the ledge remained uncovered and dry apart from spray. He had climbed down to it in warmer weather but felt no desire to do so now.

The water itself was full of drama and implied peril. Horus' ocean was black. It did not smile or beckon to pleasure, but there was an awesome beauty, an almost hypnotic fascination about it. The foam whipped up by the wind was pure white, and the spray in the air tasted powerfully of salt.

Jake Karmikel watched him for a few moments. The Arcturian had turned slightly to set more of his shoulders and back against the wind, but otherwise, he made no concession to it. He kept his body straight, refusing to cringe before it or huddle in upon himself for warmth.

Jake started to take the controls but instead left the vehicle and walked over to the wall to stand beside his comrade.

Sogan's head turned slightly at his approach. "There is powerful kinship between space and the sea, is there not? Both can be bitter foes, utterly unforgiving of folly or carelessness, harsh even with those who know and respect them, but they offer freedom and peace as well. They each draw, lure those of us with the souls to be reached by them."

His dark eyes fixed on the scarcely darker water. "Had we lived in prespace times, we would each be master of a warship on some ocean of our respective worlds. —You would have been fortunate in that respect. I have read something of the old history of your Federation's motherplanet. Terra had some fine fighting ships and fighting captains." Some fine fighting admirals.

"What about your seed world?"

"We were seafarers and sea fighters as well."

Suddenly, Varn Tarl Sogan's entire aspect altered. He stood stiffly straight and peered intently out at the water, as if he would pierce its surface to scan its inky depths.

Karmikel kept still, watching him. Islaen Connor's talent allowed her to pick up the emotions and feelings of other people, although she could not share or read thought with anyone except the Arcturian and Bandit. Sogan's version of their gift was stranger. He could touch mind with a large segment of the galaxy's nonhuman-level life forms and even influence or directly control many of them. It was an ability that had served them all well during the past two years, although it was of little use in space or in an urban setting like Horus' spaceport.

The tension left the War Prince's body but not his expression. "What big predators haunt these waters?" he asked.

"I've never heard of any, but I've had no reason to find out, either."

"No. I suppose not."

"It was something big? And a predator?"

"A predator, certainly. I could not touch thought with it at all, but I could feel its hunger and its hunting. It was not interested in keillyfish. They were not even radiating fear of it, and there were many of them around."

"Is it still there?"

"Not nearby. It has moved out to sea again." The dark eyes were troubled. "What am I going to do, Jake? I cannot announce that I have made mind contact with an unseen, supposedly large predator, yet this is a populous region."

"You couldn't bring it to the surface for a moment? If we glimpsed it, we could report it."

He shook his head. "I tried."

"You've never felt anything like it around here before?" He knew Sogan automatically checked for wildlife when he was in an area where any might conceivably exist. It was a precaution that was now almost instinctive with him and, Jake suspected, probably a pleasure as well.

"I have never detected anything in these waters except small life forms and a large variety of highly indigestible fish."

Karmikel smiled at that. The former admiral did not care for waterfood as a whole, and he detested strongly flavored fish. It was one of the very few things about which Varn Tarl Sogan was prepared to be difficult under almost any circumstances barring the demands of an actual mission.

The forced lightness faded from the other almost immediately. "There will be no swimming now, but an accident could put someone into the water—"

"You're that worried?"

"Aye, I am. I wish I knew more. It could be nothing. A large hunger and rapacious nature in a relatively small creature could give me similar readings, I suppose. I know it is an individual, at least, and no school."

"But you do think it's big enough to be a real threat?"

"I do, potentially, at least."

"We'll know better what to do if we can identify it," the Noreenan said decisively. "Bethe and I'll hit the Natural History Center and library when I get back. We'll probably have a score of candidates for you by the time Islaen picks you up."

"I should come with you, but I want to keep scanning in case it comes inshore again."

"Do that," he agreed. "You'd better stretch your legs a bit while you're hunting the hunter. It may move along the shoreline, too, and if you stay glued here, Islaen will have to chip you out of a block of ice when she arrives."

"Thanks, Jake. If it returns, I shall know it."

Chapter Five

Varn watched until the flier disappeared from sight. He began pacing after that, although he feared to move too far from the place. Karmikel was right. It was too cold to remain long in one spot. The hunter was gone now, hopefully far out to sea where prey existed to meet the appetite he had sensed. The best he could do at the moment was to leave his receptors wide open to pick up its transmissions again should it venture near once more.

That left him free to concentrate on the miserable business that had brought him here, to walk by Horus' ocean in the bitter cold because he could scarcely stand the sight of a starship at the moment.

The Arcturian felt his anger rise against himself, that and shame. It was bad enough that he lacked the strength to kill his desire for a major command when he knew he would not again hold one, and it was worse that he had permitted Islaen Connor to ever learn of his weakness. He had, on the other hand, believed his longing to be under reasonable control, merely a deeper sorrow among others for all that he had lost, another scar to match those the executioners had left on his back.

The arrival of the *Terra's Charm* had given the lie to that comfortable fantasy. The news of her coming had torn through him like the spear of a premech warrior.

The great battleship was a five thousand-class, even as his own flagship had been, and she had been his counterpart in the War. He had always expected to meet and fight her someday and would assuredly have fought against her had he not been sent to Thorne of Brandine. He had studied her closely, every detail Arcturian Intelligence could gather about her—her weapons, her style of battle, the admiral and the captain who commanded her.

He had not hungered for the confrontation he believed to be inevitable, knowing full well that either the five thousand men serving under him would die in that battle or the five thousand men and women aboard the Federation battlecraft, or maybe both ships and their crews would be gone at the end of it.

Desired or not, he had known the meeting of the flagships could not be postponed indefinitely. What could not be avoided had to be faced. He had, therefore, planned for the fight, anticipated his opponents' tactics, and laid his own to counter them. A large portion of his thought and energy had been concentrated on the Federation battleship over a long period of time as he had prepared for the duel that fate had prevented from taking place.

Now, the big ship was back in his life once more, docked in the near-space above this planet, a concrete symbol of everything that was gone. All his effort, all he had struggled to achieve, could not stand as a shadow of that which she represented for him. She was as a whip in skilled, cruel hands, the mocking reality that named his current command a pathetic splinter ship and he himself an alien in an ultrasystem that was danger only . . .

Sogan stopped himself with an oath. All of that was true as far as it went, but in honesty, he had to admit that the Federation had not used him so very ill. Trouble, he had, aye, and in plenty, but he had also found allies to help him stand against and to bear it, and not his official comrades only. Zubin's quick intervention in his cause in the supply depot was testimony to that.

Despite his foul mood, he smiled at the memory. It had been neatly done. For all his talk of mayhem, the big spacer had ended the likelihood of violent confrontation even had Gray Jack Dundee not appeared on the scene.

The War Prince shook his head. The friendly relationship between the Malkite freighter captain and himself was a puzzle, one of the many with which life in the Federation had presented him. The years of enforced interaction with mutants of all types, the direct observation of their capabilities and courage, compelled him, however unwillingly at the outset, to condemn the contempt his kind held for peoples who had altered significantly from the basic human prototype, but he shared in full the Arcturian revulsion for physically divergent races. No amount of willing, not even the knowledge of the anger it aroused in his consort, could dislodge that completely. Close association had desensitized him to a great degree with individuals he knew, but his relationship with the *Rounder*'s crew went beyond that. He liked the four men and enjoyed their company when they chanced to meet, although he also found them overpowering.

Sogan smiled again, this time more naturally. Overpowering was an understatement with respect to the freighter's master. Zubin of Malki sometimes made him feel as if he were standing in the aftershock of a planetbuster detonation.

That might be part of the answer, he thought wryly. It was only necessary to ride the crest of the tsunami and trust it to batter down all opposition before it.

The former admiral sighed. That was all part of life in the Federation—mutants, body-killing labor, danger, the numerous questions and mysteries for which there seemed to be no answer, the countless other questions he dared not even ask. He had chosen to embrace it in its entirety and had no right of complaint.

Suicide was an acceptable course for an Arcturian warrior. It was not to be used in a moment of despair or near madness—his own people would have stopped him in those dark minutes after the Amazoon disaster even as had Jake Karmikel—but a considered decision would not be thwarted. A member of his rank in the inconceivable position in which he had found himself, degraded, with no possibility of redeeming himself, living at and upon the mercy of his enemies and facing existence only without hope or purpose, such a one had no other option.

Against all reason, he had chosen not to avail himself of it. He would never fully understand why himself, save that he had borne a dark, cold anger toward his kind despite his acceptance of their judgment against him, of its inevitably in light of the stern code by which he lived. He had also, in plain truth, been too stubborn. He had survived against all odds, and he had determined to go on surviving. Even in the raw despair of the three years that had followed while he had haunted the starlanes alone, he had refused to die. At times, he had wished to do so, but always, he had fought to live.

He sighed again. His decision to go on had been real and firm. He had accepted that work and battle of one sort or another would have to be a perpetual part of his existence in this alien and often hostile ultrasystem. He had done more than reasonably well through a great deal of good fortune and his own efforts. Why could he not reconcile himself to this one loss, the loss of command and the work he had most loved? His failure to do so was demeaning to himself. Worse, it could hurt Islaen Connor. It would hurt her if he could not chain it, and chain it quickly, before she became aware of its new strength.

Damn Gray Jack Dundee and his *Terra's Charm* to all the Federation's hells . . .

Why was the desire so strong? Command was not the greatest of his losses, not nearly the greatest. It was not the worst shaming he had been forced to endure.

No, but it was the only one not in its basic nature permanent. The rest, he had been able to accept, to bury deep within himself. The dead would not rise again. The shame, the agony of the whips and in his heart, the labor and times of want that had followed, none of that could be undone or erased. Luck or work or ability just might possibly bring a man to a battleship's bridge once more, even if it must be in an alien navy.

Sogan scowled darkly. Did he actually harbor some insane hope that he might someday win back to his desire here in the Federation since the Empire was closed to him? He had gained a great deal, but laid beside this, it was a pathetic comet against a sun-star. Was he, in truth, dreaming of something more?

His face became hard, implacable as the cold, black ocean below. If that were so, he would tear it out of himself, out of existence entirely. He would wield his mind, his will, as the executioners had their accursed whips, do such violence to his spirit that no such false hope would ever or could ever rise up to trouble him again.

Varn Tarl Sogan's attention abruptly and sharply returned to his surroundings. He had felt it again, that hunger and hunting, this time far out to sea. Even as he picked up the reading, it was gone once more.

The former admiral shivered violently. While he had been buried in his thoughts and in the mental violence he had intended to work upon himself, he had at least been oblivious to the discomforts of his situation. The return of the creature put an end to that. He would have to seek actively for it now and for signs of its activities in the more normal water life of the area, to the exclusion of personal business.

He shivered again. His spacer's jacket was adequate for movement around the ships on the planeting field or for short hops in the warmer port facility. It was not sufficient protection for this place or this work now that it seemed necessary for him to remain more or less in place. He had also lost the option of contacting his consort and asking her to come out early for him. He would have to give Karmikel and Danlo the promised time in which to do their research and stick with his own job for the duration.

The Commando-Colonel arrived at last, much to Sogan's relief. She had the rover, which meant that their comrades were still in port with the faster flier.

Connor left the vehicle and joined him at the wall. The few unshielded feelings that she was receiving from him were still dark, proof that he had not resolved whatever had been riding him, but his thoughts themselves were free of it. With actual work before him, the Arcturian had pushed more personal considerations aside.

Anything? she asked as soon as she reached his side.

A couple of brief touches. Maybe a third, but I cannot vouch for that. They were all very far out. Have our friends had any luck?

To his surprise, the woman shook her head. *None. According to all the data we checked, including one live expert, there aren't any big predators around here. Near the Equator, aye, and far out in the real deeps, but absolutely nothing along the northern coast.*

I did not imagine those contacts, Islaen. The first was very strong, and even the others were unmistakable after having experienced that initial touch.

I wouldn't insult you by suggesting they weren't real. I was saying that you've found us a puzzle, Admiral, and, as you pointed out to Jake, a problem. What in space are we going to do?

Islaen shuddered under the impact of a particularly powerful gust.

Sogan put his arm around her and held her close to give her something of his warmth. Suddenly, his mood brightened and softened. *We walked here the evening before we were married. Do you remember, my Islaen?*

She smiled. *I do.* He had not held her then. *You weren't doing very much talking that evening.*

Neither were you.

The Noreenan shuddered again despite the windbreak he was providing. *I was just as cold, though. We can finish our discussion inside the rover unless you'd like to stay a little longer here.*

Lead the way, Colonel Connor.

It was warm within the small machine. Varn closed his eyes, savoring the heat as another might some exquisite luxury. *Sometimes, I do not know why I let myself in for things like that,* he confessed ruefully. *If Karmikel did it, I would accuse him of operating with all circuits blown.*

You're the one making the observation, Admiral. I won't say the same thought hasn't entered my mind on occasion.

What is that? He was looking back down along the road in the direction of the distant port.

Islaen could see the object that had taken his attention as well. It was just a speck, a vehicle of some sort, coming toward them at what appeared to be a good clip. Like Varn, she raised her distance lenses to better make it out.

It was fairly large, and they could soon discern it clearly, a civilian multiplepassenger six-wheel transport.

Public mass transit doesn't come out this far, the Commando-Colonel said. *An excursion, perhaps. There's a rock wilderness sports complex ten miles farther on.* —*Aye. I can see children at the windows.*

It is coming bloody fast. The War Prince pulled their rover off the road well into the rugged rockfield to their right. He did not like the look of the onrushing vehicle and wanted to give it plenty of room.

Islaen Connor was frowning as well. She sent her mind out seeking the driver's. Fear! *He's in trouble, Varn! I don't think he can stop that thing!*

Chapter Six

No, nor steer well by the look of it, Sogan replied. *The fool! He should turn to the right, crash into the rockfield. Better that than over the cliff.*

Islaen Connor watched helplessly. If they had their flier, they might have been able to do something, burn out the wheels with its lasers and force a halt, but this rover was only a standard spaceport vehicle they had rented for the duration of their stay.

The transport was nearly upon them. *Spirit of Space,* she whispered as she saw the rows of terrified little faces, *they're all so small.*

The road curved in the place opposite them. The bend was not sharp, but it was sufficient to prove a bad challenge to the careening transport. *The wall may not hold if they hit it dead on.*

It will not hold, he declared, *not if struck at that speed.*

The driver struggled mightily with the controls. They thought he might succeed in turning his vehicle, but it suddenly jerked into an even greater speed. It leaped forward and hurtled itself at the wall.

The structure shattered under the impact. For a long moment, the transport hung between land and air, half balanced on the remaining shards of the wall. Those crumbled as well, and the big vehicle pitched forward and down toward the rock ledge and the sea sixty feet below.

Connor caught up the first aid kit in the rover. *I'm going down now. You contact the others. Tell them what's happened and to get here on all burners with the renewer. They can summon the Horusi Emergency Service en route.*

Sogan activated the communicator strapped to his left wrist. The small, nearly indestructible device had served Commando units well during the latter years of the War, allowing the members to communicate over surprisingly long distances and also serving as a homing instrument in need.

The distance separating them proved no challenge to its abilities. His comrades responded at once, and he made his report of the accident. That done, he hurried to give whatever assistance he could to the victims, assuming anyone had survived the crash.

The Commando-Colonel half-climbed, half-scrambled down the cliff face to the site of the crash.

The first few feet of the transport were submerged. The remainder sat apparently securely on the ledge, braced by whatever obstacle had checked its advance. She opened her mind receptors. There was life inside, life and fear and pain.

The front door was under water. The rear one was farther back on the ledge. It was sprung but still closed. She wasted no time on it. Using her blaster, she burned through the hinges.

The scene within was like something returned from the War. The bloodied children were reasonably quiet, stunned by terror and the suddenness and enormity of the accident. Most, probably all, of them were injured, some seriously so.

Islaen ignored those in the rear for the moment. The major crisis right now lay up front. Several children were trapped there, totally or partly under water. They still lived, but they would not last for long more. Anyone completely submerged probably had only seconds left.

The Noreenan gasped with the shock of it as she splashed into the frigid water. It was not deep, fortunately, and the seats had held most of the six children involved partly above its surface, enough so that they had air. Only one was completely under.

The little boy was free, at least, and she was able to haul him out quickly.

She felt her husband's arrival. *Varn, get this one outside and pump the water out of him, then disconnect the drive.* Pieces of them all would be scattered throughout the next three galaxies if the transport blew while they were still in it or on this ledge beside it.

Aye, Colonel.

The War Prince did what he could for the child, then left him on the ledge and slid into the water.

The bite of the cold was so intense that he thought for a moment that his heart would stop. It drove into him like a thousand knives, but he got himself moving.

Activating the torch from his belt, he took a deep breath and ducked his head into the salty black ocean.

It was a strange, gray world in which he found himself even this close to the surface, but between the diffused sunlight and the torch, he had sufficient light to examine the crumpled face of the wreck.

The whole nose section had been mangled, broken and flattened nearly beyond recognition. How the systems powering it remained active, he could not even begin to comprehend.

The driver had gone straight through the shattered windscreen. Two-thirds of his body hung outside the vehicle, impaled on shards of plastiglass and metal. The head had been reduced to pulp in the impact.

Varn had to search to locate the connections he wanted, and his expression tightened when he did. It would not be easy to reach them.

He rose for more air, then submerged again, this time going directly to his target.

Wreckage surrounded that part of the engine. It was firmly lodged, unmovable by one man and unbreakable. Sogan had to wriggle his way through it, wedge himself into it. Even then, he did not know if he would be able to reach the last connection.

Two, he caught and pulled readily. The third remained just out of range of his fingers. He swore mentally in his own tongue and wrenched himself against the debris to pull himself closer. At last, he managed to turn his slender body enough to slip farther in. The Arcturian reached out and quickly disabled the connection, killing all power to the transport's drive. That done, he started to back out.

Varn Tarl Sogan could not move. He was held at the waist and held fast.

An instinctive panic started to rise, but he quelled that. He needed air even now but knew he could hold out a little longer.

The problem was with his blaster. It was wedged solidly, caught and held by a claw formed by two sharp prongs of twisted metal.

The War Prince hastily unfastened the holster from his belt. He was able to pull free himself, but the wreck still held his weapon in its death grip.

By that time, there was no ignoring his lungs' demand. He extracted himself from the wreck and surfaced to draw in the cold, infinitely sweet air.

Varn, I have two hemorrhaging in here!

Abandoning the blaster, he splashed out of the water and ran for the transport. Four more children lay against the rock wall beside the one he had brought out, but he did not pause to look at them.

Islaen was within and in trouble. She had moved a toppled seat off two of the victims, among the smallest of the vehicle's passengers, only to find that it had been functioning as a crude tourniquet on their terribly torn legs. They lay just enough apart at such an angle that she could not manage both simultaneously, and only a little time was left in which to offer either any aid.

Varn took charge of the boy nearest him, and soon they had the bleeding under control in both.

A third child had shared the seat. Connor studied her while the captain carried her companions outside. She was critically injured and deeply unconscious. She was also tightly wedged. It would take some effort and more time to free her.

Reluctantly, the Noreenan left her. Too many others might—no, would—perish if she delayed now to pry this one loose. The small girl was in no pain. They would come back for her at the end, although she might well no longer be living. Her hold on life was very slim.

The Commandos labored together, using their skill and the scant supplies from their rover's first aid kit and those they were able to salvage from the transport's to stabilize their small charges and make them as comfortable as possible.

Sogan's hands shook a little as he worked, although he was careful to keep his manner calm, cheerful, so as not to further terrify the little victims.

War in space was a clean business, too clean, perhaps. It was too easy to kill ships and risk ships, forgetting the crews inside them. The Grim Commandant ruled there, as on every battlefield, but death usually came in an instant when a starship and those she carried exploded into a ball of incandescent dust.

On-world combat was always worse, both in its effects on the fighters themselves and because it involved noncombatants all too frequently. There had been incidents of such slaughter on Thorne of Brandine, but they had been few. He had forbidden atrocity, and his soldiers, after years of service under his command, were singularly well-disciplined even for their race.

He had watched his own children die, but they had been burned down, not torn and broken as were many of these. It was hard to see their pain and to be able to do so little to ease it.

Miraculously, none of the victims had died, or none had died yet. Many of them were in serious condition, and if help did not come soon, their injuries could well prove fatal.

If the physical damage did not start killing, the cold would. They were laying the children together as soon as they finished treating them, using body heat to supplement the three large survival blankets. It would not suffice forever, and they dared not use the wrecked transport for shelter. There was too much danger that it would shift under the working of the water, gentle as it fortunately was today, and slide completely off the ledge.

The former admiral settled the last of his patients beside his fellows and returned to the wreck. Islaen was trying to free the last child, the nineteenth. The little girl was badly trapped and badly injured, and life was barely a spark in her. She was also neck deep in that frigid water. They had to get her out fast, or whatever minute shred of hope that she had was gone.

It was hard, tricky work, and Islaen concentrated her full attention on it.

Suddenly, a tightly held shard of metal sprang loose with the release of the pressure on it and struck the colonel's arm with the force of a well-thrown knife, going completely through the flesh to emerge on the other side.

Islaen pulled herself free and glanced at the wound. Only a little higher, and the bone would have snapped. As it was, the injury, despite the heavy bleeding, was an inconvenience she could ignore.

Connor assured Sogan, who had come in response to her mental and audible cry of pain, that she was all right, then went back to her work.

Varn Tarl Sogan hastened to help her but froze in mid step. *Get out of here, Islaen. Now.*

Varn? She could feel the tension on him.

The hunter. It is back.

Where?

Pretty far out yet. I do not know what it can do to us, but this transport may be vulnerable. An inspiration struck him. *Go, will you! You have the only blaster. Mine became jammed when I was disabling the drive, and I had to leave it or drown.*

The colonel obeyed, pushing past him as she hurried to take up the guard. He watched her go with some concern. Blood was still running from her punctured arm.

Sogan hastened to the child. Only her head was above water. Her eyes were closed, and one of them was covered by the blood that had flowed out of the long rent in her scalp to stain all the scales on the left side of her head and face.

Islaen had done good work on the wreckage holding her, and it took the Arcturian, with his greater physical strength, only a few minutes to finish freeing her.

It seemed an eternity. The hunter had come nearer. Its hunger remained sharp, but its hunting determination had turned to expectation.

He drew the little Lemuran out of the water. It was apparent that several of her ribs were broken, although the skin was intact above them. There were no other visible injuries on her, but the head wound in itself was bad enough, even without the damage to her chest. It was more than a gash, he thought. The skull itself appeared to be depressed along its line. That plus the effects of submersion in Horus' cold sea made her the most critically threatened of all their charges.

The War Prince carried her outside and gently laid her down for evaluation by Islaen.

Spirit of Space, he thought as he rose to his feet and gazed down on her, she was so tiny. She could be no more than six and was small for that and fragile looking besides.

Varn!

The strange triumph had hit him even before Connor's warning. He whirled to face the sea.

There was a deeper blackness in the dark water by the transport. Something rose out of it, not a body or a head, but a blunt, dark gray snout, the upper part of a spike-filled jaw.

Four tentacles extended from it, two situated on either side of the snout's center, two rising out of the water and probably fixed to the place where the upper and lower parts of the great mouth joined. They seemed to lie a vast distance away from the central pair. Each of the four was about six feet long and of the thickness of his thigh. They were highly mobile, coiling and twisting in the air around them.

Only for a moment was it visible. It submerged, and the transport began to shake.

The machine steadied again after about ten seconds. The jaw surfaced again, this time accompanied by its lower counterpart. The body of the driver was held between them, looking small in their ten-foot expanse.

They crunched down on it. The corpse splintered, shredded, and was gone.

Part of one leg fell free. It scarcely struck the water before the nearest tentacle, an outer one, grabbed and restored it to the mouth, then that, too, was gone.

The hunter's hunger had in no sense abated. Sogan had used those horror-filled moments to move the child and himself back to the wall. They were beyond the reach of the tentacles, but only just. If the monstrous thing could lever itself out of the water at all, it would be able to take them or take any of the others in the Commandos' care.

He threw his will against it to try to compel or induce it to leave, but he could make no real contact with it. He had never had much luck with any of Horus' native wildlife . . .

It was coming again!

A stream of energy from Islaen Connor's blaster stung the tentacles as they emerged from the water. They disappeared fast, and he felt the creature draw back from the shore.

Good work, Colonel.

Varn's eyes turned to the child. He dropped to his knees beside her in alarm. *She is not breathing, Islaen! —Her heart still beats.* Even as he spoke, he had tilted her head back, checked that her airway was clear, and started forcing breath into her.

The Noreenan sent her mind out. She remained silent while she examined the child using that part of her talent which allowed her to study a living body and determine the injuries and some illnesses that were tearing it. *She still lives. Keep it up, Varn. You may be able to hold her long enough.*

Connor looked up at the cliff. *They're here!* she exclaimed in relief, *our comrades and the Emergency Service as well to judge by the number of other readings I'm receiving.*

She activated her communicator and gave Jake a complete report of their situation. "There isn't room for the ambulance to land here. We'll have to use our flier and take them up in three trips. The little Lemuran has to come alone so Varn can keep working on her. Any real stop in that, and she's done."

"We're on our way, Colonel."

Islaen sat down. She suddenly felt dizzy, sick. She looked at her arm. The make-shift bandage she had put on it after the press of her other duties eased had finally stopped the bleeding, but it had gone on some time before she had been able to attend to herself. The drain had been too much. A little more, and she realized she would have been as badly off as these children. The renewer would soon see her right, but in the meantime, she was done.

Islaen?

I'll be all right, Varn. You worry about that little girl. I'll worry about me.

The flier was down. Connor watched it through the dim fog clouding her eyes. Bethe and Jake jumped from it. Danlo began lifting the victims into it. Luckily, all were small, and they could put a good number of them, the more lightly injured, in at one time. Those requiring more space would go on the next trip, after having had the benefit of preliminary renewer work, and finally Varn's little patient, still left to the last by the cold command of reason, by the grim need of not risking those who should live for one who all too easily might well not.

"Islaen?"

She smiled wanly up at Jake. "I'm afraid I'm a problem, too."

He bent and looked at her arm. "You go with this lot, Colonel. —No argument," he said as he lifted her. "You can hold one or two of them on your lap if that'll make you feel more useful. Bethe will stay down here and wield the renewer."

The redhead settled her into the packed vehicle and took his place at the controls.

Even before the flier started to rise, Danlo had turned the renewer on the Lemuran. It would not heal whatever injury her lungs had suffered, but it would take out the other damage including the shattered ribs that had crushed them, and it would strengthen her, buy her time until she could be brought under regrowth.

The renewer ray was one of medicine's greatest discoveries, providing almost instantaneous complete regeneration of recently damaged or destroyed skin, muscles, blood vessels, even nerves and bone. Only the organs of the chest and abdominal cavities could not be so repaired. Those required treatment with the much newer and far more complex regrowth equipment.

At the War's beginning, only a few of the greatest experimental hospitals could support the then-massive renewer systems, but development had progressed quickly until they became standard equipment on every major battleship, and then on the medium-class and many of the smaller-class vessels as well.

Federation scientists had recently produced a renewer model portable enough to be used by individuals or small, mobile parties such as their unit, which was one of the first teams chosen to benefit from and test it in the field.

The former admiral willed his fear for Islaen to subside. She was in good hands and should be restored by the time he reached the road above once more. The same might not hold true for this tiny girl he was fighting to save. Even if he could deliver her to the medics alive, she might not survive to reach the hospital for regrowth treatment. It all depended upon the severity of her injuries.

Spirit of Space, she was no more than a baby. It wrenched the heart in him to think that she might die when she had scarcely begun to live. She would die if he failed to give her breath . . .

The minutes passed with interminable slowness. The flier returned for its second load. There were fewer children to go, and it filled faster.

Bethe came over to him. "We're ready to lift again, Varn. I'm going along. I want to keep on with the renewer work. We'll be back in another few minutes."

He nodded and lifted his hand in farewell.

Those minutes would seem long, he thought as he watched the machine rise and disappear from his sight. He was tired, and even his efforts and his concentration on them could not keep the cold knifing him at bay. He had passed beyond discomfort into the realm of pure misery. At least, he was sheltering and warming the child somewhat . . .

Fear banished the cold and nearly every other feeling. The hunter was back.

The tentacles groped up onto the ledge. Their search was not blind. They, or the thing of which they were a part, seemed to know precisely where its intended victims lay.

They could not reach the humans, not quite, but they were close and struggled to come closer still. The Arcturian pulled his legs higher so that he lay more nearly parallel to his charge.

He was helpless. Only now did he recall that he had failed to ask his comrades for a blaster.

It would probably have been useless in any event. He could not fight and continue with his present work. Deprive the Lemuran of air for even a few moments too long, and everything else would be pointless. A mindless shell did not have life.

A great form rose out of the water. There was a slap like a sharp clap of thunder as it slammed down upon the ledge, not a snout this time or a jaw but the whole massive, terrifying head.

There was movement above, but it was too late now. The flier could not make it down in time, and its lasers could not be aimed finely enough. If fired, they would take out the prey along with the predator.

The descent would take only seconds, part of a minute, but the hunter would be feeding by then.

Varn Tarl Sogan deliberately moved his body away from the child, angling himself toward the sea and maintaining only sufficient contact with her to permit him to continue breathing for her as long as possible. To cover her would be worthless. They would only be taken together, as a unit. By offering himself to the predator in this manner, he would give his comrades time in which to save the child.

He could not see the creature now, but he could feel its hunger and its anticipation, and he could hear the scraping of the tentacles as they advanced rapidly over the rock of the ledge.

Jake Karmikel watched the sea thing's advance with ever-increasing desperation. It was less than a foot from Sogan now, yet the War Prince continued to hold his body still, kept to his work.

The Noreenan let off a quick bolt from his blaster on narrow beam. The creature gave some ground, but it started to advance again almost immediately. It wanted to feed, and its victim was very near.

The flier was nearly down.

There was no more time! Jake leaped to the ground. He landed well and instantly sprang between Varn and the predator. The nearest tentacle was not two inches from the Arcturian's legs.

Karmikel burned through it, then turned his weapon against the monstrous head itself.

This time, the creature did retreat. There was no sound from it, but it backed away rapidly, pulling itself off the ledge and disappearing under the waves.

Sogan's eyes closed, and for a moment, he was too swept by relief to do more than lie where he was.

"Admiral, are you all right?"

He nodded, then sent his mind out in search of the hunter.

He found it. The creature was not dead and probably not fatally injured, the former admiral decided, but it was burned, and it was hurting, and he could feel its transmissions diminish as it fled away from the coast.

He reported as much to Karmikel, who abandoned his defensive position to help him lift the Lemuran.

Jake watched his comrade feed air to the child once more. "Admiral," he said softly, "can't we trust you two to take a simple walk by the seashore without getting into trouble?"

Chapter Seven

Hands reached for the unconscious child as soon as the flier set down on the road above, and she was hurried into the remaining ambulance. There had been two others, Bethe told him quickly, but they had already gone with their load of patients.

Sogan saw now why no oxygen had been sent down to him, no forced breathing mask such as that which Jake had put on him following the battle on Anath. The ambulance's equipment was powered from the vehicle itself and could not function independently of it. A bad system, he thought. Mobile as those ambulances were, they could not go everywhere, and without their immediate presence, the medics were stripped of most of their major gear.

Islaen Connor ran to him, Bandit on her shoulder. *Varn,* she whispered, *the Spirit ruling Space be praised.*

He put his arm around her. *It is over, my Islaen.*

I had left myself until the end. I—I could not come down for you—

It is over, he repeated. *I am sound out, in better shape than you are at the moment.*

The Commando-Colonel had recovered full use of her arm, but the renewer still in her hand told her consort that she had probably treated herself. She might well not have made a thorough job of it in her worry for him.

"Bethe, run that thing over her again to make sure the healing is complete," he ordered. "Get the cover up on the flier and turn on the heat. She will freeze in those wet clothes." Connor was shivering badly even now. Much more of this cold, and she would take real damage from it.

Two men whom he had scarcely noticed before approached the Commandos. His Maintenance Sergeant and another Lemuran. He was not pleased to see the mutants and frowned. "What are you doing here, Lampry?"

"We were at the ship when your call reached Captain Karmikel, sir. He and Sergeant Danlo had just returned. We came with them." His eyes closed. "My baby, sir, my little girl. She was—"

Sogan stepped toward the other man. How stupid could he be? How many such families were there on this part of Horus? Had the Spirit ruling Space given him no spark of compassion at all?

There had been but the one Lemuran child on the transport. His hand closed on the sergeant's arm. "She was hurt, Max, but she should be all right," he said gently.

"I know, sir. I just spoke with the medics."

The Lemuran's voice failed him for a moment. He had watched from the cliff above while the Commando-Captain had worked on his child. He had seen Sogan offer his body in sacrifice for her in an effort to win her the extra seconds needed to see her safe. "You—you gave Stella her life twice over, sir."

Varn smiled wanly and shook his head. "I am entitled to little credit for that. I cannot imagine anyone acting differently under those circumstances."

He looked up as the driver's door of the ambulance slammed shut. "You and your comrade can take the rover and follow it. We have the flier."

"Thank you, Captain Sogan."

"Sergeant."

"Aye, sir?"

"If your little girl needs you tomorrow, your place is with her and with your wife. I shall throw you bodily off the *Maid* if you show up there instead."

Pete Ospry sat in the passenger seat of the rover. He felt dazed. "I take back every word I said about him. —He couldn't imagine anyone acting differently?"

"Maybe someone like him couldn't," Lampry responded. His hands tightened on the controls. "I've always liked Captain Sogan despite everything. I'd bloody well die for him after this."

The Arcturian watched them go. He sighed. Federation men were fortunate in many ways, he thought. He had never known any of his children and would never have known his daughters as individuals even had he retained his place after the War. His sons, though, would eventually have joined his fleet and served under him. His heir would have done so in a matter of a few weeks. He had so looked forward to that . . .

Sogan rejoined his comrades. Islaen was sitting on the rear seat of the flier, her legs outside its open door. She was wrapped in the remaining survival blanket and was looking a galaxy more like herself.

"That is much better, Colonel Connor."

The woman smiled and raised her head.

Her eyes widened in alarm. "Varn!" There was a coating of ice on his jacket, and he had begun shivering so violently that he seemed to be in the grip of a raging fever.

The others faced him as well. "Get that jacket off you!" Danlo commanded. "The tunic, too!"

"There are no more blankets," he protested, although he had already begun tugging at the half-frozen fastenings with numb fingers.

"Better bare skin than those things." She impatiently brushed his hands aside and soon had the garment open. The tunic had not actually frozen and gave no similar trouble.

Karmikel helped him pull off the stiffening garments. He felt his own skin crawl. It always did when he caught sight of the corrugated mass of scar tissue that was the Arcturian's back. A month's belated renewer treatment had produced precious little cosmetic improvement, although both Sogan and Islaen claimed it to be significant, and Varn stated that most of the residual stiffness and pain were gone. He must have suffered cruelly from both in the three years preceding treatment.

Anger flared inside him. He would love to get his hands on the ones who had done it. Not the executioners themselves, but the bastards who had ordered it.

Jake stripped off his own jacket and quickly slipped it on his comrade.

Varn straightened. "I do not need—"

"No comments, Sogan," he ordered. "Just get into the flier before you shake yourself into jelly. We've got it nice and warmed up for you."

"All of you, get in," commanded the sergeant. "Every one of you is a prime candidate for Quandon Fever. I don't feel like spending the next several weeks fetching, carrying, and playing the noble nurse for the lot of you."

The War Prince automatically started for the controls.

"Rear seat, Admiral," Karmikel told him. "Comfort the colonel. It's all you probably want to do anyway."

There was no sarcasm in that. The Noreenan man had seen Bethe down on a few occasions and had been near frantic himself. It was part of the price one in their profession paid for loving.

Varn Tarl Sogan leaned back against the seat. Some sense of warmth was finally beginning to return to him thanks to Jake's jacket and the flier's heater, which had been pushed up to its maximum output. It felt good. He had begun to imagine that the gnawing cold would never leave him again.

Islaen rested against him. His arm cradled her, and she welcomed its support and the comfort he was offering, but she remained quiet. The image of that sea beast coming for Varn while she could only watch helplessly from the cliff above remained a sharp anguish in her mind.

The War Prince's fingers twined with hers. *Let it go, my Islaen. It worked out well. We are a team in fact. Our comrades were there to do what we could not.*

I know. She smiled up at him. *Just hold me tighter, all the same. It was too close a miss, and I want to keep you very near to me for a while.*

With the greatest pleasure, Colonel Connor.

Karmikel glanced over his shoulder. "Are you two beginning to thaw out at all?" he asked. He did not miss his jacket. The flier felt hotter than Amazoon's miserable jungle to him, but he made no complaint. His job was to warm up his passengers fast and keep them warm.

"Just about," Sogan answered comfortably. He roused himself a little. "Thanks for the rescue, Jake. I was wishing that you would move a mite faster for a while there, but your timing was adequate in the end."

"I've been thinking about that," the redhead remarked. "You probably weren't in all that much trouble to begin with. Horus' fish most likely favor you the same way you favor them. One bite, and the poor thing would've spit you out again."

Islaen's head snapped up. "You are not being amusing, Jake Karmikel. Just concentrate on the controls and let us have some peace and quiet."

"Whatever you say, Colonel. I just wanted to make sure you both were still alive back there."

* * *

Islaen Connor's communicator pulled her out of a dead sleep. She glanced at the luminous face of her timer. 01:17. "What is it, Jake?" she demanded none too graciously.

"Bethe's sick."

Connor sat up. "Sick? What do you mean?"

"Fever. Headache. Stomach a mess. Sick. —She's had Quandon Fever before. That makes her doubly susceptible, and it's all over Horus at the moment. What if—"

"Power down, Jake. She had a very mild case a long time ago, and her shots are up to date."

"You know how it mutates."

Islaen groaned. "Give me a few minutes. I'll be over as soon as I dress and grab the antivirals. I have some the *Moon* doesn't stock."

"Please hurry."

The colonel did. It was literally only a matter of minutes before she was at the *Maid*'s hatch.

Sogan was waiting for her there, also fully dressed.

Islaen sighed. He would have picked up Karmikel's call as well. *You stay put, my friend. Bandit, too. You'd both be in the way.*

Bandit can stay. I am coming.

The Noreenan faced him squarely. *That is an order, Captain. If Bethe does have Quandon Fever, the* Jovian Moon *and all of us are off limits to you for the duration.*

He frowned. *I thought you were not worried.*

About her, no. You are another matter. I remember that bout of it you had on Thorne. The Resistance spent a week speculating about whom your successor would be. I didn't find it a particularly pleasant exercise since I was already in love with you at that stage, even if I didn't dare let any of my comrades know about it. You were basically out of action for the next four weeks, even after the crisis passed.

Islaen softened her stand with a smile. *Guard the ship, Admiral. It probably isn't serious at all. I'll let you know as soon as I learn anything.*

I will appreciate that, Colonel.

It was after 06:00 before Islaen finally returned to the *Fairest Maid*, although she had ascertained almost immediately that they were dealing with a simple local virus and not the troublesome fever whose constant mutations outfoxed the immunization shots with dreary regularity. *The antivirals are working nicely,* she reported. *She's noninfective now and should be herself in a couple or three more hours. A day or two would have done it in any event, even without treatment.*

She smiled. *Bethe says this is her punishment for saying she didn't want to play nurse for us. Jake, on the other hand, is claiming there's no justice in the universe. We two jump up to our necks and beyond into freezing water, and it's Bethe who gets sick.*

He is right. There is no justice. I am glad you are not the patient, however. I hate to see you down for any reason. He forced a smile. *Besides, I would have been quite as frantic as Jake is, and he would never have permitted any of us to forget the fact.*

You'd hide it a lot better than he does, my friend, and I do think even Jake Karmikel would turn a blind eye and show you some mercy in that instance.

Islaen looked him over. *You never went back to bed?*

No. Bandit did, but I was worried. I have had Quandon Fever myself, as you pointed out.

I had told you Bethe didn't.

Varn shrugged. *You might have lied, at least until you had an official diagnosis.*

Arcturians! She shook her head. *I am grateful you cooperated, at least.*

Did you think I would not in the face of a direct order? Even as an admiral, I had to deal with those. I usually obeyed them, with a single infamous exception. His eyes sparkled in sudden mischief. *What if I had decided to make myself difficult?*

I'd have posted you to the Rounder *and ordered Captain Zubin to lift for an extended voyage,* she replied calmly.

Zubin is a civilian, he reminded her.

He'd obey me. Besides, he'd love to get those huge hands of his on you for a while. He likes you as much as you like him, and he'd take great delight in showing you the Malkite version of life in the starlanes, and especially in the associated spaceports. I think he regards your locking yourself away on the Maid *for so much of your on-world time as rather too restricted an existence.*

Islaen, her husband said solemnly, *with a threat like that hanging over my head, you shall find me a most reasonable and docile second-in-command.*

Don't be making promises you won't be able to keep, Admiral.

He paused. *You've never asked me about that,* he said thoughtfully.

About what?

My liking for Zubin. It is not what anyone would expect from me.

It isn't my right to ask. Besides, could I get an answer?

No. It is totally inexplicable, like so much else in this mad Federation of yours.

Islaen smiled sympathetically. Varn had spoken lightly, but she knew that life in this ultrasystem must sometimes be a perpetual series of shocks for him. Everything was simpler for Arcturian warriors—unless they violated military law or the inflexible code that bound them.

She reached up and drew his head toward her so that her lips might meet his. *Let's knock out for a few hours. Hopefully, tomorrow will be a nice, boring day, but we all have enough to do to assure that it will be a busy one.*

Chapter Eight

It was 08:00 when the Commando leaders' timers forced them out of their beds. A session under the steam jets improved their mood considerably, and both did good justice to their breakfast.

Islaen finished first. She left Varn with his second cup of jakek and went over to the *Jovian Moon* to see her patient.

Sogan had already restored the crew's cabin and galley to order by the time she returned. *How is Bethe doing?* he asked.

Alive and well. —Did you have anything really pressing to do in the port today, or can Jake handle it for you? I know you were planning to go in.

Karmikel can deal with it. Why?

I want to get him away from that ship for a while. All the concern and attention may be flattering, but he's driving Bethe right out of the galaxy. I don't like leaving her completely alone, but I have to pick some things up for us both, and I want to replenish some of our medical stores. My signature's required for those, or I'd stay myself.

No problem. I will keep an eye on our demolitions expert.

Thanks, Varn. —Come on, Bandit. I know there are some shops that you'll want to visit, those with nice things for hungry gurries.

Yes!

Varn laughed and waved them farewell.

He sighed once they were gone. He had been looking forward to a cup of coffee. It was one of the few luxuries he permitted himself while in port, and there would probably not be many more chances for having any for a while. There would be no more on this planeting if their meeting with Gray Jack Dundee tomorrow meant another mission, as they all believed would prove to be the case.

He was instantly ashamed of his regret. It was a small enough sacrifice to make for Bethe, he thought. She had done more than that for him when he had been down on more than one occasion.

The War Prince stepped onto the *Maid*'s boarding ramp. He stopped in surprise to see Lampry's crew arriving. The Maintenance Sergeant was with them and approached Sogan as soon as he climbed out of their transport.

"Good morning, Captain," he said after the officer had returned his salute.

"How is your little girl, Lampry?"

"She's doing well, sir, thanks to you. They're holding her for observation today and will release her tomorrow. Her mother is with her now."

"Should you not be as well?"

"I'll be more useful home tomorrow, if that's all right, Captain."

"The time is yours. Your crew and I can finish up anything that remains to be done here."

The other's strange eyes shadowed. "There's a problem, Captain Sogan. I meant to bring it up yesterday, but with all the excitement over Stella, it went clear out of my mind. I'm sorry about that, sir."

"Come inside. Tell me about it now."

The two men went to the crew's cabin. Sogan gave the sergeant permission to sit and took his usual place opposite him. "What is it, Lampry?"

"Well, sir, some captains might not be disturbed, but I'll put credits down that you will be, and I am. It's those drive valves we put in and the alarm sensors before them. They're not what I specified."

"What! I signed for them at the depot."

"The manufacturer's different. These are a bit cheaper, but I know for a fact that none of the major civilian ships will use them." The Lemuran scowled. "They have the same model numbers as the standard parts, which shouldn't be the case, and are more or less identical. I wouldn't have noticed the difference in the depot, either, not unless the price was much lower."

"It was not. —Was there any difficulty with them?"

Lampry hesitated. "No, Captain. The sensors were fine. I just," he hesitated. "I just didn't like the feel of the valves. They fit, but they felt funny going in." His eyes met the other's dark ones. "I know it's a damn foolish kind of report to be making, but I'd be derelict in my duty if I failed to say something."

"You do not like these new valves, for whatever reason?"

"No, sir," he responded firmly. "I don't."

"Take them out, and the sensors, too. Put the old ones back until you can get proper replacements. I will put my life in your hands, not in those of the vacuum brains in that depot." The Commando-Captain came to his feet. "Start on the *Maid*. Sergeant Danlo has not been well. I want to check on her and cut power on the *Moon*. We had begun surplanetary testing on her, but there is no point in continuing if more work is to be done on her."

Varn Tarl Sogan was surprised to find the demolitions expert finishing off a light breakfast in the *Jovian Moon*'s crew's cabin.

She looked well, especially pretty in fact, with her braid resting on her back like that instead of tightly pinned to her head, but Varn regarded her with concern. "What are you doing out of bed?" he demanded. "According to Jake, you were just about signing enlistment papers with the Grim Commandant last night."

"He was exaggerating. I only felt that way." She smiled at him. "Easy on the drive, Varn. I'm sound out now. Truly. —Join me for anything?"

"No. I am fine. I came over here to do a bit of work, actually, apart from checking on our latest casualty." He told her about Lampry's report and his decision to pull out the new valves and sensors.

"It's probably totally unnecessary, Varn, but I agree. I don't like the idea of some son of a planet hugger making substitutions on things going into the drive system of my starship. Go on up to the bridge. I'll join you there in a few minutes. I'll be interested in seeing if there are any oddities in the readings from the tube in which we installed those new valves."

Sogan had only begun studying the instrument panel when the spacer joined him. Her hair was now in place, he saw, and for all her casual words below, her expression was serious.

"See anything unusual?" she asked.

"Nothing—"

A loud, penetrating gong shrilled through the bridge as it did throughout all the rest of the starship, giving the lie to his denial.

Varn's face paled, as Bethe knew her own had. No other alarm and no other emergency generated greater fear, intellectual and gut level, aboard a spacecraft. "Fire!" she whispered. "Where?"

"The third drive or tube, apparently. Some of the indicators from the former are flashing now, but there was no sign of any trouble a moment ago."

Danlo spat out an oath. "That's the one with the new valves."

"Switch on the hull scanners. I am not getting any readings here below the drive room."

Her small hands raced across the controls, and a composite image of the *Jovian Moon* appeared on the near-space viewer, which Sogan had activated to receive it. It supplemented what they were now seeing through the normal vision panels. Gouts of angry, orange-red flame were clearly visible as they erupted from the third drive tube.

In another moment, all the scanners were centered on it.

The scene they revealed was one out of a space hound's nightmare, the hot, furious tongues of a well-established fire whose intense, rather peculiar shade proclaimed its seat to be in the fuel coil itself.

"How could it have gotten so far?" the woman demanded as much of herself and of the starship as of her companion.

The War Prince cut all power to the affected engine. The visible fires died in the next instant, but the readings they were getting remained unaltered.

The maintenance crew working on the *Fairest Maid* had seen the *Moon*'s trouble. They were now racing for the stricken vessel.

"Give me your communicator," Sogan ordered. "Get a spare one for yourself and return to the bridge. I shall talk to Lampry."

"Will do, Varn."

"What's happened, sir?"

"Those blasted new valves apparently," the Arcturian told him. "One or more of them must have blown out as soon as we started testing, causing the tube itself either to overheat or to warp and flame to the point that the fuel coil went up. To top it all, the sensors went out as well. We got no warning until the blaze spread enough and got hot enough to threaten the drive room, activating the functioning sensors there."

"Open the tube. We'll pump liquid space in. That should extinguish it fast enough."

He nodded. The incredibly cold liquid had been formulated to meet such emergencies. It would gradually cool the tube and the fuel coil beyond, reducing the temperature inside until it fell below that needed to maintain the blaze.

He opened his communicator and relayed the mechanic's instructions to Bethe Danlo.

There were several moments' silence. "I can't," the spacer reported at the end of it. "Only the inner hatch is responding, the one leading from the drive room to the rest of the ship. The others won't budge."

The Arcturian's face was grim. "Open two and four. Maybe if we can freeze them out, we can cool off three. — Max?"

"I doubt it, Captain. We can give it a try."

"You can get enough liquid space?"

"A sea of it if we need it," he assured him.

"Good. Keep at number three as well if you can. You might be able to force it from out here."

Sogan gave him Bethe's communicator and showed him how to operate it. "I am returning to the bridge. We can keep in contact through this."

The Commandos watched the sensors in deathly silence for several minutes. Sogan's head lowered at the end of that time. It had not worked. The fire was too deeply seated and too hot in itself to be cooled into extinction in that manner.

The temperature indicators continued to rise, ever to rise, giving grim testimony to the inferno raging within the affected fuel coil. "Full coil involvement," Varn muttered, "and near flash temperature."

Bethe Danlo needed no amplification of that. A rise of a few more degrees, a very few, and the fuel surrounding that tube would vaporize, taking all the rear portion of the fighter with it and leaving nothing more than twisted shards of the rest.

The captain touched the communicator. "Pull back, Max. She could blow at any moment. I must do what I can in here."

He glanced at the woman. "I shall need a protection suit with space headgear. No oxygen. It would go up in that oven, whatever the lack of open flame. I shall have to make do with the air supply in the suit. After that, clear."

Bethe did not move. "Just what do you think you are going to do, Admiral?"

"Open that tube manually. It is the *Moon*'s only chance."

"Forget it," she said flatly. "You'll never be able to do it. The *Moon*'s tubes are even narrower than the *Maid*'s. You're not a large man, but your shoulders will still rub both walls. It may be only ten feet to the switch, but you would be broiled alive before you could get half that distance."

"Maybe, but the ship will be blown to space dust if I do not try it."

Danlo smiled. "I am a whole lot smaller than you, friend."

"When space turns white!"

"The *Jovian Moon* is my starship, Varn Tarl Sogan, or half mine."

"I outrank you, Sergeant."

She caught hold of her temper. "Damn it, think, Man! If you die or lose consciousness in that tube, I'll never be able to haul you out. Your flesh would burn right onto the sides before I could move you, and I wouldn't have the strength to tear you loose, not trying to work in quarters like that. Both our dooms would be sealed then. You'd be able to drag me away and make a second try yourself. —It is both our lives that we're discussing. Whatever you do, I'm not leaving. You back me if you're smart. Otherwise, I back you."

He glared at her for several seconds, knowing she was right and hating her because she was.

In the end, Sogan nodded, although everything inside him rebelled at the thought of giving over the duty before them to this woman who was his friend and his comrade.

Both of them suited up fast, working in silence for the most part, each occupied with his own thoughts.

Bethe tried to keep her hands from shaking as she set the final layer of seals in place. These garments were designed to protect their wearers in most starship emergencies. They would shield her against open flame, even of very high intensity, at least briefly, but she was not at all sure how long or well they would hold back the blistering, baking heat inside the drive tube or the touch of the white-hot titanone walls.

She was frankly terrified. It was a horrible death that she was courting and horrible ruin of her body, and an infinity of pain would precede it.

The woman gave herself a final check. Seeing that Varn was also ready, she strode resolutely toward the ladder. Any hesitation now might well finish her courage, and even were that not true, she was determined not to reveal the extent of her fear to the Arcturian. It would shame her to let him see that. More importantly, she knew that a man like Varn Tarl Sogan would never permit her to go on with this dire task if he realized how utterly she shrank from it. He would insist on making the first try himself. He would die trying, and her cowardice would be responsible for his death. Then, at some indefinite time in the not very distant future, she would die herself in the death of the *Jovian Moon*.

They reached the hatch leading to the drive room. The spacer hesitated an instant, wondering what she would find on the other side, then she drew it back with hands made huge and clumsy by the enormous gloves covering them.

She reeled back a pace under the blast of super-heated air which roared out to greet her, although she had stood aside in anticipation of it and so had escaped the greater part of its force.

Bethe Danlo braced herself and stepped inside. She knew she must move fast. If the drive room were this hot when no flame had actually penetrated or surrounded it as yet, then the fuel coil could not be far from attaining flash temperature.

Sogan followed after her. She started to seal the hatch behind them to shield the rest of the fighter as much as possible from the heat battering them, but he stopped her. "Leave it partly ajar," he told her. "We shall probably have to get out quickly if we do succeed. The climate conditioning can handle the heat load later."

There was no more time for speech. The woman's eyes closed as they went to the entrance of the tube itself. This was worse even than her imagination had painted it.

Nothing was visible of the interior. Nothing could be seen at all but the white glare of titanone brought to a state of incandescence by the inferno blazing behind its three-inch barrier. No other metal could have withstood a fraction of this much punishment without already having melted or fractured.

She had to venture ten feet into that. Ten feet? It might as well be as many leagues into the heart of a star. Could any protection, any defensive material, withstand such challenge? Could any human body endure the spill-over, the heat which would inevitably leak through even if the suit did hold? She was already hot. What would it be like in that tunnel of blazing death?

She stepped through the open lock. The heat of the place struck at her in a wave of palpable energy.

Bethe staggered under it but kept her feet. That she must do at all costs, stay erect, keep on moving, and keep away from the walls curving so closely beside her. The heavy insulation on her boots, reinforced by the magnetic oversoles, would guard her feet, at least long enough to permit her to finish the task she had set herself to do, but any other contact with the shimmering metal must be avoided. That would have to come eventually, and she could not afford to stress the suit beforehand.

Some of her uncertainty faded after the first few seconds. The shielding garments would hold, or they should, and she knew now that she could bear the spill-over heat rending her through them. It was a torment, right enough, but she could endure it. She did not even believe it was doing her real injury.

She wished she could move faster, race down the pathetically few feet separating her from her goal, but the weight of her footgear made anything more than this plodding advance impossible.

Danlo had known the magnets would do that, but they would be necessary later, and she had not been able to dispense with them. They were deactivated, at least, and she did not have to struggle against their power as well as their weight.

The switch was before her! She could just make it out through the glare, a large handle set into the wall high above her so that it would not impede the flow of the energy which should be ripping through this place.

She looked at it bleakly. Varn could have activated it with ease merely by stretching his arms a little, but it was well beyond her reach.

The spacer ran her tongue over lips parched as much by fear and dark anticipation as by the desiccating action of the heat, but there was no hesitation in her movements. She knew what must be done.

She would try to avoid the walls, but if she could not, she would have thirty seconds, at the most forty. After that, no defense would be left to her. Even if the burns she would subsequently take were not fatal in themselves, the superheated air pouring through the rent protection suit would sear the lungs out of her.

There was no time to think about that now. Whatever happened afterwards, she would have time to complete her purpose. Her companion would live and the starship would live whether she did or not. That was all that mattered at the moment or must be allowed to matter.

Bethe Danlo pressed one of the buttons set into the inner palm of her right glove, activating the magnetics in her oversoles. Marshaling what courage she had, she began walking up the shimmering curve of the wall.

She fought to hold herself away from the one behind her, but her muscles were not equal to that task, and she leaned back so that her shoulders were braced against it.

Tears sprang to her eyes as she felt the charring heat penetrate her suit.

She blinked them back and tried to ignore the pain. It was not extreme, and she knew she was not actually burning, not yet. Her garments had still not given way . . .

At last! The Commando's gloved hand shot out, yanked the handle down.

To her infinite relief, she felt it vibrate into life before she released it in the next instant. That had been an unacknowledged, ever-present canker in her mind and heart, the dread that the manual control might be disabled even as the automatics were.

Almost without conscious thought, she deactivated the magnets and dropped to the deck, landing, knees flexed, with a feral grace that kept her on her feet and allowed no other part of her already stressed garments to touch the glowing metal around her.

She had to move now, and fast, or the success of her mission would be her death. She could not be in this tube when the frigid flood of liquid space poured into it seconds less than two minutes from now.

Her lips tightened. She did not have so much time at all. The lock sealing the tube off from the drive room switched to automatic and closed fifteen seconds before that, assuming it functioned as it should.

A warmth filled her at the thought of the comrade waiting there for her, the sure knowledge that Varn Tarl Sogan would fight to give her every chance, would keep the way on manual and open for her to the last possible moment even at the cost of heavy risk to himself.

Fear followed fast upon that certainty. Suppose the fuel flashed during the interval programmed into the locks while they were on manual to give the one throwing the switch time to escape? Suppose the opening sequence aborted, and the outer hatch remained sealed?

She drove both thoughts out of her mind, although nothing could expel the doubt and dread they engendered from her heart. She had done all she could. Now she must see to her own life.

That was a race the sergeant could still lose all too easily. Much of her strength was spent, and a great part of the drive goading her on had faded with the completing of her task. She was tired and hurting, half blinded by the awful glare surrounding her and by the sweat stinging her strained, tearing eyes. The air in her suit was growing poor, too, making movement, any physical effort, an act of will.

She wanted to live! At the least, if she must die, she wanted it to be in the comfort of the *Moon*'s interior, not in the searing agony of this place or later on the teeth of the liquid space's near primal cold.

Fear and desperation drove the woman into a run, but she gained only a couple of steps before she stumbled, striking hard with her elbow against the left wall.

Bethe's suit was less heavily padded there, and she screamed under the shock of blazing energy surging into her. The pain of it drove the mists from her mind, and she righted herself once more.

Not that way, she told herself. Take it easy or she would never win free.

The woman started off again, this time holding to the agonizingly slow shuffle that the weight of her boots and her exhaustion forced on her.

Would she never get out of this accursed tube? The oxygen in her suit was almost depleted. Even in these last few moments, her air had gotten so bad that it was painful to draw and nearly impossible to find enough useable molecules in it to satisfy the demands of her lungs.

She had only about a foot to go, less, but movement was now so difficult as to be almost beyond her ability to force it, and her vision was hopelessly blurred. By will alone, she staggered on, compelling herself to take one more step and then another and another after that.

Her foot struck something. The lock at last?

Aye, but she was done. She could not move her heavily weighted leg high enough to clear it, and she had no more time to waste, no more strength with which to fight. Despair filled her as blackness, the final blackness, swept over her.

Varn Tarl Sogan reached out quickly to catch the spacer as she began to fall. He swept her into his arms even as the lock began to slide closed.

He did not know whether she was alive or dead, nor did he delay to find out. Whatever chance she had, he had to get her away from the heat of the tube and the drive room at once, though the latter would probably seem cool to her were she conscious to experience it after the inferno from which she had just emerged.

Once he set the seals on the second lock, that closing the drive room from the ship proper, he paused to release her face mask and his own. That done, he started up the core ladder.

Bethe's limp body scarcely slowed his ascent. He had long since learned how to negotiate the ways of a starship without delay, however heavily burdened he might be.

Sogan did not stop until he had reached the hatch. He darted down the ramp and ran until he felt they were out of range of an explosion's worst effects.

He could go no farther without risking losing his comrade. He settled Bethe on the ground and hastened to work her protection suit's fastenings open and pull it off her to release the heated air trapped inside it.

She was still unconscious, but after ascertaining that neither pulse nor breathing were abnormal, he turned away from her.

How was it with the ship? Most of the mechanics were still keeping their distance, but Lampry and two of the others were working the hose from one of the four liquid space tankers lined up near the imperiled starship. The spaceport's emergency crews were on hand as well, prepared to contain the flames and debris should the *Jovian Moon* go up.

The former admiral went back to the fighter and all but flew up her ladder to her bridge.

His eyes went eagerly and fearfully to those dials displaying the temperature in the drive tubes. If Bethe had succeeded and if their plan worked, he should soon be seeing some indication of it.

Varn's heart leaped. Aye! The drive room was several degrees cooler than it had been, and the sensors in the second and fourth tubes which adjoined the damaged third showed that the temperature in the affected coil was dropping. Not even that holocaust could hold out against so direct a contact with the bitter chill of the liquid space. Its heat was being bled away, leaching so rapidly through the titanone wall into the frozen tube that soon the fire would not be able to sustain itself at all.

Chapter Nine

Sogan returned to the still unconscious spacer. He touched his hand to her too-warm face, then carried her back to the starship and laid her on her bed.

He slit her tunic rather than risk further injuring tender, damaged skin.

After a few minutes, he sighed with relief. Most of this was not bad, more like deep but undramatic ultraviolet burns than the charring he had anticipated to find. The shoulders and left arm were worse, but the renewer would take care of all of it within a few minutes.

As if to confirm his diagnosis, Danlo moaned softly. Her eyes opened and met his. "The *Moon*?" Her voice came in a whisper, but it was steady.

"Sound out now. You did it for us, Bethe."

"My burns?"

"Nothing more than the equivalent of a nasty sunburn. Your suit will have to be scrapped after this jaunt, but it did its work well."

The War Prince carefully settled her into a more comfortable position. She smiled up at him. His normally stern features were gentle, as was his touch. "I'm a bother to you," she murmured.

"Not as much as I have been to you now and then." He came to his feet. "Try to rest for a little while, Sergeant. The renewer will soon set you right. Islaen left it on the *Maid* today, praise the Spirit ruling Space. I shall go for it now. In the meantime, I want to set you up on oxygen."

"Oxygen?" she asked in surprise. "My lungs are all right."

"Aye, but they should be flushed out. You were breathing that dead air for quite a while."

"Oh, very well. You're the medic on this one, Admiral, and I don't want to risk another infection. Trust me, last night was a lot worse than this."

The Arcturian smiled. "You are a far more cooperative patient than I usually prove, Bethe Danlo. I appreciate your consideration." He shuddered deep inside himself. It was an infinite relief just to have her alive and able to cooperate.

Sogan wasted no time retrieving the renewer, but one of the mechanics intercepted him on his way back to the *Moon*. "Aye, yeoman?" he asked impatiently.

She stood her ground. "If Sergeant Danlo isn't critical, Max-Sergeant Lampry could use a turn with that."

"What?"

He whirled about and saw the maintenance crew gathered in a knot beside the *Jovian Moon*. One of them was on the ground.

The former admiral broke into a run and quickly reached the group. "Max?"

Lampry lay on the pavement, his head resting on Purvis' knee. In place of hands, he had two blackened claws.

The Maintenance Sergeant's eyes were closed but opened at the sound of Varn's voice. "The renewer, sir?" He gasped rather than spoke the words. They were half-plea, half-question.

"I am activating it now, Max. Just lay quietly. You will have ease soon, I promise you."

The Arcturian glanced at the yeoman supporting the injured sergeant. "What happened, Purvis?"

"The tube hatch only partly opened, Captain. It stuck with more than two-thirds of the way to go, and we couldn't get the hoses in properly. Max grabbed it and forced it fully open. He didn't stop working, either, not until all the liquid space was in. He refused to go with the emergency people. He said you'd fix him up, and he didn't want to give his wife another scare."

Sogan's eyes closed. He doubted he would have had the same raw courage.

The renewer worked its usual seeming magic. As it had healed the children's broken bodies on the previous day, it now transformed the injured man's claws back into human hands. The pain vanished with the burns, and soon Lampry was sitting up, still supported by his comrade.

"Rest for a while on the *Maid*," the Commando told him. "When you feel up to it, one of the lads can drive you home."

He turned to the woman who had summoned him. "I want the remainder of that debris out of the *Fairest Maid* at once. We must wait for Captain Karmikel's return before discussing repairs and clean-up on the *Jovian Moon*."

"We'll take care of it, Captain Sogan," Lampry assured him.

"They will. You are on the injured list."

"I'm fine now, sir. Your renewer did the job."

"You are not fine. There is always an aftershock to serious injury that even the renewer does not lift immediately." He looked at the mechanic and realized the man was as stubborn as any Commando—and as proud. "Very well, Sergeant. You may supervise, but only that and from a sitting position. The remainder of your crew are under my direct order to see that you do not exceed those limitations."

The grins on the smudged faces around them told him the others were delighted at the prospect of keeping their sergeant in line.

Sogan came to his feet. "Bring the discards to me. I am going to take them back to the supply depot and feed them to those planet-hugging sons of Schythian apes atom by atom."

"I'd like to go with you, sir," Max said.

"If you feel up to it, aye. It will not be until this afternoon. I must watch the instruments on the *Moon* until Captain Karmikel returns. I would not want to leave Sergeant Danlo alone in any event."

"I'll be ready, Captain Sogan. You can put credits down on that." His round eyes flashed. "If you leave anything of the bastards intact, I want to be there to finish the job."

The War Prince hurried to Bethe's cabin. He apologized for the delay, explaining what had happened, then turned the renewer on her.

Once its work was done and she was resting comfortably, he went to the bridge.

Everything was in order, with the readings as he had expected. He sank wearily into the pilot's seat and sent his thoughts out to give Islaen a report of the accident. There had been no point in doing it before. The flier could not have brought the two Commandos back much before now in any event, and so he had merely closed off his thoughts until the crisis had ended.

The colonel made no comment and only said that they were on their way.

That knowledge was not entirely comforting. Jake Karmikel would not be happy about what had happened to his starship. He would be even less happy about what had happened to his wife.

Islaen's call came at last. *Varn, we're at the planeting field. Jake's flaming,* she warned. *I haven't been able to calm him down at all. Bandit can't reach him, either. His temper's too high.*

Just stay clear, Colonel. Leave him to me.

He's furious enough to kill you, Varn.

His face hardened. Connor had meant that. There was real fear for him on her. *Karmikel is my friend. He has a right to be angry, and I will not have him shamed by having an audience up here. I can handle him.* He hoped.

Sogan did not have long to wait. The Noreenan captain tore onto the bridge. He caught the smaller man before Varn could speak and slammed him against the wall.

"You cold-blooded Arcturian bastard, I'm going—"

The War Prince struck hard and fast, driving his hands down to break the other's grip. The next movement in Arcturian weaponless combat would either be to smash both arms or to drive a killing blow into his opponent's abdomen, but he merely caught Karmikel and whirled him about so that the redhead was the one pinned against the wall.

"I could not do it, Jake. Had I tried, Bethe would be dead now. Bethe would be dead because of my arrant pride and my misplaced caring. She would be dead, Jake. She would not have left me to die in that tube alone, even knowing it would have been through my own stupidity."

He released his hold and stepped back, leaving himself completely open to the other's fury.

Jake glared at him, then turned his head. For a moment, Sogan thought he would break and took a step closer to him, but the Noreenan mastered himself. "You did not leave her."

"No." His voice changed. "It killed me to see her go into that tube."

"You had no other choice," Karmikel said hoarsely. "I would've had to do the same thing. You spared me that."

Varn gave him another few moments, then touched his shoulder. "Let us go, friend. I had best assure Islaen that you have left me in one, unbroken piece, and I think Sergeant Danlo would benefit from some proper comforting right now."

Chapter Ten

Varn Tarl Sogan brought the rover to a stop before the supply depot. He and Lampry got out, the Maintenance Sergeant bringing a heavy duffel with him.

The two men strode inside. The big room was crowded, but they stalked to the counter. Lampry slammed his bag down on top of it.

Sogan nodded to Zubin of Malki, who was standing in line with his copilot, Tubal, but said nothing to him.

The sales clerk looked up in annoyance. "You'll have to wait your turn."

"I have no intention of dealing with menials. Get your manager out here at once or, better still, the owner."

Varn might be wearing the clothes of a spacer, but it was a War Prince of the Arcturian Empire who was speaking. Command was his right, and the response was immediate. The clerk jumped as if struck. He disappeared through the door behind him and returned seconds later accompanied by two individuals.

"How may we help you—"

"Commando-Captain Varnt Sogan of the *Fairest Maid*. —Sergeant Lampry, please."

Max dumped the contents of his bag out on the counter.

Sogan's eyes bore into the speaker. "You are the proprietor?"

"Yes. —Simon, please continue waiting on the other customers."

The clerk beckoned to the next person in line, but no one moved. The frigid anger on the Commando was apparent, and all waited to learn its cause.

Sogan picked up one of the valves and tossed it back onto the pile with a loud crash. "Your establishment sold this substandard garbage to us. It was not produced by the manufacturer specified by my Maintenance Sergeant."

"I assure you that this material meets all specifications—"

"I assure you that it almost killed another member of my unit and myself, it very nearly destroyed one of my unit's starships, and it caused serious injury to my chief mechanic. If we did not make it a practice to test new equipment on-world whenever practicable, the failure would have occurred upon lifting or in space, assuring the loss of crew and ship."

He leaned forward on the counter. "What you have done to me, you have done to others. You will scrap your remaining stock of this debris. You will reorder and fast-ship everything my ships require at your expense, and you will, also at your cost, replace every piece of unacceptable rubble you have sold to any other unsuspecting starship."

The other drew himself erect with visible effort. His face was ashen, but to yield was to admit guilt and assume responsibility, financially and possibly legally.

"You take a lot on yourself, Captain."

"I have taken more than that upon myself," he snapped. "My report has already been filed with Admiral Sithe and with it the recommendation that criminal charges be filed against your establishment and yourself plus civil charges for any damage, injury, or death occasioned by the failure or malfunction of any substituted items that you supplied. You acted for profit only, giving no thought to the potential cost in terms of human life."

"No one would—"

"Put it on freeze! Your fees to the Navy remained the same as those for the equivalent recommended parts."

Max Lampry smiled coldly. He knew the Horusi was completely cowed, and he was not above rubbing salt into the planet hugger's proverbial lacerations. "Listen well, you bastard. Admiral Sithe pays a lot of attention to Captain Sogan's reports, and the maintenance crews on Horus, military and civilian, pay a lot of attention to mine. Between us, we can close this flaming place down and send the pair of you to the galactic pen besides."

"You may retain this debris and dispose of it as you will," the former admiral told the man. "We have kept more than enough to substantiate our accusations."

With that, he turned on his heel and stalked out of the depot, the Lemuran sergeant at his side.

"Planet-hugging sons of Schythian apes," Sogan snarled as the door closed behind them, "and rank cowards besides."

"With all due respect, sir, I much preferred being where I was standing beside you as opposed to trying to face you down on the other side of that counter."

The door banged open, and Zubin of Malki emerged. His face was bright with glee. "I don't know how you manage it,

Captain, but I love to watch you do it. I'd have been bellowing so loud that you'd have heard me back at the planeting field, and about all I'd have gotten would be compensation for part of my repair costs. You never raised your voice. All you did was go into that high-officer performance of yours, glare at them a bit, and guaranteed you'll get everything you demanded and more. You had the sons shaking in their expensive socks."

"I would make a proper tyrant," the Arcturian said dryly.

"Naw. You don't like seeing people in trouble, and tyrants're stellar-class trouble for everyone." He glanced at the door. "I'd better get back. Tubal's holding our place in the line, but I don't want him dealing with the sons. —We poor civilian spacers don't have the Navy paying our bills, and we have to haggle if we're to eat and stay in space at the same time."

Varn wished him fortune and turned to Lampry with a sigh. The verbal assault, however devastating to the onworlders, had in no sense satisfied his temper. He had wanted to shred the vermin with his bare hands, and he still wanted to do it. "Back to the *Maid,* I suppose?"

"Begging your pardon, sir, but we're both still tearing mad. You just hide it better than I do. Let me spring for some coffee. It'll give us a chance to power down."

The dark eyes fixed on him strangely, and the sergeant came erect. "Sorry, Captain. I know an enlisted man is no company for an officer—"

Sogan smiled. "Put it on freeze, Max. What you mean is that you know I am an arrogant son of a Schythian ape who keeps to his own devices and his own unit. —Coffee sounds good. It is already late. I will stand a meal for us."

"*Isaak's*, sir?" he asked doubtfully.

"Where else?" the former admiral replied. There were other restaurants and eateries that offered the old Terran beverage, but most were expensive, and neither of them was well enough dressed at the moment to feel comfortable in any of those.

They had gone only a couple of blocks when Sogan brought the vehicle to a stop in a vacant space by the curb.

Lampry looked at him in surprise. "Captain?"

"The pharmacy," the War Prince said, glancing in the direction of the sprawling one-story building near their parking spot. "I was wondering if Islaen got everything she wanted from there."

"Well, sir, if you're going in, may I suggest that we move the rover farther up the block? We could find it flattened if we leave it here."

The War Prince nodded. The three-story building beside them was the center of heavy construction activity, and all the spaces beside it both along this side of the street and on that opposite it were vacant despite the heavy traffic in this area. No one wanted to risk being struck or having their vehicles hit by falling debris.

"I will not bother going in," he decided. "Most of the things she wanted require her signature and voice print." As field commander of the unit, Connor was entitled to requisition prescription medications. The rest of her team, including himself, did not have similar authorization.

Varn looked back at the building under renovation. "A big job going on there to judge by the size of the crew."

Max shrugged. "The owners want it done fast. They're altering it from an office complex into rental warehousing."

"You do not approve?" The sergeant did not to judge by the tone of his voice.

"Not of their methods, I don't. Neither do most of the experienced construction workers in the area. Those people you see are almost all green hands. Anyone better qualified won't stay despite the high wages. Only last week, I was talking with a woman who'd just walked out on a job in there. She said they're ripping out the place's bones along with its guts. The owners are putting in some sort of experimental support structure, but no one with any knowledge of construction work trusts it."

Sogan's brows raised. "That's a strange remark coming from you, Sergeant Lampry, considering what you and your lads have done to our ships."

"That's different, Captain. We know what we're doing, and you know what we're doing. We care about what we do. All that interests those sons of Schythian apes is that their new method is fast, and it's a galaxy cheaper than the old way. —Planet-hugging bastards. They're the same misbegotten breed as the sons who sold us those flaming valves."

The rover turned a corner, taking them out of sight of the building.

"No more stops," the Arcturian promised. "By the sound of it, you need that opportunity to power down more than I do."

The rover traveled southward for more than twelve miles before coming to a stop once more.

The area in which they found themselves was part of the great spaceport complex, but it was as different in nature from the business district they had left as that was from the planeting field it serviced. This was the pleasure district of the small freighter crews and rankless military. At night, it was rough, loud, booming with noise and frantic activity, and more than a little dangerous. Now, it was quiet and rather sad.

Most of the businesses lining the streets were still closed, waiting for the sun-star to set before awaking to life and purpose. The greatest percentage of them were drinking places, some offering eating facilities as well, but every block sported its gaming halls and brothels as well. Other things could be had here, too, but only after a careful search. The Stellar Patrol and surplanetary police both kept close watch on doings in this part of the port and made sure the worst illegal offerings were always in short supply.

Only a few establishments with pretensions of being eateries were open during the daylight hours, *Isaak's* being chief most among them. In the very late hours, it was rumored to be an outpost of hell itself, and had any of his crew members mentioned planning to go there, Lampry would simply have busted their heads for them then and there and saved everyone some credits and a lot of trouble. By day, it was almost respectable, enough so that the maintenance crews and even a few noncoms like himself would come down for the coffee and decent food, all sold at a reasonable cost.

Purvis had introduced Sogan to it about a year and a half ago after the subject of coffee had somehow come up, and Max knew the Commando-Captain dropped by here at least once or twice whenever his unit was planeted on Horus, always wearing spacer garb, of course, as he was now.

The two went inside. The place was brightly lighted, although the only natural illumination came through the large, shatterproof synthetic glass door. There were no windows, as was usual in the district.

A very large bar, currently managed by only one tender, held pride of place along one wall. A bewildering variety of liquid offerings filled the racks behind it.

Tables, some for two, others for four patrons, filled the remainder of the room. More than half of them were occupied. *Isaak's* was noted as a place where freighter captains and their clients or potential clients could meet to discuss charters. Many of the cargoes they engaged to transport were of a highly irregular nature, but that did not trouble either of the newcomers. A shipment of untaxed opaline was Stellar Patrol business, not theirs.

They claimed a table and gave their orders to the powerfully built waiter who had approached them almost as soon as they came through the door.

Lampry relaxed. He had been somewhat nervous about bringing the officer here despite his knowledge of Sogan's familiarity with it, but he realized now that, unknown as he was and in his anonymous dress, the Commando seemed a better fit for the place than he was himself. Sogan had the look of the kind of spacer who would frequent it. In his manner, he was like a wary, hunted, wild thing, one it would be highly unwise to challenge.

The food came. It was passable, and the Arcturian ate it with a reasonably good appetite. He had learned not to be too particular during those first years of his in the Federation. Any food, including even fish, had been something of a luxury then, and on occasion, one which had to be foregone. The needs of the *Fairest Maid* had to come first then, and in a choice between her requirements and his comfort, the starship had always won.

Much to his relief, they encountered no trouble. Once, a man had looked sharply at him, but the War Prince had met his gaze evenly, and the spacer had retreated. He had been neither drunk nor sure enough of himself to accost that deadly looking stranger.

The coffee arrived, and this, Varn Tarl Sogan sipped with real pleasure. He drank slowly, making himself savor the beverage. He probably would not be tasting it again for quite some time to come.

At last, they were ready to leave. Sogan paused in the door of the eatery, automatically scanning the street in either direction before he and Lampry stepped out into the open.

Everything had appeared to be as it should, but even as he moved forward, a vehicle, a rover, tore around the corner and raced, not along the street itself, but on the pedestrian walkway, straight toward them.

The Arcturian threw his companion back with a blow of his hand, leaping aside himself as he did so.

He had acted only in time and had gone barely far enough. The rover roared by, its rear wheel passing inches from his head.

Varn's heart was still pounding loudly as he came to his feet, but he wheeled to watch the machine that had so nearly run them down.

It did not stop after the near collision with them but kept going on its mad race. It appeared to want to turn at the corner but jerked about too soon and slammed into the last, fortunately closed, building on the block.

All was still for several moments as people began to come out of *Isaak's* and a few of the other buildings to investigate.

Varn gave his hand to Max, who was still sitting where the Commando had thrown him. "Sorry about the push, Sergeant."

"I'd rather be bruised than squashed, sir. What in space happened?"

"Let us have a look—"

A man's head emerged from the driver's window. The fair hair was wet and reddened from a scalp wound, but he appeared not to notice.

He would not, Lampry thought with a horrified gasp. The peculiarly red face, the blue eyes blazing from their sockets, the rigid features and set snarl of the mouth offered all the explanation necessary. "Raklik and alcohol, and the madman's armed!"

This time, it was Max who acted first. He pulled his companion down as a blast of furious energy tore through the place in which they had been standing a moment before.

Varn Tarl Sogan swore. That blaster had been set at the broadest possible beam to slay.

Screams accompanied its discharge, some of them horribly truncated, then a deadly sort of peace filled the street, broken only by the moaning of the wounded and the roaring laughter of the killer.

The chemically maddened spacer was using his rover as a fortress. His laughter ceased, and he bellowed a challenge and a promise of a quick, painful death to anyone daring or stupid enough to come against him.

Sogan rose to his knees. Those who could do so had fled, but bodies littered the street, and many of them still supported life. They would not continue to do so if the killer discharged his blaster again right on them, as he seemed to be preparing to do. "Stay here, Max. You'll be safe enough."

"Like Lemura's two hells, I will!"

"Come on, then. Keep low."

The soldiers gained their rover. "Remain on the floor until I stop," the former admiral ordered. He made as small a target of himself as possible as he started the machine. The door, he left slightly ajar.

Lampry, as a full Navy man, was armed, and Sogan tapped the handle of his own blaster. "Stun him down as soon as you get a chance, but don't expose yourself needlessly."

He had scarcely finished speaking before they reached the site of carnage. Varn braked and sprang from the rover, firing a narrow, concentrated beam as he did so.

The madman's machine was merely a port rental like his own and no well-screened and armored military vehicle. The Commando's bolt seared through the metal covering straight into the fuel tank that was its target.

Flame exploded out of it, quickly engulfing the rover and its occupant. The door was blown half open, and the raklik man was thrown partly through it. He remained conscious and dived back inside. His clothes were aflame, but he seemed little aware of them as he snapped his weapon to ready once more. His two brilliant eyes were fixed on the completely unshielded Arcturian.

Max Lampry steadied his blaster, fired. The weapon had been set to stun at Sogan's order, and the ray it emitted was invisible, but its effect was instantaneous. His opponent dropped, falling, not away from the blazing rover, but back into it.

Varn Tarl Sogan froze for a fraction-second as he stared at the inferno before him, then he sprang forward and dove through the flames sheathing the open door.

There was no time to search, but that was unnecessary. The stunned man lay just within the door. He was now a mass of fire.

Sogan gave a cry of pain as he caught hold of him. He tightened his grasp despite the cruel bite of the fire and hauled the spacer out onto the street.

"Max, your jacket!" He already had his own off and was using it to smother and beat out the flames.

Working together with frantic haste, they succeeded in extinguishing the fire just as the first Stellar Patrol flier tore onto the scene.

It was late evening by the time the two men finished giving and signing their depositions and were finally free to leave Patrol headquarters.

The Arcturian's face was bleak. "Three dead. Eight significantly injured—all for the sake of so-called pleasure," he said bitterly.

"That's why it's a capital offense to deal in raklik, sir. That son will be spending a few years in the galactic pen, too, if he survives, in body or in mind. It's deadly business mixing raklik and booze."

They stopped beside their rover.

"You will have to drive, Max," Sogan said. He did not try to keep the weariness out of his voice. This whole day had been one hell of a foul charter.

"My pleasure, sir." He opened the door for the captain. "How are the hands?"

"The burn cream is doing its job."

"You should've let the Patrol chaps take you to the hospital like they wanted."

"No. Our renewer will take care of it. —Space! That thing has had more use on this supposedly routine refitting jaunt than it gets on most of our missions."

Varn felt bone tired and allowed the seat to take his weight. He had already given Islaen a full report of what had happened in mind and a briefer account over the communicator for Lampry's benefit. She was waiting for them, and he would be glad of the relief she had to offer. Whatever his assurances to the contrary to Max, he was hurting.

He roused himself to study the Maintenance Sergeant. "You have a few singes of your own needing treatment, and you are going to have to permit my comrades to tidy you up before you go home. Your family has already suffered one fright too many this week."

"Aye, sir. I'm afraid you're right there. I am a sorry sight." He shook his head. "That was the first time I've ever fired my blaster except on the shooting range. It certainly was the first time I was ever inside a Stellar Patrol headquarters, or any police station for that matter."

Varn Tarl Sogan smiled. "I am a bad influence, Max. You should know better than to travel around in company with a Commando. We are always in one sort of trouble or another."

Chapter Eleven

Islaen Connor shook her head. They were alone in the crew's cabin save for Bandit, and Varn had recounted the events of the day in detail. He looked pretty good, she thought, all things considered. Had she been in his place, she would have been on the flat of her back in her bed, oblivious to all the universe.

Islaen smirked at him. *What was that I said about hoping for a boring day?*

That does not seem to be our lot in life. I doubt we would care for it long-term.

It would be a refreshing change once in a while. She eyed him. *Would it be amiss to ask what you and Max Lampry were doing in that pleasure district in the first place? You left that part of it out of your account, and I can't imagine a more unlikely brace of revelers, individually or in tandem.*

Not in the least amiss, he assured her. *There is no mystery involved. Max wanted some coffee, and it was past time for a meal. We were too shabby looking to go anywhere more respectable that offered both.*

The Commando-Colonel stood up. *Well, your day's adventures have cost me another trip to the port. I never got to the pharmacy, and I need those supplies. It's open all night, luckily.*

I shall go for you, he said quickly. *Just give me written authorization to pick up the prescriptions.*

No. It was my job. Besides, you really did have a nova of a day. You and Bandit relax here for yourselves. I shouldn't be gone too long.

Varn sighed in his heart. He had no right to try to prevent her from going, and no real reason, either, but spaceports could be dangerous and were doubly so at night. *Try to be careful, Colonel,* he said lightly. *Our unit has had too many incidents of note of late. I want to sleep this night through.*

I'm going to the pharmacy, not the pleasure district, Admiral, she replied tartly.

The Noreenan smiled as she turned the flier away from the planeting field. It was hard to imagine anyone worrying about the commander of the Federation's top Commando unit going into Horus' spaceport to requisition supplies, day or night, but Varn Tarl Sogan's concern was real. He had encountered so much peril in such places over the years that he could not but view them as hazardous.

Her expression darkened. Maybe more than that on occasion. Although he was always carefully shielded at those times, she had thought it had taken an act of will more than once to bring him in at all in some of the outer ports they had visited. Certainly he never ventured into one at night on his own, not even here on Horus.

Warmth filled her. Varn had volunteered to do that just now for her sake.

The nighttime spaceport was strange, the Commando-Colonel had to admit. Most of the places which normally drew her there were closed and dark. Others, insignificant by day, were now alive and bright, even up here in the business district. She had no interest at all in knowing what was going on far to the south. Even without her Noreenan prudery, basic good sense would have kept her well away.

The single-story pharmacy was brightly lighted. It looked remarkably cheerful beside its glowering neighbor.

Connor studied the three-story building. It was utterly dark. By day, it was a veritable wasps' nest of activity. New owners were completely gutting it with the intention of converting it from a maze of small office suites into a large warehousing facility. Now, it was black, silent, and empty.

Empty of legitimate workers. She ignored the free curb beside it, although there was no open space in front of the pharmacy. The woman parked her flier two doors down on its opposite side, before an equally well-lit restaurant, and she made sure her blaster was loose in its holster. Crime was not limited to the south, and she had no wish to copy Varn's visit to Stellar Patrol headquarters, that or require a session with the renewer herself.

The pharmacy was busy, as evinced by the number of vehicles parked outside it. A half-dozen people were on line awaiting service when she went inside, and others joined the queue behind her.

The people in front of her were served quickly, and the Commando soon found herself at the counter. She presented her requisitions to the pharmacist.

Islaen Connor sighed at the Horusi's frown. She was well known here to the day shift, but she had not seen this one before. The woman looked to be very young, probably not long certified in her position and with a head full of rules.

"I am sorry," the Horusi said, handing her back the forms, "but most of these require a doctor's signature."

"I am Commando-Colonel Islaen Connor, and I am entitled to draw whatever supplies are required by my unit. You have that information along with my signature and voice print on your computer. May I suggest that you check your records now?"

Space, Islaen thought, she was beginning to sound like Varn in one of his War Prince moods. "I'm sorry," she told the other, "but it is late now, and I don't want to have to come back again tomorrow. We do need these things."

The pharmacist quickly called up the Noreenan's record and found the appropriate approvals. "I'm the one to apologize, Colonel Connor. Please wait. I shall have what you need in a few minutes."

An hour's quarter later, she gathered up her sizable parcel and, after signing for the purchases, left the establishment.

Islaen stowed her supplies. She was about to enter the flier herself when a strange, rumbling sound caused her to whirl toward the dark building up the block

Almost in slow motion, its side wall crumbled at the second floor. After that, everything happened rapidly, too rapidly. The whole mass crashed down upon the lower, lighted structure beside it.

Peace returned within an incredibly few seconds. Connor had dropped and rolled beneath her flier. Plenty of debris had fallen around her, but it was chiefly small stuff. The vehicle had taken some strikes but had received no significant damage. She had suffered none at all.

The pharmacy was another matter. Nothing remained of it, or seemed to remain. When the colonel sent out her mind, she found living people within, buried under what well might prove their vast, broken tomb.

Islaen started to call out in mind to Sogan but stopped herself. Speed was needed now, and other help was closer. She would be back at the *Maid* again before her unit ever knew there was trouble here. She raised her shields and set them tightly, as she always did when facing surplanetary combat, and put in a call to the Stellar Patrol. They would be able to marshal the equipment and massive effort necessary to effect a rescue here.

In the meantime, people were alive in there, alive in terror and pain, those who still retained the consciousness to be aware of their situation. If the rubble settled, as it could at any moment, they would all be gone before any other assistance could arrive.

The Commando-Colonel examined the ruins. The debris was so braced that she realized she could get through it, through the place where the door more or less had been. Most of the patrons had been standing in line with that.

Islaen Connor was coward enough not to welcome either realization. She had no desire in all this great universe to venture into that menacing mountain of rubble.

She took her torch from her belt, activated it, and bent low, then wriggled her way inside.

Islaen advanced about four feet. She stopped. Her heart was beating rapidly, loudly to her ears. Her fear was so strong that she was near becoming sick with it. She had been in caves, in tight crawl spaces, before, but they were usually silent, or nearly so. This was different. The rubble creaked. It groaned with stress and minor movement that at any moment might become major.

Connor forced herself onward. She soon discovered three people pinned together but did not trouble herself with them. The quarter-ton slab which had struck them had left nothing of life and little of human form behind.

Another foot's crawl brought her greater success. A man was there, alive, but his thigh was impaled by a slender metal pole.

The woman examined it. The thing was immobile, driven into the floor by the impact of its fall and wedged between it and the dark mass above. Its upper end was invisible, fixed somewhere in the great mound of rubble beyond the range of her torch.

She studied the victim's leg, the way it was held. It would not have to come off, she decided with relief, and a renewer could take care of the damage she would have to inflict to free it. He was a lucky man in the face of what might too easily have happened to him.

Islaen drew her knife. It was viciously sharp and readily cut through the flesh surrounding the pole. Fortunately, the bone itself had not been pierced.

This man was a civilian, not military. He screamed and screamed loud until the pain took him, and he fainted.

Connor cut a strip from his pants to tie off the wound and began to drag him out. He was a dead weight and difficult for her to manage in the narrow crawl way, but she was grateful for his unconsciousness. She could deal with this. A hysterical man half again or twice her weight would have been a different story, maybe one fatal to both of them and to those others still awaiting help farther inside.

The Stellar Patrol and Emergency Service had arrived by the time she reached the street once more.

Turning over her patient to the latter's care, she reported to the Patrol Captain commanding the official rescue effort and described the route she had discovered to the interior and, hopefully, to more survivors.

Workers were already clearing the outermost layer of rubble. The big equipment was under order and expected soon. In the meantime, Islaen Connor was the only one present slight enough to continue with the rescue operation. Steeling herself, the Commando ventured inside once more.

Varn Tarl Sogan was deeply immersed in a nano on the early use of fireboats and torpedoes on Terra when his communicator startled him back into awareness of his surroundings.

"Aye, Karmikel?" he asked, managing to keep his annoyance over the shock the other man had given him out of his voice.

"Sorry to bother you, Admiral, but with all the excitement, we forgot to pick up the medical supplies the colonel got for us. Bethe wants to stow them tonight. It'll be one less thing to do if we find ourselves facing a mission in the immediate future."

"She did not get them yet. She has gone back to the pharmacy to collect them now."

There was a brief silence. "When did she go?"

Sogan told him. He glanced at his timer. "She is taking her time about it." She was taking a damn sight too much time . . .

Again, a silence. "Sit tight, Varn. Bethe and I are on our way over."

Once more, the War Prince looked at the timer. Had he not gotten so involved reading, he would have been pacing long ago.

A cold dread, a certainty, filled him. Islaen was in trouble. She had to be. His mind went out, not in a call that might prove a deadly distraction, but just seeking.

Nothing. Her shields were closed tight. If she were there at all . . .

"Bandit?" he asked desperately. The gurry had once told him that she would know it if one of them were dead.

He should know it! He should have felt her dying or her pain or her fear. Perhaps not, though, if unconsciousness had come too fast, especially with shields already in place . . .

Islaen's alive! the Jadite assured him. *Islaen not mind talking!*

"Thank you, Small One." It was a relief, but his fear eased only slightly. Islaen Connor still confronted some unnamed peril.

The other two Commandos arrived at that point. One look at their faces was sufficient to confirm for him that something was seriously amiss.

"What has happened?" By force of will, the Arcturian kept his voice normal.

"You didn't hear the local news?"

"No. I was reading. —Karmikel, what is wrong?"

"There's been an accident, Varn," Danlo told him quickly. "The building next to the pharmacy collapsed on it. There have been a number of fatalities, and people are still trapped inside."

Jake nodded. "We called to volunteer, but the Stellar Patrol said to stay away. They only want the big gear and trained operators in there at the moment."

Sogan drew on his will. He knew heart and soul that his consort was involved and involved deeply. "Islaen is alive," he assured the others. "Bandit has confirmed that."

"Can you reach her?" the redhead demanded eagerly.

He shook his head. "Not by merely searching, and I dare not try to push contact, no more than I would in battle, not yet at any rate."

"What about the Stellar Patrol?" Bethe Danlo suggested. "They owe you one after your afternoon's work. Contact their colonel and see if he knows anything. There may be survivor lists out by now even if they're not being released to the public yet."

The War Prince raced for the surplanetary transceiver on the bridge, his comrades following fast behind him. He soon reached the Patrol commander but was told no information was available.

Jake Karmikel swore under his breath and pushed him aside just as he was about to sever the connection. "Colonel, this is Commando-Captain Karmikel. Colonel Connor is Sogan's wife as well as our unit's commander. We're nearly certain she was on-site at the time of the collapse, and we'd really appreciate anything you can tell us as soon as there is any news at all."

The Patrol man was quiet only a moment. "I'm sorry, Sogan. I don't have anything now, but I'll see what I can do. Stay put. We'll be back to you or have your colonel contact you herself as soon as we know something."

"Thank you, Colonel. We shall be waiting here." Varn closed off the transmission with a sigh. He would give the man a little time, he decided, give Islaen a very little more time, then he would start searching himself, in mind and, if necessary, in person.

The Noreenan glared at him. "Blast you, Sogan! Don't you know yet that a personal appeal frequently gets a lot farther than some damned formal official request?"

Karmikel was sorry in the next moment that he had said anything. The Arcturian did not need a reaming from him. He had retreated behind that frigid wall of his, screened and seemingly aloof from the living universe around him. The image came to Jake's mind of a single star, the sole survivor of a galaxy otherwise totally swallowed by the insatiable hunger of a black hole, painfully bright, impossibly, unbearably alone.

"We know she's alive," Jake ventured more gently. "Why wouldn't she have contacted us, you?"

"Islaen may be . . . working on the rescue," and so in danger herself, "and thus responding as if we were in combat." He stopped but forced himself to go on. "She may be trapped within the building, either unconscious or dying and unwilling to have me endure that with her."

His shoulders straightened a little more, and he turned away from them.

"Varn, don't do this to us," Bethe pleaded. "Not now. This means too much to us as well."

Sogan drew a deep breath. Danlo was right. She and Islaen Connor were close friends. Spirit of Space, Jake Karmikel and Islaen had gone through basic training together. They were suffering, and still they were trying to help, to comfort, him. They needed and deserved something more from him than withdrawal.

He was not certain what to do. He faced them once more. In the end, he only took Bethe's hand, that and lowered the guards that kept his face a mask, only a little but enough to let them see that he shared their misery at this lack of knowledge and enforced inaction, that he, too, feared.

Fear? This was more like terror. His eyes closed. Islaen was alive, but what good was that if she were also buried, badly or fatally hurt, doomed to a slow death of want in the horror of the endless dark?

"I will not give any of them much longer," he snapped suddenly. "If I do not hear soon, I shall begin my own hunt, and if I do not contact her in mind, I shall tear that ruin apart, Stellar Patrol orders be damned!"

"Any time you're ready, Admiral," Jake told him quietly.

Sogan gripped his temper and the dread driving it. More was to be expected of him than this.

His eyes fell but lifted again. His comrades were feeling the same fear, the same rage at their inability to do more. They knew it could be no different with him. It was no shame to him to be afraid for a woman like Islaen Connor, to grieve over the possibility of losing her. He knew he was not lessened in the eyes of these two because of it. Certainly, it was no lessening of himself to try to comfort the poor little gurry, whom he now swept up and cradled in his hands. Varn looked into the tiny, upturned face. What would either of them do, he thought bleakly, if Islaen Connor failed to return this night or on any other?

Twice more, the Commando-Colonel entered the ruins and twice returned with still-breathing victims. Only one more remained, the young pharmacist sealed beneath her counter, unharmed but terrified and with her small pocket of air already growing tainted.

She prepared to reenter the crawl space, but the Patrol officer hailed her.

"Aye, Captain?" she asked wearily.

"The excavation people say that rubble's going to settle real soon."

She nodded. She had been fearing that right from the start. "This should be my last trip. I'll make it quick."

"I'm sorry, Colonel. I can't permit you to go in there again."

"I'm sorry, Captain, but you can't prevent me from doing so." Her eyes locked with his. "The counter's intact, and there is a young woman who could well be trapped beneath it. I cannot stand here and make no effort to get her out."

"How will you reach to her, assuming she's alive at all?" he asked, admitting his defeat.

"With this flame torch." She held up the implement she had already borrowed from the other workers to aid her in her task.

"Your unit—your husband—have contacted Patrol headquarters about you," he told her.

Islaen's eyes closed. Varn . . . "I'll call them as soon as I'm out," she said. She paused. "If—if I should be killed, let them know at once. Waiting is worse torture than sure knowledge."

"I'll do that, Colonel Connor," he promised. "Good hunting, and good luck."

Going into the ruin had been hard before. Now, with the Patrolman's warning of imminent doom sounding in her mind, it was well-nigh impossible. Will alone pushed her through that narrow opening.

The excavation folk were right. That she knew at once. The sounds made by the rubble were different. Something was going to happen, and it would happen soon.

It was a bit of a wriggle to get herself through the final few feet to the counter, and the Commando was glad it was another lightly built woman that she was seeking, one relatively unhurt at that. A larger person would not have found this easy.

She reached the counter and banged against it. "Keep back from this spot," she called out. "I'm going to burn my way through to you." She hoped the other woman could hear her and had the room to permit her to obey.

The synthetic wood glowed and then vaporized beneath the intense heat of the flame torch. Soon, she had a hole cut in it large enough to permit the prisoner to emerge.

A head quickly poked through it. The pharmacist's face was tearstained and strained, but she declared herself ready to proceed.

"Just follow me," Islaen told her. "It's a straight crawl and not too difficult once we pass these first few feet. They're by far the worst of it."

Connor had to fight to keep her fear and need for haste out of her voice and fight even harder to hold her pace to the slow crawl she had set for herself. She could have made better speed, but she was not sure that her charge could manage it. Overtax or panic the woman, and everything might be lost.

It seemed to take an eternity. Twice, the rubble groaned, and once there was a mighty crack. Connor licked her dry, dirt-caked lips and kept going.

She came to the entrance. Hands, the Patrol Captain's, drew her forward and out. Others reached in and pulled the second woman to safety.

No sooner had they done so than a rumbling began that did not stop. They ran, Islaen more than half carried by the officer. When they turned again, the great mound of debris had dropped a third of a story in height.

She leaned against the man, trying to catch her breath and willing her heart to resume a more normal beat. It had been close, but she had done her job. Nothing alive had remained inside that building when she and her latest charge had come forth.

Her mind flew open. *Varn, it's over. I'm covered in dirt from head to toe, but I'm sound out, and I'm on my way home.*

Islaen was not surprised to find her comrades waiting for her on the *Maid*'s boarding ramp. Jake caught her up in a rib-threatening bear hug that completely ignored the state of her clothes or what contact with them was doing to his own.

He did not release her until he had carried her up the core ladder and deposited her in the center of the crew's cabin.

Karmikel looked at Sogan. "There you are, Admiral. I always seem to be the one hugging your wife on these occasions. Now it's your turn."

Varn smiled. He stepped forward and took his consort in his arms, not exuberantly as Jake had done, but very gently. "Welcome back, Islaen," he said as his lips met hers. *Welcome home, my Islaen.*

Chapter Twelve

Wake up, Colonel. It is bad discipline for the unit when our commander chooses to sleep the day away.

Islaen opened her eyes. Varn was standing beside her, a cup of jakek in his hands. *This is real service. Thank you, Admiral.*

Yes! Bandit agreed from her perch on the dresser. *Islaen get up now! Breakfast ready soon!*

"Be quiet, you feathered rogue," Sogan ordered. "Let her enjoy her jakek."

What's this about breakfast?

I have the range programmed with a delay set on it to give you time to get ready at your leisure. I shall reactivate it as soon as you come down.

You do have my thanks, Admiral Sogan. I appreciate the meal, her eyes danced, *and even more, the sacrifice.*

Varn Tarl Sogan performed his rotation on galley duty without complaint and by far better than adequately, but it was not his favorite duty. Apart from making an occasional pot or cup of jakek, he rarely went beyond what was required of him with respect to it.

He studied her fondly. *You are so beautiful, Islaen Connor.*

I was some beauty when I arrived home last night. She smiled. *I loved your greeting, though. You're definitely improving in that respect.*

Connor felt him laugh. He closed his shields, but only to induce her to question him. *What are you thinking now?*

That I am glad I insisted upon full-sized beds for the Maid's cabins instead of bunks. They leave little floor space, but they have proven a great comfort during these last couple of years.

Sogan took the empty cup from her and set it on the half-width dresser. He sat on the bed beside her and slipped his arms around her. He kissed her deeply.

Bandit gave an annoyed chirp and flew from the cabin.

Varn rolled onto his back so that he shared Islaen's pillow. *Sometimes, she can be a less-than-ideal associate,* he grumbled.

His consort laughed. *Try to look at it from her point of view. First, she spent a pretty miserable night waiting up for me, and now she thinks there will be a long delay before she gets what is probably her second breakfast.*

Varn turned to her once more. *She will just have to wait,* he said as his mouth covered hers.

Islaen Connor smiled. She would never grow tired of seeing her husband in dress uniform, she thought, and he looked even better in the stark black of a Federation Commando than he had in the Empire's scarlet.

She said nothing to him this time. His shields were up, only enough open to permit surface communication, but she did not need to delve his closed thoughts to be aware of his already growing discomfort. *I'm sorry, Varn,* she said, *but Admiral Dundee did insist upon seeing both of us.*

I know, my Islaen. He sighed. *It should not trouble me, I suppose, but I had considered him my near equal for so long. Now, I am so much less.*

Not less, friend. You just have a lower rank.

He forced a smile. *For an Arcturian, that is one and the same thing.*

Connor watched him for a few moments. *I know this is probably a bad time for it, but I have a present for you.* She retrieved a package from the cabinet nearest her. *I picked these up yesterday, but with all the fuss about the* Moon *and then doctoring you and Max and my own bit of excitement, I forgot to give them to you.*

Varn took the package. It contained nanos, six of them. His eyes brightened when he read the titles.

He looked inquiringly at her. *Where did you get these?*

I special ordered them from The Motherworld. *They just came in.* —*Prespace Terran naval history, each on a different engagement. They go into detail on the tactics, the action itself, the equipment, and the people. I hoped they would interest you.*

They could hardly fail to do so. You know how much Terran history I read. Your motherplanet produced a mad race but a thoroughly fascinating one.

You are pleased? It was scarcely necessary to ask between the readings she was receiving and his smile.

Aye, my Islaen, that, I am. He scowled. *Now, this meeting is doubly onerous to me. I should much rather you left me on the* Maid *with these.*

Sorry, Admiral, she said sternly. *Duty must come first.*

Sogan glanced at his timer. *It also must come soon. Let us be going, Colonel. It would not do to keep the Chief Admiral waiting.*

The Arcturian kept his face a mask, his body absolutely still, as he studied the man sharing the table with them. His discomfort was sufficiently strong that he would have preferred to keep his mind completely shielded even as he was covering his closed thoughts, but he wanted to remain linked with Islaen in order to share the transmissions she was receiving from their host.

Islaen and he had just seated themselves after saluting and greeting the Chief Admiral. Dundee was watching them both intently, but his feelings were friendly enough. His interest in them was strong, and there was more than a trace of embarrassment in him. That last reassured Varn and made it easier for him to carry the part fate had given him to play.

There was disappointment in the Terran as well. "You did not bring your gurry, Colonel Connor?"

"No, sir. It would hardly have been appropriate."

He glowered. "Sometimes an admiral's supposed dignity is considerably overrated."

"It's usually best to err on the conservative side when dealing with so senior an officer, Admiral Dundee."

Gray Jack continued to study Connor as they spoke. He was glad to have had the opportunity to see that other aspect of her the other night. The woman now before him might have been another individual entirely, fully a Commando leader, competent, smart, brave, capable of bearing the responsibilities laid on her.

Islaen Connor was strong, and she had need of that strength, he thought, more, perhaps, in her personal life than in her military work. Dundee glanced quickly at the man who was both her second-in-command and her husband. That was no easy charter. The scars marring Varn Tarl Sogan's back despite a month of belated renewer treatment had to be the least of those left by the Arcturian executioners.

Sogan's record over the last two years was stark proof that the brutal injustice he had suffered had not lessened his fighting ability, and it was that on which the Terran commander needed to draw.

That was not for the moment. There was opportunity yet for more casual conversation, and he had been looking forward to this time with them.

The Chief Admiral eyed his guests. "Tell me, Colonel Connor, does your unit require at least one crisis every day to keep fighting fit?"

"It's beginning to look that way of late, sir," she admitted ruefully.

"All I know is that I am starting to truly look forward to seeing my daily reports since I planeted on Horus."

He continued more seriously. "You both are to be congratulated on that transport rescue. It was a fine piece of work. It would have been even without the addition of the trench shark."

The blue eyes flickered to the Arcturian. "You'll probably be pleased to learn that Ram has begun a full investigation of the supply depot whose operation you have questioned. It will doubtless be under new management by the time you return here again."

"I am glad to hear it. What about any other ships bearing substandard parts from there?"

"We began a hunt for them last night."

"Thank you, sir."

Dundee smiled. "Speaking of last night, the local Patrol boss called Ram well after hours to personally thank us for the job you did knocking out that raklik lunatic. You had a busy day, Captain."

Varn smiled. "Too busy, sir."

"So did Colonel Connor. The Patrol had plenty to say in praise of her, too."

The Chief Admiral began to ply his guests with questions about their various missions, asking for the details not included in the official reports.

Connor responded at first. By the simple expedient of omitting her own role in her descriptions, she forced Varn, first, to join her efforts and then to take over the task. The War Prince had a narrative ability that could turn what otherwise would be a bald recounting of events into an epic. Only when he attempted to downplay or gloss over his own contributions did she intervene.

Dundee's eyes were glowing by the meal's end. He always pumped his own Commando leaders in this manner, but he had not encountered a pair this articulate before or so interesting in themselves.

The Tamboran affair particularly intrigued him. It was one thing to battle pirates or an enemy navy in space and quite another to face the mindless fury of an erupting volcano. These two had, he knew, been on-world and on-site when the fire mountain had gone up.

He regretted when the time came to leave *The Lioness* and return to headquarters and the revelation of his plans for their unit. He wondered what the Arcturian's response would be, or whether Varn Tarl Sogan would deign to respond at all.

Colonel Barnak Fran Urtine stood by the window of the big chamber serving as their general meeting room in the suite assigned to the Arcturian delegation. It overlooked the ever-busy entrance to Federation Naval headquarters on Horus.

He straightened. "Sogan again. He is with Dundee."

His comrades joined him.

"The woman is beautiful," Captain Lassur observed. "She must be his commander."

"And his consort," the colonel agreed. "He did well for himself there. If what we have learned thus far is accurate, she is an officer of good rank and a Commando as well."

"How could she allow him near her?" demanded Trion Sorn Gidon. "She is an officer, an active military commander. Why would she have any truck with a mercenary disgraced among his own?"

"She probably pities him," Urtine said. "As for the rest, standards are different in this ultrasystem. The circumstances surrounding it make his disobedience almost acceptable here. Both Dundee and Sithe entered personal pleas for clemency at the time of his court-martial—"

"I had not known that!" Lassur exclaimed.

"Aye. The Emperor chose to ignore them. There was too much anger and pain in the military at the time, and Sogan's crime provided a good means of venting it."

"The Federation issued strong protests following the execution."

"That is so. Thorne of Brandine also granted him citizenship, I understand, posthumously as they believed."

"They can live to regret that now," Lt. Mitree said contemptuously.

"I do not believe that the Thornens would if they knew. This is a strange ultrasystem, incomprehensible in many of its ways."

Urtine gazed thoughtfully at the doorway through which the three had passed. "The Commando-Colonel is not to be blamed. She is merely following her own ways and standards."

"She has a brave man, certainly," the lieutenant conceded. "The whole port is alive with the story of that business by the coast. It is impressive."

"Varn Tarl Sogan never lacked courage."

"Except the courage to die," said Gidon bitterly.

"Aye, except that."

The Arcturian commander scowled. "She is a brave, an exceptional, officer, apparently. Her part, I can understand given the ways of this ultrasystem, but how could he have permitted her to become part of his shame? How could he have chosen to involve her?"

"You expect scruples from a mercenary?" his captain asked. "She was most likely his key into the Federation military."

"You are probably correct." Urtine sighed. "Thorne's Resistance fought well and bravely by all accounts. I can pity Sogan the situation in which he found himself. What I can neither condone nor comprehend is what he has permitted himself to become, the state of degradation into which he appears to have fallen. To sell his oath, to company even peripherally with blatant mutants, to fly a spark of a two-man fighter as if he were no more than the son of a family scarcely above the level of menials—none of that should even have been conceivable for any Arcturian officer, much less for a War Prince."

"What are we to do about him?" Lassur asked.

It was not the first time one of the party had asked him that question. "Do?" Urtine shook his head and repeated the only answer he had to give. "Perhaps there is nothing we should do or nothing that we can do. Most assuredly, we cannot involve the Empire in any private action of ours, and we have received no orders to act officially, just to transmit any more information that we may gather about the man. All that we can do at the moment is continue to watch him as best we may and conduct ourselves as the situation demands for the Empire's honor."

* * *

The Commando leaders left the restaurant and followed Dundee's transport in their flier until they arrived at Naval headquarters. There, they went to the office given over to the Chief Admiral's use.

"Sit, Colonel, Captain."

They complied, and he took his own place. "As you have probably guessed, I am interested in acquiring your services for a while."

"We assumed as much," Connor affirmed.

As the unit's field commander, it was natural that the Noreenan would talk for both, and Sogan was surprised to find the Chief Admiral turning to him. "How much do you know of general conditions along the borders of your former ultrasystem, Captain?"

"Nothing very specific, sir. We—they are struggling to regain their strength. There would not be as much trouble, probably no trouble, from internal renegades, but pirates and their ilk are no respecters of political boundaries. I imagine the Empire's rim is no better patrolled than the Federation's at this stage, and maybe less well patrolled given our losses in ships and matériel. There are those in plenty who would be tempted by the relatively easy raiding opportunities both in the starlanes and on some of the lesser planets."

"The Pirate Stars?"

"Those among the rest of the scavengers, I should imagine." The Pirate Stars were a loose confederation of systems, each basically self-sufficient but practicing raiding to keep their planetary treasuries full. They shared a common border with both ultrasystems and might well view their neighbors' postWar difficulties as opportunity. "I used to think that we should take them out as a precaution until I got too busy with Thorne's Resistance to concern myself much with incidentals."

"You chaps should've taken care of them decades ago instead of coming after us," Dundee told him. "They've grown strong and greedy during the time we were at one another's throats and are now creating all the hells along the Empire's portion of the border."

"Not the Federation's?" Islaen asked.

"No, Colonel. We won. Even more importantly to them, we don't let Arcturian battlecraft into our space. They've been going in from our side, raiding hard and fast, and darting back out again. The Arcturians want permission to bring in ships to counter them. I'm on Horus to meet with a diplomatic mission of theirs. It's a secret one, and very few know of their presence here. My crew certainly doesn't, as is apparent from that incident with Captain Sogan the other day."

He looked quickly at the War Prince, who seemed to be frozen in place. "I am not planning to involve you or any of your unit with them."

Varn relaxed only a little, and Islaen frowned. "What, then, sir?"

"The Pirate Stars. We've discovered that they've had the temerity to slip in a ship, a big one, apparently, and to establish a permanent base facility on Kyrie of Olga. My job is to knock out both the ship and the base and to do it decisively enough to convince their mother system that the Federation will not tolerate raiders within our borders, whether they're preying on our people or on those of another system, and that we most assuredly will not tolerate the appropriation of one of our planets by any alien force."

"You want our help to do that?" It was hardly necessary to ask. Why else would she and Varn be sitting here?

"For the base, at least, aye. It'll be a nasty job. I have the details ready for you on the *Charm*."

His eyes fixed on Sogan. "The *Terra's Charm* is a fine ship, state-of-the-art in every respect, and Captain Broderick handles her as if she were an extension of herself. Unfortunately, Broderick is in the Naval hospital at the moment with a bad case of Quandon Fever."

"You will be flying the *Charm* yourself?" Varn asked.

"If I must. I would prefer for you to do it."

Islaen felt the War Prince's shields slam into place around his mind. She stared at the Chief Admiral in open disbelief, but Varn Tarl Sogan made no move whatsoever.

"I am perfectly serious, Captain. As you said, my forté is overall fleet command, not the handling of a single ship. Certainly not the fighting of one. You, on the other hand, are probably the best battlecraft commander produced by either side during the War. The *Terra's Charm* is facing what may prove to be major combat. I want you on her bridge, and convention be damned."

Still, the Arcturian said nothing. He seemed more statue than living man.

Dundee's eyes did not leave him, but neither did they attempt to compel. "It will be your choice. If you decide not to do it, either because you don't believe you can or because you don't want to fly her, you need only say so, without explanation. You'll still have full part in the on-world portion of the mission along with the rest of your unit."

"I very much would like to take her, Admiral," he said in an absolutely steady voice. "There may be difficulties, however. Arcturian and Federation technology were similar, but not precisely the same. I am well familiar with your systems by now, but chiefly on the small-class level. A battleship is another matter."

"Look over the ship before deciding. I'll say nothing to the crew until and if I receive your acceptance of command."

"Thank you, sir."

Dundee hesitated. "The *Charm*'s a Federation ship. Those manning her are a well-mixed lot."

"That is the case throughout the ultrasystem. It will not be a problem." Sogan's eyes did not fall, but he cringed behind his shields at having that question raised before Islaen Connor. It was to his shame, and it was necessary.

The Chief Admiral did not press the question. Sogan's performance at the base of that cliff was a sharp assurance that he would be able to handle himself.

Dundee's eyes fell for an instant. They raised again. "I'm not going to lie to you, Sogan. This command will be for the duration of the mission only. Captain Broderick will recover and will rejoin the *Charm* upon our return. Even if she did not, a firm and excellent plan for succession of command is already in place."

"That is understood, sir."

The Terran pushed back in his chair. He returned his attention to Connor. "I shall leave for the *Charm* immediately. You will need time to secure your own ships and arrange for the completion of whatever work remains to be done on them following that fire. Report with your unit for duty on the *Terra's Charm* Thursday at 18:00 hours. That will give you two full days and part of another in which to complete your business."

"Aye, sir. Thank you."

"And, Colonel Connor," he added gruffly, "do not forget to bring the gurry."

Chapter Thirteen

Jake Karmikel stood in the entrance of the *Maid's crew's* cabin. "Morning, Colonel. Where, may I ask, is your consort?"

"On the bridge, of course. —How do I look?"

"Very nice, indeed, Colonel Connor." She did, too, he thought. Islaen was wearing a dark green day suit of lightweight Aberdeenan wool. It was a favorite of his. "You'd make a grand civilian."

"Just for an afternoon, thank you." She glanced at her timer. "Is Bethe ready?"

"Almost."

"I might as well join her."

"Have a good time."

"We shall. It's a wonderful program."

The Commando-Colonel looked at him severely. "I hope that you two will manage to keep out of trouble for a change."

His brows lifted. "Look who's talking! However, we'll do our best," he promised genially. "We plan to pass most of the day working on the *Moon*. That won't give us much scope for adventures."

"I don't know about that. You both have a strong talent in that particular area."

He glanced upward. "Our admiral was supposed to have joined me twenty minutes ago. What's he doing?"

She looked a bit surprised. Varn was normally punctual, and he rarely forgot appointments. "Pulling the communications systems apart."

"Damn!"

"Power down, Jake. He probably won't be long. Go on up and collect him."

"I'll do just that, Colonel," the redhead said. "I can't lug those replacement parts around by myself."

The Noreenan captain soon reached the bridge deck. He stood in the entrance, scowling darkly. All three consoles were wide open, and his comrade was obviously settled in for a long session with their innards.

"Admiral, just what in space or beyond it do you think you are doing?"

Varn did not look up. "Checking out the communications systems."

"You did that when we first planeted," Karmikel reminded him.

"Not thoroughly enough."

Jake's temper snapped. "Sogan, while you're up here playing at busy work, my *Moon's* down for a fact. I have three hundredweight of matériel waiting for pickup on the Navy dock, all of it necessary to set her right. You're supposed to help me collect it, among other things, this morning. If your recent experiences have left you too terrified to quit your little private fortress here, just say so, and I'll tell Bethe to cancel her concert and come with me. Otherwise, blast off your tail, and let's get going before we blow half the day."

The War Prince slammed the magpliers he had been using down on the deck and twisted himself around so that he faced the other man. "Get the bloody hell off my bridge, Karmikel," he snarled. "I shall be down as soon as I close everything up."

"Good enough, Admiral. I'll be waiting."

Jake's brows raised as he descended the ladder and hurried from the starship. He had realized the Arcturian was on edge, but he had not anticipated provoking so sharp a reaction with his barb.

Sogan was apparently not the only one in a foul temper, he thought a couple of minutes later. Islaen Connor was waiting for him beside the flier, and she was obviously in no better humor than her consort had been.

"All right," she demanded before he could even speak. "What happened?"

"Nothing, Colonel—" he started to protest.

"Stow it," she snapped. "Varn's mind was wide open."

The redhead grinned. "Our admiral possesses a remarkably imaginative vocabulary, doesn't he?"

"This isn't funny. He's furious."

"If thoughts were blaster bolts, I'd be a cinder?"

His commander did not relent. "You listen closely, Captain Karmikel. I don't care how you two choose to amuse yourselves, but I won't tolerate serious fighting among the members of my unit. Do you understand that?"

He nodded. "Aye, Colonel." Jake frowned. "I blew up and flamed him a bit, but there's no reason why he should have—"

Karmikel stopped, recalling his taunt and the manner in which he had delivered it. "I was navigating right off the charts," he confessed. "It would've been no more than my due if he'd dumped me bodily off the bridge instead of merely ordering me off."

The woman sighed. "If you don't learn to think before firing off your mouth, you're going to land us all in a galaxy of trouble someday."

The captain sighed. "I guess I should go up and apologize, except I doubt that he'll let me in."

"Give him time to cool down first. —Just wait here. I'll have a talk with Varn."

"It really wasn't his fault, Islaen."

"The last I heard, an argument requires a minimum of two participants."

"How's he doing now?"

"He's under control if not particularly happy. His shields are up tight, so I can't tell you any more than that."

Varn? Islaen decided to try mind speech, although she was not sure Sogan would accept the contact.

To her relief, the Arcturian responded immediately. *I am almost finished up here. You can tell Karmikel that I shall be down in a few minutes.*

I'm not here to check on your progress, she said when she reached the bridge.

Islaen sat on the edge of her flight chair, watching him. He was taking care to avoid looking at her. *What happened?*

Nothing.

Jake wouldn't tell me, either, she observed.

It was between us. His lips tightened. *The exchange was not creditable to either of us.*

The Commando-Colonel shook her head. They needed a furlough, all of them, she thought, not another mission. Nerves frayed under perpetual tension. It was a wonder they could hold on as well as they were doing at this point. *If you'd rather stay here, I can go with Jake. A bit of exercise would do me more good than sitting on my fins at yet another concert.*

The man smiled. *Enjoy the performance, Colonel Connor. Even if I were as selfish as I am arrogant, I could not give Karmikel a laser like that to fire back at me.*

She laughed. *The pair of you are incorrigible.* Her tone altered. *Seriously, though, Varn—*

I shall try to make peace, Colonel, and to keep it.

Good. You shouldn't have too much trouble. Jake isn't any too pleased with his own performance, either.

They left the starship together, then separated, Connor going to the *Jovian Moon* where Bethe Danlo was waiting for her, Sogan heading for the flier.

Karmikel had meekly taken the passenger seat. He kept quiet until the other man had activated the drive.

"Sogan," he said once they were airborne, "this is the Federation. The next time I go that far off the charts, remember that you're entitled to deck me."

The Arcturian smiled faintly. "I would be entitled to try. Whether I could succeed in doing it is an entirely different question."

"Let's just say that I would hate to see it put to the trial, my friend."

Jake straightened as their vehicle turned onto the public road that followed the perimeter of the planeting field. "No. We go east first."

"The docks are due north."

"They're our final stop. I don't want to have to drag a full cargo trailer all over Horus City."

"The City?"

"Aye, Admiral. I realized too late that frontal assault was entirely the wrong tactic to use on you. I plan to try open bribery instead."

"I am listening, Captain Karmikel."

"I figure if I drop you off at *The Motherworld* for an hour or so while I conduct some other business, I'll probably be able to get any amount of work out of you that I want later on."

Sogan's face brightened in real pleasure. *The Motherworld* was unique on the rim, or at least on this part of it, specializing in nanos and other media dealing with prespace and early-space Terran history. Sully, the proprietor, and the former Arcturian admiral had enjoyed many an involved discussion on some fairly esoteric subjects over the last two years.

Jake's proposal was particularly appealing since Varn had not managed to make an excursion to the shop on this planeting. He realized suddenly that he had not been doing much unnecessary venturing about anywhere on-world for some time now . . .

He forced the new darkness down and made himself smile. "An excellent suggestion from my side, Captain Karmikel, but perhaps not so stellar-class from yours."

"Why not?"

"The last time Islaen left me there for an hour, Sully and I wound up on a hunt through some new material he had acquired. I not only missed lunch, but I very nearly forgot dinner as well."

The other chuckled. "I remember. —Don't worry. I'm nothing near as nice as she is. I'll come and drag you away as soon as I'm ready."

"Fair enough, my friend. You will even succeed if I choose to cooperate."

Sogan set the familiar course almost without thinking. It was a pity he had left it so long on this planeting. Now, there would be time for only this single, brief visit . . .

Suddenly, he began to laugh. Karmikel looked at him in amazement. "You are feeling well, Admiral?"

"A deal better than I was feeling this morning. —Do you consider me a superstitious man?"

The Noreenan shrugged. "No more so than any other spacer. Why?"

"Because I have been looking at this planeting as somehow jinxed, that I am fated to have the firmament fall on my head every time I go out of sight of my starship. You were right in naming my project this morning busy work. It was. I was trying to weasel out of coming with you."

Jake stared at him, then laughed as well. "Sometimes, you're actually all right, Sogan! I wouldn't have thought you'd own up to that."

"Why not? It is too ridiculous to be disgraceful."

The Arcturian stopped at the corner nearest *The Motherworld* and turned the flier over to his comrade, promising to meet him again in the same place in an hour's time.

Rather to Jake's surprise, knowing the War Prince as he did and the strength of the temptation that particular shop represented for him, Sogan proved to be as good as his word and was waiting for him on the corner, a small package under his arm, at the appointed time.

"Did you buy out Sully's entire stock?" Karmikel inquired.

"No, not on this trip. I just got a couple of biographies and a symphony I had not heard before. It is a very beautiful one."

"No doubt." Jake made no comment on the small purchase. That dinner at *The Lioness* had to have put a large hole in the former admiral's store of squanderable credits. It did not take much in the way of sensitivity to recognize that his friend's relative poverty had to be a sore topic with him. He had blundered badly enough in savaging tender nerves already today . . .

Varn did not immediately reboard the vehicle. "Come look at this." He walked over to the window of the pawn shop that occupied the corner merchant facility and waited for his comrade to join him.

"What is it? A second river tear?"

"Not exactly. —The dagger, second row from the bottom, far right."

The Noreenan whistled. It was a striking weapon and obviously an extremely fine one. The blade was longer than those on the equivalent Commando knives. It was wickedly sharp on both edges and was crowned with a point like a needle. The ultrahard solar steel of which it was fashioned had been incised with an exquisitely wrought tracery of fine lines whose abstract pattern was repeated by the pale royal silver inlaid in the long, otherwise plain black hilt. "Arcturian, isn't it? An officer's?" It was hardly necessary to ask the last. No mere yeoman could have paid for it.

"An admiral's," Sogan answered softly. "A rank badge."

Karmikel's head snapped around. "Yours?"

"I did not lose mine to the Federation," Varn replied in cold pride. He gripped his temper. "It belonged to some other of my kind." Someone both less and more fortunate.

"It's beautiful, whoever owned it."

"Aye. A special commission, even as mine was. We were permitted that luxury with our rank daggers as long as they remained functional weapons."

"It may not be real. Look at the price."

"It is real. Who would copy such a thing?" he countered. "Besides, I know our workmanship. The fool of a shopkeeper simply does not realize what he has. Even discounting its history, it is valuable in itself as a weapon and as a work of art." Varn started for the door. "His ignorance works to my benefit."

Jake felt a surge of alarm. "Is that wise, Sogan?" he asked quietly.

The former admiral whirled on him, his dark eyes flashing.

They dropped in the next moment. "You are right. It is bad enough that I look like an Arcturian without carrying our weapons as well."

Without glancing at the window again, he strode over to the flier and took his place at the controls.

Chapter Fourteen

"North now?" Sogan asked.

His comrade smiled and shook his head. "South."

"I thought you wanted to get to work on the *Jovian Moon*," Varn said irritably.

"I do, but I also want to pick up a couple of items first."

"Very well, but it looks as if you might have left me at peace for a while longer than you did," he grumbled. "Travel along the planeting field?"

Karmikel nodded. "We might as well have a look at the civilian ships. They can usually be counted upon to provide an interesting show."

"Some of them are more terrifying than interesting." It was difficult to imagine how a few of those craft could lift or planet, much less remain at all in space.

"That, too," he agreed. "I'll tell you when to turn into the pleasure district."

Sogan frowned. "What business do you have in there, and at this hour?"

"We're just passing through. It makes a good shortcut." His eyes sparkled. "Besides, you're not all that innocent, Admiral, if you're a habitué of *Isaak's*. I must admit, I am impressed—"

"Put it on freeze, Karmikel. Max suggested the place," the War Prince told him sourly. He decided to keep quiet about his own previous acquaintance with the establishment.

Jake grinned. "I'm impressed with him, too."

"Spare him your compliments," his companion advised.

"Don't worry. I know his defenses aren't the equal of yours. It wouldn't be any fun to torment him."

Sogan shook his head in mock disgust. He glanced at the other. "Why should the fact that I am familiar with such places surprise you in any event? I had to frequent them to pick up charters. I did manage to hold body and soul together and to keep my ship in the starlanes for three years before meeting up with you two."

"True enough, but I think I'd be safe in putting credits down that you visited them only in the virtuous light of day."

Varn sighed. "I do not drink to excess, gamble, or whore," he said patiently. "What would I do in a pleasure district?"

"Arcturians never have any fun, do they?"

"Stow it, Jake. I have teamed with you for the last two years. Your off-duty existence is very nearly as circumspect as my own."

"Of course. Now. I'm a Commando officer, after all, and an old married man, but in my wild youth—"

"Under Islaen Connor's command?"

"May I remind you that we were equals at one point, Captain Sogan?"

"Islaen would still have issued the orders."

The Noreenan laughed. "Aye, she did for a fact, but I gave her a bit of trouble on occasion, all the same."

"You still do that. —Why do we have to come so far south, anyway?"

"I've finally located a supplier who stocks the same line of tools that you have. They're a deal better than Navy standard."

"Good. Buy a full set. That way, you will not have to keep borrowing mine."

"You might consider getting yourself another long-nosed magpliers while we're there. After that crack you gave it on the deck this morning, your present one might no longer be operational."

"Give it up, Jake," Sogan told him. "You are not going to provoke me a second time today."

"I was afraid of that," he said mournfully, "but it was worth a try."

The ever-changing scene in the civilian spaceport was as fascinating to the War Prince as it was to his comrade. The seemingly countless starships were planeted with the same orderly precision of place as were those in their own section. That was a port requirement to facilitate servicing and keeping track of them, but it was the sole visible similarity between the military and civilian segments of the immense field. The vessels themselves ran the gamut in appearance from craft the equal of any of their class in Navy service to a number Varn Tarl Sogan would unhesitatingly have condemned as derelict-class in his former life.

Jake shuddered at a particularly notable example of the latter berthed close to the perimeter. "I wouldn't even board that one of my own free will. If the ramp didn't collapse under me, the core ladder almost certainly would."

"She is probably sound enough. I should not care to tangle with her crew, however."

"They're hard-looking cases," his comrade agreed. "I doubt they'd appreciate too-close scrutiny by the Stellar Patrol."

"That is probably true." Varn smiled. "There is the *Rounder*."

"She's shabby enough, too."

"Only dark. Zubin cannot afford to have her skin scrubbed every time he is in port."

Karmikel made him no answer. Sogan had been able to afford even less, and he had been flying completely without help, yet his *Maid* had worn a bright skin. The sheer physical labor required for one man to keep it that way was appalling even to contemplate . . .

The diversity of condition ended once they reached the area where the large vessels were berthed. Fifty- and one hundred-class starships were big craft. They were expensive to fly and maintain, and only those captains with sufficient credits to do the job took one of them on. All of them that they could see were superbly kept, particularly those catering to passengers on a regular basis. There were no full-time liners out here on the rim such as those connecting the planets of the inner systems, but some of these came very close. They offered luxury to those utilizing their services, and competition among them was stiff enough that they took care to fulfill that commitment.

Karmikel stopped collecting stardust. A large crowd of locals and spacers from nearby vessels had gathered both within the field and at the fence marking the perimeter. Their attention appeared to be fixed on a crescent-shaped fifty-class with the red-and-black striped fins that proclaimed her Emirite registry. Suddenly, he saw why.

"Turn here," he snapped abruptly.

He was too late. The Arcturian had also seen the device the crew were setting up beside their ship and had recognized it for what it was.

Varn brought the flier to the curb and swung himself out of it.

Jake followed. "Sogan, damn it, come on! We've still got a lot to do."

If the War Prince heard him, he gave no sign of it. Pushing his way through the mass of other spectators with an authority that brooked no refusal, he soon had cleared a space for himself and his comrade at the fence.

His eyes were fixed on the strange device. It consisted of three upright metal slats braced at top and bottom by sturdy crossbeams, the whole being some eight feet tall and the breadth of a big man's body. It was not Terra's infamous old triangle or his own people's H-form equivalent, but there was no mistaking its purpose. No one with his history would have mistaken it.

A strident bell sounded. Several men emerged from the ship and marched down the ramp. —The crew was entirely male. Emir's women did not work off-world.

Others followed, two crewmen escorting a third. That he came unwillingly was evident. His companions held his arms in a powerful grasp. He was bare to the waist.

The bell sounded again when the three reached the device. The two guards, moving together in a practiced unison, fastened their charge's arms and legs to the outer slats so that he stood spread-eagled with his back to the crowd, his chest and head braced against the center beam.

Their work done, they nodded to another of the crew, who now stepped forward, uncoiling the thing in his hand as he moved.

The bell rang a third time. The disciplinarian's arm drew back. The long, flexible wire he controlled lashed out.

His victim screamed as a red stripe opened on his back as if by magic.

Again and again in measured rhythm, the bell signaled the flight of the wire and the prisoner's answering scream.

"So that is a flogging," Varn Tarl Sogan remarked, as if conversationally. "I had never actually witnessed one before now. It is even more degrading than I had imagined."

Karmikel, disgusted and already furious at the brutality of the scene playing out before him, turned viciously on his companion.

He took one look at the Arcturian, caught him by the arm, and half-dragged, half-carried him back through the crowd.

Sogan leaned against the side of the flier, bracing himself on his arms, for several minutes as he tried to will his shaking body back under his control. At last, he nodded and permitted the Noreenan to maneuver him into the passenger seat.

Jake watched him sympathetically. "You all right now?"

"Aye, or I will be in a few more minutes." His mouth twisted. "That was bad."

"Real bad."

The former admiral faced him. He knew he must look just about as drained as he felt. "I was not lying. I had never seen that. I had always been fortunate enough to serve under humane officers myself, and I never permitted violent non-capital corporeal punishment in my own command. I did not witness my execution. That, I only experienced—"

"Easy, friend. Don't think about it."

"Under the circumstances, that is a rather difficult suggestion to follow."

"You could use a good, stiff drink."

"No."

"I didn't say you'd go along. I said you need it, and badly at that."

Sogan's eyes closed. "It would not help." His expression tightened, as if he himself were taking the Emirite's lash. "I did not yell, at least not while I remained conscious. What happened after that, I do not know—"

"Let it go, Sogan," Karmikel told him softly. "It happened once, but it's done now. It's over for you."

"Is it?" the War Prince asked with infinite weariness. "I wonder if it will ever really be ended." He looked up. "It is not just the matter of the lashing. That merely hurt. It is the shame of it and the shame of my crime." Pain deep and black as interstellar space filled him, filled his voice as he spoke. "If I were to meet up with some of my own kind right now, even with those who might once have regarded me with affection, they would not deign to so much as spit on me—"

"That would be their failing and none of yours! Why in all the hells should you even care what vacuum brains like that would think or do?"

The Noreenan gripped himself. "I'm sorry, Varn. That was a stupid remark. This whole idea of mine was stupid, and you've had to pay the price for it."

Sogan forced himself to smile. "It is not your fault, Jake. You hardly arranged that performance for my benefit."

"No."

"So, I will survive the experience. I have lived through considerably worse."

Karmikel started the engine. "Let's get out of here."

Varn roused himself. "Where now?"

"Home. We've both had more than enough for one day."

"No. I am willing to forego purchasing your tools for today, but we came out specifically for that matériel. We are not returning without it."

"Sogan, don't be so damned stubborn—"

"I intend to spend the remainder of this day hard at some sort of work. I would prefer that it have genuine significance." His voice turned bleak. "I would also prefer that I not have to do it alone."

Bethe Danlo somberly watched the man sitting across from her at the table in the *Jovian Moon*'s crew's cabin. The Noreenan had just finished recounting the events of the whole wretched day for her and was now staring into his jakek. "He wouldn't take so much as a single drink for me, of course," he concluded bitterly. "I, on the other hand, could readily have downed the contents of a couple of flasks. I still feel like doing it." As if to illustrate, he drained the cup in his hands, ignoring the fact that the liquid it contained was still somewhat too hot for gulping.

He looked up. "I didn't know what to do, Bethe. I've never seen the admiral down like that."

Danlo fetched him a refill from the galley and sat down again. "This was an improvement over his normal response to his own troubles, actually. He usually walls up everything dark that he feels."

"I think he was simply too low to make the effort this time."

"It must have been a flaming shock," she said sympathetically, "a regular little vignette out of the past. No wonder it hit him hard. It came so fast that he had no chance to brace himself for it at all."

Karmikel nodded gloomily. He drifted into his own thoughts for a few moments, then recalled himself to his wife's presence. "You know, as bad as those damned Emirites were, that part of it all couldn't be helped. It's the business about the knife that's really tearing me."

"The Arcturian dagger?"

"Aye." He shook his head angrily. "I should've kept my big mouth shut. Sogan wouldn't have to carry the weapon simply because he owned it. He'd still have had all the pleasure of it."

The demolitions expert did not contradict him. "He could have paid for it?"

"No problem. He probably could've managed it when he was almost dead broke before meeting up with Islaen and me. He'd have been glad to go without a few more meals to get it."

"He really wanted it?"

"Sogan wanted it. There was excitement on him. Until I short-circuited it. —I can accept that he must forget about the big things he's lost, but it's a damn foul charter that he has to give up the little ones as well. That this particular sacrifice is my contribution doesn't make me feel any better about it all."

"We still have a couple of days on-world. Maybe—"

He just shook his head. "The admiral will never go back for it now, even if I admitted I was dead wrong."

Bethe held out her hand to him. "What's past can't be altered. Forget about it now, my friend. Varn will. Right now, I suggest that we both knock out early. Sergeant Lampry and his crew will be here at 06:00 tomorrow, and you'll have to show him what you did today. —His jaw'll drop when he sees how much the two of you managed to accomplish."

"An upset Arcturian can do a prodigious amount of labor. I couldn't very well let Sogan put me to shame."

"Perish the thought!" She came to her feet. "To bed, Captain Karmikel. Our admiral is likely to still be just as upset tomorrow, so you'll had best be well rested before renewing your own efforts."

Chapter Fifteen

Isis had not fully risen before Islaen Connor joined her comrades on the *Jovian Moon*. She sat at the table and automatically accepted the jakek and syntheggs Karmikel was quick to dish up for her despite his surprise at her unexpected arrival.

He eyed his commander disapprovingly. "You haven't been taking care of yourself, Colonel," he chided. "You look as if you didn't sleep a wink last night."

"I didn't."

"I suppose that means Varn didn't, either," Danlo said softly.

"He slept some, if it could be called that. However, you're right in the main part. He spent the bulk of the night pacing the bridge."

"There isn't room enough to pace up there," Jake interjected.

"He managed."

"More dreams, I suppose?" the sergeant asked. That was one outlet for his troubles which the War Prince was powerless to bar. Connor was usually able either to wake him and defuse the emotion driving the nightmares or to block them from his awareness, although never the last without having to bear the brunt of them herself. Apparently, she had failed in both efforts on this occasion.

"Let's just say that if there was some detail of his execution about which I was previously ignorant, that deficiency in my knowledge has now been rectified." She pressed her fingers to her eyes. Her consort had cycled into that horror again and again. She had been powerless to help this time, and she was all too well aware of what he had suffered. With his shields completely down, those dark memories of his had torn into her mind even as they were seared in Varn Tarl Sogan's.

Her head raised. She had come to the *Jovian Moon* in search of information, not sympathy. "What in space or beyond it did you two do yesterday to set him off like that?" she demanded.

"Sogan didn't tell you?" the redhead asked.

"Varn's too mortified to look at me at the moment, much less talk to me. He wasn't talking last night, either, when I was finally able to rouse him. Bandit's doing no better with him, though she's still trying."

Karmikel described their encounter with the Emirite justice system.

Connor's eyes closed. "Oh, Jake! I thought I could depend on you."

"That's hardly fair, Islaen!" Bethe Danlo snapped. "Jake didn't know those sons of Schythian apes were on-world, much less that they'd be staging a disciplinary action just as he and Varn were passing by."

The colonel drew in a deep breath and took hold of her temper. "No, of course, he didn't. —I'm sorry, Jake. Put it down to a real bad night." She sighed. "I'm glad you were with him, at least. It would've been a galaxy worse if he'd been roving about by himself at the time."

She straightened in her seat. "Varn mentioned that you didn't complete all your business yesterday and that he'd be helping you again today."

"I thought he wasn't talking."

"A brief message over the communicator. As the unit's CO, I'm entitled to know his plans."

Her eyes held his. "You're a trained observer, Captain Karmikel. Use your skills. Varn Tarl Sogan won't just come out and say that he wants no part of the universe beyond these two starships at the moment, but if you believe that to be the case, cut him a break. You can come up with some legitimate excuse for letting him off."

"Will do, Colonel. Actually, I'm surprised he's even considering coming along. I had to practically pry him off the *Maid's* bridge yesterday. I'd have thought it would take a planetbuster detonation to shift him this morning."

"He sees it as his duty. An Arcturian officer will respond to that summons, whatever his feelings, and that our comrade remains to his very core." Sometimes, she wished that was not so completely true. A little Terran rebelliousness might make life a bit easier for him, and right now, she did not believe that anything could make hers more complicated.

Karmikel opened his communicator. "Can I come up, Sogan, or am I still banned from the bridge?"

"Come up if you want, you Blackguard, but I was already on my way down."

"I'll wait here, then."

True to his word, the former admiral joined him moments later. He was already wearing his jacket. "Ready to go?"

"Aye. I've just turned Max and company loose on the *Moon*. They were impressed by our afternoon's work. —Did you have breakfast yet?"

The other shrugged. "Later, maybe. Let us go now. Islaen and Bandit have gone back to bed and are trying for some sleep. I do not want to disturb them. They-had a rough night."

"Sogan, wait up. The only thing I have to do in port today is to pick up those tools. That's not a two-man operation. You remain here and work on the *Moon* with Lampry. Much as it chokes me to admit it, you're the best mechanic in the star-lanes, myself included."

"I am going."

"Spirit of Space, why? You'd have weaseled out yesterday when I actually needed you. Today, I don't, and you refuse to stay put."

The Arcturian's eyes fell. "I disgraced myself properly yesterday," he said stiffly.

"Put that debris on freeze, Sogan!" Jake did not try to keep the anger out of his voice. "Whatever friendship is supposed to be in the Empire, around here, it entitles us to shoulder some of the load now and then."

"We try to spare one another that burden." His voice was cold. Explanations of this nature did not come easily for him, and he was mortified at the necessity of having to make this one now. He was furious with himself for the weakness which was the root of it all. "I might prefer to remain locked on the *Fairest Maid* or, perhaps, safe in our palace on Thorne, but what sort of existence would that be? I do not claim that I never yield to the temptation," he added bitterly. "I have run on a few occasions when I felt too weary to face the possibility of still more confrontation, but I have to make sure that such self-indulgence—or cowardice, to give it its proper name—remains a very rare luxury." His dark eyes met his comrade's. "I intend to finish yesterday's business, Karmikel."

"Power down, Admiral. We won't be gone long enough to make arguing about the journey worthwhile. I'll take the controls, though. I know a shortcut, and it'll be easier to drive myself than to have to keep feeding you a string of directions."

"Fair enough, Captain Karmikel."

Jake headed away from the planeting field once they had passed through the gate in its confining fence. He was not going to risk another unpleasant encounter with any of their more unsavory neighbors today. Not only did Sogan deserve a bit of peace, but Islaen Connor with probably kill him outright if they wound up in any more trouble, assuming he and the War Prince survived it.

The flier skimmed along one seemingly endless street after another. "This is a shortcut?" Varn inquired dryly.

"It will be once we get far enough south," the Noreenan replied calmly. He had to admit that it was irritating to possess an airborne vehicle capable of surface-space operation and be compelled by local traffic ordinance to hover a few inches above the ground and abide by all the rules binding conventional wheeled machines. As sure as space was black, he thought, he would not care much for a planet hugger's life, leastwise not on any halfway civilized world.

At long last, the redhead brought his flier to a halt before the shop he wanted. Half an hour later, his purchase was complete and the tools were stowed for the journey back.

Varn's inner sigh of relief died stillborn. His comrade was looking purposefully up the street. He gave no indication at all that he intended to reenter the vehicle in anything like the immediate future. "I thought that was our final errand, or have you dredged up some other job for us?"

"The work is done. The pleasure starts. We're going to have some lunch."

"It is too early."

"Not for on-worlders. We'll just have a slightly better choice of tables and faster service than we would in half an hour's time. —No use protesting, Admiral. We're mission-bound. There's no telling what the galley's like on the *Terra's Charm*—"

"It is most likely excellent."

"We are also slated for active service," he continued, ignoring the interruption. "That could mean a long stint on rations. I'm going to pack in real food while I have the chance."

"You make an excellent point, Captain Karmikel," Sogan said, admitting his defeat. "Any suggestions as to where we should go?"

"Not really. There are mostly laborers' eateries around here. One of them should be as good as another. They wouldn't stay in business if they weren't acceptable, not with all the competition. Let's have a look at that one up the street. It's the closest."

The two Commandos walked half a block to *Dorian's Kitchen* and examined the menu posted in the window. The room within, from what they could see of it, was plain but was well lighted and looked to be clean and properly maintained.

They went inside and were immediately taken in charge by the sole waitress on duty, a pretty, fair-haired young woman with the accent of Helga of Thor. Given her youth and general appearance, they judged her to be a first-year student at the Sector University.

Jake asked for her recommendations and, after receiving Sogan's nod of assent, ordered as she suggested. Spacers such as themselves frequently ate in workers' restaurants like this one when on-world on established planets tracing their ultimate ancestry to the Federation's motherplanet. The food in such places, allowing for local variation, could usually be counted upon to be hearty, plentiful, and, as a rule, not very expensive.

Dorian's Kitchen proved to be no exception. The meat curry was as good a choice as the waitress had claimed. It was served on an ample bed of boiled grain and was accompanied by a dish of mixed winter vegetables. The seasoning was only mildly hot but was richly flavored.

"Wine?" their attendant asked, seeing them well started on their meal.

"Just jakek, thanks," Karmikel replied. "We have to go back to work."

"So do those chaps," she retorted, pointing to the trio at the next table to theirs, each of whom had a partly filled goblet before him.

"Not on my starship's drive tubes, though."

She flashed him a bright smile. "No, certainly not on anything like that. I wouldn't want to drink in your case, either." She smiled again. "Why don't I bring you a full pot of jakek instead and a couple of tarts as well for your dessert? They're really very good."

"An excellent suggestion. Thank you."

She soon brought the promised beverage and the tarts and then withdrew to allow them to enjoy the remainder of their meal in peace.

The Noreenan refilled his cup. "This is good," he declared. "We lucked out in this place."

"Aye," Sogan responded absently.

"Gathering stardust, Admiral?"

Varn brought his attention back to his surroundings. "Somewhat," he confessed. "I was thinking about our destination tomorrow."

"The *Terra's Charm*?—I wonder what it'll be like aboard her? I've never been on a really big starship."

"There will be a greater measure of comfort than on a small one, assuming a general similarity with our equivalents, and more resources provided for the passing of off-duty time. The sense of crowding will be worse."

Jake nodded. "Naturally." In the confined realm of an interstellar vessel during a voyage, the members of a crew could not but be very aware of one another under even the best circumstances. The more people, the greater that effect, however big or well-designed the ship in question.

"There will be a great deal of specialization in the duty assignments, with the individuals performing them more or less limited to their own specific spheres of responsibility."

"That's true the Federation over. It's one very unappealing aspect of big-ship service, to my way of thinking. I like to do my own flying, all of it."

Sogan smiled. "That would hardly be possible on a five thousand-class battleship, Captain. Besides, we shall not have anything much to do with most of it. Commandos ride along as cargo, remember?"

"Three of us, maybe. You'll be busy enough."

"Only if I choose to accept command."

"As if you won't," he said sarcastically.

"My option to refuse is real, and at this point, I prefer to keep it open. If I believe I could have a significant problem with the technology, I shall not put five thousand lives plus our own in jeopardy."

"You want it, though? You have to want it." Space was Varn Tarl Sogan's element. After more than two years with the unit, he was now a superb Commando, but he still could not quite match either Islaen Connor or Karmikel in their on-world work and keenly felt his failure to do so. On the bridge of a starship, he was their unquestioned master, even on a tiny fighter like the *Fairest Maid*. On a battleship, his superiority should be even more evident. He had literally been bred to the command of vessels like the *Charm*.

"Aye, of course, I do." His every nerve was alight with his eagerness, but battling it was a gnawing fear. Five years was a long time. In his case, it had been a small eternity. He had lost so much. If the skill that had once been his was gone . . .

"My credits are still all on your accepting, my friend."

Sogan did not reply. He drew a sharp, hissing breath.

Karmikel followed the direction of his gaze. "Spirit of Space!" he whispered. He glanced at his companion. "I'm sorry, Varn."

A large party had just crowded into the restaurant, spacers, an even dozen of them, all tall and powerfully muscled, although not disproportionally so. Their complexions were olive, several shades darker than the former admiral's, their hair and eyes also dark. Despite that, they would not be taken for Arcturians even apart from their size, which was considerably greater than the average for the Empire's slender race. Their features were coarse, heavy in the jowls and lips, and generally square in shape. All of them wore the black-and-red colors of Emir. Only a couple were armed with standard blasters. The rest carried their kind's trademark weapon coiled at their hips.

Sogan shrugged, although he forced his eyes away from the newcomers only with visible effort. "This is a free-access port. Let us confine ourselves to our own concerns. They should attend to theirs."

The newcomers were a rough lot in themselves and were making an early start on what they intended to be a full night of celebration once the pleasure district woke up. Right now, they were boisterous and loud and open in their contempt for the planet-bound people around them.

As soon as they were settled, one of them slammed his big hand on the table before him.

The rest of the group had arranged themselves around it and around several of the other tables near the door and also noisily demanded service.

The waitress hung back, her eyes wide with alarm, until the manager, who was also the restaurant's owner, pointed to the kitchen door. She gratefully seized upon the offered retreat.

The Horusi went over to his customers to take their orders himself, but the girl's hesitation and withdrawal had annoyed them.

"Send the wench back," the apparent leader of the band ordered in a surely tone. He was their crew chief to judge by his arm band and was minded to treat the on-worlder as he would a disfavored rankless hand aboard his ship.

"She's just gone off rotation, sir."

"Pay her overtime. She's prettier than you."

"True, but she is also under age, working on a scholar's permit. The minor protection laws forbid back-to-back shifts. Besides, an inexperienced waitress like that couldn't serve so large a group as this as efficiently as you deserve."

The two Commandos relaxed as the Emirites settled down. There could have been trouble. The spacers had been drinking some, enough to fuel already rowdy temperaments while not perceptibly reducing any of their abilities.

"A good man," Varn commented in a low voice. "He managed that well."

"Aye. The girl overreacted, but I suppose she never encountered anything like our friends over there back home on one of Helga's farms."

"They are no friends of mine!"

"Easy on the drive, Varn," he warned. "We'll finish our jakek and beat a retreat ourselves."

"Bad move. They would notice us. If they are still feeling touchy, they could assume we are leaving because of them and view our departure as a slight. This place would probably wind up a surplanetary war zone, whatever the outcome."

"Aren't you ever wrong, Admiral?"

"Too often. —Space! A run-in with a few pirates will seem like planned entertainment on a rest cruise after these last several days."

Jake smiled, but he watched his comrade somberly. Sogan was forcing that display of normalcy, using it as a mask. Behind it, the War Prince was as tightly drawn as if a blaster set to slay was turned directly on him.

The workers at the next table were openly nervous. They hastily downed the last of their meal and, not waiting for the bill, put a measure of Horusi specie on the table. They came to their feet and started for the door.

They had to pass between the Emirites' several tables to reach it, and their step automatically quickened as they approached that perceived gauntlet.

The spacers watched them contemptuously. Several smiled unpleasantly. "You planet huggers are in a bit of a hurry to go, aren't you?" the nearest to the trio observed.

"Let them be. They must return to their jobs." Sogan's voice was cool, almost indifferent.

"They're going on sick leave, not back to work!"

The Emirite had uncoiled his whip as he spoke. Suddenly, his arm snapped back.

He gave a yelp of fright as a pencil-thin beam of furious energy sliced through the lash.

Every eye riveted on the War Prince. Jake's astonishment was no less than that of the other witnesses. It was simply not possible to draw, set, and fire a blaster in that span of time, much less to strike true with it on so slender and fast-flying a target. It should not have been possible.

"Let these men pass," Sogan commanded.

There was no trouble this time, and the on-worlders were quick to make their escape.

The Arcturian did not lower his weapon even after they were gone. "Your comrade is apparently the worse for drink. Take him back to your ship and keep him there until he is fit to associate with human beings. By rights, I should hold you here until the Patrol arrives, but I shall take that much pity on you and permit you all to go now."

None of the spacers moved. They would not risk drawing a bolt down on themselves, but they were no cowards. They were not minded to give up all ground just yet.

"If we don't, are you simply going to burn the lot of us down?" the man he had disarmed demanded sarcastically.

"With the Stellar Patrol on the way?—I suppose that Horusison scurried off to summon them."

"If necessary."

Once again, a deathly silence gripped the room. Karmikel kept his own expression impassive. Varn Tarl Sogan was one of the least bloodthirsty individuals he had ever encountered, but there was that about the War Prince when he spoke in that tone of voice, with that imperious look and manner, that made people unfamiliar with him ready to believe him capable of nearly any fell, violent deed. It was a trait that had worked well in the unit's cause before now.

Once again, the off-worlders rallied. It was obvious to them that their opponent preferred talk and the law to violence, whatever his very real deadliness. He would have dropped the whipman rather than cut the lash otherwise.

"You're a brave enough holding a blaster," the crew chief said more reasonably. "Why not settle this like men, with whips, you against any one of us you choose? As you said, we've had some drink. That should balance out our greater experience with the weapon."

Varn's answering smile was cold. All of them knew full well that the supposed balancing the man mentioned would not make enough of a difference to even be perceptible in such a contest. "I do not engage in adolescent duels. If that fact generates an illogical feeling of superiority in you, I do not grudge you the joy of it."

"You're one arrogant bastard."

Sogan smiled again, this time naturally, and a flicker of laughter momentarily brightened the chilling eyes. "So I have been informed." His voice dropped so that only his comrade could hear him. "It does not sound quiet so offensive when you call me that."

Karmikel had drawn his own blaster. The off-worlders were too widely spread for his comrade to cover them adequately without a backup. There was no sense in offering them any temptations. "All right, you sons," he commanded. "A few of you at a time. Out the door and keep going unless you want to mess with the Patrol, and I really wouldn't recommend that." He, too, had seen the proprietor slip into the back and knew the authorities had already been summoned. "Cause real trouble, and you'll be checking out your quarters in Emir's particular hell."

The spacers obeyed. The two Commandos carefully directed their withdrawal so that there would be no bunching at the door, no confusion that might encourage some shooting star to try to turn the situation to his party's favor.

At last, *Dorian's Kitchen* and the street outside were clear. Jake breathed a sigh of relief. "That could have been quite nasty."

"Aye, and over nothing." The Arcturian sounded a little dazed. "How can such people remain in the starlanes? How did they survive long enough to reach the stars?"

"They cut loose when in port. Other spacers do that, too, though usually in a more harmless fashion. That's why we have pleasure districts. Emirites are well disciplined on their own planet and aboard their ships."

"We witnessed something of that discipline," Sogan said stiffly.

"I imagine second offenses are pretty rare," Karmikel remarked, then quickly switched back to their more recent encounter. "You handled that well."

"I wondered for a while there."

The other man eyed him speculatively. "How did you learn to draw a blaster like that? I didn't believe it was possible to move that fast outside of space-awful adventure tales. I still don't believe it's possible, and I saw you do it."

Varn's eyes brightened. "I practiced, my friend. I practiced a great deal. It was a useful skill to develop during my first few years in the Federation. Once a number of people saw me in action, I was faced with significantly fewer challenges."

"That, I can well believe," he said dryly.

"All looks quiet now. Let us go before the Patrol shows up. We can call in our report from the *Maid*."

"They're somewhat too late as usual," Jake remarked.

"I did not say that."

"No. —Maybe we should wait around for them. At this rate of going, they should be offering us commissions and salaries."

"Spirit of Space forefend! I do not mind doing their job occasionally. It is the four hours, minimum, of legalities which inevitably follow that are setting me running."

"I'll gladly join you in that flight, comrade." He shook his head. "We military types do have some advantages over our less fortunate fellow citizens, don't we? Just a quick, or not-so-quick, report to our own superior officers and leave the details in their capable hands."

Chapter Sixteen

The Commandos left *Dorian's Kitchen* after receiving the owner's thanks. They started down the block at an unhurried walk.

Karmikel stopped abruptly at the window of a shop a few doors away from the place where their flier was parked and peered intently at the goods displayed there.

"What now?" Sogan asked wearily.

"Oh, nothing. That hair scarf over there's the exact shade of blue that Bethe likes so much—"

"Get it for her. She merits an agreeable surprise now and then in place of the kind we two usually inflict on her."

"It'll only take a few minutes," Jake promised.

"Go ahead. I shall wait by the flier."

The former admiral continued walking. Now that he was alone, without the need to maintain a strict guard over himself, he allowed his thoughts to return to their most recent incident during this star-crossed planeting. He wanted to analyze and try to make some sense of it.

Varn shook his head almost imperceptibly. He would never be able to comprehend illogical, useless violence, whether the perpetrators were his own kind or offspring of the Federation. Blood could have been shed back there, and for no purpose at all. For no reason. Those men had been drinking, but they had not been drunk. Even had they been, they had received no insult, no provocation whatsoever, to so enflame their malice.

Malice, it had been, too, a dark, ugly cruelty . . .

Varn Tarl Sogan's mind returned abruptly and completely to his present situation. There was a mouth-drying fear on him, the anticipation of sure danger ahead. It was a familiar feeling, a warning such has he had experienced countless times on Thorne of Brandine when he had ventured forth at the head of his Arcturian invasion force to confront the merchant planet's deadly, Commando-led Resistance.

This time, the alarm had sounded too late. He had been walking unaware like some novice recruit and so had missed its early signals. Now, even as he tensed to meet his peril, he found himself confronted by three men, who had stepped out from the shadows of a narrow side street to intercept him. The blasters in the hands of two of them were trained directly on him.

"This way, space hound," the man on his left commanded. "No strange moves and no fast moves, or you're a cinder."

The War Prince obeyed. The Emirites would fire if he did not. They would fire anyway, eventually, he decided. He did not need Islaen's or Bandit's gifts to recognize that they meant to vent the full of their spleen on him.

The blame for his present difficulty lay entirely with himself, he thought bitterly. With a dozen potential foes free and conceivably still very near, he should have been traveling as if on a mission deep in enemy territory. Instead, he had shown less caution than he evinced at times on the grounds of his Thornen palace. Karmikel would not have behaved so stupidly . . .

How had the bastards known where the flier was parked, or the direction in which the Commandos would walk, for that matter?

Obviously, they had not known, save that their quarry had to go either up this street or down it. A mirror image of this ambush was probably set on the opposite side and two others like them above *Dorian's Kitchen.*

"Stand against that wall, space hound," the Emirite ordered once they had moved in several feet, out of sight of the main street. "Keep your hands raised and away from your blaster."

"Fetch it?" the centermost of his captors inquired.

"Leave it be. He might grab you. We'll just burn him through if he makes any sort of suspicious move. —You heard me, you son," he snarled. "Hands on top of your head! Clasp them."

Sogan obeyed. He kept his face an emotionless mask. Arrogant, brutal, stupid fools! They had given him his chance, or, at the very least, a hope of vengeance. As his hands joined in compliance with the other's command, the fingers of the right seemed to casually touch the left wrist. They slipped under the sleeve. In the next moment, their mission was accomplished.

The communicator was open. Jake Karmikel would hear every word now. Perhaps, he would be able to come in time . . .

The Emirite nodded in exaggerated satisfaction. "Good, spacer. I am glad to see you can follow orders as well as dish them out."

The former admiral made him no answer. He had not spoken at all since his capture. His silence would soon begin to anger them, but he expected no kindness from these three in any event. He would not demean himself by bandying useless words with vermin. Over that part, at least, of his fate, he still retained control.

The other read or sensed his prisoner's contempt, for he reddened. He spat. "You'll talk to us soon enough, or maybe I should say that you'll be making noise. The damage you might've avoided in a real, open fight if you'd been skilled or lucky, you'll take for a fact now, and a galaxy more with it. We sons of Emir despise cowards."

"Tie him?" the third Emirite ordered, pointing to a couple of conveniently placed metal spikes jutting out from the wall against which Sogan was standing.

"No. He has to be free to get on his knees, doesn't he? He'll be doing that long before we're finished with him."

"Strip him?" The speaker uncoiled the implement he had just detached from its place at his side.

"Your whip will take care of that, comrade."

He turned to the War Prince. His smile could have marred the face of the commandant of some vicious hell. "We'll start with the front, high and low. Don't worry, though, space hound. We'll attend to the back, too. You'll still match, fore and aft."

Varn Tarl Sogan braced himself. He would have to endure the first cut, and his body would be expected to react to it. So he would respond, but not in the anticipated uncontrolled jerk of agony. He would get to the weapon the sons had rightly feared to try to take from him, and he would drop at least two of his tormentors with it, those holding the blasters meant to cow him into the docile acceptance of torture. The third, the whipman, he would either have to fell with a third bolt or, perhaps, with his hands. The cold rage burning inside him willed that it be by the latter means.

The Emirite's arm went back. For all his readiness, Varn felt his stomach twist with his shame and with pure terror. To endure this again . . .

In that moment, Jake Karmikel appeared, almost literally appeared, it seemed to his comrade's relieved eyes. His control held, and he gave no warning to his enemies of the blaster-armed man racing up behind them like some fury incarnate.

The Emirite's arm jerked forward, driving the wire lash cracking through the air.

Even as it fell, Jake cast himself between the Arcturian and his foes. The Noreenan, too, had set himself. He could not stifle entirely the scream the unexpectedly sharp stroke wrung from him, but the blow did not delay the discharge of his blaster or the accuracy of his aim. His bolt seared through the whipman's chest.

Sogan heard his friend's cry as the lash bit home but did not glance at him. He seized upon the chaos of the moment, drew and fired his own blaster, throwing himself aside as he did so to avoid the Emirites' bolts. Twice, his weapon discharged in so rapid succession that the two bolts seemed to spring like forked lightning from the single pull of the trigger. His targets screamed, crumpled, and lay still on the dark, blood-stained pavement.

The War Prince went from one to the other of the felled Emirites.

"Breathing?" Jake asked him.

"Aye. They will make it, though yours will require regrowth, I think."

"Bastard! I wish I could've done a bit more to make the rest of his life a misery, or, better still, a short misery."

Sogan shrugged. "Trust the military courts. They will not view this attempt very kindly."

The Arcturian took the trio's whips, severed the lashes at the hand grips, and used the supple wires to bind the prisoners, fastening them somewhat more tightly than was strictly necessary. If they roused, he wanted them to feel the additional pain . . .

In truth, all three were deeply unconscious, and binding was probably needless, but he was not about to take further chances. His carelessness had caused them enough trouble already, for Jake more than himself.

Only when the prisoners were secure did he leave them and rejoin his comrade.

"How are you doing?" There was no attempt to mask the concern in his voice or in his expression. A bloody stripe marked the whip's course from the Noreenan's shoulder, across and down the chest, to the opposite hip.

Karmikel looked up. "The jacket and tunic're both sliced clean through as neatly as if a knife had done the damage. I guess that means the Navy owes me replacements. Or maybe you do." Jake made himself give a genuine smile as he said the last, not a grimace of pain. —Space, but the damn thing had hurt! It still did. He had taken one cut, only one, and his clothing had absorbed much of its bite. What had it been for Varn, stroke after countless stroke down on a bare, ever-more-terribly lacerated back?

Sogan swore. "It sounds as if you will live as well," he said in mock disgust. "Come on. I shall drive you to the hospital—"

"For a cut like this? When space turns white, Admiral! Islaen can take care of it later." He grimaced in disgust. "It'll be much later, I fear. I put in a call to the Patrol while you were trussing up our acquaintances. They were still at the restaurant but will scout around for other ambushes before joining us to collect this lot. We can report to the colonel while we're waiting."

"I shall do that and tell her to bring the renewer to us here or to meet us with it at the Patrol station."

"Oh, aye. Our second home these days."

The former admiral examined his comrade's injury and found it to be slight despite its impressive appearance. His clothing had spared him much worse. The fact remained that it was undoubtedly quite painful. He recalled all too sharply how painful . . . "That was a damned stupid thing to do,

Karmikel," he snarled suddenly. "I knew what to expect, and I was braced to receive it."

Jake's blue eyes met his. Their expression was unreadable. "No," he said, "it was not stupid. No one is ever putting a lash on you again. —Now, please shut up, Admiral. From the sounds out in the street beyond, I'd say the Stellar Patrol has arrived."

Chapter Seventeen

"Where in all the galaxy has Karmikel gone?" Varn fumed. "We have only three-quarters of an hour before we have to leave if we are to reach the *Terra's Charm* on time."

"He had an errand to run," Bethe Danlo told him calmly. "Don't worry. He'll be back in good time."

"He's here now," Islaen informed her comrades. The redhead had been successful to judge by his exuberant transmissions.

Jake has something nice? For Bandit?

The colonel shook her head. "You're one spoiled gurry, but, aye, he said he would pick up a bag of honey triangles on his way back especially for you."

She gave an ear-splitting whistle of delight. *Jake's nice!*

"See, Varn," his consort said. "Jake's nice. You can't disagree and spoil the pleasure of the moment for her. We won't be able to buy her treats for some unknown span of time to come, after all."

"Poor, deprived gurry," he said sourly. "She's not likely to find anyone at all aboard a five thousand-class battleship willing to rob the commissary for her delight, is she?"

Bandit gave a chirp of alarm. *Charm's crew not like Bandit?*

"Varn! —Everyone loves you, Bandit. Varn's only jinking you."

"What's this Arcturian blackguard doing to my little girl?" Jake Karmikel demanded as he all but erupted into the *Maid*'s crew's cabin.

Islaen described what had been going on between her consort and the Jadite.

"Imagine teasing a poor little gurry like that!" he declared dramatically, then produced a honey triangle from his pocket with the flourish of a stage magician. "Maybe this will comfort you."

Honey will! she enthused.

"Only one, Jake," Connor cautioned. "She's already had lunch."

Varn had waited somewhat less than patiently and now broke in. "Karmikel, what in space moved you to go gadding about today? You know full well—"

"Power down, Admiral," the redhead said in amusement. "Anyone not knowing you would think you were having a stellar-class case of nerves."

Both women glared at him, but Sogan gave him an acid smile. "You do know me, of course."

"Naturally, Admiral. I realize that you're just being thoroughly disagreeable."

Danlo caught her husband's attention. "Mission accomplished?"

He nodded, then turned back to the War Prince. "Sogan," he said, speaking more seriously now. "This one really is a different charter for all of us. I picked this up as a luck token for you. Just please do us all a favor and don't go parading around with it."

He handed the other man a long, slender package.

Varn opened it. He stared inside.

For a moment, he could say nothing. The Arcturian dagger . . .

Sogan's fingers lifted and caressed the beautiful weapon. "Thank you," he whispered at last, softly, almost to himself.

He resolutely lay it back in its box and closed the lid over it. He looked at Jake. "Get your gear, Karmikel. If it is not in the flier when we are ready to lift, you will find yourself without a few things like spare clothing for the duration."

Jake grinned. "I'll be ready as soon as you are, Admiral."

Barnak Fran Urtine read through the report he was about to file. It was a discouraging one. Chief Admiral Dundee had departed from Horus on a mission which he declared had arisen suddenly. He had apologized for the interruption to their deliberations but had stressed its unavoidability, and he had promised to give them the Federation's response upon his return in a couple or four weeks' time. None of the Arcturian delegation believed that it would be a favorable one.

He looked up to see both his lieutenants hurry into the room. They approached him immediately and froze into salute.

Urtine granted them ease and smiled. "You have news for me, it would seem."

"Aye, my Colonel," Mitree responded. "Sogan's gone."

"Gone?"

"Aye, my Colonel, along with the rest of his unit. Their starships remain in port, but they themselves have vanished."

The Arcturian commander pondered that intelligence. "It would appear that Admiral Dundee is off on a legitimate mission after all and has taken his prize Commandos with him."

"So we must wait?" Harnid Form Lassur asked in disgust.

"We must, since we have no other choice. We can amuse ourselves by keeping watch on Sogan's starships. The Commandos will return to them eventually." If they returned.

His dark eyes were somber. Perhaps that was how it would end, he thought. Perhaps Varn Tarl Sogan would perish on this assignment, relieving them of the responsibility of deciding what, if anything, to do about him. It would also give the fallen admiral a soldier's death, however poor his reasons for courting it or how little he now merited the honor. The opposite had once been true. The man had fought well, heroically, in the Empire's cause for so many years. Urtine found that he did not grudge him that grace.

Mitree interrupted his thoughts. "Sogan was involved in another incident the other day. We heard a couple of civilians discussing it." He went on to describe the Commando-Captain's capture of the raklik user.

"We went to examine the site where it happened ourselves," the other lieutenant reported somewhat uncomfortably. "It is in one of the port's less desirable locations, one that becomes unruly at night, I understand. Actually," he went on delicately, "it is what is called a spacers' pleasure district. That is where—"

"I know what a Federation pleasure district is, Lieutenant," the colonel said dryly. "Sogan went there?"

"Aye, my Colonel. He had been frequenting one of the establishments there, apparently." His expression darkened. "What would bring him to a place like that? No officers are reputed to visit the area."

Captain Lassur shrugged. "The obvious reason."

Barnak Fran Urtine said nothing for a moment. An infinite sadness filled him. It was only to be expected, he supposed. The renegade War Prince could not but retain some embers of what he had been. He had to feel the depth of his shame and know that there could be no escape from it, no way to bury his degradation, save in temporary oblivion. He must at last have grown weak enough to seek that relief now and then, or perhaps frequently, even at the cost of further disgrace.

Urtine sighed. Varn Tarl Sogan had been one of the Empire's greatest war commanders. He wished that fate had not called upon him to witness the ruin of such a man. In his own inner heart, he would have preferred learning that Sogan had done well in their enemies' ultrasystem.

Sogan's weakness, if it were one in truth and not but a single aberration sparked by some particularly sharp thrust of despair, could be the means of putting him into their hands, especially if it was his habit to visit the pleasure district by day when it was relatively deserted. At this stage, Urtine believed that they would probably leave the man to his misery, but should they be ordered or decide to eliminate him, that pleasure district dive would be the ideal place to make their attempt. Logic declared that his Commando associates probably had little to do with the renegade save in the field and certainly would have no part of this sort of conduct, which even in their own ultrasystem was seen as unfit for an officer. If they could find their quarry in such a situation, he would almost certainly be on his own and, in all probability, be weakened by excess as well. He would be alone and very vulnerable . . .

"We will watch that establishment along with the ships," he told the others wearily. "If it is his wallow, he will return to it. This could be our key to taking him if we decide to move against him."

The War Prince checked once more that the space seals were in place and firm before taking the flier out of Horus' atmosphere. Although primarily a surface vehicle, the versatile Commando craft could function in space for short distances, giving the unit access to a target without exposing them to the greater risk of detection a more conventional vessel would have entailed.

No one spoke. Karmikel and Danlo, in their customary places on the rear seat, were occupied with their own thoughts. Neither was happy with the way in which this mission was shaping up, either the little they knew of it or the vastly greater part still in darkness.

The Arcturian, as usual, was at the controls. They had passed into the velvet blackness of true space, and he was straining his eyes for his first glimpse of the *Terra's Charm*. His ship, perhaps, if only for a few, painfully short weeks.

Connor gently stroked the gurry nestled in her lap. Like her Federation-born comrades, she was worried about nearly every aspect of this assignment, and her expression was as bleak as the questions she was considering.

Bandit raised her head to look at Sogan. *Is* Charm *nice? Varn's excited!*

He did not bridle at this broadcast of the emotion on him. His shields were only loosely in place, and his mind was open for Islaen's reading. He did choose to respond in thought rather than in the more common verbal speech. *She is a very big starship. I used to command one something like her before-before I joined the Commandos. I might be allowed to hold her bridge as well for a short while if I can handle her.*

Islaen stirred. *Varn Tarl Sogan, you know very well that you can handle anything that flies, floats, or rolls!*

It has been five years, Islaen. Longer—

You'll do fine.

He would with the *Terra's Charm* herself, the colonel thought as she slipped behind her shields once more. If problems arose, they would not be with the battleship.

Gray Jack Dundee had been right to voice that question of mutants, she thought somberly. Tambora's volcano and even more so their concern over the injured gurry had stripped away the barrier with respect to the *Rounder*'s crew, but with that one exception, Sogan was in no sense immune to the Arcturian revulsion for those races who had significantly altered from the basic human prototype. It was the one trait she truly detested in him, although she knew that he did not permit it to rule in his interactions with them.

Still, the fault remained. It was powerful because it was instinctive and irrational both, and at times he was helpless before it. She had seen an unexpected contact physically sicken him, and on that occasion, he had only barely been able to hold on until they were alone before giving way. What would happen in the close, forced associations inevitable on a battleship?

She would have to trust Varn Tarl Sogan. His sense of basic justice was stronger than he himself realized, and, if nothing else, a War Prince of the Arcturian Empire would not permit a recognized personal flaw to imperil an active mission.

Islaen ran her finger across Bandit's head and down her back. *We'll be needing your help, Little Bandit,* she said in her closed thoughts so that Varn would not hear her. *The Charm's crew may not like having a new captain while their own one is sick. You'll have to help make friends of them for Varn and for all of us, especially Admiral Dundee.*

Bandit help unit! she responded serenely in kind.

The Arcturian straightened in his seat. "There she is," he told his companions. "She is a beautiful ship."

She was that, his consort agreed. The *Terra's Charm* was disk shaped, the usual form of major battlecraft, and she hung before them against the ebony, starlit curtain of space like a silver moon. She was also immense. The little flier was scarcely a speck beside her.

Islaen opened the transceiver for ship-to-ship and requested permission to board, which was instantly granted.

The transport hatch opened, and Varn carefully guided his vehicle into the great hull.

Chapter Eighteen

The yeoman who greeted them as they stepped into the starship proper was a veteran of long service, but he stared like a recruit at the four Commandos. The Navy was not generous even with its decorations. Few people in the vast ultra-system had ever so much as seen the famed star of a heroism citation, first class, yet seven of them sparkled on the uniform of this Commando-Colonel. Her second-in-command carried eight, and the man and woman with them bore six and three respectively. His breath caught. Only one unit in all the Federation could claim that tally.

He recovered himself quickly and gave them salute. "Welcome to the *Terra's Charm*. Admiral Dundee will see you at once in his office."

He led them through a seemingly endless maze of corridors. At last, he stopped and knocked on one of the doors. Dundee responded at once and bade them enter.

As was usual aboard these large vessels, the fleet admiral and the battleship's captain each occupied suites, one room of which was a personal cabin, the second an office. This one was as big and well-appointed as that in which Gray Jack had spoken with the unit's commanders on Horus.

The newcomers saluted. He returned it and ordered them at ease. "Welcome aboard the *Terra's Charm,* Colonel, Captain, and you as well, Captain Karmikel and Sergeant Danlo."

His features broadened in a smile. "I see you remembered the gurry this time."

"Aye, sir. Bandit is part of the unit. We wouldn't start a mission without her."

Helping unit easy, Islaen! Jack likes Bandit!

The Jadite fluttered to the pile of papers cluttering the center of the ample desk. She looked up at the Terran and whistled expectantly.

"What does she want?" he asked.

"Attention, sir. That's what she usually wants. A rub of your finger on her head or back will satisfy her."

Dundee did both and was rewarded by a storm of ecstatic purring.

For the moment, the only thing the four Commandos were concealing was their laughter as they watched their strange comrade work her customary magic on the Chief Admiral.

Dundee regretfully turned his mind back to the business at hand. "Our first task will be a tour of the *Charm*. Captain Sogan can decide then whether he will assume command of her or not. Leave your packs here. I'll have you taken to your quarters when we get back."

It was a long time before the Chief Admiral and the Commandos returned to his office.

"Well, Captain Sogan?"

"I am very glad I did not have to face this ship in space, Admiral Dundee."

"That makes us a pair," he responded dryly. Gray Jack's eyes fixed on him. "Do you believe you can fly and fight her?"

"I do."

"You'll assume command?"

"Aye." He hesitated. "Will your crew accept that? They know me only as a Commando."

"They'd accept your gurry if I ordered it."

"I shall take her whenever you wish."

"I'll announce your appointment immediately. —I'll be here if you need me, but the *Terra's Charm* is yours. Start working her as soon as you're settled in."

Varn Tarl Sogan nodded. "I intended that." Every starship had her strengths and weaknesses, her quirks. The time to learn them was not at the height of a battle.

"You'll occupy Captain Broderick's quarters, Captain Sogan. That will provide your unit with working space as well as underline the reality of your authority. Colonel Connor, you and your other comrades will have the three cabins beside it. My officers will have to endure the change for one mission."

That'll make us popular, Islaen muttered.

We do not have to be popular, Colonel Connor. As Dundee says, we shall be inconveniencing the crew for this one mission only.

Dundee summoned a yeoman and instructed her to escort the Commandos to their quarters for the voyage.

His hand touched Connor's arm as she was about to quit the office with the others. "A moment, Colonel."

Go with Varn, Bandit. I'll come on soon.

Yes, Islaen!

The woman waited with the Chief Admiral, remaining quiet until they were alone. "Aye, Admiral Dundee?"

"Your unit's been busy again, Colonel."

"Sir?"

"The Emirites, Colonel," he said with exaggerated patience. His face darkened. "Sons of Schythian apes! They're trouble everywhere they go off their own ever-suffering planet, in the Navy and in every spaceport unfortunate enough to be visited by them. I was more delighted than you can imagine to learn that a few of the whip-swinging bastards got fried by your lads."

"Captains Sogan and Karmikel share the credit on that one, sir."

"Credit, it is," he affirmed. "I am also pleased that they did spare the sons. If the three of them, and the ones the Patrol rounded up at the other ambush sites, receive stiff enough sentences, maybe their planetmates'll get the idea that they're not going to be permitted to ride roughshod over the locals whenever they venture abroad."

"Admiral Sithe is pressing for maximum sentences, sir."

"He'll get them. Back-alleying military personnel is not popular with Navy tribunals. Planning to flog officers to death or half to death will be even less well received."

Connor nodded. Whips were detested throughout most of the Federation. She had seen the reaction of the Patrol officers. Ram Sithe's had been less visible, but his fury had seared into her like the bolt from a blaster. "I know, Admiral."

She felt the man's eyes on her, piercing her, and raised her own to meet them. "Sir?"

"Captain Sogan has experienced no…difficulty?"

"No, sir."

"I'll be blunt, Colonel Connor. He can't like whips."

"Of course, he doesn't. Neither do the rest of us, as you yourself have pointed out."

"I am not turning my battleship over to the rest of you, Colonel," he said sharply.

"Varn Tarl Sogan is a Commando officer, and he is a War Prince of the Arcturian Empire."

"And so his control is absolute?"

"No, sir. That would make him a god, not a man, but he can be depended upon to keep himself well in hand. There is no danger of his jeopardizing this or any other mission because of an unfortunate on-world incident, however unpleasant he found it or whatever memories it aroused."

"That confirms my own opinion. I just had to hear you say it. —Captain Sogan is one of the finest officers in our military. He was the finest in his own as well."

"Aye, sir."

"I freely confess that I wouldn't trust anyone else with this assignment under the same circumstances. I simply couldn't be sure enough of him, and I don't exclude myself from that statement."

The Noreenan's head lifted. "You can count upon Varn. We all can."

"Aye, Colonel. Power down. I wasn't doubting or belittling him." He shook his head. "I wouldn't want to be around if his hold ever did slip, though," he told her, then he smiled. "Thank you, Colonel Connor. I did need to check with you."

"Of course, sir."

"I'll have you taken to your quarters now. I'm sure you'll want to settle in and check with your command."

"Thank you, Admiral. I do."

Islaen was quiet as she followed her escort to the cabin she would occupy for the duration of her stay aboard the *Terra's Charm*. She mulled over her conversation with the Chief Admiral. Dundee liked the War Prince, but he would not want to be near should Varn's seemingly titanone control shatter for a fact. That was the difference between him and her, she thought, between him and the rest of her unit. They would want to be there, to lend a hand or simply to hold one if there was nothing more that could be done.

Nothing short of palatial, Islaen said admiringly as she looked about her consort's cabin. It was, too, compared with their minute quarters aboard the *Fairest Maid*. There was plenty of floor space here even with a full-sized dresser and a real armchair fixed beneath the primary wall light. All the furnishings were fastened to the floor including the moveable pieces when not in use. Nothing could be left loose on a starship to become a potential missile during turbulence or combat.

What about yours?

Quite nice as well. It's not as big, and there's only the one room, of course. Very adequate facilities. I've stowed everything away already. Varn apparently had not realized the subject of her discussion with Dundee, and she decided not to go into it. There was no need to do so. He seemed to be happy, and she did not want to throw even so small a shadow on his mood. Cares would be coming to them all quite soon enough.

Fast work. —You did bring the renewer, I presume?

Foolish question, Admiral. The Terra's Charm *may possess a fully equipped and excellent Sick Bay and may even boast of regrowth equipment, as her Medical Staff was quick to point out to us, but Commandos don't survive by neglecting their own gear.* Their renewer had saved their lives and permitted them to continue as an effective unit on more than one mission already and could help them again on this one despite the availability of more complex medical care. Islaen Connor had not been about to leave it behind.

They rejoined their comrades, who were waiting for them in the outer, office room.

"Quite a setup," Jake remarked. "Do your chaps enjoy something similar, Admiral?"

"Just about. There are some design differences, but the basics are more or less the same."

Bethe's fingers ran around the high neck of her tunic. "It's dress uniforms for the duration, I suppose, Colonel?"

"I'm afraid so," her commander informed her. "We're dealing with the Regular Navy now."

"I thought that would be what you'd say," the spacer said glumly. "What next?"

"Our admiral takes over his battleship, and we begin reviewing this material. There's a proper mountain of it. We'll have a war council at 06:00 tomorrow. That'll give us good time to fill Varn in on anything he doesn't get a chance to read himself, maybe make a few decisions if we're lucky, and still get him on the bridge at the appointed hour."

She paused. Running a five thousand-class battleship preparing for combat was no small task. Even Varn Tarl Sogan was going to have his hands full with it. *Maybe you should concentrate on the* Charm *and leave the on-world work to us on this one,* she suggested.

No.

Expect a lot of late nights and early mornings, then, Admiral.

He smiled. *I do, Colonel Connor.*

Sogan went to the door. His hand seemed to freeze for a moment as he reached out to open it.

Islaen's mind brushed his. *You'll do fine,* she told him, repeating her earlier assurance. *You're the best there is, Varn Tarl Sogan.*

It was 23:05 when the Arcturian returned to his cabin.

Islaen was waiting for him in the office. She handed him the jakek she had been keeping hot on her plutonium disk. *I thought you might want this.*

He took a long drink. *I needed it. You are a thoughtful commanding officer, Colonel.*

I do my humble best. She sat on the edge of the conference table. *How did it go?*

I think the crew was somewhat surprised by the thoroughness of my inspection, and I believe no one is too pleased with the schedule I have announced for tomorrow. He shrugged. *I want to see how she flies, what she can do. I want to see what the crew can do as well.*

The War Prince opened his mind to her. His tiredness was not of a nature that he minded her observing, and he wanted to share the rest with her.

Spirit of Space, but he was happy, she thought. This was where he belonged . . .

He brushed her cheek with his fingers. *Thank you for the confidence earlier. Mine was somewhat shaky.*

She smiled. *You just needed to get your space legs again. You won't have any problems now.*

Not with our side. The pirates may try to supply a few.

You'll manage those, too.

She was not quick enough to completely mask the darkness that touched her at the mention of their opponents. Sogan glanced from her to the pile of data littering the table. *A bad one?*

She rose to her feet. *You'll hear plenty about it in the morning. Knock out now. You've had a day, and there's too much of this for you to assimilate in a quick scan.*

I shall have a look at it. He smiled. *I am soaring too high at the moment to sleep right away in any event.*

Chapter Nineteen

Varn Tarl Sogan was waiting for them when his comrades came to the office the following morning.

Islaen did not have to ask if he was prepared. He would not look so grim if he were not. He also looked tired. *Did you get any sleep?*

Enough. —I wish your Federation would not try to mingle political concerns with combat strategy.

It's 'our' Federation, she corrected for what seemed like the thousandth time since their initial meeting. Someday, Varn Tarl Sogan would realize he was part of this ultrasystem in fact. Until then, she would have to hold her temper and not give in to the urge to choke him.

The War Prince felt her annoyance. He shrugged and at the same time disarmed the gesture with a smile.

Karmikel watched the pair with some aggravation. "I believe I've mentioned before that having a mind conversation while in other company can be plaguey rude. This is supposed to be a war council."

The colonel apologized. "Varn was just saying that he wished the Federation wouldn't mix politics and war."

"It's unanimous, then. The rest of us said the same thing yesterday."

"Sit, all of you. Let's see if we can't come up with a plan for dealing with this little mess Dundee has dropped on our heads."

Connor waited until the others were settled before going on. "To recap, the Pirate Stars, or one or more of their member systems, have moved a ship of significant size into Federation space and have set up housekeeping on Kyrie of Olga to maintain her long-term.

"Olga has only the one planet and a smattering of small satellites and space rubble. Kyrie is little more than a moon herself, but she's extremely dense for her size, giving her an acceptable gravity and atmosphere. She has a small amount of surface water and considerably more underground. There are a few plant species, two of which could serve as food crops, but little fauna apart from some bugs that feed on the plants and a couple of predators to keep them in line. There is an abundance of the common heavy metals and huge stocks of the rarer ones.

"At present, the planet has received Settlement Board approval as a mining colony, and no fewer than three groups of eager would-be colonists are ready to come to blows for the right to claim her.

"Our job is to remove the base without doing drastic damage to Kyrie. No planetbusters neatly fired from near-space. In this case, the name would be too apt. If she didn't shatter outright, she'd be a seismic nightmare.

"Neither can we engage in a long-term pitched battle. The Federation wants to use this situation to make a statement. We want the Pirate Stars to realize gut level that we will not tolerate the invasion of our territory, most particularly not for use by pirates to work ill on other systems or on our own. The ship and the base are to be eliminated simply and quickly, as one would slap a stinging insect, or so reads our directive.

"Varn and the *Charm* will handle the former chore, one ship to sweep away one ship."

"No need to mention that ours happens to be a full battleship, of course," Jake said dryly.

"The base is the chore of the unit as a whole," his commander went on without seeming to hear him. "You've seen the reports. It'd be a stellar job for the four of us to take that place even without the demand that it be done in one fast, seemingly effortless move."

"How did we collect the data?" Sogan asked. "I did not have time to go over the peripheral information last night."

"Navy Intelligence. One of their people brought it in. — The Commandos should toss a net over that particular agent. She'd be a prize."

Islaen returned to the problem immediately before them. "We'll almost certainly have to take out the ship first since the *Charm* doesn't lend herself to concealment the way a little two-man fighter does. That means the base will be on full alert by the time we're ready to make any move against it."

"It would never do to make a Commando's life simple," Jake remarked.

"May I continue, Captain Karmikel? This is Varn's first morning as the *Charm*'s captain. It would be nice if he got to the bridge on time."

"Of course. Please proceed, Colonel," the redhead told her graciously.

"This is no small operation that we're facing. The power of at least one star system is behind it, and we can assume there will be proper antimissile and antienergy screens. There's likely to be surface-to-space artillery as well. We don't know what sort or how its placed. It's a domed installation, completely enclosed, and our agent wasn't able to get inside for a look-see.

"We know they'll fight and fight hard. The Federation executes captured pirates, home grown or imported. These chaps won't surrender."

"Given the constraints on us, it seems more the work of a Regular assault force than a Commando team," Danlo said in disgust. "They'd do everything we can."

"No," Connor disagreed. "They'd take too long, and they couldn't do it without a pitched battle. We can blast our way in there fast, hopefully without having previously given our presence on-world away, and we can blow the place up. Besides living facilities and warehousing for supplies and loot, there are stocks of fuel, either solid or liquid, all of them almost certainly stowed above ground. That base was built quickly, and Kyrie's solid rock. There wasn't time for the sons to have drilled out proper tanks. There will also be arms stockpiled on-world for use during raids. Ignite either of those, and we'll have the whole place."

The others listened in silence. It was the obvious solution but not a welcome one. It was unlikely that any of the attackers could escape the inferno they would create in the enclosed space of the domed installation.

Sogan thought for several seconds. "I have a couple of projectiles," he said slowly. "There are only the two, worse luck, but if managed well, they should do the job for us without our having to go inside at all." The old-time weapons were hopelessly antiquated for space war, but they served very good purpose on-world, and it annoyed him that a battlecraft the size of the *Terra's Charm* was not adequately equipped with them.

"They'll do half of it, at any rate," his colonel agreed.

"Half? One will suffice to blast a hole in the wall. The other will follow fast after it to blow the fuel."

"We don't know where it's stored in there," she reminded him. "It won't help us just to pass through thin air and smash through the opposite wall again."

He flushed. "Sorry. I did not think."

The Arcturian left the table and stood in the doorway to the sleeping room, his back to his comrades.

Islaen waited for a few moments before turning toward him. He was not sulking. The War Prince would not pull that at a council like this, and besides, she would be picking it up. "Living in the past or the future, Admiral?" she asked.

He roused himself out of obviously deep thought and faced them again. "The past. Military history." He returned to the table. "I may have an idea, but I want to work it for a while. I am not sure enough of it yet to present it."

"Have at it, friend. In the meantime, you've given us our key in."

"Perhaps," Sogan warned. "I have no idea of the actual condition of those projectiles or if they will prove suitable."

"Finding out's my job," Bethe Danlo told them decisively. She had spent her Wartime Navy enlistment as part of Demolitions and had first encountered the Commando team in that capacity on Hades of Persephone. Any work involving explosives or explosive devices naturally fell primarily to her.

"Come with me, then. I shall turn them over to you for your study before I start making life miserable for the *Charm*'s crew."

He would, too, Karmikel thought with a touch of sympathy. Admiral Varn Tarl Sogan had been a strict taskmaster, demanding the utmost from both his machines and his men.

The redhead chuckled. "I'd love to be around to watch you at it, provided you left me alone, of course."

Varn paused for a moment. "That might be arranged," he said at the end of that time. "Remember how we spied on the *Free Comet*'s bridge?"

"You wouldn't!" Bethe exclaimed.

His dark eyes sparkled. "Why not? The *Charm* is my ship, and Bandit could use a little more practice in the ancient art of espionage."

Bandit scout bridge! the gurry responded enthusiastically. She had kept silent, as she usually did, during her unit's battle discussions, but she was pleased to be offered an opportunity to be of assistance.

"Aye, Small One. No one would suspect a friendly little gurry of passing on information." He stroked her feathers with the tip of his fingers and smiled softly.

His attention returned to his human comrades. "It will not be as effective a contact as we have had before. I shall not be able to physically link with her or even to share thought with her or with Islaen at all times, but she will be able to stay in contact with our colonel and describe what is happening. Islaen can translate her transmissions for Jake and Bethe."

"It sounds good to me," Connor told him. "I'd rather have some information coming in than none."

"Let us go, Sergeant. You will probably enjoy this task whether the things will serve our purpose or not."

She laughed. "There's little doubt of that, Admiral."

Sogan and Danlo took their leave of their comrades, both of them already deep in a technical discussion of projectile innards and potential.

Jake Karmikel laughed softly as the door closed behind the pair. "His projectiles. His ship. Making himself right at home, isn't he?"

"He'd better if he's going to fight this monster," the Commando-Colonel told him dryly. "Now, you big space tramp, it behooves the two of us to make ourselves even more at home with this mass of information. We still have to figure out what we're going to do once we blow a hole in that dome."

Varn left Bethe with the projectiles, already so deeply absorbed that she scarcely noticed his departure.

He did not go directly to the bridge but, rather, made his way to that part of the ship housing the various maintenance departments. The day shift would be on duty by then, and he should be able to locate the unit he wanted without too much delay.

He spotted the noncom he sought, the Weapons Maintenance Sergeant. The man, a Lemuran, had a familiar look, and the War Prince, now that he made the effort to study him, vaguely recognized him as the one who had accompanied Max the day of the transport accident.

"Sergeant Ospry, is it?"

"Aye, sir." Pete came to full attention. He had remembered Sogan much more quickly than the Arcturian had placed him and had started in near shock when Dundee had introduced the Commando as temporary master of the *Terra's Charm*.

"I'm looking for the unit that has charge of the *Charm*'s projectiles."

"That's mine, sir."

"Good. I need to meet with all of you at once."

"That's easily arranged, Captain Sogan. The others are in that cabin up ahead grabbing a mug of jakek and laying out the day's duties. I'll bring them to your—"

"I have no time to waste. I shall speak with all of you here."

"Very good, sir."

The maintenance crew snapped to attention at the appearance of their new commander.

"At ease," he told them. "I need information about the two projectiles, what they can do and what you can do with them."

The Regulars eyed him warily. Their own captain would have summoned them to the bridge or to her office if she had need to confer with them. She assuredly would not have come to them like this.

They shrugged off the breach of custom. This Sogan was a Commando, after all. He could be expected to display some unconventional behavior, whatever the almost grim formality with which he had thus far conducted himself.

They were prepared to give him a chance, at least. Pete Ospry had related the tale of how this man had fought to save his own mechanic's child and of his response when the father had attempted to thank him. He could not be entirely a machine. Even if he were, his courage and proven humanity deserved some return, not to mention the fact that it was his right to meet with his crew anywhere he chose aboard the *Terra's Charm*.

Varn Tarl Sogan remained standing by the door of the minute assembly cabin. Of all the six hands before him, only the woman to his right was on prototype. The others, including two reptilian Sarvans, were very apparent mutants. In these close, crowded quarters, his awareness of them as such was overpowering.

The Arcturian recognized the stupidity of it all, but at this stage, it was beyond the power of reason to quell the sense of revulsion inside him. He felt soiled merely by being in the same room with so obvious mutants, breathing the same air that had filled their altered lungs. Sogan shuddered inwardly. Many officers he had known in his former life would simply have drawn their blasters and burned every one of these people down, the woman along with the others for her shame in associating with them. He had spent more than a few sleepless nights since his arrival in this ultrasystem wondering if he would once have been one of their number and hoping fervently that he would not.

Be that as it might, for the moment, irrational and shameful as he knew them to be, he could neither banish his feelings nor flee the room to escape them. He could only try to deal with the situation as best he might, that and give no outward sign of his discomfort. The Spirit of Space knew, it was real enough.

Varn steeled himself and moved farther inside. This much he could manage, but he would have to watch the six. If one of them should come too near or touch him unexpectedly when he was not braced to meet the contact, the surprise could snap his already badly threatened control over his body. Only a moment's break would suffice. He would be forced to quit the room then, fast, and face an unpleasant session in the corridor outside if he could not reach a sanunit quickly enough.

Anger steadied him. Not again, he told himself savagely. That had happened once, and he still reddened at the memory of Islaen's anger and disgust. If it occurred here, it would destroy his effectiveness as a commander and would almost certainly identify him for what he was as well.

Sogan concentrated on Ospry. The sergeant was a Lemuran, not much different from Max Lampry and his daughter. He was accustomed to his Maintenance Sergeant and had no difficulty remaining in his company even in close quarters.

He liked and respected the man. Space, at this stage, he looked upon Lampry as a friend. There had never been a problem at all with little Stella. All he had seen in her was a small, hurt child desperately in need of the help he was glad to provide.

As for the others, none of them approached his Malkite friends for sheer ugliness of form.

He tried to imagine Zubin of Malki standing behind him, an invisible ally in this battle with his own irrationality.

The struggle became easier as time went on. The War Prince had continued questioning the six, and most of his difficulty vanished as he involved himself more completely in describing what it was that he wanted them to do, what he intended to do himself.

The Regulars simply stared at him.

The situation had reversed itself, Sogan thought with wry humor. At this point, they were the ones having trouble. All six of them were sure they were trapped in this room with a total madman.

He smiled for the first time. "It is not so unreasonable if we can get it to work," he told them. "The potential loss of one life against the certain loss of four is an equitable trade. I must at least investigate the possibility."

Pete Ospry nodded. "We can't give you an answer right away, sir. That'll take investigation and some figuring, but we'll work as fast as we can."

"That's all I ask at the moment, Sergeant. Please keep me informed as to your progress."

With that, the Arcturian left them and hurried to take his place on the bridge of the *Terra's Charm*.

Chapter Twenty

The crew of the *Terra's Charm* had been disgruntled at first at the driving their temporary commander was giving them, but their mood soon altered. They quickly realized that the man their admiral had so inexplicably set over them not only knew the bridge of a battleship, he knew the rest of her systems and the complex duties and interactions required to keep her in space and functioning as her designers intended, as need demanded. He understood the intricacies of the *Charm*'s drive and controls, her weapons banks and screens, as if he had been born in command of such a vessel.

He worked well with them. As a man, he seemed aloof, distant. The fact that he did not participate in the noisy democracy of the crew's cabin, that he rarely went there at all save for a hasty breakfast, was not taken amiss, for everyone understood that what time he had away from his duties to the starship had to be spent with his own unit, preparing for the work they would have to assume when they reached target. As for the rest, if their new commander was not affable, he was ever courteous, and he showed his respect for the abilities and experience of those serving beneath him.

Varn Tarl Sogan pressed the ship and her crew over the next several days, and in the final stages of her testing, he made trial of her utmost capabilities.

On the final day of his shakedown, his commands caused the hearts to beat hard in the breasts of the Regular officers on the bridge, and several of them looked inquiringly at Dundee, but the Chief Admiral stood silent, watching the performance of his flagship.

In the end, it was over. The *Terra's Charm* moved once again serenely toward her ever-nearing targets, and her officers and crew exulted in the new knowledge of her that they had gained and in the pride of her blazing in their hearts.

The Commando unit shared in the starship's victory and in Sogan's thanks to their feathered intelligence agent.

"Bandit reports that there is polite pandemonium taking place on the bridge," Islaen Connor announced triumphantly.

"What's Varn broadcasting?" Bethe asked.

"He's pleased."

Jake laughed at that. "Pleased? He's probably outflying the battleship."

"Very nearly."

"He's got a right. He's good. Space, I've seen what he can do on the *Fairest Maid*, but he's nothing short of a magician here."

The Arcturian and a happy-looking Bandit returned to the cabin to find their comrades waiting for them.

"Not bad, Admiral," Jake told him. "It looks like you haven't quite forgotten everything about big ships after all."

"Coming from you, Karmikel, I accept that as a great compliment."

"It is," the sergeant declared. "We were in on all of it thanks to Bandit. You were wonderful."

"The *Charm* was wonderful." His eyes were glowing. "She is about the finest ship I have ever flown."

"Well, I echo Bethe's judgment," Islaen declared. "It's the commander walking the bridge who makes or crashes the starship."

Yes! seconded the gurry, who was basking in her own share of the glory.

Her head cocked to one side. *Jack's coming!*

Immediately, the four drew apart and were already at partial attention when the Chief Admiral knocked on and opened the door almost in one moment. His order for ease came in the next.

"Relax," he told the four. "I just wanted to repeat my congratulations to Captain Sogan." He eyed the Arcturian. "I also want to pick your brains." Dundee shook his head. "For a while there, I was certain I'd turned a madman loose on my bridge."

"Thank you for permitting me to continue, sir."

"A captain must run his ship." He smiled. "You did that, sure as space is black. Things were moving fast at times. Come to my office and explain—slowly—how you got the *Charm* to make that fourth turn. According to her specs, that wasn't quite possible. I know. I just reread them to be sure my memory wasn't failing me. A number of the other miracles you managed to coax out of her weren't supposed to be possible, either."

"Initially not, perhaps, but the *Terra's Charm* has been upgraded many times since she was built. I believed the newer technology would give her the additional capabilities and speed."

Dundee scratched Bandit under the bill and offered her a sugar triangle, which she happily accepted, then he departed, taking Sogan with him.

Jack's nice! the gurry enthused. *Jack talks to Bandit! Pets Bandit!* —

"Feeds Bandit!" Islaen Connor mimicked.

Bandit's careful! she protested.

"Bandit, if I were the same kind of careful as you, I'd be one huge, round ball with a head, arms, and legs attached."

Bethe Danlo rescued the Jadite, whose feathers were beginning to expand in exasperation. "Never mind, Pet. Islaen's only jinking you. We all know you deserve a little treat now and then, especially with the wonderful job of scouting that you're doing for us."

Yes!

The spacer's expression grew grave, and her eyes were somber when she turned them to her colonel. "Maybe I shouldn't raise the question, but what will we do when this is all over?"

"All five of us will go back to living in the real universe!" Islaen snapped.

The Noreenan woman gripped her temper. "Sorry, Bethe. I'm thinking of what still lies ahead, and you can put credits down that Varn is as well. He may be having a wonderful time at the moment, but he knows he's going to have to fight this ship for real in the near future, and then we'll all have to depart on what promises to be one nasty hell of a job. Let him enjoy what he has for the next few days. It won't last any longer than that."

Jake followed Bethe to her cabin. "Why did you start that business about going back?" he asked curiously. He also wanted to ask why Islaen Connor had responded so sharply to her question.

"Because I think we're going to have a stellar-class problem when we do."

"With Sogan?"

She nodded. "Aye."

"Spirit of Space," he said hotly, "the man's enjoying himself thoroughly for once in his life. What's so flaming bad about that? I, for one, happen to be glad to see it."

"Varn is happy. He's so happy that he doesn't even mind letting us know that he is—"

"He should be. He's doing what he very obviously should be doing."

"Jake, a butterfly doesn't crawl back into its cocoon. Varn Tarl Sogan is not going to want to return to a splinter ship like the *Fairest Maid* after all this. He wouldn't be the man he is if he did. He wouldn't be human at all."

Karmikel was silent for some moments. "Maybe that won't be necessary," he reasoned in the end. "Our admiral's more than proven himself thus far. The brass might give him a battleship. It won't be the *Terra's Charm*, maybe, but the Federation Navy does boast of more than one of them."

The sergeant sighed. "I'm hoping for that, too, Jake."

"But you don't believe it will happen?"

She shook her head. "Dundee would've said it if there was a chance, I think. He didn't even try to use the possibility as a lure to induce Varn to accept command of the *Charm* for this mission. Islaen said he stressed that this was to be a temporary posting, for the one operation only, and that's all I believe it will turn out to be."

The redhead's eyes dropped, and he sighed. "We'd best brace ourselves, then, if that's the way of it. —He'll adapt again, I suppose."

"Aye. He will adapt."

His expression was dark. "That's not good enough, is it?"

"Good enough, no, but probably inevitable. I'm just not going to enjoy watching the process."

The Commando Sergeant's shoulders squared. "We've got a galaxy of troubles closer to hand," she said bleakly. "We've still got to blow that Pirate Stars base and get ourselves back from there again before we can even begin to worry about any more distant difficulties."

Chapter Twenty-One

Short term, things were going very well, Islaen Connor thought as her eyes scanned the cheerful activity in the *Charm*'s huge, ever-busy crew's cabin. None of the potential problems she had initially envisioned had developed in fact. The War Prince was simply too self-disciplined to create avoidable trouble with his officers and crew, even with two distinctly off-prototype individuals sharing bridge duty with him. She had felt him recoil or cringe in mind on several occasions, but he had not permitted anything of his distaste to become visible. On only one occasion had she felt him experience real difficulty, but he had managed to fight his way out of that without betraying himself. He had never mentioned it to her, nor had she raised the subject with him.

Even the invisible wall he used to distance himself from most of the Federation's denizens and the strict formality with which he ruled the bridge were not now taken too amiss, in a large part thanks to Bandit. Everyone liked and welcomed the gurry, and their temporary commander's open affection for her humanized him a little in the Regulars' eyes.

Something else did as well. The crew regarded their own part in the coming engagement as an easy ride, nothing more really than a clean-up job. Word was out that the Commandos faced an entirely different charter.

Her eyes shadowed. So they did, and thus far, she had been able to come up with nothing that would alter its probable outcome.

She resolutely put the problem from her mind. The guerrilla unit, its commander included, had come to the crew's cabin this evening for the express purpose of relaxing for a while. Four of them were present already, Bandit included. Varn should be joining them in a few minutes, as soon as he officially left the bridge for the day.

Connor gave a little shake of her head. The War Prince was coming solely because she had commanded him to do so. He did not like the big, noisy, crowded room. He took his breakfast here, she knew, thereby avoiding the even worse clamor of the mess, but he would not voluntarily have appeared here at this hour. Islaen had insisted. He was stretching himself too thin, driving himself too hard, trying to fulfill his double responsibilities as battleship commander and Commando, and she wanted to force him to relax, if only for a short while. He would be working in one way or another anywhere else on the *Terra's Charm*.

Islaen felt her husband's greeting. She replied with pleasure as she instinctively looked in the direction of the door.

The buzz of conversation momentarily stilled when the Commando-Captain entered the room and paused to survey the activities going on within. He was carrying himself as straight as if an iron bar stiffened his uniform and looked every bit as unbending. His gaze seemed cold, disapproving. In truth, she had to admit, it was.

"Space," muttered Karmikel. "He can kill an evening's fun real fast, can't he?"

"Shut up, Jake," Danlo ordered. "What are you picking up, Colonel?"

"They respect him. They don't actually dislike him."

"But they don't like him, either?"

"Some do, those chaps from the Maintenance Service, for instance." That was a little surprising. Five of the six were obvious mutants. Varn's behavior with the *Charm*'s off-prototype crew members had been scrupulously correct, but, to her knowledge, invariably distant.

"You have to show at least a glimmer of basic humanity for people to like you," the redhead observed, "unless you're an adorable gurry, of course."

"Jake!" Bethe frowned. "Smile at him, Islaen. Hold out your hand to him when he gets here."

Her colonel looked startled for a moment, but then nodded. Of course.

Sogan's face brightened and gentled at the woman's visible greeting, and his step quickened. He took the hand she raised up to him, and Islaen could feel a small but perceptible softening in the transmissions around them. *Good suggestion, Bethe Danlo*, she thought, even as she gave Sogan a verbal welcome.

"Don't get comfortable yet, Admiral," the demolitions expert told him after offering her own greeting. "Since you're on your feet already, you can fetch a replacement mug of jakek for each of us three, and a first one for yourself, of course."

The Arcturian was eyeing the nearly empty platter in the center of his unit's table with unfeigned interest. "What is this?"

It was a totally unnecessary question with his eyes and nose already giving him the answer. Morovian black mushroom caps, five inches in diameter and three thick, with a cup an inch deep. The latter was stuffed with the finely chopped stems and the traditional mixture of delicate Denevan spices.

He cut one in half and bit into it. "I am beginning to think this may not be a bad idea after all, Colonel Connor."

She laughed. "I know. I would've ordered you to come even if hadn't already ordered you to come when I found out these were on the menu. We've decided to make our dinner on them and skip the formal mess entirely."

"Another capital idea."

"I'm glad you approve, Admiral. —Now, fetch that jakek. Go along with him, Captain Karmikel. Bring back more mushrooms for us and a plate of however many of them you think Varn can eat."

"I'll need a crane," Jake responded, eyeing his comrade.

The Noreenan headed for the perpetually open galley serving the crew's cabin. Sogan started to follow, but he noticed a yeoman heading for their table and waited.

The man, or boy, rather, to judge by the softness still apparent in his round face, saluted hesitantly. The dark-eyed officer's more relaxed demeanor had encouraged him to approach the Commandos, but now that he was here and it was too late to back out, he feared he had made a bad mistake.

The War Prince read his discomfort and smiled. "Aye, yeoman?" he prompted. He wanted a crew that was disciplined, not terrified. Besides, from he direction of the boy's gaze, he thought he know what he wanted. Every man and woman aboard the *Terra's Charm* was thoroughly gurry-smitten.

"Bandit, sir," he managed. "Would she like peppermint? I have some, and—"

"Bandit loves peppermint. You have permission to give her one piece."

The little Jadite expressed her delight with her usual enthusiasm, and the shipman returned in happy triumph to his own companions.

"They probably bet him he wouldn't dare come within blaster range of us," Islaen remarked.

"Doubtless. I can be intimidating, I suppose."

"You can be outright grim," Bethe Danlo told him, recalling his entrance into the room.

"I thought you were my friend."

"I am. I just have to keep you in practice and fill in for Jake when he's not around. He'd never have resisted that shot."

Varn shook his head. He looked at the table where their recent visitor was once more sitting. "Has your Navy dropped the enlistment age a couple of years, or is there a less happy reason why he looks so young?"

His consort smiled. "He is young. Recruits can join up at sixteen with parental consent. That's what I did. It wasn't a common practice during the War, needless to say, but I think it'll become much more so now. Navy pay and benefits, not to mention the training and educational opportunities, stand well against civilian standards." Her eyes danced. "I wouldn't give Jake an opening like that if I were you, though."

"Do not worry, Colonel Connor. I do possess some rudimentary survival instincts."

The Arcturian joined his fellow captain at the galley counter. "Did you put our order in?"

"Aye. —What was that about?"

"Another of Bandit's conquests."

"I figured as much. She should be made President of the Federation. All political squabbling would instantly disappear."

The galley orderly came over to them. "May I help you, Captain Sogan?"

"Three mugs of jakek, one of coffee, please," he told her absently.

"By the way," Jake said, "while there's still time, would you like me to have them do up a few mushrooms Noreenan style?" He knew Sogan favored them that way, just quick fried in a lot of lightly salted butter.

"Let it be. Temporary commanders are not entitled to ask for special treatment."

The other grinned. "I was sure you'd say that, so I already did."

"Why did you ask me, then?" he grumbled.

"Just being polite, Admiral."

Varn withdrew from the verbal duel. He scanned the list of offerings posted above the service counter. The mushrooms were the day's special and were apparently going very well, but all of the usual temptations were there as well, everything from sensible syntheggs and traditional sandwiches through sweets of various sorts and a good mix of hot and cold nonalcoholic beverages.

"It is a wonder the entire crew does not waddle instead of walk. Our soldiers would not have believed this."

"Didn't your chaps eat well?" Karmikel asked. He was a bit surprised, for he knew life aboard equal-class vessels had been fairly similar in both Navies.

"We had good food and plenty of it, even at the end, but it was basically standard, and under normal conditions, it was available only at official mealtimes."

"No snacking?" he asked in mock horror.

"No."

"You poor blokes were absolutely deprived!"

Sogan was spared the need to reply by the arrival of the orderly with their food. He glared at Jake when he saw the size of the platter supposedly intended for him. It contained more than twice what he could hope to eat, though he supposed his comrades would be more than pleased to heroically step in and assist him in finishing it off.

"You will need help with those," he observed. He glanced at the orderly. "Hold the beverages here, yeoman. I shall be back for them."

"I'll bring them along for you, sir."

"No need," he said quickly. Self-service was the rule in the crew's cabin, regardless of rank.

"It won't be any trouble, Captain," she countered pleasantly. "I'm going off duty and will be passing your table on my way out. It'll give me a chance to talk to your little gurry."

"Very well, yeoman. Thank you."

The Commando-Captains were scarcely seated before the orderly arrived, expertly balancing a loaded tray.

"Three jakek," she announced. "One coffee." She glanced at Varn. "Black. Strong. No sweeteners. Is that right, sir?"

"Aye." He wondered that she should remember. He always ordered and ate his breakfast quickly, never lingering unnecessarily in the galley or at table, and he certainly was not alone among his temporary shipmates in his preference for the old-fashioned beverage that anyone should mark him for it. He sipped the steaming liquid. "Perfect, yeoman. Thanks."

"My pleasure, sir."

The woman left them after rubbing her finger down Bandit's neck and receiving an ecstatic purr as her reward.

Jake watched his comrade disapprovingly. The very thought of coffee made his mouth pucker. "How can anything which smells that good taste so bad?"

"I find the flavor interesting," Sogan replied defensively. "Besides, coffee is rare on the rim and readily available here. It is good to change from our normal fare now and then."

"Cease and desist," their commander ordered. "If you two start what you euphemistically term a discussion over the respective merits of jakek and coffee, Bethe and I are going to be more than a little annoyed. I wanted us to come here for some peace, remember?"

"Oh, very well, Colonel," Karmikel said. "We'll switch the conversation to the mushrooms. The admiral and I can unite in praise of those."

"We'll much appreciate that, Captain."

They fell to eating, giving their full attention to the food in the manner of seasoned spacers who never know when some emergency might interrupt or terminate a meal.

As she ate, Islaen Connor automatically continued to monitor the mental transmissions of those around her. She gradually became aware of an interest, an eagerness, overriding the less focused readings she was receiving from the bulk of the cabin's occupants.

She concentrated and discovered that the source of the transmissions were the six Maintenance Staff hands whom she had noticed earlier.

Varn felt the change in her and saw the direction of her gaze. *What is it?* he asked sharply, his old wariness surging back to its customary strength.

Nothing dire, the woman assured him. *Those six are paying us some significant attention, that's all. There's nothing unfriendly about them. The opposite, in fact.*

Anything else?

They're excited. I don't know if we have anything to do with that.

Varn Tarl Sogan's pulse quickened, but he took care to conceal his own response behind carefully raised shields.

He, too, studied the Maintenance crew. Their attention was, indeed, fixed on the Commandos, on him, and it took no mind talent for one who knew something of them to see that they were aroused. The little forked air tasters kept darting in and out between the two Sarvans' lips . . .

The Arcturian was prepared and had no difficulty in mastering his distaste before he made any show of it.

Why should he react like this, anyway, he thought in anger at himself. It was only another sense organ, and a useful one. His revulsion was even less logical than usual in this case since he happened to like snakes and thought them beautiful in their own way.

There was no reasoning with his feelings in this matter, and he thrust them out of his awareness. Those people were damn fine weapons mechanics, and they had all been putting in long, hard hours on his pet project. They deserved more than a cursory nod of respect from him.

They might also have news for him at last. By the look of them, they did have news, and he did not think it was bad.

"I'm going to have a talk with them," he said aloud.

Varn—

Power down, he told her a little irritably, annoyed by the warning she had been about to voice. *If nothing else, it will put to rest the rumor that Captain Varnt Sogan ignores his mutant crew members.*

The six rose to their feet at the Commando-Captain's approach. He waved them back to their seats and pulled a chair over from another table to accommodate himself. His attention was focused on the Maintenance crew, and he was not aware of the interest he had aroused in the other occupants of the cabin, all of whom were well aware of his reputation with respect to off-prototypes.

His smile was real, reaching and brightening his eyes. "It is good to see you doing something besides hard work," he told them. "By the look of you, I'd say you have some information for me."

"That, we do, sir!" Pete Osprey declared triumphantly. "We've got it licked at last."

His heart leaped, not entirely in pleasure. If the thing was operational, he was going to have to use it. "Fine work! When will you have my projectile ready?"

"It's ready right now, Captain, or ready for you to see what we've done with it, at least." He said that last a little more quietly. The Lemuran liked this man. He liked him a great deal after having had the privilege of working closely with him, and he knew that his crew's success well-nigh sealed Sogan's doom.

"You should have come over at once—"

The sergeant shook his head. "We didn't want to interrupt your dinner. We figured it'd hold until you were done."

The Arcturian eyed the large fruit tart awaiting division on the table and the fresh pot of jakek accompanying it.

"We should be finished by the time you dispose of all that," he told them. "You can show me then."

"Very good, sir. Thank you."

"Thank you, Sergeant. Thank you all. To say this job was a challenge is more than an understatement."

He would keep quiet about the project for a while longer, the former admiral decided as he returned to the other Commandos. He wanted to be sure he had something for a fact before he made any mention of his plan. It would be poorly enough received as it was.

Chapter Twenty-Two

Islaen, Jake, and Bethe joined Varn in their office. He seemed quiet this morning, subdued after the excitement of the previous several days, but he smiled readily in greeting.

The Arcturian sat down only after the others had taken their places. They waited expectantly. By this time, they knew when he had something on his mind, and none of them liked that he seemed to be hesitant about revealing it, especially when it pertained to a mission.

"I have not been occupying myself solely with the management of the *Terra's Charm*," the War Prince said at last. "It has taken me time, but, the Spirit of Space and Fortune willing, I believe I can assure us both the successful conclusion of our mission and the survival of all or most of the unit."

"We're listening, Admiral," Connor said. There was something in his manner that told her she was not going to entirely like his plan. His tightly shielded thoughts would have proclaimed that in any event.

"Our problem was never really the initial entry to the base. The projectile all but guarantees that. Our difficulty has been finding a way to eradicate it once we are in. The second projectile would take care of that, but we had no way of sending it to its target."

"Aye," Danlo agreed. "I can't rig a distance control system on them, not one fine enough. Those things are just meant to be fired at something and explode on contact. They're not baby rockets."

"True, but some study confirms that a simple manual control to direct gross movement, basically right, left, and forward, can be installed easily enough on one of them along with a superstructure for the operator to grasp. Only a minor adjustment of balance—"

Karmikel stared at him in disbelief. "Ride the flaming thing? Sogan, not only has success gone to your head, it's fried every circuit you had in there!"

The other man smiled. "It was not a difficult procedure. My mechanics completed the job yesterday evening. I have inspected their work and am satisfied with the result. —I do want you and Bethe to give it a thorough going over, though," he added. "These technicians are good, but they normally work on the battleship's weaponry for use in space combat. This is a Commando mission, and I would prefer to have you two double check their efforts before I must trust myself to it."

"You're making a broad assumption as to the eventual rider, aren't you?" the blond spacer asked calmly. "I'm the demolitions expert."

"No one is touching the detonation mechanism. It will still be activated upon firing and go off upon impact."

"You're going to have more than enough fun fighting the battleship, Admiral. Let—"

"Sorry, Jake. My idea. My right to carry it out. —Islaen?"

The Commando-Colonel nodded. "It's his baby."

Sogan nodded and went on smoothly. "I shall follow the initial projectile, delaying only long enough for it to detonate. That way, I shall be through the breach before the shock and confusion abate enough for anyone to become aware that I am there."

"You'd be crisped," Islaen told him flatly. "The whole breach'll be a mass of flame."

"I shall be wearing a protection suit. All of us must. There will be a lot of fire loose before we are ready to withdraw."

"Good thought." She sighed. "Go on."

"I shall not delay inside. Once I spot a target, I shall throw the controls for it and jump off, then race back outside on all burners. I will not be far from the breach, probably no more than a few feet. The flier can pick me up at that point."

The former admiral paused, then went on. "It will be a risky rescue. The base's weapons should be dead by then, but the whole place will be a bloody inferno. Do not try to land. Drop me an insulated cable with a couple of foot loops at its end and lift me out. I can hang on until we reach a point where you can safely set down or from which you can at least haul me in. Do not use rope," he added. "It might burn through. Naked metal will also be unacceptable. It could get too hot for me to hold."

The others nodded. It was a valiant fiction. Neither Varn Tarl Sogan nor any of his companions believed he would emerge from the burning hell he intended to create, but they would go on with it. If some miracle did occur, they would be there for him, whatever the danger to themselves.

"One other bad time will be our initial approach," Karmikel said. "We'll planet at a distance and work our way in, so, the Spirit of Space willing, we shouldn't be spotted then, but we'll need a minimum of time to get the projectiles into firing position. The base will be on the alert and braced to meet our attack after their ship's defeat. We could well be seen before we're ready to make our move."

Connor nodded. "They'll be expecting trouble, and we should give them some. —Varn, can we have the shuttlecraft flit about, as if to test the sons' firepower? We should be able to finish them off before they start wondering why the *Charm* doesn't try to fry them for real."

"The shuttles are yours," Sogan told her. "We should not have a problem finding volunteers to man them."

A knock prevented further discussion.

Jack! Bandit exclaimed happily. She hated battle talk and hoped the interruption would bring a change to a happier topic of conversation. At the very least, it would bring her a snack.

In that last, the gurry was not disappointed, but the Chief Admiral was grave when he addressed the Commandos. "Have you a tentative plan of action, Colonel Connor? We're getting pretty near target."

"We do, sir, in a great part thanks to Captain Sogan." She described their intentions, as far as they had developed them.

"A daring suggestion, Sogan," he remarked after the woman had finished speaking.

"It is not actually novel, sir," he replied. "Similar tactics were known even on prespace Terra, and we-the Arcturians used them during the War. We used small ships, not projectiles, but the principle is the same."

One Arcturian admiral had used them. Dundee had good reason to recall that particular assault. It had wrought havoc with the unfortunate fleet on the receiving end. "Just as a matter of historical interest, Captain, did any of your people survive the attack?"

"No, sir, but they were the equivalent of Regular Navy, not Commandos." The War Prince smiled grimly. "Guerrillas have different survival skills. Those are simply better suited to this sort of warfare." At the very least, he thought, this time, the man proposing the plan would be the one to carry it out and to bear its consequences.

"Well, you four seem to have everything worked out to cover your part of our mission."

"Not everything," Connor said. "We still have some detail to consider, and, of course, chance could force us to scrap everything and start fresh at the end. It's happened before."

"That's not an occurrence unique to any one branch of the service, Colonel."

Gray Jack turned to the Arcturian once more. "Everyone knows you Commandos are facing a fight, but the general opinion is that the *Terra's Charm* will float through her phase of the operation. I don't believe you share that notion, Captain Sogan, not to judge by the way you've begun working with our weapons crews."

"No, Admiral, I do not. It simply does not compute with the facts as we know them."

"How so?" Dundee accepted the chair Jake vacated for him.

"The Empire reports that four colonies have been totally obliterated. Every man, woman, and child butchered. Everything not fixed to bedrock taken. Two of those were well-established, flourishing settlements several generations beyond first ship each. What about their defense?"

"Menials don't fight."

"One at least out of the four would have had some sort of garrison," Sogan said impatiently.

"Would Arcturian warriors fight for dirt-grubbing farmers or miners?" the Terran countered.

"Aye. They would, in any event, fight to live, but, aye, they would fight for their charges. Like the most of your Federation's denizens, you are well aware of the services our menials provide to my caste but not of that which we owe them. We are their defense and would stand their cause with the same dedication, if not the same passion, that we showed in the cause of the Empire itself."

Varn Tarl Sogan had spoken as a War Prince to an opposing military equal. He recalled himself to their true positions and compelled his manner to change, although he did not offer an apology. "Arcturian soldiers are consummate fighters, sir. What happened? They died, obviously, but how? It is my belief that the ship they faced, and faced suddenly, was no brig or cruiser but something far larger, a full battleship, one thousand-class, or greater, or else that they were confronted by more than a single major vessel. In either case, they were wiped out by this greater force very quickly, and none were permitted to escape to carry report to our-their Navy. I do not intend that the *Terra's Charm* should fall victim to the same fate."

Chapter Twenty-Three

Tension rose aboard the battleship as she drew ever closer to target, to Olga's space.

The sun-star at last appeared in their distance viewers, a bright star with her clutch of rubble and small moons and the one glorified moon that bore the description of planet by default.

"What a rock!"

Sogan agreed with the Communications Officer. Kyrie appeared as an undramatic tan ball under magnification. There seemed to be nothing about her to excite or exalt the soul, yet three separate peoples were vying for the privilege of making her their homeworld.

It was not a small planet that they had voyaged so far to find. The former admiral's heart beat faster as the seconds passed into minutes, and those minutes increased inexorably. They could see the planet clearly. Anyone scanning this part of distant space from her surface or environs should see them. The watchers might not immediately identify the *Terra's Charm* for what she was, but they could not but note her presence and the fact that she was moving toward their base. They should investigate.

Even as the thoughts formed in his mind, a spark of light that could only be another starship appeared on the *Charm*'s viewer.

The distance between the two vessels closed rapidly until they could get good readings on the newcomer.

"By Siren's towers!" Once again, it was the Communications Officer who spoke. "That monster's as big as ourselves. No wonder those Arcturians were wiped out. The poor buggers didn't stand a chance."

"Activate screens," Sogan commanded. He felt a little numb, although his voice was steady and cool. He had anticipated meeting a large ship, a battleship, but not one of this, the greatest, class. It was as if the War had returned. If the opposing commander were any good at all, it had.

Immediately, the *Charm* seemed to double in size as the field of glowing energy that was her protection formed and enveloped her hull. A similar shell of light expanded from the strange vessel almost in the same instant.

"Weapons banks at ready." There was no trace of emotion or concern in his voice, as if this were no more than he had expected, no more than a training exercise. Nothing more than that order was needed, nothing beyond luck and the favoring will of the great Spirit ruling Space. His crew was good. They would respond as they must. They would fight as they must.

"You're fluent in Arcturian, I presume, Captain, like most Commandos?" Gray Jack Dundee asked smoothly.

"I am, sir, of course," Varn replied with a mental smile. So were his comrades, even Bethe Danlo now. They all practiced on him, and Varn Tarl Sogan would tolerate no sloppiness in grammar or diction. He was no more lenient with himself when he spoke Basic or the languages of Thorne or of Islaen and Jake's Noreen.

"Identify us and demand their surrender and that of their base. Use both Basic and Arcturian. They'll understand one or the other, and probably both."

"Aye, sir. —Open ship-to-ship."

A chill fell over the bridge when he delivered Dundee's ultimatum in his own language. Most of those assembled there had some knowledge of it, but hearing it from him seemed to recall once more the dark days when the Federation was in close battle for its very existence.

That cloud soon passed. The real threat before them left little room for fancy.

The other starship made no answer, and the two vessels drew ever closer, ever nearer to the duel that would end in the destruction of one or perhaps both of them.

For an instant, the stranger was visible on both the distant and near-space viewer screens, then she vanished from the former.

They could see her clearly now, or see the muted outline revealed by her screens.

Sogan straightened. She was an odd specimen indeed, square in form and coming for them with one edge serving as a great, tall prow. Her screens seemed brighter, stronger, there, like the pads sometimes used to defend or brace a corner. He felt that was probably their precise purpose, to provide still greater strength to what was already powerful beyond measure. His practiced eyes could detect no indication of weakness anywhere in her gleaming defenses.

The pirate warcraft made no delay. The moment she entered reasonable range, she opened up with her lasers, bank after bank of them in a sudden, concentrated volley meant to seek out and penetrate any soft place, any still-untightened seam in the Federation battleship's energy screens.

Varn Tarl Sogan's eyes flickered from the visual screens to the various gages supplying readouts of conditions aboard his own ship and what could be monitored of his enemy's. The Pirate Stars battleship was powerfully armed and powerfully defended, and her gunners handled their weapons expertly. They would find and exploit any flaw that existed in the *Charm*'s screens.

The War Prince knew he had taken a chance in allowing his enemy the first strike, but he had needed to see something of them in action, both that strange, square warship and the equally unknown crew who flew and fought her.

His confidence in the *Terra's Charm* had not been misplaced. She and those manning her were prepared. The vicious bands of energy searching and pummeling her defenses could find no flaw or weakness, no shadow of unreadiness, upon which to batten.

Combat in space between major battlecraft usually began thus, with their lesser rather than with their greater armaments. A pletzar bank's charge was finite, and no captain would squander any of their precious store of power if lasers would suffice to do the job at hand.

His eyes narrowed. The pirates would soon realize their attempt had failed, and the second, also predictable phase of the duel would commence.

Lasers bore within themselves a deadly inherent weakness. They could not be fired through their own vessel's screens. The energy plates had to open the barest fraction to permit passage of their rays, and at that moment, a starship became vulnerable. Opposing gunners would sight on a beam as it tore outward and, the moment it faded, would try to send one of their own directly into the spot from which it had emerged. If they succeeded, if the smallest amount of their energy made it through their target's screens, then the weapons bay behind them was no more. On splinter craft like the *Fairest Maid* and *Jovian Moon*, that spelled the death of the ship. Major vessels could usually absorb several such hits, depending upon the location, before being dangerously afflicted, provided the damage within the ship could quickly be limited and contained.

The glare of the pirates' lasers abruptly ceased.

"Hold fire!"

Every eye on the bridge fixed on Sogan in consternation. Now was the time for the *Charm*'s bolts to rip into their opponent, to batter through to her unprotected laser ports before her screens fully converged once more over her own retreating beams.

In the next instant, the Pirate Stars battleship again blazed with furious light.

There was a collective gasp on the bridge of the *Terra's Charm*, and once more, eyes rested momentarily on their commander. This time, they were filled with awe.

Varn's attention was entirely fixed on his enemy, on the unknown man or woman on the bridge of that square ship. A clever bastard and a daring one, daring almost but not quite to the point of madness. Sogan shivered in his heart at the narrowness of their escape. He had very nearly gone for that, had nearly danced the traditional step and opened the *Charm*'s laser ports just in time to receive the full of the pirate's renewed broadside. Had he permitted the *Terra's Charm* to return fire, she and all those aboard her would even now be a cloud of incandescent dust slowly expanding and dispersing into the infinity of interstellar space.

"Gunners, select your own targets. Fire at will."

Bridge officers and gunners started at that quietly voiced command. All knew that the time of the big broadsides was now ended. The battle would be conducted during this stage on many smaller fronts with individual marksmen striving to break through their counterparts' defenses on the opposite vessel. That was always the way of it when opponents survived thus far. Such complete independence of action by the disparate weapons bays of a major battlecraft was not Federation Navy standard procedure, however. Only the Arcturian fleets with their unfailingly superb gunners had used the tactic consistently and with consistent success.

Varn Tarl Sogan smiled. His move was unconventional in this ultrasystem, aye, but he had taken the measure of the *Charm*'s weapons crews. Their level of excellence was the equal of anything he had encountered on his own side during the proud years of his service during the War. They would do well.

Short-lived strands of furious light darted through the space separating the two great ships. Three minutes went by until his gunners rewarded his trust with a direct hit. Another followed seconds later.

A blaze of light and a frantically flashing indicator proclaimed the death of one of their own bays near to the bridge.

"Damage contained," a tense voice informed him a couple of seconds later.

The medics would be on-site even now, but Sogan knew they would find no life. There never was anyone left after so solid a strike. He tried to recall the faces or even the names of those who had held that station but could not. He had been aboard the huge starship too short a time to know every hand, by sight or by post. Perhaps he had seen them in the crew's cabin at one time or another and had disapproved of their pleasure . . .

That last thought would come later. Now, only the *Terra's Charm* and the Pirate Stars battleship existed for him.

Another of the enemy's laser ports blew out. Ten minutes later, a fourth went up.

The War Prince tensed. His gunners were very much the superior. The square ship had to be hurting, maybe severely so if the damage had not been rapidly and well contained inside. The pirate commander would have to make his move soon if he was not to yield or die.

Very soon now, Varn thought. He watched the pirate. Soon . . .

The other ship seemed to shimmer.

"Cease laser fire! Full pletzar screens!"

The *Terra's Charm*, too, shimmered. The hearts of the officers and rankless crew alike beat fast. The real trial was about to burst upon them.

Light seemed literally to roll out from the pirate battleship as her pletzars, those lining her huge sides and those heavy banks she had massed one upon the other in the prow, discharged in one immense broadside.

The wild energy struck the *Terra's Charm*, deforming her screens almost to the hull.

She responded, but her fire flowed harmlessly over the reinforced corner screens like water over a jetty on Lir.

The battle continued thus for fifteen minutes. Thirty. Neither ship gained or gave way, not yet, but the fight could not go on forever. The defenses of one or the other must shatter under the incredible pressure being brought to bear against them.

The War Prince watched the viewer screen and watched the gages revealing the status of his screens, and he knew the *Charm* would lose this fight. Her screens were weakening already, and once they opened even an atom's breadth anywhere, the Federation starship was dead and all those on board were dead with her.

She would die very soon now if she continued to fight using his present tactics. He rapidly made several calculations in his mind and then issued a series of orders to his astonished crew.

The battleship began to spin rapidly. Her pletzar banks switched to rest when they passed out of range, activated again just as they were about to face her foe's brutally armed prow.

For almost five minutes, the strange maneuver continued, then, with no forewarning, the screens over the enemy's prow flickered and were gone. In the next instant, all of space before them erupted in a fury of light that rivaled Olga for brilliance in the seconds that it lasted before the individual components comprising it cooled and dispersed into the infinite blackness of the realm between the stars.

A breathless silence gripped the bridge for several long moments. At last, Varn Tarl Sogan drew and released a long, deep breath. "Thank you," he said. "A battle well fought."

Admiral Dundee stepped up beside him. "Sogan, what in the name of space or beyond it did you do?" he asked in a voice low enough that the words remained between the two of them alone. "How did spinning our ship kill theirs?"

The Arcturian smiled. "We have become so accustomed to fighting our wars with energy that we sometimes forget mundane mechanical facts. When a civilian cannot open a jar of food in the more normal fashion, a few sharp taps with some implement applied with sufficient force to the side lip of the lid will usually be enough to break the seal and do the job. The pirate's corner screen cap was like such a lid. Our pletzars striking its edge as each bank reactivated and shot forward provided the force. Fortunately, it was sufficient, and the lid lifted."

Bandit flew to him from the perch where she had waited out the battle. *Fight over? Renegade ship gone?*

Aye, Small One. It is all over.
Varn saved us!
All the crew fought well.
Varn's idea saved us! Varn's the best captain!

He stroked her gently. He felt no sense of elation. One fight was over. Another, worse one would soon begin. A worse fight for him. No one else should have to die, at least.

One responsibility remained to him. *Bandit, you are to stay on the* Charm *when we leave for Kyrie,* he reminded her.

Bandit not leave unit! Not fight! Stay near unit! the gurry protested.

You know Islaen has ordered you to remain here, he responded severely. *Usually, you have no place of safety, no one to care for you, so you must come with us into battle. That is not the case here.*

Yes, Varn.

You have told us gurries can bond again. Would you stay with Admiral Dundee if we did not come back? It was already arranged that she would go with Jake and Bethe if both Islaen and he should fall, but circumstances were different here. It was criminal that they had not thought to make arrangements for the Jadite before now. *Is there someone else that you would prefer, on the* Charm *or elsewhere?*

Nooo! she wailed. *Unit not die!*

Bandit, please. I cannot face what I soon must without knowing that you, at least, will be safe and well. Do not force me to do that. —It is only a precaution, Small One.

Jack's nice! —Everyone won't die?

No, the others should not, the Spirit of Space willing. They should suffer no hurt at all.

Will Varn die?

He hesitated. *Probably,* he responded truthfully. *I shall try to live.*

She was deathly quiet for a moment. *Bandit loves Varn! I love you, too, Small One. Very much.*

"You're awfully quiet, Captain. Gathering stardust, or is something amiss? You certainly called that battleship right."

"I was thinking, sir. May I ask a favor of you?"

"Of course."

"Would you be willing to keep Bandit for us until we get back, or permanently if none of us make it?"

Dundee stroked the little creature and took her from Varn. "I can promise to do both readily, Captain. I'm uncommonly fond of her." He made himself smile. "I hope to be returning her to her intact unit in a very few hours' time." To her unit, he thought, but both of them knew that the dark-eyed man was not likely to be with it.

Sogan formally turned over command of the *Terra's Charm* to the Chief Admiral and hurried to join his unit for their phase of the assault.

Chapter Twenty-Four

Varn Tarl Sogan made his way quickly to the staging area where his comrades and the shuttlecraft crews were waiting.

The Commandos were already clad in the protection suits he had ordered. They would not defend against everything, but they would keep off a lot, more than any of them except Sogan himself should have to meet unless fortune went badly against them all.

After pulling on and fastening his own suit, he turned to the Regulars. "You all know what is expected of you. I want no shooting stars. Your mission is to distract the enemy, not try to do battle with them. You would not stand a meteor's chance.

"Those pirates will be fully alert and presumably sitting by their weapons. They will be in considerable shock over the loss of that battleship, but their brains will not have stopped functioning. No one would send shuttles to fight a battle. They will figure we want to trick them into revealing their firepower and the location of their weapons, and that they will not do unless you attempt something altogether unnecessary and foolish. Just keep them occupied until we strike and then clear fast."

He wished them luck and took his place in the driver's seat of his unit's flier.

All too soon, it seemed, they were in space and en route to Kyrie of Olga. Varn flexed his shoulders to ease the tightness that had been growing between them. It felt good to be at the controls and actually flying the vehicle, and he realized with some surprise that he had missed that direct contact between pilot and starship while he had been on the *Charm*. He had certainly missed it during the battle when he had been forced to wait, losing precious fraction-seconds while his will had to be relayed through verbal orders for implementation by others.

The Arcturian laughed to himself. He was a difficult man to please, it seemed. He wanted it both ways.

His consort's mind had been linked with his, and she laughed as well. *Typical admiral,* she declared. *Impossible to satisfy.*

Varn's mood became serious once more. He told her the arrangement he had made for Bandit.

Thank you, Varn, she said quietly. *She does like Dundee. I should have thought of it myself.*

Sogan remained quiet for a couple of seconds. *I love you,* he said then. *The others, too.* He had to force that last, but he knew there was little hope that he would have the chance to say it again.

They know that, she answered softly. She wanted to give him the rest in return, their comrades' feeling for him, but his shields had tightened over his mind, not to close her out but in response to the discipline they had assumed from the first discovery of their abilities lest one distract the other at the wrong moment in combat with disastrous consequences. Kyrie was very close.

"She is a rock," the War Prince said aloud in agreement with the *Charm*'s Communications Officer's earlier judgment. She was that, he thought behind his shields, a miserable rock for which to have to die. There was no population for whom he was sacrificing himself, not even a fauna of any significance, just the Federation's damned decision to make an example out of this situation. He did not want to die for that. He did not want to die at all. He sighed then and made himself banish that regret. Better him than Islaen or one of the others.

Jake leaned forward. "Take us in, and let's make this quick, Admiral. After it's over, we have to have a little policy discussion. You're going to have to stop hogging all the fun on our missions. The rest of us're just about superfluous on this one."

There was no lightness in Karmikel's heart or mind to match that which he had forced into his voice. Danger came part and parcel with the work of a unit like theirs, but it was understood that they all shared equally in it in one way or another. This time, that was not so. He and the others were going to have to stand back and watch while his friend went ahead into almost certain death.

Sogan smiled. "Hardly superfluous, Captain. Bethe has to finish setting the projectiles, someone has to handle the flier, and if my brilliant plan proves a dud, you will all have to go in, lasers blazing, as we originally intended." Though the flier was officially considered only a transport vehicle, the Arcturian had mounted two artillery-class lasers on its nose. He still grinned to himself at the memory of Dundee's expression of shock when the Chief Admiral had first seen them.

All fell silent as the War Prince began his approach. He planeted smoothly, well over the horizon from the pirate base. It was hilly country, fortunately, and they would be able to come fairly close before reaching the final acceptable cover.

Varn hesitated momentarily, then turned the controls over to Islaen. The Noreenan woman was still the better Commando. She should be the one to bring them to the actual site from which he would launch his attack.

Flitting from cover to cover, from shade to shade, the flier crept its way ever closer to the Pirate Stars installation. If they should be discovered now . . .

After a seeming eternity, Connor brought the machine to a stop. "This is it. I can't take us any nearer. The base should be just over that ridge above us."

The Federation soldiers got out and wriggled their way up the short, steep rise until they reached its crest.

All were quiet. Their target was below, a plain dome overlaid now with an umbrella of light, a screen against assault from space. Its occupants were strictly ignoring the five shuttlecraft buzzing above, ostensibly tempting the defenders to fire. In front of the place, lying between it and the ridge where the four watchers lay, was a small, roughly made planeting field for use by the two shuttles berthed on its perimeter. The monster starship those had serviced would, of course, never have set down on-world.

The Commandos breathed one collective sigh of relief. The first test to their plan had been met and passed. The installation's screens were massed against attack from above. The defenders anticipated no trouble from the surface, and the lower sides were completely uncovered.

The four off-worlders worked silently to unload and make ready the big projectiles. They were afraid, all of them, and all held silent about it. Anyone who did not feel fear in the moments before combat did not belong in a unit such as this.

Bethe Danlo quickly completed the fine setting and arming of each missile. She looked up. "All ready to go, Admiral."

His eyes fixed on the one he was to ride, on the superstructure he and the *Charm*'s mechanics had devised. Superstructure? There was a long, low, backward-sweeping transparent shield to deflect the force of the wind generated by its movement, a couple of plates against which to brace his feet, handles for his fingers to grasp, a simple directional rod, and beneath all, an enormous live bomb. He must be as mad as Jake had declared him to be when he had first proposed his plan.

Islaen shuddered in her own heart. Spirit of Space, do not let her lose this man, she prayed deep inside herself. He was the finest thing that had ever happened to her, and they had been together for so short a span of time.

She made herself smile, in face and in mind. *Hurry back out of there, Varn. In one piece, preferably.*

I shall do my best, Colonel.

The sergeant's fingers brushed his hand, then she took her place beside the first projectile.

Karmikel steadied him as he scrambled onto his odd vehicle. The redhead winked and stepped back.

Varn stretched out full length, making himself as much as possible one with his vehicle. He pressed himself against the cold skin of the projectile and grasped the handholds with punishing force. He tried to will his heart to pound less loudly and at a saner rate. His eyes closed. Not only was he scared green, but he felt like an utter fool.

Maybe he would prove a fool. If anything was amiss with the design, he could find himself lying in midair with his weapon speeding ahead right out from under him . . .

The first projectile shot forward. In seconds, moments, it tore downslope and across the planeting field. In the next, it slammed into the wall of the pirates' base. With contact came detonation.

Fire, noise, and flying debris filled the whole scene in front of them.

The Arcturian was given no opportunity to study the damage or plan an approach. The impact of the first missile signaled the flight of the second. It shot forward with a roaring speed that filled him with exultation and terror. This thing was more elemental force than human-made craft, and he had little more hope of controlling it.

The broken, burning wall was near. Sogan buried his face in his arms so that only the hooded protection suit would confront the flames directly, and he drew a breath deep enough to see him beyond the breach. Pull any of that fire into his lungs, and he was done before he even began.

A moment of searing heat, and he was through. He looked up, scanning the installation within the broken dome. He knew what he wanted and found it to his far left, a sturdy, square blockhouse designed to shelter the volatile substances that kept ships flying between the stars. Its sides were metal sheathed as an additional guard against accident, but that would provide no defense against the explosive power of his projectile.

The War Prince shoved the control rod to the left and jumped. He landed hard and clumsily, bruising both shoulder and hip badly enough to wring a cry of pain from him.

Sogan did not so much as attempt to get to his feet. He rolled. The burning breach was near. He had to reach and pass through it . . .

A blaster bolt sizzled above him. A second scorched along his back, but the protection suit deflected the worst of it.

There were no more shots. An explosion melded with an infinitely greater one, and a geyser of flame tore through the dome to claw far into the sky above.

Everything flattened under the blast wave that followed immediately upon it. Varn had been down, prone, already, or he felt he must have been shredded by it. As it was, the breath was driven from him and, for a moment, awareness as well.

His will held onto consciousness, compelled it to return. He fought for and claimed the power to breathe.

In so doing, he destroyed himself. He was at the breach, and it was fire that he drew into his lungs.

The Commando-Captain continued to roll, into the fire, beyond it, and yet once again.

No blasters challenged him. He started to crawl but gained only a half dozen yards. His airway remained partly open, but his lungs were functioning badly and already starting to fill.

Sogan willed himself to move again. He made another two feet, then collapsed, beaten, to lie waiting for death in the midst of the sea of his pain.

The remaining Commandos had leaped into their flier before the discharge of the War Prince's projectile. They would have to be airborne by the time he entered the base either to begin their own attack in the event of his failure or to effect a rescue in the unlikely event that one would be required.

Islaen watched the column of flame erupt through the suddenly shattered dome. "Mission accomplished," she said softly. "Keep well away from it, Jake," she told the redhead, who had the controls.

"No fear that I won't! —Do you see anything?"

"No." She straightened. "Aye! There!" Incredibly, impossibly, Varn Tarl Sogan had made it out.

He was hurt, and hurt badly. The colonel concentrated and sent her mind out, not to touch thought with her husband's thought but to examine his battered body.

"His lungs are almost gone." She unfastened her belt. "I'm going down after him. He won't be able to hold onto the cable." He might not even be capable of grasping it, and they could not put the flier down. Flames were shooting furiously out from the ravaged installation, and there were munitions within which had not yet blown. When they did . . .

Luckily, they had fashioned two loops in the cable. Connor pushed her foot into the uppermost one and tied her belt around the cable as an additional brace. "Get down as far as you can, Jake."

Karmikel nodded grimly. Sogan's loop would have to touch ground. "As far as necessary," he promised.

"You'll have to planet with us. I doubt we'll be able to haul him in over the side."

There was no time for anything more. The flier dropped quickly. "Go, Colonel," Karmikel told her at last.

Islaen wriggled over the side and started her descent. It was not a pleasant sensation to drop ever lower, ever nearer to that barren surface with those flames reaching out, coming closer and closer to her and to the seemingly unconscious man below.

Varn! Varn, can you hear me?

The War Prince lifted his head. He saw her and struggled to his knees only to fall once more. *Go back, my Islaen. I am done. There is still too much danger for you all—*

Fight, Varn! Damn you, fight to live! If you stay here, I stay with you.

Her words struck him like the lash of the executioners' whips. Sogan fought his way to his feet. He staggered to the cable and, with Islaen to help him, managed to get his feet into the loop.

"We're set! Take us up!" Connor called into her communicator. After that, she concentrated on Varn. Her arms were around him, supporting him while she used her body to shield him from the huge tongues of fire licking around them, seeming to reach for them. *Hang on,* she whispered. *Hang on a little longer. We're almost home.*

The War Prince rested against her. He need do nothing more. He was safe now, safe in the midst of the madness of flames around them.

An explosion greater than any of the previous ones rent Kyrie's atmosphere, and fire rode with it.

The munitions! Islaen instinctively tightened her hold on her husband, then screamed in an agony no will could block as a wall of flame struck her, fire of such intense heat that even the protection suit could not completely thwart its will.

Her pain tore into Sogan's mind. He was untouched himself. The woman's body had covered him, and the flier had pulled them free before the fire could engulf them both.

It had been on them for no more than a couple of seconds, but to what effect? Frantically, his mind sought his consort's and could find nothing, no shadow, no answering spark whatsoever.

She might still be in there, he thought desperately. His own broken body could not sustain the effort of deep delving, not without driving himself into unconsciousness as well, and that he could not risk. As Islaen had held him, now his arms fastened about her. If his support relaxed, she would slip from the cable, drop into the inferno below.

It must be a living woman and not a corpse that he held! Tears were in his eyes, on his cheeks. *Islaen, please, live! You made me fight. You forced me to fight. Now, you have to fight as well!*

Chapter Twenty-Five

Varn Tarl Sogan tried to concentrate. He could not. His mind was a fog from the heavy sedative they had given him.

It could not blunt his fear. Why were they keeping him like this? Was it that they did not want to tell him, feared to tell him, before they could bring him under treatment?

He tossed his head. What was the use? If Islaen Connor were dead, there was no point to any of it. There was nothing at all . . .

She had been alive in the flier. Bethe had told him that much . . .

"Sogan? Varn, can you hear me at all?"

His eyes opened. They would not focus, but he saw a badly blurred, double image of Jake Karmikel.

Whatever shred of hope that he had held died. She was gone, then, or Islaen would have come . . .

Drawing on a nearly numb will, he kept his face a mask. Speech was impossible, but he gave an almost imperceptible nod of his head to acknowledge the other man.

Jake's hand grasped his. "She'll be fine, Varn. They've got her under a renewer now, a big hospital-class one. You had to be stabilized enough for the regrowth to start working on you, or you'd already be under treatment yourself." That stabilization had been a galactic job. The renewer had quickly healed his airway, but the damage to the lungs was severe, and the Arcturian had kept slipping away from them.

Varn's will could not block the sob that rose to his throat in relief as he had been able to screen his grief. He turned his head aside.

"They didn't tell you?" There was surprise and anger in that, although the Noreenan tried to muffle the last. "She's been under sedation, too, or she would have contacted you herself."

The War Prince faced his comrade. "Thanks, Jake." His lips formed the words, although he had no power to voice them.

He was so tired that he had to fight to keep his eyes open . . .

Once more, the other man's fingers pressed his hand. This time, they remained. "Your turn's next. Go to sleep now, Admiral. I'll stick around until they come for you."

Bethe Danlo faced him anxiously when the redhead finally returned to their office. He had been gone so long . . . "Varn?"

"He'll make it now, I think." The anger boiling inside him surfaced. "Damn, bloody fools! Everyone on that medical staff has to be denser than a white dwarf! No one told him Islaen was alive. They informed him that he had been stabilized, but they never said a word about what mattered to him. He was going under regrowth hoping to die and not to live, and it'll be close enough as it is."

"They probably thought he was too heavily sedated to be aware of anything. No one could fight the dose they gave him."

"Well, Sogan was fighting it. He was too sick with fear for Islaen to give way to it."

"You stayed with him until they took him?"

He nodded. "They weren't too happy to find me still there, but as far as I was concerned, they could all go off on a long voyage to nowhere. Given those sons' performance with him already, I figured he could do with having a real friend around. As it was, I hated turning him over to them."

"Well, we'll have to assume greater medical competence on their part. You've done yours."

"They should manage," he replied bitterly. "It isn't easy to foul up a regrowth treatment."

He strode over to the cabin wall and slammed his hand against it. "I hate feeling this helpless!"

Bethe went to him. "I know, Jake. So do I. —Let's get back to Sick Bay. They should have some real answers for us soon."

The War Prince awoke to find Islaen sitting beside him. He smiled, although he was embarrassed that she had caught him asleep again. He had been back in his cabin for two days now, but it seemed that he could remain up for no more than a couple of hours without having to knock out once more. It was the fault of the treatment, of course. A renewer healed almost instantly, without aftereffects. Regrowth drained every ounce of a patient's energy, and it did not return again in full for some time.

He sat up and took a playful poke at Bandit, who had fluttered to the bed beside him. "Have you been taking care of Islaen for me, Small One?"

Yes! Varn, too!

Sogan glanced at his consort. *You should be getting some rest as well.*

I just had renewer work, remember? I'm probably in better shape than I was when we started this jaunt, which is more than can be about you, as usual.

Islaen spoke lightly of it now, but he recalled all too vividly how she had been when he had clasped her to him on that cable, not knowing whether she lived or was dead.

His eyes closed. All his terror for her, all his vast grief, roared back over him. His universe had grown very small since his fall. It held four stars only, and this woman was its center. It had been so monstrously close this time . . .

The horror and misery had returned to him so suddenly that he had not been able to raise his shields rapidly enough to block them from his consort's awareness. She took his hands in hers. *I'm sound out, Varn. It's over. It's all over now.*

I thought I had lost you, he whispered. *When no one would tell me anything, I was certain of it. If it had not been for Jake—*

He handled it better than those dolts in Sick Bay, she agreed. *That's why we got you out of there so fast. We figured you'd make better progress with us watching out for you. It was mostly rest that you needed at that stage anyway.*

I have been getting plenty of that, whether I will it or not, he said ruefully.

His eyes dropped. *How is the ship doing?*

Just fine. Why shouldn't she be? She's on her way home, after all, and no longer engaged in preventing murder and mayhem.

He did not respond with a smile as she had hoped. After a moment, he sighed. *This is a graceful way of restoring command to Admiral Dundee, I suppose.*

That isn't precisely the word I'd use to describe it. The woman shook her head, half in amusement, half in exasperation. *You probably could take over the bridge again in an emergency, but do you really feel up to that at the moment?*

No. All I seem to feel like doing these days is sleeping.

He gave the lie to that by swinging off the bed and going to the office.

Varn sat somewhat dejectedly at the table. *I dislike being just so much worthless cargo.*

Aren't you exaggerating just a wee bit? she asked, barely succeeding in masking her smile.

The War Prince made her no answer. His mood had darkened, and he did not seem to want to look at her.

Varn, what's the matter? Connor asked in sudden concern. Something was riding him badly enough that he was not battling to conceal the shadow it put on him.

I am useless now and will be for some days to come—

You don't imagine you are valuable to us only when you're in a state to fight well? she demanded, angry now.

No, but being like this has made me think. His lips tightened. *When I could stay awake long enough to think.*

She felt his shields start to rise, but he willed them to stay down. She could read the trouble on him, the embarrassment.

Sogan made himself face his colonel. *It is not just the regrowth,* he said at last. *I am so tired, Islaen, body and mind. I have been fighting since I was twelve years old and have had no peace at all since I was ordered to invade Thorne of Brandine.* He looked at her wearily. *It has to be as bad for the rest of you. We have had one mission on top of another for the last two years, and little enough rest in the scant time we have been permitted between them. No unit can continue like that indefinitely.*

His eyes dropped. *I had hoped to be able to keep going, to be a help to you others if any of you should start to weaken. Now, I do not know—*

Do you want out, Varn? she asked quietly. *Say it, and we'll do it. There will always be plenty to keep the four of us more than busy and challenged on Thorne when we're ready to go back to work again.*

No, he said slowly. *I want the Navy. We are needed here.* He gave her the shadow of a smile. *I would just like to be left quiet for a while, for long enough to recover more than merely my basic physical strength again.*

You will be, she promised almost fiercely. *We all will. I was planning to hit Sithe up for an extended leave. Now, I'm going to demand it. On medical grounds, and not just based on your records, either. You may be the worst off, but we're all facing the same trouble. I'll take the unit to Thorne and have Harlran Lanree lock the planet up so tight that the Federation and the Empire together couldn't win through to us.*

He smiled more naturally. *The Doge would do that for you.*

He'll do it for you, she snapped. Her eyes closed. *Varn— Even you think of Thorne as home. Or has that changed?*

Of course, it has not.

She felt his weariness, his discouragement, and did not press him further. *I know I couldn't give you the vengeance I promised, but I won't let you down on this. I can't. It's the whole unit, myself included, that's at risk.* She looked at him somberly. *You wouldn't have said anything at all, would you, if that weren't the case?*

No. It would have been only my own difficulty then and mine to bear it. I could not risk failing you or our comrades.

Space will turn white and black again before you'll ever do that, Varn Tarl Sogan, Islaen told him firmly. She touched his arm to make him face her. *Varn, will you trust me to take care of this?*

Aye. He sighed. *I should have known you were too good a commander not to be aware of it. It was wrong of me to have bothered you at all.*

Arcturians! she said in exasperation. *You're all hopeless! —Admiral Dundee has been asking for you. He'll probably drop by tomorrow. He'd have come sooner, but we wouldn't let him near you.*

You what?

Islaen laughed. *We Commandos look after our own, Varn Tarl Sogan, whether that means pulling one another out of an inferno or keeping temporarily unwanted brass at bay.*

She scooped up the gurry. *Bandit and I are meeting our friends in the crew's cabin. Shall we bring anything back for you?*

Coffee. Strong. Black. No sweeteners. Except for Bandit. My stockpile is running low. He pretended to glare at the Jadite. "Have you been raiding it when I'm asleep, you little feathered rogue?"

Nooo! Bandit wouldn't—

Varn! —"Power down, Love. He's only jinking you. I guess that means he's starting to feel a bit better."—*As for the mystery you mention, Admiral Sogan, your stocks are so low because you've been amusing yourself by giving her double rations ever since you got out of Sick Bay.*

"Very well. I apologize, Bandit."

Good!

See, she forgives you. You don't deserve her.

I never did. He stroked the gurry. "Do not let her forget my coffee, Small One."

Nooo!

Islaen laughed. *All right. We're going. —You really like that stuff, don't you?* That had become a regular request of his, and she recalled now that Varn had been drinking a lot of it before his injury as well. Even the orderly in the crew's cabin had served him often enough to be aware of his preferences. Most of those who used the old beverage drank it colored and with sugar.

Aye. I do. I have since I discovered its existence on Dorita. It had been one of the few pleasures of which he had been able to avail himself in those very early days of his in the Federation. Coffee had been in good supply on that particular colony, and he had not realized then that it would be only relatively rarely that he would be able to indulge himself with it. *It is basic issue on the* Terra's Charm, *so I can allow myself the luxury.*

The Noreenan felt a touch of annoyance rise in her. *You might have mentioned your interest in it before. Coffee may not be common out here on the rim, but it's not exactly impossible to find in big ports like Horus. You are entitled to enjoy a few nonessentials, you know.*

He shrugged. *No one else cares for it.*

She quelled her irritation. A War Prince in good standing would not seek what he took to be favors, either. Of course, given the fact that a War Prince normally had the income of star systems at his command, it was highly unlikely that one of them would ever have to depend upon anyone else's interest for the fulfillment of any of his desires. Varn Tarl Sogan retained all the pride of his kind. He merely had been stripped of the means to support it.

A knock interrupted the reply he would have made. The colonel went to the door, spoke briefly with and thanked someone, and returned with a covered container in her hands.

First drink this, then you'll get your coffee.

What is it? he asked suspiciously.

A high-calorie supplement. The Charm's *medical staff isn't any happier than I am about the discrepancy between the weight you should be carrying and the weight that you do. You'll be on this stuff until we reach Horus.*

She removed the lid and groaned in her mind. She knew her husband's opinion of fish even when he was feeling enough himself to be somewhat tolerant. This concoction reeked of it.

The Arcturian's reaction was just about what she had anticipated. *If this is some sort of jest, Colonel Connor, it is far from amusing.*

It's just following an old Federation tradition that any medicine worth taking has to taste terrible. Her eyes shadowed. That medical report had her worried. Sogan had lost more ground all around than she had suspected since Amazoon, and this latest dose of trouble had not helped. *I think it's a tradition we should continue on the* Maid, *too, for a while.*

No! he snapped. *The least I should have is some peace and comfort aboard my own starship, whatever her deficiencies in other respects.*

Islaen realized she had hit a nerve and backed off, but Bandit was alarmed. *Nooo!* Maid*'s home!*

The Arcturian was instantly contrite. He hated to upset the gurry, and this was his failing, his problem. None of the others should have to suffer for it. "Of course, she is, Small One," he agreed soothingly. "We all know that."

He glared in none-too-friendly fashion at his consort. *That does not mean that I am going to consent to being poisoned, there or on the* Terra's Charm. *Dump that potion out now and see to it that no more of it arrives.*

Islaen Connor pushed the container toward him. *Dump it out yourself, then! I'm not your servant. —Sometimes you're worse than any five-year-old on Noreen, and we tend to spoil our small children!*

Nooo! Don't dump food, Varn! Bandit swooped down to the container and perched on its rim. She dipped her bill into it.

Bad! Horrid!

The gurry shook her head in an effort to clear the last drops of the liquid from around her beak, then launched herself into the air with such force that she toppled the container.

The Arcturian jumped to avoid the spill but was too late.

He swore in his own language, then switched back to Basic. "Bandit, if I get my hands on you—" He glared at his consort. *Is it necessary to laugh, Colonel?*

I'm sorry, Varn, but she looks so disgusted.

She *is disgusted?* He started to laugh himself. *Get that misbegotten ball of feathers out of here and find her something decent to eat. There is no reason for her to suffer because I apparently must.*

Never mind being a martyr. You win. I can't be cruel enough to stand against both of your opinions. No more Medical Service cocktails.

Good! declared the gurry emphatically. *Chocolate better!*

What about this mess? the woman asked.

I shall take care of it, the table and myself. —Go on and feed her. She did me a favor, even if I do smell like a fish at the moment.

I'll bring you the coffee as a peace offering, she promised.

That, I shall accept with pleasure. He paused. *Are you sure I am entitled to special service now that I am no more than a passenger?*

Islaen started to bridle until she felt his laugh. *You're a worse rogue than Bandit is.* She eyed him. *As for special service, Varn Tarl Sogan, if anyone aboard this battleship thought you might fancy a bottle from Hedon's top vineyard, all five shuttlecraft would promptly be dispatched to hunt it up, and every one of them would probably return with an entire case!*

Chapter Twenty-Six

Varn lied! Bandit declared as soon as the door closed behind them and Islaen's mental prohibition against speech lifted. *Varn doesn't want* Maid!

He does, really, the woman assured her, speaking in mind as well since there were others, crew members, present in the corridor. *Give him a little time to get used to the idea again.*

Nooo! the gurry protested. *Varn wants* Charm, *not* Maid!

Islaen stroked the agitated gurry. *Varn's very tired, Love, and he's still sick. We'll both just have to be patient with him for a while.* She only hoped she was not the one who was lying, to the Jadite and to herself.

But, Islaen—

Quiet now, Love. You'll be attracting attention. I don't want to have to deal with any more problems at the moment. I'm tired, too.

Bandit subsided, and her spirits rose again once they reached the crew's cabin and located their comrades, both of whom still had interesting things on their plates.

The colonel sat down. "Did you leave anything for us?"

"A bit," Danlo said. "We'd just about given up on you."

"Is there jakek in that pot?"

"Aye, Colonel." Jake poured a good measure of the dark liquid into the mug they had fetched in anticipation of her coming.

She sipped it. "This is good." She set it down again and smiled. "I feel like I should raise a formal toast to modern medicine. Do you realize that at the War's beginning, both Varn and I would've been in the hospital for months after this one?"

"You'd both be in boxes," Karmikel informed her dryly.

The sergeant glared at him but turned back at once to her colonel. "What's the admiral doing?" she asked the other woman. "Sleeping again?"

"Under the steam jets. Bandit didn't like his high-cal supplement any more than he did and managed to spill it all over the cabin and its occupant. It smelled exactly like a large, long-caught, and poorly preserved fish."

The redhead's smile was beatific.

"Don't say one word, Commando-Captain," his commander warned sternly.

"All right, Colonel Connor. I won't say it." He grinned. "I'll regret until my dying day that I wasn't present, though."

"You have no compassion for another's misfortunes, Jake Karmikel."

"None whatsoever."

Bethe brought her commander a sandwich from the perpetually open galley. "Sink your teeth into this. There's more than enough in it to cover for dinner, too."

Islaen compressed the mountainous offering sufficiently to permit her to bite into it. "The Regulars do eat well, don't they?" she remarked appreciatively, not for the first time during the voyage.

"Aye." The spacer's eyes dropped to her hands. "They're not going to give Varn a ship, are they?"

"There was never a question of that," Islaen Connor answered carefully.

"He deserves a major command," she protested. "He belongs here. I hadn't realized how much until actually seeing him in action."

"If Gray Jack Dundee could swing it, he would."

"No chance?" Karmikel pressed.

She shook her head. "It's one thing to give a cashiered Arcturian admiral a Commando-Captain's commission out in a rim Sector and another to turn a battleship over to him."

"If there were any justice in this universe, he'd get that ship," the Noreenan man hissed.

"If there were any justice in this universe, Varn Tarl Sogan would still be wearing the insignia of an Arcturian admiral and would have all the battlecraft he could desire under his command." Doubtless, one of them would be captained by his heir son at this point. Five years. The boy would have been nineteen or twenty now had he lived, more than old enough to have gained that rank if he had shared anything at all of his father's ability. The same might be true of his brothers of the same age. Space, she thought, how had the War Prince retained his courage, his fineness, through all that had happened? How could he still love or trust at all?

Her companions' expressions were dark, their anger all the sharper because they knew full well that they were powerless to help their comrade.

Jake swore. "So Sogan gets back-alleyed by his own lot and by the Federation, too?"

"Enough, Jake," the colonel warned. "That's enough. This is the way of it, and we'll do no one any good running our mouths about it here." She did not sound any more content than her companions.

Bethe sighed. "Does the admiral know?"

"Not officially yet. Dundee will tell him tomorrow."

"What will he do?" she asked softly.

"Varn Tarl Sogan will accept it, because he has no option except to do so, the same as he has had to accept every other injustice, betrayal, and disappointment he has endured during these last five wretched years. —Space! I'm beginning to hate that word! Sometimes, I wish he would really explode. I wish by all the Federation's gods that he would go out and get burning drunk as you sometimes suggest, Jake, when you're being particularly insufferable." Except that she would then have to live with her consort's sense of guilt afterwards, and, the Spirit of Space knew, she had to put up with enough of that already on occasion.

The others stared at her, stunned by the depth of the bitterness in her sudden tirade.

"Easy, Lass," Jake said gently. "We've been forgetting that you've been having a rough time, too."

The colonel gave him a wan smile. "Sorry about that. — I don't really have it so bad. I can always relieve the pressure by grousing at you two now and then."

She frowned. "I am going to have at it with Admiral Ram Sithe when we get back to Horus, though. We're all tired right down to our bones, and I want a real furlough for the unit, a month, minimum, excluding travel time, and no new assignments half way or a quarter through like we've had in the past."

"On Thorne?"

"Aye. I'd really like to take us all away from the Sector, from the rim entirely, and go someplace completely without associations of war and the memory of war for us, but that's not possible, and Thorne of Brandine will more than suit the purpose." The merchant world was not only one of their official bases but their home, and it was the sole planet in all the galaxy where Varn Tarl Sogan had nothing to hide and nothing to fear. Thorne had given this former enemy who was her greatest hero full refuge and complete welcome.

"Especially when you can have a few words with the Doge, and he'll seal the port against any roving Federation brass with extraneous missions on their minds?"

"Precisely, my friend." Sithe had other Commando units to utilize. At this point, she had to work for her own, or none of them would be good for much of anything.

The captain came to his feet. "You just sit here for a while and work out the details with Bethe. I'll take some dinner back to our patient." His eyes sparkled. "I won't even run him over the jets. Too much."

"I'll bring him food later," Connor said. "Bandit will be expecting her share of it. Just take the coffee he wanted."

"Anything to please, Colonel. —When did he start liking that stuff, anyway?" The redhead definitely did not. "I couldn't believe my ears when I heard him order it the other evening."

"Just about since he arrived in the Federation, apparently."

Her eyes darkened as she watched him go. Let Varn enjoy it, she thought. He still had an admittedly foolish spark of hope. By this time tomorrow, that would be extinguished, and he would be taking little pleasure in anything for a while, maybe for a great while to come.

Gray Jack Dundee found the Commando leaders waiting for him in their office. Islaen was already on her feet. Sogan started to rise at his entrance, but the Chief Admiral waved him back. "Sit! By all rights, you should still be in Sick Bay. You both probably should."

The colonel smiled. "We're well mended now, sir."

"Besides, Commandos prefer to take care of their own? Aye, I think I've noticed that." He laughed to see the Arcturian's color rise. "So you know about your three watchdogs? They were extremely polite about it, but the President of the Federation wouldn't have gotten through that door for the past few days."

Dundee squared his shoulders. He had always been a man who dealt fairly with his equals and subordinates, who rewarded ability and valor, and he was more ashamed of his inability to do so in this instance than he was of any other act or failure to act in his long career. The injustice of it was enough to sicken him.

"My congratulations, Colonel, Captain, and my thanks. Your unit did a fine job on every front. That space battle and your assault on the base both promise to become part of Navy legend." So, too, did the rescue that had followed the last. The shuttle crews had watched in disbelief as the little flier had descended into the jaws of the inferno with the colonel dangling from the long cable and had watched in even greater disbelief as the two Commandos had risen through that final vicious blast, each clasped in the other's arms. No one had imagined that either of them would be brought back still living to the *Terra's Charm*.

He studied the Arcturian somberly. "The Federation is making a miserly showing of its gratitude in your case, Captain Sogan. —Damn it, you're the best battleship commander we've got. You deserve a real command. Space, you deserve a fleet, and I have to send you back to Horus with a few warm words."

This was it, then. Everything was over. Varn Tarl Sogan felt that a planetbuster had detonated far inside him, leaving everything that had mattered of him in ashes.

He concealed the depth, the bitterness, of his disappointment. Dundee had not led him to expect anything else. "That was the understanding from the beginning, sir," the War Prince said smoothly. "Whatever I was in the past, I am a Commando now. That work is challenging." He made himself smile. "It is also uncommonly interesting."

Islaen sighed in her mind. Challenging and interesting, but he had not said it was sufficient. In this moment, she knew that, for him, it was not.

The uncomfortable interview ended shortly after that, and the Commandos were left alone in the office.

Both remained silent. Sogan's thoughts were walled behind impenetrable shields. His face was a mask.

"I'm sorry, Varn," Islaen said softly, aloud since he would give her mind no entry into his. Ability and courage had won so much for him already that he had let himself hope against hope and against all reason. He was now paying the price for that daring in bitter disappointment.

"I knew it would only be for a while," he replied dully. "I was fortunate to have been given the opportunity at all." In point of fact, he was not. This brief taste of major command had only recalled the past more vividly, only sharpened the longing.

He would accept none of the comfort she wanted to give. He had no right to it. It was his shame that he needed it and more shameful still that he had permitted Islaen Connor to suspect the dream whose death was such misery to him.

"I had hoped he would be able to arrange a more suitable command for you, too," his consort said. "The unit would still have remained intact. The Patrol carries Rangers now, and I think most major Navy craft will soon start carrying Commandos. You could have ordered that in any event. I've always followed your orders in space, so there wouldn't even have been any adjustment of practice involved."

He made her no response. Maybe she should have held quiet and said nothing, she thought, but she had wanted him to know that she had at least been willing for and not against him.

The War Prince battled his disappointment and unhappiness and the despair they brought with them. He still had his duty to his position and his duty to this woman. Answer her, he must, and answer as befitted who and what he was, what he had once been. "Your Federation has been a generous enemy. I had no right to expect the favors I have been granted, much less seek anything further. It is time that our unit returned to our own ships and our place on Horus."

He had spoken firmly, decisively. Islaen Connor might almost have believed him had he not still used verbal rather than mental speech, had he not continued to lock her so completely away from his thoughts and feelings, from himself. "Our work is important, Varn," she told him softly. "You have to know that. You've known what failure would have meant on every one of our missions."

Sogan willed himself to smile. He brushed her cheek tenderly with his fingers in his familiar caress. "I do not merit you," he said, "but go on now, my Islaen. Bethe and Jake are waiting for you."

She nodded. "Shall I send Bandit to you?"

"No. I am-tired. Let her remain with you, where she can have some enjoyment." She would find nothing of that at all in the darkness that was now his universe.

Chapter Twenty-Seven

The Commandos' flier emerged from the *Terra's Charm*'s transport hatch. Varn Tarl Sogan resolutely kept his eyes fixed ahead, on Horus. He had no wish to look back at the starship he had commanded so briefly.

Planeting in the little vehicle was always a tricky procedure even in cases like this when there was no need to make the entry in secrecy. He was glad of that fact now, for no one spoke, lest they distract him. He had little heart for the role he must forever play and was grateful for this respite before having to resume it.

They touched down smoothly, as if they were doing no more than returning from a visit to the port facility.

It was barely dawn, but the light was strong enough to clearly reveal the starships berthed on the planeting field, the *Fairest Maid* and *Jovian Moon* among them. The Arcturian could summon no feeling of joy or even a sense of comfort at the familiar sight of them. Splinter ships, such vessels were often called, and splinters they were, insignificant little sparks in place of the proud battleship he had been compelled to quit. It was a species of death to know that he would never again have better . . .

There was no need to feign the emotion his comrades had a right to expect from him. Another perfectly genuine one filled his mind, as it did those of his comrades. Even at this hour, there was a flurry of activity about the two fighters.

Scaffolding had been thrown up around them, and large maintenance crews were busy with both of them.

"Spirit of Space, what now?" Jake Karmikel demanded. "All the work was supposed to be finished long ago. Their skins certainly didn't need another scraping."

"We shall soon find out," Sogan said grimly as he sent the vehicle into high surplanetary speed.

They were not long in reaching their starships. The four were out of the flier almost before it had come to a full halt.

Maintenance Sergeant Max Lampry stepped forward to meet them and snapped into a full salute. The hull lights sparkled on the scales of his head and hands.

The Arcturian gave a sketchy return salute. "Max, what is going on here?"

"Busy work, sir," the Lemuran responded in a low voice. "May I board with you?"

"Of course. Islaen, Jake, Bethe, come with us."

Lampry stayed a pace behind Sogan, walking near him but making sure that he did not brush against or jar him.

Connor's eyes narrowed. Max was always careful about that, she recalled suddenly, and she had seen the two men work closely together many times during the unit's frequent stays on Horus. There were few secrets maintenance crews like these did not share about the starships and crews they serviced regularly. How much did the man suspect—or know—about the Commando-Captain?

She had no further time to ponder the matter. They were already in the crew's cabin, and Varn was facing the mechanic. "Well? What are you all doing here besides busy work?"

"Keeping an eye on the ships, actually, sir. We've arranged it 'round the clock, and we may be nothing more than vacuum brains for doing it," he finished honestly.

"I doubt that. Sit, and let us have the whole of it."

"There isn't much to tell, Captain Sogan. We've just noticed strangers, civilians, watching the ships a few times. The night crews have seen them three times. I've gotten a glimpse of them on a couple of more occasions during my shift."

"Civilians, you say?"

"Aye, sir, or so it seems. They're always cloaked. There are usually two of them, but once, four came. I saw them that time."

"People do come to take a look at the ships," Jake pointed out.

"The big ones, aye, Captain Karmikel, but not these little splinters. They wouldn't bother returning, would they, even if they did it once?"

"Not likely," the War Prince agreed. "Have you reported the sightings to Security?"

"Aye, sir," Lampry answered with a trace of disgust. "They dismissed it as nothing. They're probably right, too."

Sogan swore sharply. "Security should have given your observation more weight. Didn't the Commandos and Resistance fighters prove during the War that no starship is completely secure on-world?" He reined in his anger. "What did you do then?"

The Maintenance Sergeant was gratified by the strength of the dark-eyed captain's reaction. "What you see, sir. The *Maid* and the *Moon* are our babies. We've all put a galaxy of work and even more thought into them, and we weren't about to chance letting anything happen to either of them. You weren't here to take care of them, so we resolved to do it for you."

"You've just earned yourselves a unit commendation," the War Prince informed him. "Colonel Connor will have a word or two with Admiral Sithe and with Security, and I have a feeling your suspicions will receive a much closer hearing this time. False or true, this is a Naval base. Such a report as yours should never have been ignored."

"Thank you, sir."

"No, Sergeant. I thank you. We all do, and we thank your crews with you."

Sogan glanced at his own comrades. "I want energy pickets set around both ships immediately, and they are not to be dropped until we are actually lifting from Horus."

No sooner had Karmikel, Danlo, and Lampry quit the ship than the War Prince headed for the bridge to activate the *Fairest Maid*'s powerful picket.

Islaen Connor sighed. A crisis already, and Isis was not even fully up in the sky. This was not a promising start to what she had hoped would be a peaceful, restful day. *I'm programming the range, Varn. Syntheggs all right?* Space, they had not even eaten breakfast yet!

"Fine with me." The answer came over the communicator.

The woman bit her lip. She decided to continue with mind speech. Sogan was receiving it, at least, even if he still refused to respond in kind. That was an improvement over the total block to mental communication which he had maintained these last few days. *Stow our packs when you come back down.*

"Very well."

Varn returned from the bridge. He stood glaring in the direction of the hatch. "That vacuum-brained rabble this port calls Security should all be burned down," he fumed.

Easy on the drive, Varn. As you told Max, I'll speak with Sithe.

"Easy nothing," he snapped. "You heard Dundee say there are Arcturians on Horus, and your honorable Federation will never have the sense to keep them locked up. Some shooting star might burn a circuit and decide to avenge the Empire's fallen fortunes by blowing a Navy ship or two. The real ones would be relatively impossible targets, but these small craft could be viewed as having vengeance potential."

That's a little farfetched, Admiral.

"Is it?" he countered. "You chaps taught us the drill."

All right, she responded more thoughtfully. *You make a good point. I'll raise it, too.*

The War Prince nodded, satisfied, and caught up the two packs. He dropped down the ladder to the next deck with a spacer's ease and deposited the colonel's gear in her cabin.

The floor beneath him suddenly seemed to tilt, and he caught at the edge of Connor's desk for support.

In another moment, his sense of balance returned, but an unutterable weariness filled every part of his mind and body. He slowly slid his pack from his shoulder and rested it on Islaen's. Sogan's eyes closed. Damned regrowth! He had been doing well enough the last few days and thought he was over its effects, but all at once, here he was, completely drained again, like a blaster whose charge was spent.

He would have to knock out when he got to his own cabin, he decided. Postponing breakfast was no hardship. With his spirits so low, he had little interest in eating anyway and did so only out of necessity, under the lash of his will. The worst part of it was that this latest relapse would set Islaen worrying again . . .

Moving slowly, Varn reclaimed the pack he had been compelled to set down and crossed the deck to his own cabin. He dropped his burden on the floor beside the bed. The damn thing filled nearly the whole of the little space between bed and desk.

His face hardened. A proud final command for the admiral—former admiral—of the Empire's finest fleet, he thought bitterly.

The minute cabin seemed to close in on him. Forgetting his weariness, he headed for the hatch and only gripped himself as he was about to pass through it to the ramp. "Hold my share," he told his consort in what hoped was a reasonable approximation of a casual tone of voice. "I am going to the port for a while."

No problem, she answered, although he felt her question.

Sogan hesitated. "Would you mind if I did not return immediately? I would like to walk for a while."

Take whatever time you need. She paused and then went on, seemingly as a second thought. *Don't sever contact completely. I may need you.*

"I shall keep my receptors open," he promised. "Call if there is any trouble here."

Varn not leave! Islaen, stop Varn! Help Varn! The last was a plea.

"I can't, Love. Neither of us can. Varn needs some time to himself. All humans do now and then."

Islaen—

"He has a battle to fight, just as he must sometimes fight battles in space or with enemies on-world, and he won't let us help him. We'll just have to trust him, that and wait. Whatever move he makes will have to come from him."

Chapter Twenty-Eight

As he had not looked back at the *Terra's Charm*, Varn Tarl Sogan now refused to look at the *Fairest Maid*.

He gasped as a sharp gust of wind drove the already bitterly cold air through his jacket and seemingly into his very bones. After that, he ignored it. If he walked rapidly enough, he would keep warm, and it was his intention to walk, fast and far.

The War Prince left the planeting field itself and followed its perimeter until he reached the area where the larger vessels were berthed. He paused for a few minutes to watch the activity around them but moved on swiftly after that. He had no particular interest in these ships, but they reminded him too strongly of the minor status of his own and even more keenly of the unobtainable dream he had left in Horus' near-space.

Turning on his heel, he set his back to the planeting field altogether and moved into the port itself. He had no goal but kept traveling southward, generally following the flow of the already heavy pedestrian traffic.

At first, he attempted to block all thought from his mind but gave up on that. It was cowardice, and it was useless in any event. He would do better to face himself openly.

His efforts to bury the past and the desires, the hopes, that were its baggage had proven a stark failure. Now, he compelled himself to recall it, to relive the whole wretched business.

Most of his history had been bright. He had fought from boyhood and had gained victory after victory, and with them honors and rank. All would have been well had he had the fortune to fall in any one of those engagements, as befitted an Arcturian officer.

The end had begun, he supposed, when he had received the onerous assignment of invasion duty on Thorne of Brandine. He had fought that planet's powerful Commando-led Resistance and had fought them well, too, despite his guilty, ever-increasing respect and sympathy and his even more dangerous liking for the merchant people. His doom had been sealed when he had refused to burn off the valiant, vital world at his deranged commander's order at the War's end but had instead turned her and his own fleet over to Federation Admiral Ram Sithe in compliance with the treaty between the two combatants, the treaty his Emperor had signed.

Sogan recalled the numbing, bitter misery, the grief, of the surrender and his return in defeat to his own ultrasystem. His betrayal by his own aide and the court-martial whose verdict had never been in question had followed fast upon it.

There had been little delay between sentencing and execution. His consort and concubines had at least been able to embrace their own daggers and do it in private. Their offspring, his offspring, had not been so fortunate. They had been executed by blaster in compliance with the order to eradicate his seed from the race lest the weakness he had displayed be perpetuated.

He had watched them die, all of them, from the exquisite little seven year old, the daughter born of his last leave home and whom he had never seen before that cursed day, to his eldest son, only weeks away from the man's estate that would have spared him. The boy's eyes had met his in those last moments. They had not held despair but contempt only.

After that had come his own physical disgrace. Rank insignia and honors had been torn from his uniform and the tunic ripped from his body. Then the final stage of the execution had begun. Those endless whips were the last memory he had of his life in the Arcturian Empire. He had been condemned to be flogged through his fleet, maximum lashes on each vessel, beginning on his own flagship, and he had retained consciousness until about half way through the sentence on the third battleship.

In the end, his supposedly lifeless body had been cast adrift in a near-derelict lifeboat so that not even that should remain to pollute Arcturian space.

It had been an unexpectedly harsh and brutal sentence, but he had understood and accepted it. A War Prince's disobedience of a direct command from a superior was intolerable in itself, and his people had desperately needed a scapegoat, a target against which to vent their pain and grief over the first major defeat in their ultrasystem's long history of warfare, a defeat which had negated all the heroism, sacrifice, and loss that had preceded it. He had provided that.

Fate had shown him little kindness even then. His aged craft had carried him through most of the Empire and through the better part of the Federation until it had been pulled from space near the mining colony of Dorita, where he had been taken for a victim of his people rather than a renegade officer of their hated warrior caste.

His mouth hardened. He had to count that as the scene of his second failure, his second disgrace, he supposed, though he would no more alter the decision he had made there than he would reverse his sparing of Thorne of Brandine. He should have died. He should have put his blaster to his head at the earliest possible moment, yet when he had regained sufficient clarity of mind and strength of will do so, he had refused, and he had clung to that refusal through the three dark years that followed.

His meeting with Islaen Connor and Jake Karmikel on Vishnu had brought him the prospect of returned purpose and honor, and that he had seized.

He recalled the oath he had given to the Federation when he had accepted the commission the Commando-Colonel had procured for him, first in the Navy, then in the Commandos, and the more personal oath he had given to Islaen herself when they were joined here on Horus by the priest of her people's faith.

Those oaths were his answer and his command. The Arcturian War Prince had given them willingly, and they bound him now. He owed service and strength to both the woman and the ultrasystem.

There could be no running. He knew what he wanted, aye, an admiral's rank and an admiral's command, but that starlane was irrevocably closed to him. He had been set upon this other course, and it was his raw duty to travel it and travel it well. He had to return to his assigned place and responsibilities, to the sometimes bloody, always hard and dangerous work that was now his to do, and he had to return in such a manner that he would seem to have buried the false hopes and worthless longing of the past. It was a role he would have to carry for the remainder of his life. That much consideration, at the very least, he owed to Islaen Connor and to his other comrades, as he owed dedication to the cause and system he was sworn to uphold.

The former admiral's decision was a conscious one, an acceptance of mind ratified and supported by will, and with it came the determination to carry it through.

His mind and spirit felt lighter if no happier, and the boiling energy that had been driving him evaporated.

To his shock, nothing remained behind it. His muscles, his very will, seemed completely bereft of strength.

Sogan stopped. He fought to get a grip on his suddenly rebellious body, but he only swayed, and his knees started to buckle beneath him.

Islaen Connor carried her jakek back into the galley. It was stone cold, and she wondered if she should reheat it or just dump it out. Rewarming it would do no good anyway, she thought. It would just go cold again. She had contacted Admiral Sithe as soon as she had believed the hour to be decent and had turned her attention to making the *Maid* livable again after their absence, but through all that and ever since, her thoughts and Bandit's had been centered on the still-missing War Prince. This reacting and waiting was a new role for her, and she found that she had no liking at all for it.

The woman sighed as she felt her comrades' familiar patterns. More questions, she thought wearily, and she had precious few good answers to give.

"Up here!" she replied to Jake's call.

Karmikel was glowering when he joined her a few moments later. "Where's Sogan?" he demanded.

"In the port."

"That's the same answer you gave two hours ago and an hour-and-a-half before that and three hours before that. Now, where in space or beyond it is he, Colonel Connor?"

"He is somewhere in the port. I have no idea in the universe where. He left here this morning after setting the picket, and I haven't heard a flaming word since."

"That was twelve hours ago!" Bethe exclaimed.

"I am aware of that fact, Sergeant."

The range was already programmed for jakek. Islaen poured two cups and carried them into the crew's cabin. She did not particularly want to see anyone at the moment, but she knew she was not going to be able to send the pair off again, not this time. "He was hurting badly. He wanted to do some thinking."

"He always locks himself up on the bridge when something's riding him that hard," the captain reminded her. "The *Maid*'s his refuge, his little fortress against the rest of the universe."

Bandit gave two short, sharp whistles. Karmikel's head snapped in her direction. That was the rudimentary code they had worked out between them during the crisis on Tambora. One whistle meant yes. Two was no.

He looked from the dejected gurry back to his commander. "Would you care to elaborate on that, Colonel?"

"No, not at the moment, and you keep quiet, Bandit. I have problems enough right now."

The Noreenan man's eyes clouded. "Sogan has always loved this ship, Islaen. If he's rejecting her, he's in real trouble." A galaxy worse trouble than he had feared. Why in space or beyond it had Connor let the War Prince go off anywhere feeling like that, much less go off alone? "He shouldn't be wandering about the Spirit of Space only knows where," he said bluntly.

She bit her lip. "I know, Jake, but what could I do? I was between a nova and a dark hole. He couldn't work this out here with Bandit and me picking every other thought out of his head. Besides, how could I stop him? He's got the right to go into the port, and to stay there for a while if he so desires." She grimaced. "Isn't it spacer tradition, military and civilian alike, to vanish on the equivalent of Friday afternoon when in port and not return until sometime in the wee hours of Monday morning?"

"Space, you don't think—"

"No. I don't. Varn will be back when he's ready."

"He hasn't contacted you at all?" Danlo asked.

She shook her head. "No."

"You haven't tried to reach him?"

"No. I promised him the time. I haven't let Bandit try, either."

"I think you should start, Islaen, better still with all of us in the flier," the spacer said.

"Varn would be furious, and with reason."

"Think, Woman! By the time your talent tells us Sogan's up to his neck in something dire, it'll be too late for us to get to him," Karmikel told her. "I can put up with our admiral's temper. It's standing in the morgue identifying what remains of him that I couldn't take."

"That is enough, Jake!"

"Easy on the drive, Islaen," Bethe said quietly. "Jake wouldn't have said that if he weren't worried. So am I. After what you've just told us, I'm very worried."

The colonel pressed her fingers to her eyes. "Aren't you both forgetting that Varn Tarl Sogan isn't exactly a tyro? He's tough, he's smart, and he's able."

"He also gets jumped every other time he ventures into a new port, or an old one for that matter, for being exactly what he is."

"That's not precisely accurate," she snapped.

"Pretty nearly at times."

"All right, Jake!" his wife warned. "It isn't just that, Islaen. Even if he were fully himself, we'd be concerned at this point, but he patently is not. Varn's too driven by a sense of responsibility to let it go this long without contacting you. Space, he loves you too much to do this to you. I don't have to be able to read minds to see that you're in Alarm-One mode yourself."

The colonel gave up. "Aye, of course, I am. —I promised him time. I'll give him another hour. If we haven't heard anything by then and if Bandit and I can't reach him right away at that stage, we'll start a manhunt."

Chapter Twenty-Nine

If he had not been standing so near the wall, Sogan would have fallen. He leaned against it, as if casually, and tried to will strength back into his muscles.

He also took real note of his surroundings for the first time in many hours, and he recognized where he was with some alarm. If he had gone down here, no one would so much as have noticed, except, perhaps, for a moment's surprise that he had started his evening's celebration so early. Unless scavengers were about . . .

He had traveled an incredible distance. He was well to the south, more than fifteen direct miles, and he had not walked a straight route. The Navy portion of the planeting field was well to the north, as was the business district. Even the portion of the pleasure district used by the officers of military and larger civilian craft lay more than six miles north. This was the territory of the small spacers, the rankless crews. It was asleep yet, but soon, it would awaken. It would be alive then with light and noise and enough danger that patrons did not wander its ways alone, and at least half the members of any group remained sober to watch that nothing befell their more fortunate companions, a duty normally drawn by lot at the start of an evening's roving.

It was almost dark now, and it had grown bitterly, perilously cold. He had to get out of here at once, but the

Arcturian knew full well that he would never be able to make it back to the *Fairest Maid* under his own power.

His expression was bleak. Hired transports did not come into the district. He would have to get much farther north to have a hope of finding one, a journey also well beyond his present capabilities. The way he felt right now, he would be on his face before he had gone a couple of blocks.

Sogan looked about him. It was with reason that he had identified this block so quickly. Fortune had favored him in this, at least. There was a ready refuge only three doors away.

The War Prince reached *Isaak's* door. The room within was not crowded as yet, but the big bar was now manned by four tenders, all of them moderately busy. Most of the familiar tables had been removed to make space for the transient evening customers, but a few remained at the rear. None of them were occupied. That suited him, he thought. He always preferred to sit as much out of the main traffic lane as possible and with his back to a wall where it offered no tempting target to would-be assassins.

The Arcturian went inside. The heat, simply the absence of the wind, felt wonderful, and he had to check himself from just standing still to glory in it for a few minutes.

He went to the rearmost table and claimed it, then gave an order for coffee to be brought to him at once. The first cup, he downed immediately, using it to drive the cold from his body. He would sit a while with the second.

Sogan started to open his jacket but stopped himself and left it fastened save for a small space at the neck. It covered the uniform he had not bothered to remove. A Commando's tunic was likely to attract attention in this place, and right now, he wanted anonymity. He wanted oblivion.

He stared into his cup. Food would help, he knew, and so would this rest, but at some point, he would have to get himself back to his ship. There was little hope of his making anything like a full recovery in the time he would be able to remain here. In the worst instance, he supposed he could always contact Islaen and ask her to come for him in the flier, but the shreds of pride he had left at the moment rose up against calling for any such rescue. He would just have to wait to see how much of his own strength came back before this place became a danger in itself.

Varn looked up dully at the sound of loud laughter from the bar. It was a warning that he should be leaving now.

He lowered his head once more. That was impossible. His eyes closed in weariness and a return of despair. Spirit of Space, where was he going to find the inner strength to function as he would have to do when he could not even summon the ability to walk the six or seven miles to find the transport he needed to get back to the *Fairest Maid*?

Zubin of Malki slowed his rover. "Plenty of places to berth her." He announced the obvious to his shipmates in their own language.

"Don't put her in front of any doors this time, or some son'll puke all over her again," Gad told him.

Zubin pulled over to the curb and put on the brake. "All out."

"Cold night," Shadrak grumbled. "Gad and I'll warm up soon enough, at least. Too bad you and Tubal have to keep your navputers programmed."

"Our turn comes next time," the freighter captain replied. "Someone has to be able to keep you two out of trouble."

"And tuck you into your bunks sometime around dawn tomorrow," added the *Rounder*'s copilot. He looked around. "Nothing much seems to be going on as yet."

"We have to line our bellies anyway," Zubin said. "By the time we finish eating, the place should be alive. *Isaak's* over there should do. They make a solid meal."

They walked the half block to the eatery. As they neared it, Gad nudged his captain's arm. "Seems like the local scavengers are at work already. Those two have found their night's prey by the look of them."

"Anyone in a state to be of interest to those sons at this hour deserves what he'll get," Zubin said, although he eyed the cloaked pair with distaste.

"Anyone in that state this early isn't out having fun," Tubal corrected. "He's got half a galaxy of trouble to drown. — They're watching *Isaak's* for him to come out."

The copilot walked over to the door, as if checking out the place.

His shoulders straightened, and he swore viciously, although he kept his voice low. "You'd better have a look, Zubin," he said. "We're not letting the bastards have this one."

Zubin joined him. "Where?"

"The table at the rear."

A good few customers were at the bar. He ignored them and fixed his attention on the single man seated at the back. His head was bent over his cup. He seemed oblivious to the universe around him, or nearly so. Some stimulus, probably a burst of laughter or other noise from the bar, caused him to glance up for a moment to look at the revelers with dead eyes before lowering his gaze and sinking back into his private mist once more.

"Space!"

The Malkite captain pulled open the door.

"Time to go, Captain."

Varn looked up at the sound of the familiar voice. "Zubin?"

The big spacer blinked in surprise. "You're sober?"

"I am, of course," he snapped, then quelled his temper. "This is all I have had all day."

Zubin eyed the full cup. "You haven't had much of that, either."

"It is my second."

The Malkite's voice dropped. "Are you working?"

"No." He nodded to the chair opposite him. "Join me if you have a few minutes."

The spacer complied. He beckoned to Tubal. "Come on! Call the lads!"

The other Malkites were quick to obey. They settled themselves around the War Prince's table, Shadrak hooking a chair from the next one to accommodate himself.

Zubin glanced at the door. "Gone?"

"Aye," his copilot replied. "As soon as you came over here. —He's all right!"

Sogan flushed. "I am," he growled. "Captain Zubin, would you kindly explain what is going on?"

"A couple of port rats were real interested in you. They were stationed outside, across the street. —You hadn't spotted them?"

Varn shook his head. "No," he said grimly. "I was gathering stardust, I am afraid. I owe you again."

"Captain, what are you doing in a dive like this?"

He shrugged. "The coffee. I needed a break, and *Isaak's* was close. —What about yourselves?"

"We just wanted a change from our own cooking and came for a look around before going back north for a proper meal," he lied smoothly. "We spotted those back-alley boys and decided we'd do someone a favor."

"You did that," he said.

"Good. You can repay us by being our guest."

That was a statement, not a question or request, and Sogan sighed to himself. He could not in courtesy refuse, not in the face of the fact that he owed them on more than one count.

He knew the ritual. "My pleasure, but I pick up the first round." He would bend tradition so far as to order wine for himself, but he would have to go through with the rest of it.

At least, his problem of transport was solved, Varn thought wryly, and he made no further delay in sending out his mind to Islaen.

He found the colonel almost before his search began. She had obviously been waiting for contact from him. He could sense the anger in her but also a worry, a fear, that made him cringe to his soul. He was a damned bastard! Why had he been unable to remember the weight of dread he had felt the night of the building collapse on the pharmacy? He had been in no similar danger, aye, but to have kept silent for this long had been unconscionable . . .

Sogan apologized quickly and explained the situation in which he found himself, then severed contact again after promising a full accounting upon his return. He anticipated and deserved a thorough reaming, but he could not deal with it now, not and maintain any semblance of normalcy before his present companions.

Zubin glanced around the room. The place was beginning to fill up. "Finish that stuff if you want it, Captain. We'd better be getting out of here." He saw the smaller man's surprise. "*Isaak's* may be fine by day, but it's not for the like of you even now, and it'll be getting a lot worse real soon. If we don't move on, you could be explaining yourself to the Patrol."

That could very easily happen. The Stellar Patrol kept a close watch on Horus' port facilities and toured the various portions of the pleasure district frequently. The *Rounder*'s crew would draw no particular interest, but Sogan was different. With whatever darkness that had shadowed him gone, he looked to be as dangerous as they indeed knew him to be. A Patrol unit would be all over him the moment they spotted him. The uniform they could just see at the neck of his jacket would probably spare him any serious difficulty, but Zubin of Malki believed that the Commando would care for the embarrassment even less than for an open fight.

Varn nodded in immediate agreement. He did not want to have to add an encounter of that nature with the Stellar Patrol to the already long list he would have to recount to his colonel in a few hours' time. Fortunately, between the stimulus of the meeting with the Malkites and the brief rest, his strength had returned, at least to the point that he could trust his body not to give way again in the immediate future. "I am ready now, Captain Zubin."

"Where's your transport berthed?"

"I am on foot."

The other gave him a sharp look. "You walked from the *Fairest Maid*?"

"I like to do so, particularly when I have something to think through."

"There's plenty of room in ours."

Sogan and Gad led the way out of the eatery. They soon reached the street, but such a blast of wind caught them that both men were thrown off balance and forced back several steps. Had their companions following behind not steadied them, they might well have gone down.

"Space, what a night," the crewman grumbled. "I'll be glad to get back under a roof again."

The War Prince echoed that sentiment in his own mind as he set himself against yet another blast. He was glad now that he had met with the four. Travel in their rover was going to be a galaxy more pleasant than a long hike through this gale.

Four pairs of eyes watched them until the rugged machine turned the next corner and disappeared from their sight.

"He is not quite as drunk as we thought," Sivor Dord Mitree said.

"Very nearly. Besides, a little less, a little more, what matter?" asked his fellow lieutenant in disgust. "Did you see what accompanied him? By the gods, I would spend my life intoxicated as well if I had to companion with such things."

"This cannot be permitted to continue," the Arcturian colonel declared decisively. He was sick with shame for the man, sick that he had been forced to witness his disgrace, sick that it had occurred at all. "It is well that you summoned us."

"We still have received no orders to proceed against him," his captain warned.

"It is our duty to preserve the honor of the Arcturian Empire. That renegade flaunts it by the fact of his existence and even more by the manner of it. Varn Tarl Sogan has refused a soldier's death, and his conduct here is disgrace only. We shall watch. When we can take him alone, he will die, and in such a manner as befits the sorry thing he has become."

Chapter Thirty

Jake Karmikel looked at his timer. Islaen's hour was almost up, but he knew she would not try to reach the missing War Prince before the specified time was spent. "Gray Jack Dundee may be a fine commander, but I wish he had left us alone," he grumbled. "Sogan was doing grand until he hauled us onto that blasted battleship."

"No, he wasn't, Jake, not really," Islaen said glumly. "He hasn't been since that debacle on Amazoon. He was fighting, right enough, but he was losing." Her heart felt cold, empty. Maybe now, he had lost the whole damn war . . .

Suddenly, her head lifted, and she raised her hand for silence.

Have fun, Admiral! she concluded a short while later as Sogan broke contact again.

The Commando-Colonel laughed heartily. She shook her head. How in space did the man do it?

Her comrades looked at her in no good humor. "If that was the admiral, you might consider sharing the news," Jake told her sourly.

"It was," she informed them. "Varn will be late. It seems he's gotten himself kidnapped by the crew of the *Rounder*. He apologized and promised me the full story when he finally does get back."

Karmikel laughed as well. "It couldn't have happened to a more deserving War Prince."

"I'm mad enough at him right now to agree." She smiled at the image in her mind. "Seriously, though, Jake, he genuinely likes those four. It might not turn out all that badly."

"At any rate, they won't let him brood over lost opportunities."

"Well, he won't get into any trouble, at least," Bethe said wearily. She was tired now that the emergency was over, and she was not quite as inclined to be forgiving as her two companions appeared to be. Varn Tarl Sogan had given her a bad scare.

"No one's going to think a War Prince of the Arcturian Empire would be walking around with that particular bodyguard," Karmikel agreed. His face brightened in a smile of pure anticipation. "However, there is always the Malkite delight in a good, old fashioned, straight forward portside brawl."

"Forget it," Islaen told him, chucking herself at the idea. Varn did deserve a bit of punishment for all he had put them through today. "They wouldn't consider it sporting to involve an officer. That would put too much of a damper on their opponents' fighting spirits."

"All too true, I suppose," he admitted sadly. "I guess you won't want us to stick around to hear the tale first hand?"

"No. I want him all to myself, or to myself and Bandit, tonight. You can have your fun tomorrow."

The redhead took his wife's arm. "Good-night, then, Colonel. We'll leave you to your vigil."

* * *

The food was plentiful when it came and surprisingly good, although Sogan kept his eyes away from his companions' plates. Malkites liked meat, and they liked it in a far rarer state than an Arcturian considered acceptable.

The wine was fair. It was good for its type, but he did not favor the chewy, superfortified reds popular on Horus, nor did he care for it in such quantity. It was served almost brimming over in a goblet that would have been used for water in another setting.

The eatery itself was good enough. It was many degrees superior to *Isaak's*, but it was no *Lioness*, and he kept a wary eye on the other patrons. There was celebrating going on here as well. It was of a more restrained nature than was the norm farther south, but he was not about to let his vigilance lapse again.

His care was soon rewarded. Two men came inside, gave an exaggerated shiver, and headed for the bar. Their eyes made a casual sweep of the room's other occupants. Those of one fixed on the Arcturian and widened in disbelief. He yanked on his shipmate's sleeve to draw his attention.

Varn sighed and loosened his blaster, slipping the catch to stun, but the Malkite captain's big hand covered his before he could draw.

"Look there, Lads," Zubin whispered.

The four flashed wide, sharp-toothed smiles at the bristling spacers.

The pair stared, spoke together, and hastily turned away.

"See, Captain," Zubin said calmly. "There'll be no mistakes about your supposedly unpleasant origins while you're in our company." He grinned. "Or nobody'll try doing anything about them, at any rate."

Varn Tarl Sogan settled back in his chair. He was going to enjoy this evening, he decided. For once in his life since his arrival in the Federation, he did not have to concern himself about challenges because of his antecedents, and if someone did happen to raise the question, the Malkites would handle the situation swiftly and effectively. They had dealt with those spacers so deftly that he almost hoped he would have the chance to watch them at it again.

"That happens fairly often, does it?" Tubal inquired. The incident had amused him as well.

"Often enough to have lost its novelty." The Arcturian grimaced. "I did not become one of the toughest brawlers on this part of the rim because I coveted the reputation."

In the strictest sense, that was not accurate. He had been able to talk or bluff his way out of most confrontations, but the few occasions on which he had been compelled to fight had marked Varn Tarl Sogan as a man better left alone unless one had business with him, a man it was unwise to cross. Unfortunately, there had always been a steady stream of newcomers unaware of his reputation to keep his skills sharp.

Tonight, that would not prove the case, the War Prince told himself again. He compelled himself to relax and so far succeeded that he was able to fall in with the conversation of his companions and enjoy it without the drain of the perpetual guard he would normally have felt compelled to maintain in such surroundings.

The four men all eagerly pressed him for the details of the fight he had led in defense of Noreen of Tara, Islaen's homeworld. The nature of his answers as much as his ability to tell a story well held them enthralled. He had a fleet commander's ability to view the full battle, not merely the experiences of his single vessel, and so was able to describe the action in its entirety.

For the most part, though, he held quiet, listening to the others and himself prompting for detail. The life and outlook of a small rim trader differed drastically from that a military fighter crew. These men were often truly alone in a hard and dangerous lifeway. Some of their adventures, their escapes, stood well beside any Navy equivalent. Some of the others caused him to laugh heartily, freely, as he rarely did in these days of exile, save in the company of his own unit and not often even then.

Near the end of the evening, Sogan grew more serious. He questioned his hosts about the men they had seen watching him but received no satisfactory answers.

"Just a couple of port rats, Captain Sogan," Shadrak told him. "We couldn't so much as get a look at them with the cloaks they had on. You wouldn't have been able to track them down even if we had seen them, or charge them, either, if you'd caught them. They hadn't actually tried to do anything to you."

He smiled. "Thanks to you four." His expression shadowed. "There was a security issue at the ships. I was wondering if there might not have been a connection."

The Arcturian saw his companions start and went on quickly. "There was not much chance of it. We had just returned after a mission at daybreak, and I left almost immediately after setting the *Maid*'s picket. No one knew my plans for the day." Including myself, he thought wryly.

Varn decided to go a little farther. Between his admittedly illogical behavior and some of the responses he had given to the Malkites' questions, they had to be thinking he was operating with a few blown circuits. An explanation, he was not about to give, but an excuse should suffice.

"I had required heavy regrowth treatment at the end of the mission and underestimated the aftereffects. I suddenly ran completely out of fuel. That was why you found me in *Isaak's*. It was a matter of sitting down or falling down."

Zubin nodded sympathetically. "I've known chaps who did nothing but sleep and eat for a month after major treatment, big, healthy men like myself." In his personal opinion, the Commando had not done anything near enough of either of late.

"Can we hear about the mission?" Tubal asked eagerly.

Sogan hesitated. "I do not know how much of it the Navy will want to classify."

"Say no more. We don't want to be walking around with any Federation secrets in our heads."

Varn's eyes dropped as the memories rushed back. For that brief span of time, he had been alive, whole, as he had never thought to be again in his life. He had been more complete than ever in the past. This time, he had the battleship, and he had Islaen Connor. —Damn it, he had flown that ship and fought her. He had blown the Pirate Stars battleship. Without him, it was the *Terra's Charm* and all aboard her that would have been space dust . . .

"A rough one?" the Malkite captain asked with surprising gentleness.

"Aye." To cover himself and to counter the unwanted emotion, he drained the scarcely touched goblet before him.

It was replenished quickly. The Arcturian carefully moved the big glass a little away from him. His own comrades would not have done that without his request, knowing him as they did, but these were spacers. They would not force, but they would facilitate, particularly if they felt he wanted or needed it. If he was not careful, he could find himself in as bad a state as they had first imagined.

That was too strong a possibility with the effects of the regrowth still on him. It was dramatically enhancing the power of the wine. His head had suddenly begun to swim, and he had to fight the impulse to shake it.

The dizziness should pass soon, he thought and hoped, but Varn was very grateful right then to have the Malkites with him and grateful that they were showing restraint themselves. This place was not *Isaak's*, but danger could arise all too quickly here as well. He would not want to be in it alone with any shadow on his capability or control.

He wondered that anyone could consciously lessen or deaden his ability to react well in a setting as potentially perilous as a rim spaceport, even in the company of sober comrades. How did they dare, with danger ready to strike at any time and in completely unexpected form?

He had been incredibly fortunate today, he realized, both during the hours when he had wandered, oblivious to his surroundings, and later. Had Zubin's party not found him, he almost certainly would have had to deal with those scavengers. He might not have been drunk, but with his strength as reduced as it had been then, he could still have been taken down.

Varn glanced up too suddenly in response to exceptionally loud talk at the bar. The room before him seemed to shimmer, as if he were viewing it through a layer of water.

A surge of pure panic shot through him. He was almost certain his head would clear again well before the remainder of the meal was done, but anything could happen in the meantime. If he had to fight now . . .

He willed his fear to recede. His companions had been doing a fine job of keeping trouble at bay since they had encountered him in *Isaak's*. He could trust them to continue doing it until he was capable of his full defense once more.

They had apparently been prepared to step in for him when they had believed him to be helpless. Curiosity pricked him. "What would you have done if I had been tight like you thought back there?" he asked, although he knew it was the alcohol working in him that pushed him to do it. Before now, he had never so much as imagined finding himself in such a situation . . .

"We thought you were a lot more than just tight," Tubal informed him.

Zubin silenced his comrade with a glare. "The same as we'd have done for any other friend," he replied. "We'd have hauled you back to the *Rounder* before the Patrol came snooping around, sobered you up, and let you sleep as long as you liked before delivering you to your ship armed with a good story to explain your absence."

Sogan's smile caused the Malkite to frown. "Is it so strange an idea?"

"It would have been an absolutely unique experience for me."

Zubin gave him a look of pure disbelief. "You've never been—"

"No."

The spacer shook his head in genuine pity. "You've led a sad life, Captain."

The wind had eased off considerably by the time the Malkites' rover at last rolled to a stop before the *Fairest Maid*. The cold had increased, if anything, but the War Prince did not mind that. He would not be out in it for more than a few minutes. At least, there was no longer the danger of being blown off the boarding ramp.

He thanked his hosts and took his leave of them, then touched his mind with Islaen's. She had been aware of his arrival, of course, since he had opened his surface shields when they had reached the planeting field, but she had waited for his contact before speaking.

At last, Admiral! You're sober, I presume?

Aye, and I do not want to hear that fact questioned again tonight. He was not about to admit how close he had been to being very much otherwise for a while there, to the point that at one stage, just before his system had finally settled down again, he had feared he would have to request a temporary berth on the *Rounder*. It would have been preferable to presenting himself to his colonel in a less-than-steady condition, but he would not have cared to have had to pass what little remained of the night on Zubin of Malki's starship. He would have cared less still for having to return to the *Maid* some time the following day and face explaining that extension to his already excessive absence.

I sense a story.

One that will give you a laugh at my expense, he admitted a bit wryly.

I'll be looking forward to hearing it, my friend. —Come on aboard. I'll be with you as soon as I pay my respects to Captain Zubin and the others.

The Commando-Colonel gave him a quick smile as she passed him on the ramp, but she was careful to shield her inner thoughts. She felt anger on the Malkite captain, and it was not directed at Varn Tarl Sogan.

"Stretch your legs," Zubin told his comrades as Connor reached the rover. "Sit for a few minutes, Colonel." He gestured to the seat beside him.

She complied. "What is it, Captain Zubin?" she asked quietly.

The big man's eyes locked with hers. "Maybe I shouldn't be telling a Commando officer how to run her unit, and it isn't any of my business to ask what's wrong, but every spaceport out here on the rim is a dangerous place. A man doesn't belong roaming around in one if he doesn't have his wits about him. Your captain wasn't aware that a couple of the local microlife were stalking him proper. Space, he didn't even realize I was in the room until I spoke to him. That means he shouldn't have been there, not alone. He wouldn't have been if he were one of my lads."

Islaen quelled her instinctive rush of anger. There was no mistaking what lay behind that rebuke. They owed him as well. Space, if what she had read in Varn just now was true, the Malkite had not done them a favor. He had helped work a bloody miracle.

"You're right," she admitted. She decided to give him a full response. His consideration, his friendship, merited that, and she could do it without betraying Varn. "Varnt likes time to himself. I try not to overcrowd him, but I called it wrong on this occasion. I didn't expect him to go so far or for so long, and I didn't take the effects of his recent injuries and treatment into consideration."

"He mentioned a turn under regrowth."

The Commando nodded. "He inhaled fire. His lungs and throat were badly seared. It was still a near thing even half way through the treatment. —I hardly need say that I'm grateful for the rescue."

Zubin smiled. "That was my pleasure. Your Captain Sogan deserves a break he doesn't have to fight for himself every now and then."

Islaen Connor entered the crew's cabin to find the War Prince in his usual place at the table. He was trying without success to calm the gurry, who was pinned to his chest, her wings fully extended as if she were trying to embrace him. Her thoughts were coming with a speed that rendered them incomprehensible, and her whistle sounded like a small, shrill siren.

The woman frowned slightly. *You might take off your jacket, or are you planning to leave again?*

I cannot remove it. Bandit has impaled me right through it. I would have to break her legs to get it off.

"Bandit," she said sternly, "let him go and power down. You're giving him a headache. You're giving me one, too, and I just got here."

Bandit worried! Islaen worried! Bethe, Jake worried!

"All right, Bandit. Varn knows that."

Sogan's head bowed. "I am sorry for that, Small One."

Why not tell me about it? Islaen prompted. *You needn't go into everything.* She smiled. *Just don't leave out any of the parts with the Malkites.*

The Arcturian complied. He began with his near collapse, gliding over the bulk of the day by merely stating that he had been walking. He had so little actual memory of most of it that a description would have been impossible anyway, and he could not bring himself to discuss the thoughts that had occupied him.

He did not spare himself in detailing the events in *Isaak's*. That lapse had been serious, and he would allow himself no excuse for it. After that, he told her about the remainder of the evening with better humor.

Islaen was smiling by the time he had finished. Varn's ability to tell a tale did not diminish when it happened to be one on himself, and she liked the readings she was picking up. *You're amazing, Admiral.*

I was criminally careless and a fool besides, he said with a sigh.

Aye. You had a good time tonight, though, didn't you?

I did. His eyes darkened. *It was time that I needed, Islaen. I am just sorry for what it cost you.*

You're feeling better? Really better?

Aye. His mind closed briefly. Now that he had stopped being sorry for himself, but he was not going to confess that to anyone, not even Islaen Connor.

He smiled ruefully. *I was braced for a proper reaming, Colonel.*

You do deserve one, but Jake will take singular delight in your night's adventures. That will be revenge enough for me and sufficient punishment for you. Her face grew grave. *Or would you truly prefer to say nothing to the others? They do know you were with the* Rounder's *crew. They were with me when you contacted me, and I had to tell them that much.*

The War Prince shook his head ruefully. *They might as well hear it from me. With the way my fortune has been falling since we planeted here, they could too easily run into my Malkite friends and be treated to a somewhat different version.*

Chapter Thirty-One

Varn Tarl Sogan sipped his jakek and pretended to ignore the latest of his fellow captain's comments. In actuality, it was very effective. By this time, Jake Karmikel knew him well enough to hit just about any nerve at which he chose to aim, and the Arcturian's pride and sense of dignity were always prime and vulnerable targets.

He normally preferred to rely on his own sharp tongue and quick wit for his defense but had chosen selective deafness this time. He had earned a measure of punishment and should have to endure it. Besides, there was a dull ache gnawing away behind his eyes . . .

Islaen had left the ship early, taking the flier with her, leaving him to face their comrades' grilling alone. Bandit was with him, but she was too busy devouring the treats he was doling out to her to bother rising to his defense. She had heard Jake and him at one another too often to be concerned now.

He glanced at the Commando-Sergeant. Danlo was quiet, making little response to Sogan's story or, now, to her husband's verbal assault. Her anger must still be sharp, he thought, or her disappointment. He had been running yesterday, however he might prefer to label it or whatever benefit he had derived from it. She had come to expect better of him, and she had a right to expect better . . .

Bandit's demanding whistle recalled him to what she considered to be his responsibilities, and he hastily offered her another sugar triangle from the store in his hand.

Bethe's eyes narrowed. "What in space or beyond it are you doing?" she demanded. "That's the third one you've given her."

"I had a fair dinner last night," he explained defensively. "She has had to wait this long for her donation."

"Donation, aye. Orgy, no." The demolitions expert snatched the remaining triangles out of his hand. "You drove me straight out of my flaming mind yesterday, and you seem determined to begin the process anew today!"

The gurry squawked. *Is Bethe mad at Bandit?*

"No, Small One. Bethe is not angry with you. I think she would like to ream me within a micrometer of my existence and is nobly resisting the temptation. That makes her snarl at everything else."

"Actually," Bethe Danlo informed him coolly, "now that I see you're in one piece, what I'd like to do is strangle you, Varn Tarl Sogan."

"The reaming, I would have to endure. Strangulation is a bit extreme."

"Not from my bridge, Admiral."

The transceiver alarm interrupted the answer he would have made. "There is some mercy in the universe after all," he declared as he hit the response button to trigger the announcement that he was on his way to the bridge.

* * *

To the War Prince's surprise, the call was coming in neither on the interstellar nor the surplanetary transceiver but on ship-to-ship, which was normally used only for relatively close-range hailing between vessels in space.

He activated the controls. "Federation Starship *Fairest Maid*. Commando-Captain Varnt Sogan."

"Admiral Varn Tarl Sogan, rather, is it not?"

The War Prince's heart went cold, at the language used and at the voice that addressed him.

He compelled himself to answer evenly in the Basic he now spoke nearly as freely as his own native tongue. "That is a strange question posed in an even stranger language."

"It is one that you obviously comprehend."

"I am a Commando. Most of us are fluent in Arcturian."

"Enough! You know who speaks to you, but if five years have so dimmed your memory, I am Oburn Tarl Formin."

"I recognized the Emperor's voice." This time, his response was in the precise Arcturian of his caste and former rank.

"It is no longer 'my' Emperor?"

"I am no longer part of the Arcturian Empire," Varn Tarl Sogan responded coldly. "Citizenship was stripped from me along with rank, honor, and the seed of my body."

Sogan owed this man no allegiance, certainly not personally and none by reason of his oath to the Federation, yet he had come to stiff attention at the sound of the Arcturian ruler's voice, and he did not attempt to link his mind with Islaen Connor's.

Formin's voice was hard. "I did not have the Communications Officer of this battleship arrange this transmission to bandy words with you, Varn Tarl Sogan."

That was obvious, the Commando-Captain thought. The technical challenge of establishing such a link across the better part of the galaxy was immense. Why would Formin go to such lengths to contact a cashiered officer, dregs vomited from his ultrasystem five long years previously? How did he know to do so?

Sogan would not raise the questions. He had precious few advantages in this exchange. He would give the other man no opening, no sign of uncertainty, on which to build. Most assuredly, Oburn Tarl Formin would receive none of the instantaneous submission and compliance he could not but be expecting.

For the first time, the Emperor seemed uncertain. He had anticipated a quick offer of service or, at the lest, given the man's circumstances, eager curiosity. Sogan displayed no sign of either.

He tried another course. "You are to be congratulated on your survival, though I fail to understand how it could have come to pass." Or how it could have been permitted to continue.

Varn smiled coldly. He did not have to hear his former ruler's unvoiced question to recognize it. "I was sentenced to flogging, not death, although I was obviously not expected to live through the procedure. I found myself unwilling to sacrifice anything more in my defense of my Empire's—and

Emperor's—honor against a madman's unworthy command." He allowed his anger, his bitterness, to sharpen his tone.

"That madness had not been discovered at the time."

"No. Only the madness of the command."

Formin said nothing for the moment. "That is past. You are probably aware of the difficulties we are experiencing with the Pirate Stars as well as with other renegades, small-wolf packs, I believe they are called in the Federation, which are nipping at our rim trade and planets with increasing ferocity."

"I am." His lips curved into a humorless smile. This, the Emperor could not have learned yet. "I have just blown one of the Pirate Stars' battleships and the installation servicing her into space dust."

"With a two-man fighter?" the Emperor demanded.

"With a battleship," Varn Tarl Sogan replied contemptuously, "five thousand-class." He had little behind him in fact. Let Formin believe there was more. —Why was the ruler of the Arcturian Empire toying with him? What could he want with him? Such effort would not be made merely to torture an already broken man, nor was that pettiness in Forman's nature, whatever his other faults.

Once more, there was a pause. "You are apparently better situated than I had been given to believe."

"Seemingly so."

"Will you hear my offer, Admiral Sogan?" It was demeaning to speak like this here in the presence of his officers, but for the Empire's sake, it must be done. The renegade obviously did not intend to comply with any unadorned order of his.

"I will." Here it was, then, but the Commando's eyes were shadowed. That was a strange phrase for the Arcturian ruler, for any member of the warrior caste, to use.

"Since being apprised of your survival, I have learned something of your recent activities. You have done well with the Federation military, and, of greater interest to us, you have done well for them in space. It is my understanding that you have fought a number of engagements either with that spark ship of yours alone or in command of rabble fleets of small vessels, always against vastly larger forces and always with success.

"I have a plethora of fine space commanders, but none of them possesses your particular talent against the type of foes we are presently facing and must expect to face for an extended period of time to come. You are to head our war effort against them, Varn Tarl Sogan, as High Admiral of the Arcturian Navy."

The voice grew smoother, less authoritarian. The Federation had bought Sogan with that captain's commission. He could be bought again, bought back, for a higher price, and it was not difficult do deduce the lure that would move the former officer. That payment plus a call to the duty he had been bred to uphold should suffice to command the War Prince's services once more. "Naturally, you will not be expected to return without place or resources. You will be promoted to your new rank immediately upon your acceptance of it, and your honors will be restored, as will the star systems previously taken from you. As High Admiral, you shall, of course, have your own choice of flagship and her companion battlecraft in your personal fleet."

The War Prince was silent so long that Formin grew impatient. "Admiral Sogan, are you still there?"

"I am." He willed his voice to hold steady. "I have given my oath to the Federation."

"A mercenary's oath to the Empire's recent enemies? Sever it. —Varn Tarl Sogan, you are an Arcturian of the warrior caste, and you bear the responsibilities of a War Prince. The Empire's need of you is real and grave. Your duty requires your immediate return to active service. I, your Emperor and ultimate commander, order you to do so."

Chapter Thirty-Two

Jake stowed their emptied cups in the cleaner cabinet and returned to the crew's cabin. He did not sit again. It was time he and his copilot were getting back to their own starship.

Sogan rejoined them. He moved slowly to his place but remained standing beside it.

Bethe looked up in annoyance. "Don't hover, Admiral—" She stopped, her eyes narrowing. "What's the matter, Man? You're dead white."

"I have just been having an extended ship-to-ship conversation with Oburn Tarl Formin."

Karmikel hissed. "your Emperor! What in space or beyond it did he want?"

"Me." He took a deep breath. "He has chosen me for High Admiral of the Arcturian Navy to deal with the Pirate Stars. My star systems to be returned. Full rank and honors restored. My choice of flagship and the others comprising my personal fleet."

An expression of horror crossed Danlo's face. She quickly regained command of herself and masked it with a smile.

The Noreenan forced a smile as well. "Pardon our shock, Admiral. Congratulations seem to be in order."

"They would be unfounded, Captain Karmikel. I told the Emperor to go to hell. I specified which one. I—"

The War Prince sat down abruptly and covered his face with his hands.

Bethe slid along the bench to sit beside him. Her fingers closed on his arm.

Spirit of Space, Jake thought, where was Islaen? He rested his hand on the other man's shoulder.

Sogan lowered his hands to the table. His head remained bowed. "Sorry."

"Put it on freeze, friend," Jake said softly. "You've just taken a pletzar broadside straight in the gut. If you weren't winded, you wouldn't be human."

"Dropping a planetbuster on my own head is my concern, but what if I have rekindled the War?"

Danlo and Karmikel glanced sharply at one another.

"Varn, have you contacted Islaen?" the woman asked quietly.

He shook his head. "You do it." The communicator would be as fast for this. It had to be. He was not about to lower his shields. He dared not do so. If he did, he would shatter, and strength was required of him now.

He roused himself. "Admiral Sithe will have to be informed. Dundee, too, I suppose. That must be my task."

"No," Jake told him firmly. "Islaen first. We'll call in the brass once we've heard all the details. In the meantime, just sit there and power down for a bit. You've got one hell of an interesting report to give."

* * *

The Commando-Sergeant quit the crew's cabin for the galley before trying to reach her commander. Sogan did not have to hear this.

The colonel opened her communicator at once. "Aye, Bethe?"

"Islaen, get back to the *Maid* on all burners. The Arcturian Emperor has just contacted our admiral. They want him back. He's refused to go, and he's scared green that he's rekindled the War. His words."

"Space!" She was quiet for several seconds. "Damn him! His shields are set so tight that even Bandit can't get through them. Stay there with him, you two. I'll be back as fast as this misery of a machine will bring me."

Islaen Connor braked the flier before the *Maid*'s energy picket and spoke the release command that was keyed to her voice pattern, then sped through the space that opened briefly to admit her.

She came to a stop at the ramp. The work crew was there, busy with the tasks they had manufactured to cover their self-imposed sentry duty.

"Sergeant Lampry," she called.

He stepped forward and saluted. "Aye, Colonel?"

"You and your crews are armed?"

"We are."

"Admirals Dundee and Sithe will probably be arriving shortly. Admit them, but no one else is to board either of these ships or so much as approach them without my knowing it." She met his strange eyes steadily. "Be subtle about it, but this is important, Max."

"You four can depend on us, Colonel Connor."

The Commando-Colonel wasted no further time. She took the steps of the core ladder a brace at a time until she reached the crew's cabin.

All three of her comrades looked tense and grim.

Varn was deadly calm. He was pale, and his shields would have deflected a fleet assault, but he had braced himself for the ordeal ahead of him.

"All right," she said briskly, "what happened?"

"The Emperor offered him a job. He turned it down," Jake told her.

"Tell me everything you can remember, Varn."

Sogan repeated the interview very nearly verbatim. Only of his own thoughts, his own feelings, did he not speak. He spared himself nothing of the rest.

Karmikel swore fluently when he had finished, drawing upon all the languages in which he was proficient for material, including Sogan's own.

The War Prince seemed scarcely to have heard him. "I should have held my tongue," he said dully. "All the innumerable lives—"

"Easy on the drive, Varn. You have not restarted the War," his consort told him with an assurance she did not feel.

Varn did right! Bandit declared indignantly.

"Aye, Small One, but I did not speak wisely. Many others may suffer because of my words."

"For whatever it's worth, we're all damn proud of you," Bethe Danlo said softly.

He looked at her, surprised, but said nothing.

Bad Emperor hurt Varn? Bandit asked Islaen, speaking to her closed thoughts.

Aye, Love. Very badly, I'm afraid. She stood up. "I'm going to contact Sithe and Dundee. I've already told them that I might have something of major importance to report and asked them to stand by. Sithe'll be waiting, and I imagine Gray Jack Dundee will as well."

It was not long before the colonel returned to her comrades. "Both were there," she informed them. "I gave them a nasty start."

"We are to go to them now?" Sogan asked.

"They're on their way to us, as I figured they'd be. Our orders are to sit tight until they arrive."

The two admirals reached the *Fairest Maid* in a span of time that indicated they had shown no regard for Horus' speed limit on the way from headquarters.

In accordance with Islaen's orders, they entered without challenge and hastened up the core ladder of the small starship to the crew's cabin deck.

The Commando unit was waiting for them inside. Connor and Danlo were sitting on either side of the Arcturian. Karmikel was leaning against the wall, close enough to touch the other man. He looked angry enough to burn down anyone daring to enter the cabin. Even the gurry seemed ready to launch herself into attack.

The three started to rise.

"Stay put," Dundee growled. "Let's have the story, Sogan."

Varn Tarl Sogan faced them with an almost frightening control. He repeated his account of his exchange with Oburn Tarl Formin, speaking in the precise manner of an officer making a report. Had it not been for a certain deadness in his voice and his stark pallor, he might have been describing an incident of no direct interest to him.

Only at the end did his mask fail momentarily, and that through amazement. When he reiterated his response to the Emperor's demand, Gray Jack Dundee gave a crow of pure triumph. Even the more reserved Sithe laughed aloud in delight.

The War Prince looked warily from one to the other of them. His guards had slammed back into place almost as soon as they had wavered, but Islaen had read his bewilderment. She felt sorry for him. He had often said, only half in jest, that the denizens of the Federation were stark mad. Now, he was just about convinced of it.

His lack of comprehension was equally apparent to Dundee. "I'm sorry, Captain. We haven't quite blown our circuits. It's just that you have joined a long and distinguished line in the ancient Federation tradition of giving succinct replies to would-be tyrants. Your comrades will be happy to recount some prime examples for you when life calms down again."

The Terran smiled. "As for the possibility of renewed hostilities between our ultrasystems, you can rest easy on that."

Varn said, "Formin is fond of his dignity, sir, and if that was a true ship-to-ship transmission, there were almost certainly witnesses."

"All you Arcturians are fond of your dignity. That is a most useful weapon for us right now. The Emperor is not going to want this particular incident broadcast among the rank and file, is he?"

"No," Sogan admitted. "If he had been completely alone, he would say nothing about it at all. The fact remains that he was given insult in the presence of his officers."

"He's not such a fool as to go to war over it. He just admitted the Empire is in no way ready. He—and those officers—know we'd smash them again, and then the Pirate Stars would snap up the remnants.

"He can't protest through diplomatic channels, either, not after having tried to subvert a member of the Federation military into desertion. As for trying extradition, you are a full-fledged Federation citizen with three highly legitimate planetary affiliations. You can't be touched by an alien system."

"I could give myself up voluntarily. To prevent another War, I shall."

"That will not be necessary, nor would it be permitted," the Chief Admiral snapped. "It could not be permitted. That would create too deadly a precedent. You were in the right on all counts, not Formin."

"They could reveal Varn's identity to cause him and the Navy stellar-class trouble," Islaen pointed out.

"Aye, but I doubt that they will after we subtly outline the story we have to follow any such announcement. First, there is the matter of what they did to him for sparing Thorne, then, five years later, they realize their mistake and want him back to fight their battles for them again, after he's made himself our most highly decorated soldier, and lastly, they try to use gross bribery to influence a man with a history of integrity like Varn Tarl Sogan's. Spirit of Space! They'd come out of it as nothing short of the fools of the galaxy, individually and as a race!

"There is the outside possibility of a shooting star or two trying to seek revenge and personal advantage. We'll watch for those and neutralize them, but they won't be allowed to create any intersystem incidents."

Ram Sithe nodded, but he looked grave. "The worse danger is that of a personal attack on Captain Sogan. An odd man could slip in and cause considerable trouble if he were determined enough and clever enough."

"I have always had to guard myself against back-alley work, sir. It is part of life on the rim."

"I'm aware of that. You'll have to be even more cautious for a while. —I shall assign a watch on your ships as a precaution."

"We already have one, sir," Islaen Connor told him.

He looked puzzled, then his brows lifted. "Your mechanics?"

"They're Navy soldiers, too, sir, and well trained, although we all tend to forget that fact. No one will get through them and our pickets. Once we're back on Thorne of Brandine, no strangers will reach us at all."

Dundee nodded. "Well done, Colonel. —We two had best be going now. Ram and I have some transmissions to make."

His eyes rested sympathetically on Varn. "I realize it isn't much comfort at the moment, but you made the right decision, Captain Sogan. Speaking from my old preNavy days as a trader, that wasn't as good an offer as it sounded."

"I know that, sir."

The Chief Admiral smiled. "You'll have to stay on the *Maid* until we get some details settled, just so we can reach you fast should we need you, if for no other reason. I suggest that you all try to relax for the next few hours and then knock out early. It's been nova of a day, and tomorrow may be as busy if not as bad if we admirals fail to accomplish as much today as we intend." His eyes sparkled. "I'm only suggesting, mind you, not ordering. I don't want to risk having Captain Sogan consigning me to the same spot as he did his former boss. We'd make terrible neighbors. Right now, I'd probably throttle the son of a Schythian ape if I could get my hands on him."

Jake scowled. "Dundee would have to wait in line," he stated once Islaen assured her comrades that they were alone in the starship once more. "I'd love a crack at that bastard. I wouldn't leave enough of him intact to allow for a proper burial."

He gripped his rage with visible effort, and his expression became more thoughtful. "What I don't understand is why he handled it like that, like a—purchase." He spat the last word out. The humiliation of it left him sick. That might have been done to anyone else in either ultrasystem, but not to Varn Tarl Sogan.

Varn's eyes raised. They looked infinitely tired. "It was only natural, I suppose. That is the way he sees me, as a renegade mercenary in the pay of my system's enemies." The words all but choked him. "Perhaps I am that in truth—"

Bethe Danlo's hand caught him hard and sharp across the face. "No more of that rot! No more of it ever again!"

She stopped in dismay. Her fingers touched the place where his cheek was already reddening after her blow. "Varn, I'm sorry! I wanted to tear Oburn Tarl Formin, and I tore you instead."

"It is all right, Bethe. I want to tear someone myself."

He came to his feet. "It is not likely, but another transmission might come in. I had best wait on the bridge for a while."

"Link with me if you do hear anything," Islaen told him, "and open your communicator. We'll keep ours ready to listen in, just in case."

"I shall."

Do you want to be alone, Varn?
Aye. —No, not completely. Maybe not at all later.
Call when you want me, in mind or in person.

Chapter Thirty-Three

Varn Tarl Sogan woke slowly. A flight chair did not make the best bed, and, as always, his back protested his spending the night there. He had been warm enough, at least. Islaen must have spread the spider silk blanket he had just brushed aside over him after he had finally drifted off.

He sat up. The colonel was standing beside him, a cup of steaming jakek in her hands. Bandit was perched on her shoulder, openly disgruntled because no food accompanied the beverage.

He accepted it gratefully. *Thanks. I can use this.*—"Never mind, Small One. I shall have a proper breakfast soon for you to share."

Good! Very soon?

"You greedy little thing! Let him have some peace first." Islaen watched her husband. He did not look too bad, more tired than anything. *How are you doing?*

A bit stiff. He hesitated. *Our two comrades yesterday,* he began uncertainly. *Their anger seemed greater than mine. I— did not expect that.*

You shouldn't be surprised. An insult, an injury, to oneself is easier to bear than a similar hurt to someone we— to a friend. Her eyes met his. *More than need and battle skills unite the five of us, Varn. You know that. You've proven it yourself often enough.*

His fingers brushed her cheek. *Aye, I do know it, Islaen Connor. I find it hard to remember on occasion,* he added ruefully.

Bandit flew to the arm of his chair and peered up at him. *Varn's staying on* Maid?

"I am, Small One. If I left, who would I have to spoil? I could not have brought you and Islaen with me, you know."

Her feathers ruffled in alarm. She had not considered the possibility of a real, permanent separation from either of her humans. *Varn needs Bandit!*

"Power down!" he laughed. "Of course, I do."

The gurry relaxed. *Varn spoils Bandit! Islaen spoils Varn!*

"Bandit!" The woman shrugged. *In point of fact, I want to do just that. You could use a massive dose of it—even if you do have a bad habit of scaring the starlight out of me with remarkable frequency.*

He smiled. *It comes with the job.* The man sighed. *Speaking of that?* He glanced at the transceiver.

Nothing from that source, obviously, or it would have woken you. Admiral Sithe himself dropped by early to let me know that all the necessary arrangements have been made to shut out trouble. That means we're free to go about our business again.

Early? What time is it now?

Half ten, as we Noreenans phrase it. Don't worry. Jake's still snoring away, or he was when I came up. He and Bethe stayed on the Maid *last night.*

* * *

Their comrades were just starting breakfast when the pair came down from the bridge.

The sergeant promptly fetched two filled plates for them and sat down again herself.

"Good morning, Admiral," Karmikel said casually. "I hope you don't have another such interesting day planned for us?"

"Perhaps," he responded thoughtfully. "I cannot permit you to grow bored and lazy." His eyes fell. "I-wish we could have managed it without drawing in Dundee and Sithe." Whatever the control he had exerted over himself, he had been in poor condition to face them, in poor condition to face any outsiders, yesterday. He had wanted only his own.

The other man shook his head. "Never mind. They should have to earn their exalted salaries now and then."

"That they should," Danlo agreed. She scowled. "I'll never be able to hear that flaming transceiver go off again without leaping out of my hide."

Jake studied the other man. "Don't answer if you don't want to, Sogan, but what did it feel like to tell Formin where he should be residing?"

"Damn good." He smiled, savoring the moment. "Then the universe novaed on me."

"You did a nice job of doing that to us, too," Connor told him.

Both turned to their plates and ate quickly, slipping choice portions to the seemingly ever-hungry gurry.

Varn raised his cup. He frowned at it, then shrugged and drained the jakek.

The Commando-Colonel straightened. "I understand from Max that the work has been completed on the ships. Admiral Sithe tells me that all we have to do is wait for Dundee to boot his Arcturian diplomatic party off-world with a stiff lecture on the impropriety of trying to corrupt Federation military personnel ringing in their ears. Apparently, they don't want us sharing Horus' near-space with them. After that, we can go anywhere we like for a while. I've already said Thorne, for four uninterrupted weeks, minimum."

Sogan laughed. "It will never happen. Sithe will stumble onto some problem or other before half that much time passes and send for us."

"It'll happen, my friend," she told him firmly. "I gave you my word on that. Besides, I think he'll be happy enough to keep us buried for a while this time. We're responsible for stirring up the entire Federation High Command and upper government, even though he and Dundee have worked a not-so-minor miracle and managed to keep our names out of it, praise the Spirit of Space. I want to lift as soon as we get permission.

"Jake, Bethe, you two see to picking up whatever supplies we still need to acquire for both ships. Varn, you said you had business at the supply depot?"

"Aye. I am canceling the other part of our order. It was not fulfilled as promised even after we filed our complaint, and Max had to scrounge and trade to meet our requirements."

"They'll be pleased to hear that," Karmikel commented.

"As you have pointed out on occasion, I can be an arrogant bastard. If they want to continue our previous discussion, I shall be willing to accommodate them. It will not end to their satisfaction."

"What about you, Colonel Connor?" the redhead inquired.

"I'll be attending to Thornen business. The Doge asked me to check on luxury silk prices before we lift. Bandit and I'll pop over to the market and see to that."

Varn frowned. "Thornen textiles, particularly the silks, are far too fine to move well on the rim if he attempts a straight penetration. Harlran should try to get them into the inner-systems first, to Hedon, if possible, and to Terra herself. Establish them there, and they will soon work their way back out again as luxury imports already known and fashionable among the ultrasystem's elite. It seems indirect, but I believe that will be our best course in the end."

He stopped in embarrassment when the saw the way the others were looking at him. "What is the matter?" he demanded testily. "Why should planning a merchant campaign be different from planning a military one? As long as I am not expected to engage in any of the actual bartering—"

Bethe Danlo rolled her eyes. "The Lady of Traders forefend! You're hopeless at it."

Karmikel gave an exaggerated shake of his head. "It looks as if you're going to prove an asset to this unit after all, Admiral."

"Back off, you two," their commander ordered. "I believe Varn happens to be reading it right. However, I've been requested to check the prices, and check them, I shall. Harlran wants to sign up those freighters now, and he needs to know where to send them with what."

"Well, our job's easy," the demolitions expert declared as she came to her feet. "We pretty much know what we require. Are there any special requests?"

"Coffee," Sogan said. "Genuine Terran. Do not stint on the quality."

Jake stared at him in amazement and groaned.

Danlo stared as well, then smiled her approval. "Excellent idea, Admiral. We could do with a change now and then, and I happen to make an excellent cup of it. My father and brothers all loved coffee when we could acquire a supply, and I'm hardly adverse to it myself."

"Traitor," muttered her husband.

"Put it on freeze, you big space tramp," she said archly. "You don't have to drink the stuff. You can always program the range for jakek." She smiled again. "Anything else, Admiral?"

"Chocolate."

"I know," Jake said. "Also genuine. To replenish Bandit's supply. It would never do to have to ration her treats."

Karmikel and Danlo dropped off, first Varn and then Islaen, before starting to collect the items on their fairly extensive lists.

The War Prince was not long in concluding his business at the depot. As the Noreenan had predicted, the cancellation of the order was not well received, but Varn Tarl Sogan had his will, and the business was soon concluded to his satisfaction.

That done, Varn was free of other duties. He would seek out his consort, he decided. She should not be long, either, and they could rejoin their comrades at once or perhaps spend some time together in the port. The day was cold, but it was bright and clear, a fine one for walking. He would enjoy seeing the silks as well. Perhaps there would be something for Islaen . . .

He moved briskly until he came to the place he sought. It was a street, a long alley really, that would cut the distance between this district and that of the cloth merchants by more than half.

Sogan studied it carefully before venturing inside. This was the first day of the weekend, and the office and commercial establishments lining it were all closed and silent. There would be no witnesses to anything happening within and no one to summon assistance, Patrol or medical.

The alley, since it truly was a commercial byway, was clean enough and reasonably clear of debris, but refuse crates and bins lined the walls near most of the buildings. There was some loose garbage, but not a great deal. The worst place that he could see lay about one hundred yards in. There seemed to be a lot of glass there, bottles in various states of destruction, and he figured that some sort of target competition must have taken place there the previous evening. That was a popular form of entertainment for spacers and civilians alike on most rim worlds. No one objected as long as reasonable precautions were taken to prevent accidental injuries to participants and bystanders.

Everything seemed to be quiet, and the light was good with Isis well up in the sky. He loosened his blaster and slipped off the safety, then entered the passageway. He walked rapidly, determined to get through it as quickly as possible, but he paused to glance at the glass-littered place. There were a great many small pieces and a number of larger shards. Some person or persons who understood the handling of a blaster had been at work here. If a contest had been held, it would have been interesting to watch, he thought.

Four cloaked men had seen the Commando-Captain go into the supply depot. They entered the small eatery opposite it, ordered and paid for unwanted jakek, and watched. When he came out still alone, they rose and, after waiting a few moments, left their make-shift spy hole as well.

When they saw their quarry enter the alley, Barnak Fran Urtine nodded. "This is our chance, I believe. It may be our only one, so let us not waste it."

The colonel felt relieved now that the moment was come. Varn Tarl Sogan had once been too fine an officer, too fine a man, to go on as he was. His would be a hard death, an execution of sorts, since he had proven himself unworthy of better, but it would be an act of mercy as well. He hoped it would bring the renegade peace in the end.

The Arcturians entered the narrow space after their quarry, moving quietly as shadows, quickly as thought. They knew better than to try to hunt a Commando down in such a place, and that the former admiral now was. Their only hope of success was to strike fast and strike hard, before he realized they were there.

Sogan had barely gone one hundred yards before Urtine's blaster spat fire.

Varn cried out in pain and crashed down as the angry, narrow beam seared through his legs inches above the knees.

His attackers, four of them, were upon him almost in the same moment. Two hung back a little. Two came on.

The first to reach him slammed his boot into the downed man's abdomen in a blow that left him winded and momentarily helpless.

The men dropped their cowls as if on signal. Sogan's heart went cold. The stern cast of feature would have told him what they were even without the short, narrow beards skirting their jaws such as he himself had once worn. His own kind, and there was an implacable purpose on them, purpose and disgust, as if they were in the presence of something foul and debased.

Urtine looked down on his victim, not without compassion. He hated what his duty required of him. In truth, had they been alone, he would have given the man a decent death, little though he merited that grace, but he could display no such weakness before his subordinates.

"You lacked the courage to die as an Arcturian warrior, as one who had been an officer." He spat out the words, making a sentence of them. "You consent to exist in a manner that is a shame to our entire race, aye, to the lowest menial of our race. You shall die now, not as the man you once were but as the debased renegade you have become."

Once more, he struck down with his foot, this time brutally hard against the ribs.

The Commando tried to gather his strength, his wits. He knew what was to come. They would break any power of his to struggle against them with another couple of blows and perhaps burn through his arms as well to insure his complete helplessness. Then they would finish him slowly. Arcturian officers, as he knew this one, at least, to be by his speech, were skilled in weaponless combat. They could inflict a lot of punishment, a galaxy of pain, before killing an opponent, and these appeared to be determined that he should know the full of it.

Varn Tarl Sogan was not minded to accept that. He had walked meekly to his execution because he recognized his guilt and the right of the court-martial to pass sentence. He granted no similar authority to these back-alley would-be murderers.

Sogan sent out his mind, found and grasped Islaen's, which had been desperately seeking him since the first waves of his pain and fear had seared into her. He described his situation and location and then severed contact. For now, for the next critical seconds and minutes, whatever poor hope he had of survival depended upon himself alone.

His enemies did not believe that he could fight with the damage he had already sustained and with his blaster trapped beneath his body, but the War Prince had skills beyond even those of an Arcturian officer. He had also been schooled in the Federation's rough rim ports where only survival mattered in a fight. Commandos killed cleanly. These four preferred torture and so had given him his chance.

The bolt that had felled him had been a straight hit. It had cauterized as it had burned, stopping most of the bleeding, but the pain of it was intense. He allowed his face to show his agony, his hands to clasp and unclasp convulsively with it.

The boot raised to slam down on him again. As it did, he grabbed for the half-shattered bottle that had been his target, grasped it by the neck and flung it in one desperate motion.

The unwieldy weapon flew true. Its jagged shards ripped through Barnak Fran Urtine's neck, tearing open windpipe and arteries, tearing everything nearly back to the bone.

Even as he threw, Varn rolled, freed and fired his blaster, felling the second near assailant.

The remaining two flung themselves aside and dove for cover.

Sogan half-crawled, half-rolled to the crates, fortunately full, stacked beside the wall closest to him. He wedged himself behind them and waited for the attackers to make their next move.

Chapter Thirty-Four

Islaen Connor gasped and froze as her consort's pain ripped into her. More pain followed fast and with it gut-wrenching fear.

Varn's hurt!

I know, Bandit! Be very quiet. See if your mind can find him.

His call came. He gave his information calmly and severed contact again.

The Commando-Colonel activated her communicator. "Jake, Bethe, Varn's under attack and wounded. Arcturians, four of them." She gave the location and ordered the pair to head for it as fast as the flier's drive would take them.

Bandit, find Varn, she commanded. *Tell me how it is with him and with his enemies, but don't get involved yourself. There are too many of them.*

Islaen was running as she spoke, but she was desperate. There was no way she would be able to reach the Commando-Captain in time.

She turned a corner, and her eyes widened. A rover was just coming to a stop at the curb ahead of her, its driver an ugly man who seemed to her in that moment to be a vision from the bright paradise of her people.

She raced to the vehicle. Its hood was retracted to take advantage of the bright, brisk day, and she did not waste the time needed to open the door. She vaulted over the side. "Zubin, Varnt's under attack!" She told him where to go.

The big spacer threw his rover into high speed. He asked no questions, but he drew his blaster with his free hand and moved the setting to slay.

"These are Arcturians, Zubin," Connor told him quietly, "not just port rats."

The Malkite stiffened, but the weapon stayed steady in his hand.

Fire burned along Sogan's neck beneath his jaw. A near miss. A sear, maybe. It was nothing more. A real strike there, even a partial strike, and he would be a dead man or so injured as to be out of the battle.

His answering bolt came fast. It was a hit, but the vehemence of the curse it drew told him no significant damage had been done.

He shifted his position so that he could not be targeted along the line of his bolt, bracing himself as he did against the pain even that slight movement elicited. His face was grim. He would continue to give battle as long as possible, but this was a fight he could only lose. His enemies were whole and fully mobile, whereas he was confined to the place in which he now lay. All they need do was to keep him pinned down until one or the other of them could move into a spot from which he could get a clear shot at the Commando. Space, the Arcturians knew how badly he was wounded. They need only wait for pain and shock to overcome him and then finish him off at their leisure.

* * *

Islaen and Zubin sprang from their vehicle but approached the alley carefully. The sound of blaster fire told them the battle was still on.

Renegades see Varn! Burn Varn soon!

Connor's lips were a hard line. With Sogan badly injured and visible to his enemies, his life was measurable in seconds only. If she and Zubin failed to take the Arcturians down in their first attack, her consort was a dead man.

Islaen leaped inside. She spotted the hunters. They were maneuvering to make their kill. One was preparing to fire.

Her blaster discharged first, and he crumpled.

The second Arcturian jumped back into better cover. Lassur saw the two newcomers and realized he was probably finished, but he raised his blaster again to make an end of the man he had come to slay. There should still be time for that . . .

His body jerked violently under the impact of Zubin of Malki's bolt, his weapon falling from his already lifeless fingers.

Bandit, any more of them?

Nooo! Renegades dead! Help Varn! Hurting bad!

I'll try, Love. Keep watching for other enemies.—"Zubin, check those sons. Give them another bolt if you're not sure of any of them."

"Will do, Colonel."

Sogan leaned back against the nearest crate. His face was white and lined with pain, but he smiled when his consort approached. *Perfect timing, Colonel. Thanks.*

Varn—

I shall be fine now, he assured her.

She glanced up. *The rest of the troops have arrived.*

Islaen raised her communicator. "It's all right now," she informed their comrades. "We've cleared out the lot here, and Bandit says there are no more. Pretend to look anyway. Zubin's with me. Bring the renewer. Varn's hit pretty badly."

The Noreenan turned her mind on Sogan. He made himself lie still. It was a strange sensation, as always, as if tiny, careful, knowing fingers were touching and studying every cell in his body.

Islaen stopped suddenly. She looked at him sharply. He had taken more than those blaster burns through his legs.

I was not to be given a clean death, he told her tightly.

Her eyes dropped, and she continued her examination. *You were lucky,* she informed him at last. *There's been no major internal damage, though we'll have to conceal our knowledge of that fact until Medical confirms it.*

Zubin went from one corpse to the other, gazing pensively into their faces. His brows raised when he saw the torn throat of Varn's first victim and the neat hole through the forehead of the second.

He joined Sogan and Connor as the two newly arrived Commandos finished their supposed check of the area.

The Malkite whistled when he saw the War Prince's legs. "You did that with those burns?"

"Commandos are supposed to be tough, Captain Zubin."

"So are Arcturians."

Varn gave him a quick look but detected no sign of double meaning. He scarcely cared at that point. Where was the renewer?

Jake was carrying it. He handed it to Islaen and knelt, drawing his knife to cut away the remaining shreds of cloth from around the wounds.

"The tunic, too," the woman told him. "The sons of Schythian apes went to work with their boots after incapacitating him."

Karmikel swore bitterly. He could make a good guess as to the reason and did not want to look at his injured comrade.

"Why?" Zubin demanded hotly. "Why any of this?"

"Because he's worth ten times their whole accursed ultrasystem, and the maggot's spawn are well aware of that fact!" Jake Karmikel hissed through set lips.

"Easy on the drive, Jake," Islaen warned hastily. "He's not dying or anything near it."

Both he and Bethe Danlo relaxed, realizing the assurance she had given them was based on her real knowledge.

The renewer bore her words out as first the burns and then the bruises vanished under the action of its healing rays. The tension left Varn's body as the pain receded and finally disappeared entirely.

"Jake, help Captain Zubin dump what's left of those back-alley boys into his rover. Bethe, you ride with him. Follow us to headquarters and see that he doesn't have any trouble with Security. I'll let Admiral Sithe know what's happened now and tell Medical that we're coming in with an emergency."

She felt the fear rise in Sogan and moved fast to quell it. He had endured too much already without having to suffer still more. "Those four have done the Federation a stellar-class favor," she announced contemptuously. "First, their Emperor pulled that phenomenal blunder yesterday, and now, Arcturian officers, supposedly while on a diplomatic mission, have not only assaulted Federation military personnel but have also endangered a helpless civilian. None of their battlecraft are going to be permitted anywhere near our starlanes after this debacle, whatever their problems with the Pirate Stars."

Zubin grinned to hear himself described as a helpless civilian. "What else can I do for you, Colonel?"

"Your testimony will be required by Admiral Sithe, but don't go talking up any of this. We've all walked into something that should have stayed with the high brass. That's how Varnt ran afoul of them."

"I'll keep my mouth shut." His eyes rested on Varn Tarl Sogan. "I wouldn't want to—embarrass my friends." He reached down and touched the War Prince's shoulder. "You're going to have to stop getting battered about like this, Captain. It's bad for your health."

Sogan smiled. "I shall try to bear that in mind, Zubin."

Islaen straightened. "Jake, before you go off with Captain Zubin, lift Varnt into the flier."

Varn shot a sharp look at her. *That is not necessary.*

It is, though. As far as we're supposed to know, your innards could be kicked to a pulp. We're required to treat you as potentially very seriously injured. —Make up your mind, Admiral. Jake or Zubin?

Karmikel's eyes sparkled as they met his. The redhead did not have to read their thoughts to be well aware of the discussion that must have just passed between his two comrades.

"Give me a hand up, then," Sogan said sourly.

In truth, he was willing enough to accept the help. With the battle energy faded and the abrupt release from pain afforded by the renewer eliminating that unwelcome stimulus, he felt drained and more than a little light headed. His eyes closed and stayed shut when Jake settled him into the flier's front seat, although he remained fully awake and aware of his surroundings.

Karmikel was gone some time. At last, he slid into the driver's place. "You can do an impressive amount of damage even without the use of your legs, Admiral."

The Arcturian smiled. "Even by Commando standards?"

"Surpassing them, comrade. You could write the manual, but I'd shudder for the rest of us who'd have to follow it. — How are you doing?"

"Tired to my bones. No problems otherwise."

Jake hesitated. "I'm sorry for some of the things I've said lately. I try not to foul mouth your kind."

He faced the Noreenan. "Those were not my kind, Jake. You three are." He was silent a moment. He had opened himself to that attack by coming in here. Would Karmikel have done that? "If I can ever make the grade—"

"You set the grade, my friend," the other man said softly. "We're the ones who have to measure up."

Varn lapsed into silence once more, this time through sheer exhaustion. He knew he was radiating the full weight of his weariness, but he could not summon the strength of will to raise his shields to block it.

Islaen's mind was incredibly gentle when it touched his. He accepted the comfort she offered, let himself be held by it.

"Try to rest for a while," the woman said aloud to warn Jake to say no more. "You'll be facing a battery of questions once we get to headquarters."

He nodded and closed his eyes once more. The gurry had been perched on the seat back beside him, watching him anxiously. Now, she moved closer to him. She rubbed her face and bill against his cheek.

"Bandit, let him rest," the colonel commanded.

Varn roused himself. *No. I want her with me. I want you. I have almost lost you both so often. I could have thrown you away—*

They arrived at headquarters at last, too soon for Varn, but he straightened dutifully. "Back to the wars."

He looked at Jake, then over his shoulder at Islaen. "I think I could appear enough recovered to walk in under my own power."

The colonel smiled. "Your stubbornness is well known to Horus' Navy medical staff. Have it your way, Admiral. I think the presence of two apparently very concerned comrades will suffice."

It was late evening by the time the Commando unit returned to their starships. Jake and Bethe went directly to the *Jovian Moon*, leaving their commanders and the gurry with the *Fairest Maid*.

Islaen gave a long sigh of relief as the hatch closed behind her. *I don't want to have another day like this one for a long time to come.*

I would prefer to forego that pleasure entirely, Islaen Connor.

She smiled sympathetically at her consort. *I'll put credits down that you would. —Knock out now, Varn. It's not all that early, and you have to be dead spent.*

Stop fussing, Colonel. I am sound out.

Varn gave up. He was simply too tired, too worn in mind and body, for any argument. For now, he was perfectly content to be second-in-command to Islaen Connor and to follow whatever order or half-order she chose to issue.

Chapter Thirty-Five

It was past midday when Sogan awoke the following day. He gave himself half an hour under the *Maid*'s steam jets, allowing the moist warmth to drive the remaining soreness and stiffness out of his muscles, and then joined his consort and comrades in the crew's cabin.

"Welcome back to the living," Karmikel told him after studying him fairly critically. "Will you be having breakfast or joining the rest of us for lunch?"

Varn was about to say that a cup of jakek would do him, but Islaen's glare and Bandit's hopeful whistle caused him to retreat. "Lunch. I presume there is enough left in the range."

"Plenty. Coffee, too. Bethe brewed it especially for you."

The Arcturian filled his plate in the galley and sat down with it. The coffee tasted wonderful, and he smiled his thanks to the sergeant.

He went at the food with real interest. "Did I miss any excitement?"

"No, praise the Spirit of Space," the colonel told him. "We were just discussing our upcoming furlough."

"We did have a visitor," Jake told him. "Captain Zubin dropped by. He said he figured you'd still be asleep and not to disturb you, but he wanted us to know that we'd have no trouble from the *Rounder*'s crew."

Varn's eyes darkened. "He does know about me, then. I thought he might have guessed yesterday."

"Well," Karmikel said, "he's not a fool, he's not blind, and he had four Arcturians on hand for comparison. They wore beards, and they were dead, but otherwise, I'm afraid the similarities were pretty apparent."

"He's a sound friend, Varn," Islaen assured him. "He won't betray us, and he doesn't care. He would probably have eventually come to suspect anyway."

He nodded. There was simply too much about him that did not fit . . .

"Zubin's a friend, all right," Jake declared. "He's promised you a proper night in the port when you're really feeling up to it. He took me personally to task for grossly neglecting your education and said that someone had better teach you the ropes before you got yourself in major trouble."

Sogan responded with an oath that caused even Karmikel's brows to raise.

Jake smiled. "Zubin also claims that there is no need for a man who is reasonably careful and who has a few good friends on hand to be afraid of his own shadow in a spaceport pleasure district. He intends to make it his special business to cure you of that."

The War Prince flushed scarlet. "Karmikel—" he threatened.

"That's enough, Jake," Bethe Danlo commanded. "You're having entirely too much fun. The admiral hasn't recovered his fighting form just yet."

Islaen studied her consort, taking care that he should not observe her doing it. He seemed considerably more relaxed, easier in his mind, than she had expected. She smiled.

"Speaking of admirals, Dundee called to say that he'd be here in a couple of hours' time, so eat fast, my friend. We'll want to have the *Maid* in order and ourselves in proper uniform to greet him."

Connor's communicator activated. "Aye, Max?"

"Captain Zubin's here again, Colonel. Let him in?"

She glanced at Varn, who nodded his assent. "Of course, Sergeant. Tell him to come up to the crew's cabin."

Karmikel stretched his long limbs. "That's our signal to depart. We know whom he wants to see, and Bethe and I have a starship to ready for space."

Islaen rose as well. "I'll say hello to him and then join you. —Bandit, are you coming with us?"

Zubin likes Bandit! the gurry protested.

"Zubin feeds Bandit, too, usually cake." The colonel shook her head. "Stay, then, you cadger. —Space! You have all Horus and her visitors feeding you."

Bandit's careful!

Sogan smiled. "We know, Small One."

Zubin of Malki spoke for several minutes with Connor, then went up to the crew's cabin. He seemed to fill the whole of it.

"The colonel said I'd find you here." He smiled broadly. "And the little mote, too."

Bandit whistled in pleasure. She flew to him and happily took the nugget of cake that he held out to her before returning to her place near Varn.

He studied the War Prince closely. "You look better than you did yesterday."

"That is scarcely an achievement," Sogan responded dryly. "Sit down, Zubin."

The spacer complied, producing more cake as he did so. "She likes this."

Yes! Bandit exclaimed as she hopped over to accept his latest offering.

The Arcturian watched her for a moment, amazed as always by the amount of food the tiny creature could eat. He turned his attention back to the other man. "It seems that I am more deeply in your debt than ever," he said.

"Naw. Killing back-alley boys is a spacer's duty. It comes naturally. Like breathing."

"I hope you shall never be in a position to require my paying you back in kind, but I may be of concrete use to you all the same, or we all might."

"You don't have to be of use to me," he growled, "but what do you mean?"

"How does a permanent Thornen charter sound to you?"

"Thorne of Brandine doesn't export much."

"That is about to change. Harlran Lanree, her Doge, wants to move into the ultrasystem market." He leaned forward. "It will be luxury-class cargo—silk and other textiles, some fine metalwork and jewelry, a couple of beverages—to start. Thorne will not have her own merchant fleet for a long time to come. In the meantime, she will need to charter good, fast freighters with crews that can fight and can be trusted with cargo of that quality. Harlran has asked my help in selecting the ships to use, and I have put the *Rounder* at the top of the list." His eyes held the other's. "You may believe that I studied her record well before doing it. A fair portion of some of those goods will belong to my unit. I want you handling them."

"This is for real, isn't it?" the Malkite asked. A charter such as the Commando was describing was the dream of every small freighter captain in the ultrasystem, one precious few of them would ever see fulfilled even in the smallest part.

Varn nodded. "It is real. The Doge wants to start a few test shipments within the next couple of months."

"The conditions of the charter?"

"Those must be discussed."

Zubin sat straight. "Let's talk business, Captain Sogan."

Varn smiled. "Not with me. That will be Bethe Danlo's role. I would not stand a chance in a bargaining session with an experienced trader like yourself, and I am well aware of my deficiencies in that respect."

His eyes fell suddenly. He was aware of his other deficiencies, too, those he had brought with him into the Federation. "You know what I am?" he asked bluntly.

"What and who," the Malkite answered calmly. "Tubal makes a study of the War. He's been kicking himself since yesterday for not making the connection sooner. He did it fast enough once we realized you're an Arcturian. —Why didn't you give yourself a better name?"

"I was more than half delirious when I was asked and heavily sedated besides. Fortunately, my tongue was a blurred as my mind. I did not dare to try changing it later."

Sogan flushed as a thought struck him, and he looked quickly at his companion. "The Thornen charter is legitimate, not a bribe to hold your silence."

"If anyone else had raised that question, he'd be needing renewer work to fix his jaw just about now," the freighter captain told him evenly.

"I am sensitive on that subject at the moment," the War Prince said by way of apology. "Someone tried it on me recently, and I did not like the experience."

Zubin's eyes narrowed. His brows raised suddenly. "I thought Colonel Connor spoke rather vehemently when she mentioned the Emperor yesterday," he observed.

"Colonel Connor should not have mentioned him at all, nor should you mention him," Varn Tarl Sogan warned. "There was bloodshed enough in the War without risking starting another one."

"People who don't know when to keep their mouths shut don't survive long in space or on the rim."

Zubin of Malki studied the former admiral. "Varnt Sogan ate and drank with Malkites, but he had a disguise to preserve. Would Varn Tarl Sogan be willing to do the same?"

The question struck him like a blow, but the War Prince concealed the sharpness of his hurt. "Aye, and with pleasure." He now watched the other. "It is more my place to ask if you are still willing to have anything to do with me."

Anger deepened the red of the spacer's face. He mastered it in the next moment. "I deserved that one," he conceded gruffly. "I'm sorry for the insult, Captain. It wasn't intended as such."

"None taken," he said with an almost inaudible sigh. "My kind have a bad reputation in this ultrasystem."

"Now that we have settled that, we'll be here for you at 19:00."

Varn started. "We may be lifting—"

"Naw. I spoke with your colonel. She says she can spare you for a couple or three hours tonight. We can't be out much longer than that ourselves. We plan to lift tomorrow as well." He gave the Commando a smile that displayed his sharp teeth to full advantage. "Be ready, Captain, and be prepared to answer some questions. Tubal's very interested in an action of yours, a sneak attack where you used small fighters to blow up major battlecraft before they could get their screens raised."

Sogan nodded. "I used much the same technique on this last mission, save that it was a projectile that I rode."

The Malkite's jaw dropped. "You—rode a what?—19:00, Captain. Never mind Tubal. This, I have to hear myself."

The big man came to his feet. "Now, about Sergeant Danlo?"

"She is on the *Moon*. Go have a talk with her. I shall inform her that you are on your way." He smiled. "I shall also warn her not to let you bargain her out of all our potential profits."

Chapter Thirty-Six

Gray Jack Dundee returned the Commandos' salute and ordered them to sit.

He sighed in his mind when they complied. The Federation-born members of the team had once more drawn close to their comrade. It was unconsciously done this time, but they were determined to stand as a unit against any perceived threat to one of their own. In this case, that was himself. Sogan, with his Arcturian ability to accept the inevitable, might forgive him for putting him on a battleship and then pulling her away from him again. It would be a very long time before the other three did.

Bandit read the tension in the room and remained concealed because she was unsure how to proceed. *Jack not hurt Varn!* she protested in Islaen's closed thoughts. *Jack likes Varn!*

Jack didn't want to hurt Varn, but he did it anyway. The rest of us can't forget that.

Jack sad when Varn went to fight! Worried when Varn sick!

I know, Love.

Bandit, Jack not talk anymore? she asked unhappily.

No, the colonel said decisively, *that wouldn't be fair to you, or to him, either, I suppose. Besides, we need him to be friendly to us.* She felt the gurry's continued uncertainty. *Go on, Bandit. Jack will be very unhappy if he thinks you're mad at him, too. He feels badly enough that the rest of us are.*

The Jadite immediately fluttered into view. She went first to Sogan and accepted his caress, then flew to Dundee with a happy whistle.

The Chief Admiral held out his hand to receive her and stroked her gently before turning his attention back to her human comrades.

He looked from one to the other of them, then sat down himself. "Now, I understand why Ram has guarded you four so jealously. My life hasn't been this interesting since the War. It hasn't been this interesting since those fools in the Arcturian Tactical Command ordered you to assume invasion duty, Captain Sogan. I'm not willing to give that up again at this stage. I've already informed Ram that I'm kidnapping all of you for a while."

Dundee saw the look in Connor's eyes as she braced herself for war. He smiled. A tigress set to do battle for her cubs. "Aye, Colonel, I am aware that your unit is scheduled for furlough and that it is a necessity. I've seen the medical records, too. It would be a good idea to keep the lot of you out of sight and trouble for a while in any event." His eyes danced. "How would you like to recuperate on Hedon? I may have something for you to do at the end, but you'll have a full month to yourselves. If you see me before its end, it will be socially. I would very much enjoy that." He smiled again. "You'll be quartered in the Crystal Tower Suite, by the way."

"On a Commando's pay?" Islaen shut her mouth. She realized she had been led into that.

Hedon was the ultrasystem's pleasure planet par excellence, and the Crystal Tower was unquestionably its most famous and most expensive hotel. Planetary rulers used that exclusive topmost suite, not colonels in the military, Regular or Commando.

"That is Harlran Lanree's contribution. I had a long talk via interstellar transceiver with the Doge of Thorne this morning. —He's a fine, sensible man." The blue eyes flickered to the Arcturian. "He also possesses a positively Terran appreciation for short answers given to unworthy emperors.

"Lanree wants you positioned well on Hedon. He intends to start moving Thornen luxury products into the inner-systems and believes Hedon is the best place to begin. He would like you, Colonel Connor, as his adoptive daughter, to put out some feelers and to represent Thorne if there is real interest. Naturally, he'll send in professional merchants if you do open anything up. —This is to be strictly secondary to your primary mission of restoring yourselves, but he did mention that you have a personal interest in the project, something about nectar." For the first time, Dundee sounded puzzled. He was aware of most of Thorne's products but had not heard of this one.

"Our unit brought the crop to Thorne," the colonel explained. "It is flourishing there and promises to become one of her leading exports. We have seventy-five percent control among the four of us."

"Plus some of the silk trade as well?" the Terran asked carefully. Sithe had mentioned that.

Varn smiled. "Islaen-Colonel Connor does. Five percent. The same preinheritance portion as his natural daughters'. His adoption of her was genuine, not honorary."

Dundee cleared his throat. "I hadn't realized how well set you four are. You can afford that retirement-at-will clause in your service contracts, can't you?"

"Aye," the colonel agreed evenly. "We can, though any real wealth still lies somewhat in the future."

She watched Dundee stroke Bandit, who was treating him like a lost friend unexpectedly found. "It all sounds wonderful, sir. It's precisely what I had wanted for us, as a matter of fact, but it is a six-week voyage each way to Hedon even in a fast ship like the *Maid*."

"No problem. You'll be working. Not fighting baring something completely unexpected, but working."

"This work?"

He sat back. "No one at High Command believes we've seen the end of the Pirate Stars. The thought is that we may eventually face a war with them, though that would be in the future. In any event, with the Arcturians barred from defending themselves in our space, we're honor bound to keep those sons off their backs, not to mention our own wolf packs. Some of those have been getting pretty daring in that direction, too.

"Intelligence is gathering everything they can find out about the Pirate Stars, and all our Commando units, including yours, are going to become experts on the subject, including full oral and literary fluency in their chief language. Those twelve weeks traveling time will provide a fine opportunity for assimilating that knowledge. Learn well. You are to become our key team with respect to them."

Islaen Connor nodded. "Aye, sir." She, too, had believed their single encounter with their troublesome neighbors would not be the Federation's last.

Dundee turned his attention to Varn Tarl Sogan. "I'm going to repeat that I will not give you a battleship, Captain Sogan, however much you might think you want one. I won't throw you to our particularly vicious brand of high-level wolves."

"I accept that, sir."

"I do not want to lose your knowledge and tactical abilities. I'll give you everything we can gather about Pirate Stars ships, arms, fighting styles, the whole lot. Are you willing to work out what we'll need to counter and overcome them?"

"I am, provided it is not on another captain's starship," he replied evenly.

"You have my word on that."

The War Prince flushed. "I was off the charts, sir," he apologized stiffly. "I shall naturally work under whatever conditions are required."

"My word stands, Captain Sogan."

The Chief Admiral came to his feet. "I shall meet with you again before you lift, and I sincerely do look forward to seeing all of you on Hedon." He smiled at them. "If that job I mentioned develops and I do have to call on your services following your furlough, I have a feeling you'll shake up the inner-systems as much as you have the rim during these last two years."

Chapter Thirty-Seven

Varn turned as Islaen Connor stepped lightly onto the bridge. *Welcome, Colonel.*

He need not have said it. She felt his joy in her coming. *I knew you'd still be up here.*

She stood beside him watching the black, star-bright vastness of space. The *Fairest Maid* and *Jovian Moon* were en route to Thorne of Brandine. From there, after Islaen conferred with the Doge, the unit would move onto the *Maid* for the long voyage to Hedon.

It's always so beautiful, she said softly. *It's our real element, more so than any planet, even Thorne.*

Aye. Sogan turned to look at the starfield, then back to her. *I have had some second thoughts about this Hedon venture.*

She felt the mischief in him and went along. *Really, Captain?*

I shall accompany you only if you will indulge me in their gem market. You would look lovely in Terran emeralds. Or Lemuran sea stars. —The latter, I think. They are more luminous.

They cost a galaxy more, too.

Colonel Connor, I may no longer possess a War Prince's resources, but I do have some few credits at my disposal. It is that you do not trust my taste?

Your taste is wonderful. It's just also very expensive. She shook her head, growing serious. *Hedon may not be the place—*

The Arcturian only laughed. *Power down, Islaen Connor. I shall have Bethe with me to do the talking. No one, inner-system or rim, will take her. —Now, do you consent, or do I keep the* Fairest Maid *on Thorne?*

That's blackmail, Admiral! She smiled. *Of course, I consent. —You're getting very spoiled, Varn Tarl Sogan.*

The woman felt a change in his mood. He said nothing for several seconds while he fixed his attention on the panorama outside.

When he did speak again, she was not surprised to find that he had switched to verbal speech. "Formin ripped the heart out of me with that order of his. He named me a mercenary for what I do here, but I should have been that in truth had I proven false and gone back."

"Formin's only a man," Connor said carefully. "Just because he's Emperor and head of the Arcturian warrior caste does not mean he fits your people's ideal." Her eyes met his. "You do."

"Fury caused me to answer him as I did, but my decision had already been made. I wanted you to know that."

Sogan moved a little away from her. "I shall never cease longing for a battleship, for a fleet," he said slowly. "I had my opportunity back there, but this time, it was not taken from me or kept from me. I rejected it." He looked at his consort. "It was not pride, Islaen, not anger, not even duty entirely, although that would probably have been sufficient to force me to it. I chose for myself, as I willed and wished, for the life I wanted. I wanted you, Bandit, our comrades, everything we are fashioning here. When set against all that, the other promise could not stand, not for me."

Varn saw the sudden brightness of tears well into her eyes. "Did you doubt my love for you, the depth of it?"

The hurt in him was so sharp that the Noreenan came into his arms and reached out her mind to take and hold his. "Your love, no," she answered in a low, tight voice, "but your scars go so terribly deep. I had never thought I would see you whole enough to be able to say that, to act on it."

His lips brushed his consort's forehead, her hair. *This is also an old Federation tradition, is it not, to work together and strive and fight for the life we would have?*

Aye, Varn Tarl Sogan. It's as old as humanity on Terra herself.

Let me have the chance, my Islaen. Let me have Bandit and the help of our comrades. Let me have you beside me. There is nothing else that I ask, nothing more that I need. He smiled tenderly and corrected himself. *There is nothing more that we need.*

About the Author

Pauline (P.M.) Griffin was born in 1947 on a quiet tree-lined street in Brooklyn, NY. The daughter of Irish immigrant parents, she arrived fully equipped with an Irish love of storytelling as well as a passion for accuracy and research.

Initially breaking onto the science fiction scene with her twelve-novel series "Star Commandos," she rounded out her career by publishing thirty science fiction and fantasy novels as well as twelve short stories and a host of nonfiction pieces, winning two Muse Medallion awards and Editors' Choice for Excellence awards.

Pauline always loved the natural world and the animals that filled it, and she infused all her stories with the same wonder. She lived quietly in Brooklyn with annual visits to her beloved Ireland to refresh her creative drive, but in many ways she also lived in realms beyond the stars and in magical kingdoms of mystery, fighting epic struggles and engaging with heroes and villains. She remained in Brooklyn with her cats and tropical fish until her death in 2020, but her literary legacy continues throughout the world.

Coming Soon!

Star Commandos *series*
Book 11
PARIAH
BY
P.M. GRIFFIN

While traveling to Hedon for a much needed furlough of R&R, the unit is stranded on Elaine of Avalon when their fighter encounters mechanical problems. As they begin making repairs, Varn Tarl Sogan, former admiral and still War Prince of the Arcturian Empire, finds that he is none too welcome. An escalating conspiracy is formed to humiliate, injure, and finally destroy him and his comrades. Yet the greatest danger on Elaine of Avalon may not be its human inhabitants, but the monstrous creatures of its barracands, nine to sixty-foot eating machines; and an over one-hundred-fifty-foot leviathan with teeth the size of sabers. From every quarter the Commandos must defend one another from a hostile populace and a deadly environment if they are to escape back into the safety of space, and it is obvious on all too many occasions that they may well not succeed.

**For more information
visit: SpeakingVolumes.us**

Now Available!

P.M. GRIFFIN

STAR COMMANDOS
BOOKS 1 - 9

**For more information
visit: SpeakingVolumes.us**

Now Available!

AWARD-WINNING AUTHOR
PATRICK DEAREN

**For more information
visit: SpeakingVolumes.us**

Now Available!

KEVIN D. RANDLE

SCIENCE FICTION / FANTASY

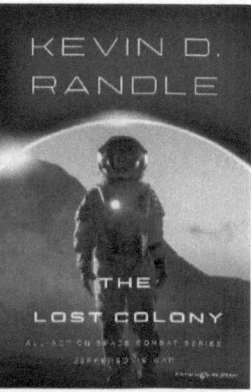

**For more information
visit:** SpeakingVolumes.us

Now Available!

JORDAN S. KELLER
SCIENCE FICTION / FANTASY

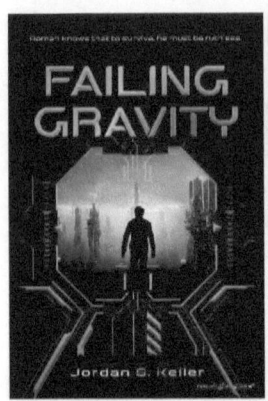

**For more information
visit: SpeakingVolumes.us**

www.ingramcontent.com/pod-product-compliance
Lightning Source LLC
LaVergne TN
LVHW091617070526
838199LV00044B/825